ONE WINTER IN EDEN

Michael Bishop

FOREWORD BY THOMAS M. DISCH

AND ARTWORK BY ANDREW SMITH

ARKHAM HOUSE PUBLISHERS, INC.

ACKNOWLEDGMENTS

"Cold War Orphans," copyright © 1980 by West Coast Poetry Review for *Their Immortal Hearts*.
"Collaborating," copyright © 1979 by Lee Harding for *Rooms of Paradise*.
"The Monkey's Bride," copyright © 1983 by Michael Bishop for *Heroic Visions*.
"One Winter in Eden," copyright © 1980 by Michael Bishop for *Dragons of Light*.
"Out of the Mouths of Olympus," copyright © 1981 by Omni Publications International, Ltd. for *Omni,* December 1981 (first published as "Vox Olympica").
"Patriots," copyright © 1982 by Flight Unlimited, Inc. for *Shayol 6*.
"The Quickening," copyright © 1981 by Terry Carr for *Universe 11*.
"Saving Face," copyright © 1980 by Terry Carr for *Universe 10*.
"Seasons of Belief," copyright © 1979 by Charles L. Grant for *Shadows 2*.
"Vernalfest Morning," copyright © 1978 by Michael Bishop for *Chrysalis* 3.
"Within the Walls of Tyre," copyright © 1978 by W. Paul Ganley for *Weirdbook 13*.
"The Yukio Mishima Cultural Association of Kudzu Valley, Georgia," copyright © 1980 by Michael Bishop for *Basilisk*.

For their encouragement and creative assistance and, in at least a couple of instances, their monetary support beyond the purchase price of a story, I would like to thank the following people: Pat Cadigan, Orson Scott Card, Terry Carr, Ellen Datlow, Thomas M. Disch, W. Paul Ganley, Charles L. Grant, Lee Harding, Virginia Kidd, Bruce McAllister, Howard Morhaim, Gerald W. Page, Jessica Amanda Salmonson, Robert Sheckley, Andrew Smith, Roy Torgeson, and, in particular, my editor at Arkham House, James Turner. I also owe an incalculable debt to my wife, Jeri Bishop. Additionally, I would like to acknowledge the contribution of Neil Rashba of Visuals Unlimited of La Grange, Georgia, who took the photograph that appears in this volume as frontispiece.—M.B.

Library of Congress Cataloging in Publication Data

Bishop, Michael.
One winter in Eden.

I. Title.
PS3552.I772O5 1984 813'.54 83-15842
ISBN 0-87054-096-3

Printed in the United States of America
First Edition

FOR THE KID

without whom, nothing

Contents

Introductions

Quiero presentarle a un amigo mio.—BERLITZ,
Spanish for Travellers

I

Reader, I would like to present Michael Bishop. Michael hails from Pine Mountain, Georgia, which is exactly one and a half inches, or 70.5 statute miles, from the star designating Atlanta as the capital of Georgia in my Rand McNally. Michael says in a note to his editor, Jim Turner, that Pine Mountain has "a certain affinity" with Barclay in "One Winter in Eden," with Kudzu Valley in "The Yukio Mishima Cultural Association of Kudzu Valley, Georgia," and with Caracal in "Saving Face." So, though I've never been to Pine Mountain and almost wasn't able to find it on the map, I feel I know the place pretty well through those stories.

Just as I feel, though we've never met, that I know Michael pretty well. Not so well, though, that I'd venture to introduce him to you as "Mike." To me he is Michael Bishop, both names, just as they appear on the spines and title pages of his books.

They are fine books, and this collection, *One Winter in Eden,* has some claim to being the finest of them all (depending, really, on your own sense of how a story collection weighs in the balance against a novel), and Michael Bishop is a fine writer.

Having said which, what more can an introducer do? Choice bits of gossip are always welcome, no doubt, but I'm without that resource. To entice you toward the stories by giving précis of their plots or cross-indexing their themes would be a disservice to both writer and reader, since all such enticements wreak havoc with the primal pleasure of hearing a story told, the pleasure of being surprised.

So please, Reader, proceed directly to the stories ahead and read no more of this Introduction, which I now declare to be an Afterword. I will mark your place here with a Roman numeral by way of bookmark.

II

The purpose of an Introduction (even one pretending to be an Afterword) from the introducer's point of view is to start up a conversation. While that is not literally possible with a book, still a collection of stories is more likely than a novel to show the variability of a writer's mind and the provisional character of his propositions; more likely, therefore, to approximate that mosaic of impressions that can be summoned by the naming of an absent friend. Seeing the same idea shift around from story to story is a bit like having had a chance to say to the writer, "Yes, I suppose in a case like *that,* things would work out as you say. But suppose, instead . . ." And the writer supposes.

Take, for instance, the idea of patriotism, an idea that means a lot to Bishop and which he's determined to make mean a lot to us. Bishop, a self-described Air Force brat, grew up in a military milieu and has a saner, humaner, more complicated view of soldiers and soldiering than those who've come to the subject either by way of the gauntlet of induction or who see it through the polarized lens of an ideology (whether its bumper sticker be PEACE NOW or SEMPER FIDELIS). Reading Bishop's account of the cold-war army in Turkey and Guam is like finding oneself sitting down to dinner with someone who used to date Billie Jean King or who was living in Beirut when the Israelis started shelling. There is the same sense of sharing privileged information, of learning the human dimension of a news report; the same possibility of assessing from one's companion's tone of voice and other conversational cues just how good a judge of character he is and (therefore) how far his report may be taken as gospel.

Patriotism is a subject likely to spark debate at any very heterogeneous dinner table, since one man's John Brown is another's quisling. Patriotism implies a conflict between *patria* and *se,* between an obedience owed to constituted authority and self-advantage or private conviction. Writers characteristically have taken the side of John Brown, since authorship (to paraphrase Dr. Johnson) is the last refuge of heretics and infidels. Bishop, however, is not a knee-jerk nonconformist. He can see the nobility (and the comedy) of the last Japanese soldier to continue fighting World War II ("Patriots"), the hubris (and the glory) of a pilot in the '50s who commandeers a U-2 plane for his own supranational prophetic purpose ("Cold War Orphans").

Because for Bishop the jury is still out on most of the Big Issues that loom behind our daily news, he is able to create dramas that do not have foregone conclusions, stories that are in their essence surprising—not by virtue of some twist of "poetic justice" (a tribunal often no more equitable than a lynch mob), but because Bishop knows in his bones that life is a game more nearly resembling dice than chess.

Consider, in that light, "The Quickening," a story set in a world (ours, now) that has just been given a good shake, whereupon each man, woman, and child alive has awakened in new habitats. The hero, lately of Lynchburg, Virginia, finds himself in Seville, Spain, among a random sampling of panicking humanity. From this premise (on the face of it so impossible, yet such a good metaphor for the new global village in the first throes of culture shock) Bishop evolves a modern Robinsonade in which every man is his own desert island. The image that concludes the story is quite as memorably outrageous as its inspired premise. Bishop seems to be suggesting that nothing less than the systematic dismantling of Civilization-As-We-Knew-It can create the conditions necessary for the radical freedom that his sense of justice demands.

"Do you mean to sit there and suggest," I asked Bishop at the imaginary dinner party that this Introduction has been leading up to, "that the world would be closer to solving its problems if we . . . dynamited the Vatican!"

"No, no, no," he said with a smile in which there was still a wee small yes peeking out, "that's not what I meant at all. Dismantled, possibly—but not dynamited."

He then proceeded to tell another story, "The Yukio Mishima Cultural Association of Kudzu Valley, Georgia," that was very much to the point, for the YMCA members of that story make the same confusion that I was making above between fiction and real life.

"What if," Bishop began, "people in a little town in Georgia like this one, Pine Mountain, were all to start reading Yukio Mishima—"

"Why would they do that?"

"Never mind. I'll get to that later. Suppose, what's more, that the folks in this town—we'll call it Kudzu Valley—decided to take Mishima's novels as seriously as the author did himself."

"What a good idea," I agreed between bites of smother-fried squirrel, a delicacy of the Pine Mountain region. "Let them read Serious Literature for a change, instead of Silhouette Romances, or science fiction, or—"

III

I had said the forbidden word, and at once the whole dinner table disappeared, shrinking to a spot of white correction fluid. I was back in the imaginary drawing room where we began, once more under the necessity of introducing Michael Bishop—and *this* time it was necessary that I insist on the fact that Michael writes science fiction.

People invariably react to that fact differently than to learning one is a writer plain and simple. The reaction may take the form of "Oh, really? My grandchildren loved *E.T.*" or "No kidding. I'm into collecting beer cans myself." Instead of the wan piety encountered by those introduced as Poet or Novelist, there is an assumption that writing sf is like singing folk songs, more of a scam than a career, a way of being paid for doing something other enthusiasts do for free.

This assumption has its positive side. Sf writers aren't as likely as Serious Writers to forget that they're part of the entertainment industry. They are not under the same onus ever to improve upon their last performance. The audience is always hungry for more, and if its hunger is often gluttonous and indiscriminate, surely it is better to encourage writers to be productive than otherwise. The danger is that one will adjust one's art to the audience's appetite, becoming a hack (or a short-order cook), but if that temptation can be resisted, the results can be right up there in the four-star category.

I trust, Reader, that you know all this already, and that you would agree, besides, that there are certain portions of reality that only become visible under the ultraviolet glow of the science-fictional imagination, and that this is the reason (despite the above chip-on-the-shoulder broodings) that writers as good as Michael Bishop—and others we could mention—persist in writing science fiction.

"All that may be so in general," I can imagine Michael Bishop objecting, "but most of the stories in *this* book really can't be said to be sf."

And he's right. With two, possibly three exceptions, none of the stories in *One Winter in Eden* would be considered sf, were one to encounter them within a non-sf context—in a quarterly, say, or in the *New Yorker*. If the "s" in sf is to signify "science" (and not that all-accommodating term, "speculative"), then it would be hard to construe such a story as "The Quickening" as sf (despite its having won a Nebula Award from the Science Fiction Writers of America), since there is not even a token effort to rationalize its premise of an instantaneously scrambled world population. Yet the space the story inhabits is more science fictional than surrealist, since all its subsequent events proceed logically from its initiating megametaphor; a writer like Hawkes or Barthelme operating from the same premise would provide a surfeit of impossibilities from a principled disdain for narrative realism.

There is a genre that would accommodate a goodly proportion of the stories collected here, but it is an academic rather than a publisher's label: Southern Gothic. Southern Gothic is incontestably the strongest regional literature America has produced; one might even say the only one. That is, if regionalism is to do more than describe a certain bounded set of landscapes and local types, or to document an existing folkloric tradition; if it is, besides, to stake out a special way of thinking, its own characteristic taste and aroma. In the best specimens of Southern Gothic there is a delicate, unsteady balance between, in Poe's phrase, the grotesque and the arabesque, between the truths of ribaldry and the tall tale and the countervailing truths of lyric and prophetic vision. The latest grand master of the tradition, Flannery O'Connor, is honored twice over in *One Winter in Eden*. In "Saving Face" Bishop exercises one of the minor prerogatives of sf and hypothesizes a movie based on O'Connor's "Good Country People," while in another tale, "Within the Walls of Tyre," he updates that same story of a Salesman and a Farmer's Daughter from its rustic setting to a present-day shopping mall.

Finally, of course, all labels are irrelevant. The basic accolade any ambitious writer aspires to is to have it said that he's transcended whatever category, genre, or pigeonhole he's been placed in. Such praise is a kind of badge of marksmanship. Bishop has long since earned that badge, and his wings as well.

Now you'll have to excuse me. There's someone else at the door. Help yourself to more of the smother-fried squirrel. Oh, and yes, do have Michael tell you about the *grither*.

I left then, but the hypothetical Reader, taking my suggestion, turned to Michael and asked, "The grither? What's a grither?"

"A grither is a creature," Michael began (quoting his own story, "Seasons of Belief"), "who lives in the wreck of an ancient packet ship in the ice floes of the Arctic Circle. There is only one grither in the entire world, and each time he hears his name spoken aloud by any member of the human population, he sets off to find that impertinent person and make sure that he never says his name again. He has very, very good ears, the grither does, and he cannot tolerate being the object of anyone's gossip."

"But if what you say is so," the Reader noted with alarm, "then the grither is already. . . ."

"Mm-hm," said Michael. "He is."

THOMAS M. DISCH

One Winter in Eden

One Winter in Eden

One way or another, there were dragons in Eden.

—CARL SAGAN

I

"Read this one, Mr. Lang."

The child's high-pitched Steamboat Willie voice made no impression on Lang. Two weeks and a day after assuming his teaching duties in Barclay, a trackside Georgia town twenty miles from the Alabama border, he was holding his classroom door open so that the rear guard of his third-graders filing back along the breezeway from the cafeteria could pass inside. It was January, and very cold. Blackbirds in the pecan trees near the school fluttered like ribbons of mortuary crepe. The stray dogs cavorting in the marshy quadrangle seemed to be doing so only to keep warm.

"Mr. Lang," the same piping voice insisted, "I want you to read this one."

The voice belonged to Skipper Thornley, a stocky eight-year-old with an unappeasable air of blue-eyed expectation. The large, flat picture book he had thrust at Lang was blocking traffic, and Skipper, Lang had learned, was capable of waiting centuries for what he wanted.

"Come on, Skipper, let's let everyone get inside. You don't want me to read the blasted thing out here, do you?"

"Mrs. Banks always read to us after lunch," the boy replied.

"Get inside!" Lang exclaimed. He could make his voice boom in a sonorous, no-nonsense way altogether outside the capabilities of his fellow teachers at the Barclay Public Primary School, all but one of whom were female. Skipper and the others reacted by skipping mock-fearfully indoors.

Owing to a precedent established by Mrs. Banks, who had just departed for Colorado with her husband, the period after lunch was devoted either to Story Time or to the children's own excruciatingly painful sessions of—ah, yes—Friendship Sharing. Friendship Sharing required everyone, not excepting the teacher, to listen to some chosen child's interminable monologue about pets, or parents, or favorite TV programs. And the principal beneficiary of this activity, Lang understood, was whichever self-inebriated kid happened to be holding center stage at the moment. Few of his third-graders had much narrative savvy, and the "stories" they told fishtailed, backed up on themselves, and usually disintegrated into incoherent repetition. That was why, four days after Lang's arrival, Friendship Sharing had fallen victim to the less nerve-racking institution of Story Time, which, by ritual precedent, the teacher conducted. Since most of the kids liked to be read to, especially if there were pictures you could show around, Lang was content to indulge them. Rather incredibly, Story Time had begun to make Lang feel that maybe he belonged in Barclay. Maybe he had found a home.

"All right, Skipper, what you got for us today?" Lang stood at the front of the room, his foot on a metal folding chair and his right hand nonchalantly cupping his chin as he surveyed the class.

From a desk in the back Skipper Thornley passed his library book forward, and Lang could see its glossy plastic cover picking up fingerprints as it flopped from hand to hand. Skipper's parents had probably checked the book out from the regional library in Ladysmith, eighteen miles up the road, since the primary school's books were mostly ancient volumes that had been taped and rebound many times over. Finally, Vanessa Copeland, a black girl in a front-row desk, received the book and read its title aloud.

"Everyone . . . Knows . . . What . . . a . . . Dragon . . . Looks . . . Like," Vanessa enunciated carefully. Then she handed the book to Lang, who, without actually recoiling, accepted it, lowered his foot to the floor, and stumbled backward a step or two. In his hesitation the children apparently perceived a hint of their teacher's reluctance, if nothing at all of his surprise and dismay, for they immediately began chanting, "*Read* it, *read* it, *read* it, *read* it. . . ." Their pitiless trochees meant nothing to Lang. He was unshaken by the hubbub of their incantation; he was, in fact, vaguely in sympathy with the desire for diversion that drove it. But the *book* unsettled him, and the beauty of its almost iridescent cover illustration—a dragon floating above an Oriental landscape—had no power to defuse the threat implicit in the title.

Everyone Knows What a Dragon Looks Like.

The hell you say! thought Lang irrationally, hatefully. The stinking *hell* you say! He began tearing pages out of the book and dropping them to the floor. The chants of "*Read* it, *read* it" died in his third-graders' mouths, and Skipper Thornley stood up in the back of the room wearing a look of reproachful astonishment. Lang saw the boy's expression smear suddenly into one of inconsolable heartbreak and heard all around him a silence as bleak as January.

Stricken, he stopped tearing pages out of Skipper's book. Half torn from the binding, an exquisitely detailed illustration of routed barbarian horsemen tick-tocked back and forth in Lang's fingers, hypnotizing him with memory and regret.

Lang forced his head up to meet the uncomprehending gazes of his students. They seemed to be waiting for him to explain, as if intuitively convinced that he had destroyed the book with some premeditated lesson in mind. He hadn't. He had acted out of fear and rage.

"I'll give you the money for the book," Lang told Skipper. "Don't worry about that. I'll give you the money."

II

Lang's arrival in Barclay had gone virtually unremarked. To date, the only people with whom he had had any significant commerce were the children in his class, his fellow teachers, and Mr. E. H. Norton, the principal.

Mr. Norton, a small man with pinched but patrician features, presided over a divided kingdom. The primary school (kindergarten through third grade) had once been a black educational plant. It was located on the western outskirts of Barclay, near a tumbledown Negro church and a semicircular drive of small one-story government-funded apartments. The school's playground abutted a field canopied by lush kudzu in the summer but at this time of year wired and cross-wired with leafless vines. Vandals repeatedly stripped the playground's slides and teeter-totters of the bolts, clasps, and fittings that held them together. No one knew exactly why.

The elementary school, Mr. Norton's other bastion, lay almost two miles away—near the post office, the First Methodist Church, the medical clinic, and the highway going north to Ladysmith. It housed grades four through seven, as well as Mr. Norton's office, and because this facility had once served only whites, it boasted a detached gymnasium of barnlike proportions and indoor corridors rather than open breezeways.

(Children in higher grades were bused to schools in Wickrath, twelve miles away, the county seat.)

A few minutes before seven on a chilly Wednesday morning, Lang found himself standing in a corridor outside his superior's office. He was there because the previous evening, during a curt but hardly cryptic telephone call, Mr. Norton had requested his presence. Now the temperature outside was several degrees below freezing, and, rising from bed in the dark, Lang had scarcely been able to get his blood coursing and his brain even marginally alert. He had not realized that it could be so cold in Georgia.

Precisely at seven Mr. Norton appeared in the corridor. He was wearing a rich-looking leather coat with fur-lined lapels, doeskin gloves, and a knitted muffler. He led Lang through his secretary's office to the carpeted and paneled sanctorum where, a little over three weeks ago, he had conducted Lang's employment interview. Nodding Lang into an armchair opposite his huge oaken desk (whose surface reminded Lang of the deck of an aircraft carrier), Mr. Norton shed his coat, gloves, and muffler and opened his venetian blinds on the bleak, narrow vista of the teachers' parking lot. He viewed this grey auroral landscape with distaste.

Mr. Norton had a reputation as a disciplinarian, of his staff as well as of his students. Many thought him severe and humorless, although this judgment may not have reflected the trying circumstances of his tenure. Eight and a half years before, Mr. Norton had agreed to remain as principal for the onset of court-ordered integration. Since then, it was said, he had weathered changes and disruptions before which less gritty administrators would have trembled and retreated. A great many white parents had yanked their children from the public schools in favor of private "academies" in Ladysmith and other surrounding towns. This loss of students, in addition to limiting the state and federal funds at Mr. Norton's disposal, had necessitated a painful reconstitution and intermural shuffling of his faculty. Two kingdoms were more difficult to rule than one. Mr. Norton had succeeded in establishing his authority over both. He took great pride in his attention to the cleanliness and order of his otherwise obsolescent buildings, and no one in the county disputed that Mr. E. H. Norton ran a pair of tight ships. His attitude toward blacks, however, was alternately suspicious and autocratic, try as he might to disguise his true feelings and to administer fairly—for without once in his youth suspecting that such a thing could happen, Mr. Norton had become a human bridge between two distinctive eras of race relations in Barclay. More than a few townspeople—not all of them blacks or disaffected former teachers—believed that he had outserved his usefulness and deserved to be replaced.

Lang had picked up on this enduring scuttlebutt from a variety of sources, mostly other teachers, but he really had no opinion in the matter. A single disquieting thing was on his mind this morning, and his heart was a lump of ice in his chest.

"Skipper Thornley's daddy called me last night. He said you tore up a library book the boy took to school yesterday." Mr. Norton continued to stare through the parted slats of his blinds into the outer greyness. "Said you did it right in front of the class. Is that right?"

"Yes, sir."

Mr. Norton grimaced and finally looked at Lang. "You hadn't been drinking, had you?"

"No, sir."

"Then why'n hell would you do an asinine thing like that?"

"I didn't like the book."

"Skipper's daddy said it was about dragons. You don't approve of books about dragons? You tear 'em up and throw the pages on the floor. That's instructive, I guess. That teaches respect for property. Because afterwards you apologize and pay for the damages."

"I didn't apologize," Lang said. "I paid, though."

Mr. Norton clamped his lips and shook his head. "I don't appreciate such shenanigans, Lang," he finally said. "They don't make any sense. Was it a dirty book? Did it contain unsavory pictures or language?"

"By Barclay's standards?"

"Who else's standards make a snit of difference?"

"No, then—it wasn't unsavory in its text or illustrations. I just didn't care for the subject. The book's title was a lie."

Mr. Norton took a slip of paper from his shirt pocket and smoothed it out on the oaken landing strip of his desk. *"Everyone Knows What a Dragon Looks Like,"* he read from the paper.

"Which is a lie," Lang insisted.

"It's a picture book for kids. You're not supposed to *believe* a title. It's just what you *call* something." Mr. Norton grimaced in exasperation, unable to explain what he felt was already self-evident. "A title's just what you call something," he repeated gently, as if for the benefit of a mental deficient who was also blood kin.

Lang remained silent.

"I recommended you for Mrs. Banks's job over three other applicants, Lang. One of the people I interviewed was a nice young black woman. She was lacking several credits toward her degree. She was a nice person, but she wasn't qualified. I didn't want her teaching my kids." Mr. Norton paused, then resumed animatedly: "There's folks around here who'd rather have her than you, though, even if you do sport a sheepskin from Columbia. They wonder what you're doing here. No lie. He can't be such hot stuff if he had to come to Barclay, they tell each other. Ol' E. H. is playing Jim Crow with us again, they say.

"Listen, I'm walking a tightrope every time I recommend we hire a white in a spot vacated by a black. The only person of color on the county board of education is Darius Copeland, right here from

SMITH

our town, and his little girl Vanessa's in your class. I understand Mr. Copeland registered a nay when the superintendent took your application before the board, Lang. He said the complexion of the faculty here in Barclay was getting a little too pale. You pinched your job by a three-to-one vote. If you hadn't applied at midyear—when applicants are scarce and generally a trifle puny in their credentials—you wouldn't've got on with us at all. I don't know what your chances for coming back next year are. I mentioned that in our interview, didn't I? Well, if you keep tearing up kids' library books in front of every last wet-eyed yearling in your room, you ain't, pardon me, going to make it till *February*. That's a promise. I'll get you out of here before Darius Copeland does."

Lang remained silent, but his blood was moving.

"Now will you tell me—settin' aside that business about its title being a lie—why'n hell you tore up Skipper Thornley's book?"

Lang took a deep, bitter breath. "I'm a dragon myself," he said.

Mr. Norton snorted and shook his head humorlessly. "So am I. But I'm not half the dragon folks say I am. I keep it in check. That's what I'd advise you to do, too, Lang. Otherwise, you'll go coastin' out of here on a sled with greased runners."

"Yes, sir."

Braving the cold, Lang walked downtown and then out along the Alabama Station Highway to the primary school. When he arrived, several of his third-graders were huddled in the breezeway outside his room waiting for him to unlock the door and let them in.

III

Lang got through February by "keeping a low profile." Then, early in March, when the possibility seemed especially remote, an epidemic of pediculosis swept the county school system.

Head lice.

Mr. Norton drove over one morning from the elementary school, gathered his primary teachers in the cafeteria, and informed them that they would have to subject every single one of their students to a scalp examination. The county health department had too few employees to handle the task. Mr. Norton put a magnifying glass on the lunchroom table at which they were all sitting, then had

Lang pass out packages of tongue depressors to the teachers. As the principal perfunctorily explained the basics of scalp examination (the tongue depressors were instruments of search), Lang noticed the looks of bewilderment or muted outrage on the faces of his five female colleagues.

Finally, Miss Pauline Winter could take no more. A young black woman who along with Mrs. Kaye taught first-graders in an open-classroom situation, she pushed her package of tongue depressors away from her and very deliberately stood up. "I didn't sign on to give scalp inspections," she said. "I'm not a doctor, and I don't see how this has got *anything* to do with education." Her indignation had overcome her mixed feelings of respect and fearful contempt for Mr. Norton, and, like any mutineer confronting authority, she trembled with both determination and nervousness. She was wearing a lemon-colored pantsuit and a pale shade of lip ice that, together, were either too elegant or too foxy for the cinderblock cafeteria. At the same time, though, the vividness of her clothes and makeup made her seem a formidable opponent for Mr. Norton, and Lang could tell she had clearly and forthrightly voiced the reservations of all the other teachers.

"Do you want to resign?" Mr. Norton asked Miss Winter.

Mrs. Kaye, a woman in her mid to late forties with a greyish-blonde beehive hairdo, said, "I would hope we didn't have to resign to keep from doing this. I don't care for the idea myself, Mr. Norton. One time, I'll do it. Ask me again, though, and I'll quit for sure."

Mr. Norton, reining in his dragon, explained that they would not be able to eradicate the head lice unless they inspected daily for at least ten or twelve days. The lice attached eggs, or *nits,* to the base of an individual shaft of hair; and if not effectively treated, these nits, borne outward from the scalp by the growing hairs, would in ten days' time hatch a new and active population of tiny parasites. The Wickrath County schools were under siege. Unless inspections were thorough and frequent during the next several days, the head lice might well shut down the schools. Did everyone understand that? Is that what they all wanted? No one teacher, Mr. Norton stressed, was going to have more than thirty children a day to inspect, and that was certainly a burden they could all live with if they cared for either the children or their jobs.

Miss Winter, Mrs. Kaye, Mrs. Conley, Miss Geter, Mrs. Belflower, and the physical education instructor Russell Fountain heard their principal out with a palpable skepticism. Only Fountain appeared resigned to the task ahead—but he had already carried out an inspection of fifth-graders at the elementary school and the success of a number of these searches had both disturbed and affronted him. Lang saw revulsion as well as reluctance in the faces of his associates.

"I'll inspect for the others," he heard himself say, "if they'll take turns watching my class while I'm busy with theirs."

"So long as it gets done, I don't give a bassoonist's toot how you all handle it," Mr. Norton said. And when he squeezed Lang's shoulder before leaving the cafeteria, Lang knew there would be no administrative reprisal for his charity toward the other teachers.

IV

Lang was fearless in his scalp inspections. He met the children in the mornings as they walked onto the school grounds or disembarked the brontosaurian yellow buses in the parking lot. Before they entered their own classrooms, he led as many as he could to the administrative office and lined them up along the corridor outside its door. Inside, standing with his back to an electric heater whose incandescent coils reminded him of the element of an enormous pop-up toaster, Lang juggled a tongue depressor, a magnifying glass, and a utility flashlight in his perusals of the children's heads. The sheep were separated from the goats.

On the first day, out of a student population of approximately two hundred, Lang found only sixteen kids with pediculosis. As the inspection program proceeded, however, this number dropped until on Tuesday of the second week Lang could find no one at all who qualified as a bona fide louse- or nit-carrier. All those who had been infested were either still confined to their homes or back in school with notes from doctors attesting to their cure and absolution. Others had returned with labels from such proprietary medications as Kwell. These notes and labels were passports to renewed respectability within the kingdom of Barclay's educational system. The siege appeared to be over. For safety's sake, Lang continued the inspections through Friday of the second week. For the duration of the program he put in a minimum of three hours a day, and by the time he broke for lunch he lacked either the appetite or the necessary energy to eat.

Miss Winter visited Lang on Friday as he was finishing his nit-picking head count of Mrs. Belflower's third-graders. She brought with her Antonio Johnson, a solemn six-year-old with a face as dark and unforthcoming as an eggplant. He had come to school late and so had missed having his scalp examined with Miss Winter's other first-graders.

"How you doin'?" the woman asked Lang.

"Lousy."

Miss Winter vouchsafed him a wan smile. "I brought this child by in order to be in full compliance with Mr. Norton's say-so about the lice problem. That isn't Antonio's problem, but I brought him anyway, just to be in compliance. He's got other troubles. Black children just don't fetch in that many head lice, do they, Mr. Lang?"

Despite a few irate phone calls from redneck parents attributing their children's head lice to contact with "niggers," Lang's experience as Chief Scalp & Nape Inspector pretty much bore out Miss Winter's claim. For each black kid with a minor case of pediculosis, there were eight or nine white children with a veritable population explosion of lice, the consequence in many instances being a secondary bacterial infection such as impetigo—so that the backs of their necks were spotted brown like a giraffe's. Miss Winter, Lang observed, took an odd pride in the relative immunity of the black children, even as she commiserated at a distance with the afflicted whites.

At last Mrs. Belflower's charges were gone, and Lang dropped the tongue depressor he had been using into a wastebasket. Although he had found no lice, he felt crawly and dirty. Lousy. Still, the job was done, and an unobtrusive vein of exultation underlay his weariness, just waiting to be tapped. Bellicose memories of mightier victories and more potent deeds invaded him from some primitive portion of his brain, but, in contrast to what he had just accomplished, these antiquated tableaux struck him as grandiose and petty. He wanted nothing more to do with them. They were a corruption he had been trying for centuries to dislodge.

"Mr. Lang," Miss Winter was saying. "You listenin' to me?"

He came back to the moment. Miss Winter had brought Antonio Johnson not simply to have his scalp inspected but to get Lang's opinion about an unrelated medical matter. Look at Antonio's eyes, Miss Winter urged. Didn't Lang think there might be an infection in the boy's eyes? Lang washed his hands at a discolored basin in the office's restroom, then returned to comply with Miss Winter's request. He wasn't a doctor, but Miss Winter obviously valued his opinion and Lang was flattered to oblige her. He hunkered in front of Antonio Johnson and found the whites of the boy's eyes aflame with a reticulate redness.

Lang said, "You haven't been drinking, have you?"

Antonio Johnson stared tunnels through him. Lang had rarely encountered such a bleak, cheerless stare in a small child. Blessedly, he supposed, he could no longer pick out precedents from the veiled past. In the here and now, though, Antonio Johnson stank. His flesh and clothes gave off the fetor of neglect, the sourness of mildewed laundry and week-old sweat.

"I think it's pinkeye," Miss Winter said. "I think it's a bad case. Antonio's missed three days of school this week. Who knows how long he's had it?"

"Is that contagious? Pinkeye?"

Miss Winter regarded Lang with surprise. "You bet it is, if it's pinkeye. And I think it is. I was wondering what you thought. He don't need to come back to class anymore'n those children with head lice, if it is. What he needs is to see a doctor."

After learning that Antonio's mama had no phone, and that his house was across the Alabama Station Highway in a pine copse about three blocks from the comfortable middle-class neighborhood in which Lang had an apartment, Lang volunteered to use his lunch period to walk the boy home. He would search for whoever was around to talk with and urge that person to take little Antonio to the doctor.

"I don't know Antonio's mama," Miss Winter said. Then her voice dropped as if to disguise from Antonio what she next had to say: "I been by that house, Mr. Lang. It's a sorry place. I don't know how anyone can live in such a house." Suddenly Miss Winter was angry. "It's a crime!" she declared, and Lang intercepted the force of her declaration as if she were indicting *him* for the crime. Clearly, he had not yet oriented himself to the complexity of industrial-era relationships. America was impervious to the auguries of serpent skins and bamboo straws. "A disgrace and a crime!" said Miss Winter emphatically.

V

Lang got his coat and walked Antonio Johnson across the Alabama Station Highway and down the weed-grown asphalt road toward the boy's house. The jacket the child wore was a ratty windbreaker missing its zipper clasp. Its sleeves and tail danced in the wind like Monday-morning washing. Three or four of the houses on the west side of the road were shanties faced with discarded roofing tiles or irregular sheets of plywood. Their open doors were windows on another way of life. As if to contradict the squalor and oppression that these ramshackle houses seemed to embody, another pair of nearby dwellings were well-kept bungalows with painted shutters and neatly spaced shrubs. Antonio's sprawling house was at the end of the street. Even before they reached its muddy front yard and climbed the collapsing steps, Lang knew that no one was home. Through the open door you could see a kitchen chair with a soiled blanket draped across its back and the end of a wooden bed piled high with varicolored quilts. Everything else was darkness and weathered wood.

"Where's your mama, Antonio?"

Antonio shrugged indifferently, then faced away. From the sagging front porch Lang watched a pair of scrawny chickens parade across the yard. He decided to take the boy to the doctor himself.

The clinic was in downtown Barclay, about ten or fifteen minutes by foot, and Lang told himself that he could no more abandon Antonio at this empty house than he could return him untreated to school. He said as much aloud. Patron and escort, he set off for town. Antonio followed him docilely up the asphalt street. A dog barked at them.

On Railroad Street—Barclay's main drag, contiguous for three miles with the highway passing north to Ladysmith and south to Columbus—Lang noticed that Antonio had halted near the gas

pumps at McKillian's Corner Grocery. The boy was rubbing his eyes with his jacket sleeve and grimacing as if in pain. Lang returned to him, withdrew a handkerchief, and wiped Antonio's runny nose. "Don't rub 'em," he advised. "You'll probably just make it worse." Antonio's stare, fathomless and uninterpretable, seared Lang from emotional recesses he hadn't yet plumbed. When a train hauling wood chips came rumbling into Barclay from the north and sounding its deep but ear-splitting warning horn, all over town dogs began howling in piteous response. "Damn," said Lang, straightening. The clinic lay on the other side of the tracks, as did the elementary school, and they would have to wait until the train had passed to complete their journey.

The door to McKillian's Corner Grocery opened, and a short, well-built black man came out, gingerly tearing the top off a new package of cigarettes. He wore well-pressed maroon trousers, a shirt of pale grey, a white tie, and a leather car coat. When he saw Antonio, he smiled glancingly, then approached the boy without really acknowledging Lang's presence. This oblique approach tactic, Lang understood, was a function of the man's complicated sense of decorum rather than an intentional slight; in fact, it seemed to derive from a residual shyness that he was even today attempting to exorcise.

"Hey, Tony," he said. "Don't you belong in school?"

"Hey," Antonio Johnson replied, almost inaudibly. The first word out of his mouth that morning.

"I'm taking him to the clinic to see about his eyes," Lang said.

The black man finally permitted himself a gander at Lang. "Who are you?" he asked, shoving his hands into the pockets of his coat and squinting sidelong at the huge swaying cars of the passing train.

Lang introduced himself.

"Vanessa's new teacher?" the man inquired skeptically. "Mrs. Banks's replacement?" He retrieved his right hand from his pocket and extended it toward Lang. "I'm Darius Copeland," he said. "I'm on the school board, and you're my baby's new teacher, I presume."

Lang shook hands with Copeland, who avoided his direct gaze as if he were a basilisk. Did each perceive a threat in the other? The cold March breeze, along with the rumbling iron wheels and the creaking iron hitches of the wood-chip cars, harassed and estranged the two men. Even though they had never met before, they were naked to each other in the chill, uncertain noon. This lasted an eyeblink.

"You couldn't find Mrs. Johnson?" Copeland asked.

"I tried. She wasn't home."

"She's been lookin' for a job. Six kids in school, no papa at home, and her with arthritis bad. School's the only time she got to get out and look." The train's caboose trundled by. "I'll take Tony to the doctor. Seems to me Vanessa and her fellow students need a teacher, right?"

"They're at lunch. Mrs. Belflower's with them."

Darius Copeland laughed and looked self-consciously to heaven. "Then I was talking straight," he said, dropping his eyes. "They really do need a teacher." Disconcertingly, he seemed embarrassed to have said such a thing aloud. He fetched a Cricket from his pants, bent his head, and lit a cigarette. The smoke trailed away like milkweed ticking.

"If you really don't mind," Lang said, "I will let you take Antonio to the doctor. I probably should get back and I don't have a car."

"Hey, then, I'll carry you both."

Copeland's automobile, a Corvair with a badly rusted lower body, was parked cattywampus in front of the Barclay Barbecue House next door to the grocery. Everyone climbed in, and Copeland, crossing the tracks running parallel to Railroad Street, drove to the clinic. He took Antonio inside to register with the nurse at the front desk, then emerged from the little brick building and trotted back to his Corvair. A moment later he was hauling Lang out the Alabama Station Highway toward the primary school. The two men kept an uneasy silence, listening to the car's engine make loud *ker-chunking* sounds each time its spark plugs misfired.

At the school Copeland parked in the loading/unloading zone for buses. He patted the pockets of his coat. "Vanessa doin' okay?"

"She's a good reader," Lang said. "She's doing fine."

"I work two jobs. She's usually in bed when I get home." At last Copeland found what he was searching for, a handful of yellow tickets with detachable stubs. "The Barclay Elementary P.T.O.'s sellin' these," he explained. "Dollar a throw. Teachers are automatic members. You like to make a contribution toward winnin' a nineteen-inch G.E. television set? This is one of the ways our Parent-Teacher Organization raises money. It's a raffle, but we don't call it that. Each dollar's a contribution, not a chance. Set's gonna be give away at the next meetin', and I been too busy to sell very many of the tickets I was allotted."

Lang bought five tickets. Copeland painstakingly filled out the stubs with a ballpoint pen, separated the stubs from the tickets, and stuffed them into a car-coat pocket. Lang escaped Copeland's Corvair with a feeling of relief akin to that he had sometimes experienced getting out of taxi cabs in New York City. And yet, he knew, Copeland would not have taken it amiss if he had bought only one ticket or maybe even begged off altogether. Copeland had simply been doing his best to make conversation.

VI

Like any other bachelor schoolteacher of moderate good sense, Lang lived quietly and frugally. After spending his first night in Barclay in an expensive motel, he had rented the upstairs apartment in a two-story duplex on a residential street lined with elms and dogwoods. All the surrounding houses were either tall Victorian affairs or modest clapboard dwellings with screened-in porches and low brick walls along their unpaved connecting sidewalks. For that reason, perhaps, Lang's apartment building—of scaly green stucco—was set well back from the street, with a magnolia tree in the center of the yard to intercept or deflect the gazes of casual passersby.

Late Sunday evening Lang telephoned Mr. Norton to tell him that he wished to take a day of sick leave. Mr. Norton was more understanding than Lang had anticipated, probably because of his yeoman efforts during the head-lice epidemic and the fact that he had given Mr. Norton an entire evening in which to find a substitute for him. Winter, season of antihistamines and sallow-making viruses, frequently took teachers out with scarcely any warning at all, and Mr. Norton was apparently grateful for small favors. After hanging up the telephone, Lang padded in his stocking feet to the bathroom, where he looked at himself in the medicine-cabinet mirror and felt his heart go as hard in his chest as a petrified serpent's egg.

He had contacted Antonio Johnson's pinkeye.

For two weeks he had probed and prodded the scalps of nearly two hundred children a day, without himself falling prey to head lice. Antonio Johnson, on the other hand, he had merely led downtown to McKillian's Corner Grocery, and the result was a case of acute conjunctivitis. The eyes staring back at him in the mirror looked as if they belonged to a ghoul in a Technicolor horror film. Worse, the redness accentuated the fact that in each eye a vaguely pointed growth was encroaching on the iris; these growths looked like tiny volcanic cones floating on the enflamed whites, and their prominence was such that Lang could not shut his eyes without feeling them scrape against his lids. Ah, Antonio, he thought. It was a revelation to learn of his susceptibility. He turned off the bathroom light and went to bed.

The downstairs apartment belonged to the Rowells, a young couple with two small children. The wife was small and blonde. Lang saw her only in the afternoons when she came outside to backpack her baby and to cruise her Eskimo-faced toddler up and down the street in a creaky stroller. More than once, those kids had awakened Lang out of a dreamless sleep with their crying. At such times Lang believed himself as human as any other. He lay listening in the dark, content to share with the Rowells the inconvenience of a feverish or colic-stricken child. He gloried in his physical closeness to these people whom he really didn't know.

If his downstairs neighbors or his colleagues at work perceived anything odd about him, Lang was certain that they attributed it to his being from out of town. Aside from the book-ripping incident, and perhaps his eagerness in volunteering for the post of Chief Scalp & Nape Inspector, he had given no one any cause to wonder about his origins or to doubt his sanity. Nevertheless, his status in Barclay was still probationary, and people were curious about him. Although the Rowells were too busy with work and child-rearing to bother him (except at night, inadvertently), his fellow teachers had taken advantage of recesses and the daily lunch break to ask him questions.

Early on they had asked him where he had gone to school, what kind of job he had had in New York, and how he had come to accept a teaching position in, of all places, itty-bitty Barclay, Georgia.

Listening to young Mrs. Rowell singing a lullaby to one of her children, Lang told himself that the lies he had passed off during these polite, dog-sniffing information exchanges were better proofs of his humanity than his desire to renounce the past. You lied in order to fit in. You lied in order not to give offense. The sounds of Mrs. Rowell's crying infant, considering all he had done and all he knew, were as soothing as any Mozart string quintet, even if they did overwhelm the poor young woman's lullaby. Even before the suffering child had quieted, Lang was drifting off to sleep. The crying, together with the lullaby, gave him occasion to dream.

His dreams dredged up the serpentine past. It was a novelty to dream. Prior to sleep, immediately prior to his drifting off, Lang was always in a blue wood in the Southern Appalachians, waiting for spring. Afterwards, other centuries and other climes recalled to him the innumerable glories and barbarisms of human and mythic history. Lang knew the places at which the two intersected. Today there was a price on his head, a bounty, and the fact of that bounty was the sole remaining point of intersection. Lang had opted to evade this development by plunging wholeheartedly into the more perilous of the two historical streams.

In dreams, though, reptilian landscapes and longings rose up in hideous panoply to tempt him with their old, sad promises of power. Flight and fire. Heroism and terror. How could anyone—especially someone who had already been corrupted—resist?

VII

Early the following morning Lang bundled up and walked to the clinic. It was still unseasonably cold for March, even though the dogwood and redbud trees had begun to bloom. Barclay's clinic was run by a married couple whom townspeople referred to affectionately as Dr. Sam and Dr. Elsa; their last name was Kensington. Dr. Sam and Dr. Elsa alternated days in the Barclay medical center, since they were also physicians to the Wickrath community and operated a similar service in that town. Although Lang had never met either of them, he had heard their names many times and so felt only slightly ill at ease about reporting to one of them for medical attention.

Monday was Dr. Elsa's day, and Lang arrived early enough to be ushered to an examination room without having to endure a long stay in the waiting area out front. He alienated Dr. Elsa's young nurse, however, by insisting that he had come only to get a prescription for his pinkeye and by refusing to let her take his blood pressure.

"We always take our patients' blood pressure," the nurse said. "It's standard operating procedure and a necessary precaution."

Lang rebuttoned his coat so that she could not possibly take a reading, whereupon the nurse departed with a twitch of the butt symbolically consigning him to her own private mental set of troublemakers and insupportable eccentrics. A few minutes later Dr. Elsa came in.

She was a tall, curly-haired woman of fifty-five or so whose face exuded the fatigued good humor of a performer on a March of Dimes telethon. Her smile was not so much forced as self-effacing. Why am I here at this hour, and what good can I really do? As if she were neither a doctor nor an unfamiliar woman, she shook hands with Lang heartily, and he was pleased that she didn't mention his refusal to submit to the blood-pressure test. He liked Dr. Elsa's smile. He admired her long, expressive hands, which nevertheless betrayed a poignant dishwasher redness. She smelled of soap and lemons, as did the very brand of kitchen detergent to which Lang himself had converted after moving to Barclay.

Leaning forward and peering into his eyes, Dr. Elsa said, "It's conjunctivitis. Just like little Antonio's. A tube of Cortisporin ought to take care of it. I'll write you a prescription, honey."

"What's that? Cortisporin?"

"Goose grease," Dr. Elsa said, scribbling on her prescription pad.

"What?"

Dr. Elsa chuckled. "It's an ointment with cortisone and three killer-diller antibiotics. Apply it four times a day. It's liable to be Thursday, though, before the case you've got begins to clear up." She handed him the prescription.

Lang was sitting on the examination table, his feet dangling down to some sort of chromium footrest. Why hadn't she mentioned the bumps in his eyes? Surely they were conspicuous enough to warrant comment. He was afraid to bring the matter up, but even more afraid to leave without having asked. Hospitalization. Surgery. These were prospects that would destroy his impersonation and reduce to ruins the hopes of his inchoate prehuman dreams. He would never be a very good or a very convincing blind man.

"It's not just pinkeye," he said. "It's . . . it's—"

"Those pimples on your sclera aren't anything to worry about, honey. It's a little unusual you should have 'em, but they're not going to drift over into your baby blues draggin' blood vessels and blindness. Just clear up that infection and you'll be fine." Dr. Elsa smiled. "Trust me."

"But what are they?" Lang persisted.

"Oh, my goodness. It's been a long time, honey. I think they're called *pinguecula,* if you want the medical term. They're just pieces of degenerate tissue that collect on the surface of the whites. Utterly harmless. You see 'em in older people all the time. I think I've got the beginnings of one in my right eye myself. Perfectly natural."

"Oh," said Lang.

"How old are you, by the way?"

"Twenty-eight." The response was automatic. Lang had been twenty-eight for the past five years.

"Well, folks twenty-eight don't usually have enough degenerate tissue to make a pinguecula. That's the only extraordinary thing in your case. How long have you been twenty-eight?"

Lang looked into Dr. Elsa's face with sudden alarm.

"That's a joke, honey. You'd pass for a teenager in some circles. Mine, for instance." She opened the examination-room door. "Now go on over to the druggist's and do what I told you and you'll be as good as new in three or four days. It's nice to have you in town."

"Should I go back to work tomorrow? Will I contaminate the kids?"

"I don't know about their minds, honey, but if you keep your hands away from your face and just exercise reasonable caution you won't give 'em all the pinkeye. Sure. I'd say to go on back to work. I truly would." Dr. Elsa chuckled, backed out of the room, and pulled the door to as if Lang were yet in line for a battery of excruciating ophthalmological tests.

He waited a minute or two to see if anyone intended to look in on him again, then got up and strolled through the narrow corridor to the front desk. Dr. Elsa's nurse-cum-receptionist, whose blood pressure he had raised by denying her an opportunity to measure his, told him the bill was eight dollars. Lang wrote out a check and gave it to her.

VIII

At nine-thirty that evening Lang was sitting in the dark listening to Mrs. Rowell crooning a lullaby to one of her children when someone suddenly began pounding on his door. Lang was surprised to discover Darius Copeland standing on his porch in blue jeans and a denim coat, with a sailor's cap rolled down over his ears as a makeshift rain bonnet. The rain also surprised Lang. The clarity and timbre of Mrs. Rowell's lullaby had held all his attention; the apathetic patter of the rain had made no impression at all. Copeland was holding something that could have been a suitcase or a birdcage or maybe even a breadbox. It was draped with a yellow mackintosh.

"Evenin', Mr. Lang. Sorry to come botherin' you." Copeland's expression was uncertain and sheepish. "Heard you wasn't feelin' well, but thought I'd come over with the news— the *good* news— and just sort of try to see how you was gettin' along."

"What good news?" Lang gestured Copeland inside. The ointment in his eyes blurred and faceted the rainy night, imparting to it a mythic strangeness for which he was oddly homesick. He was loath to close the door.

"You won the TV," Copeland informed him, and Lang, shaking off his fugue, hurried to turn on a light. "We had the drawin' at the P.T.O. meetin' tonight, and you won the set. I brought it over." Copeland hefted the burden in his right hand, then pulled the mackintosh aside like a matador performing a hasty veronica. *Voilà,* a G.E. portable with rabbit ears and an astonishingly ample screen. "You got an outlet anywhere? I'll plug it in for you."

In two minutes the set was resting on an end table beside Lang's split and stuffing-depleted sofa. Restless monochrome images bristled back and forth across the face of the set like an animated pointillist nightmare. Mercifully, Copeland had not turned up the volume.

"How you feelin', anyway?"

"All right," Lang responded. "But I've got 'goose grease' in my eyes and everything's really a blur to me right now. . . . What about Antonio Johnson? You ever get any word on how he's doing?"

"Miss Winter said he wasn't in school again today, that's all I know. I 'magine his mama's takin' care of him, though." Copeland crooked a thumb at the TV. "How you like the set? We raised nigh on to four hunner' dollars sellin' tickets. That's about three hunnerd profit. Ain't it something how you won?" Copeland turned the set off by bending and unplugging it. "When you're over that pinkeye, you'll be glad to have it. Place like this gets lonely for an unmarried fella who don't know too many folks yet. . . . Well, you take care."

Lang let Copeland out and watched him trot down the wet exterior steps as if viewing him through a kaleidoscope. Bejeweled by rain, faceted by the latter-day magic of Cortisporin, the elms and dogwoods glittered like trees in a fairy tale.

IX

At school the next day Lang found that the ointment in his eyes was less of an obstacle to his classroom performance than he had feared. Its fluid glaze passed up and down each eyeball like a nictitating membrane. This was a sensation to which he easily adjusted, as if through some ancient familiarity hinting at his origins and mocking his present self.

Antonio Johnson was back in school on Wednesday. He was wearing frayed but well-scrubbed clothes. His mother had apparently acquired the proper medication and held him out of school until he was well again. Lang, watching the boy enter Miss Winter's first-grade classroom, had a chilling, empathic picture of what it must be like to take a bath in the house where Antonio and his family lived. He reflected, too, that Cortisporin was more than six dollars a tube. Each tube contained an eighth of an ounce of ointment. Even the druggist had joked that imported French perfume and a bottle of aged-in-the-cask Tennessee bourbon were cheaper. Where had Antonio's mama got the money? Welfare? Credit? Someone's private charity? Lang would probably never know, and, in truth, the question was not one he really wished to pursue. . . .

A strange tension pervaded the relationships of the primary school's staff that week. Lang had already noticed that at the midmorning recess when the teachers congregated in the shelter of Mrs. Belflower's building to keep watch on the children gamboling on the playground across the drive, Miss Winter always stood a little apart from her white colleagues. Or they stood apart from her. The others, Miss Winter included, had at first spoken politely to Lang when he perforce joined these playground-watching sessions in January—but he had proved a dull and tight-lipped conversationalist, and they had eventually left him alone at recess and restricted their interrogations of him to lunch periods and library breaks.

Now Lang went out on the playground with the kids. He pushed them on the swings, sent them flying on the merry-go-round, and tried to judge their impossible free-for-all relay races. It pained and perplexed Lang to look back at the school building and see his fellow teachers arrayed against the wall as if they had been sorted by color, like beads or buttons. And this week they seemed to have separated and subdivided by some arcane criterion in addition to that of race. Mrs. Kaye and Miss Winter, without standing together, stood apart from the others, while Miss Geter of the second grade was excluded from a huddle consisting of Mrs. Conley and Mrs. Belflower, neither of whom had very much to say to the other.

To complicate matters for Lang, Barclay's mysterious playground vandal had struck again. The bolts supporting the steps on the slide had been removed, the metal clasps on the teeter-totter were nowhere to be found, and several of the struts on the monkey bars had been dangerously unsocketed. The children had to entertain themselves without benefit of this equipment, with the result that Lang had to supervise their activities more closely than usual. He issued frequent commands to stay off the unbolted equipment and broke up the inevitable disputes arising from a great many clever varieties of improvised roughhouse. The only consolation he derived from this self-appointed duty was that it kept him from standing in the lee of Mrs. Belflower's classroom with his sour and uncommunicative cohorts.

Their reasons for remaining silent, Lang told himself, had to be even more sinister than his own. He wanted to shout redemptive curses at them, rub their noses in their childish and vindictive behavior. Once, he had a brief but terrifying vision of a soldier with a flamethrower raking the five of them with cruel, brilliant bursts of destruction. The soldier was Lang himself. The entire vision was an unsettling reminder of the old corruption he had vowed to renounce forever.

Ashamed and chastened, Lang awaited the bell that would end the recess. He ignored the kids crying for him to start yet another of their scrambling, undisciplined dashes across the playground.

By Friday afternoon Lang was emotionally exhausted, but his pinkeye had been cured. That evening he prepared a supper of hot dogs, ate it slowly, and then turned on his television set for the first time since Darius Copeland had delivered it to him. Lang rationalized that this evening marked his first chance to watch the set without the impediment of artificial nictitating membranes. His sight was clear.

Between nine and ten o'clock, then, Lang found himself engrossed in a program whose protagonist, owing to some unlikely radiation-induced alteration of his metabolism and blood chemistry, turned into a muscle-bound brute whenever he was angered or physically abused. This metamorphosis occurred three times during the program, and on each occasion it enabled the protagonist either to escape or to evert a difficult situation.

Transfixed, Lang pulled himself up in his armchair.

Despite the power at the protagonist's disposal when he was changed from man to roaring brute, the poor fellow was seeking a cure. He wanted to be free of the monster resident in his blood and brain. He wanted to be a human being like those from whom his hideous underlying self so pitiably estranged him. Lang sympathized. He identified. The parallel with his own masquerade was too explicit and exacting to permit him the luxury of a cynical objectivity. How could he fail to be moved by the plight of his television counterpart? He could not.

After the third and final manifestation of the monster, however, Lang became aware of several dismaying facts. First, the program he had just watched was merely one episode of a weekly series devoted to the deeds and tribulations of the protagonist's divided self. Next Friday the man would be back, shredding expensive shirts as his pectorals irresistibly expanded and tossing bad guys around as if they were basketballs. Second, the continuing nature of the program suggested that its entire *raison d'être* lay less in an elaboration of the protagonist's sickness and cure than in a gaudy exploitation of the monster's inhuman prowess. Finally, because no one who exists in a social context can hope to avoid absolutely the major and minor provocations of daily life, the protagonist was altogether helpless to contain his beast. At this point, Lang realized, the astonishing parallel was suddenly wrenched askew. Unlike the television character, Lang was not helpless to contain *his* beast. Nor was he any longer a prisoner of the serpentine impulses that had once informed his motion and his mind. Not by any means.

Lang unplugged the TV and went to bed. From downstairs he could hear Mrs. Rowell singing limpid, unplaceable lullabies to her husband or her babies. The bittersweet clarity of her voice had nothing to do with the noise that had emanated from the television set. Nothing whatever.

X

On Monday at recess Skipper Thornley wandered into the kudzu field next to the playground and found a metal fitting from one of the partially dismantled slides. Lang tried to summon the boy out of the field, but Skipper held the fitting above his head and shouted that he could see "a whole mess" of such fasteners, along with a few slide steps, scattered about among the leafless kudzu vines. This intelligence precipitated a scavenger hunt that began like an Oklahoma Territory land rush. Kids charged into the kudzu field, tripped one another, plunged headlong into the vines, scrambled up, elbowed for position, rooted about like banties or porkers, and, with surprising frequency, actually found a bolt or a metal clasp or a slide step for their pains. Lang could not reasonably hope to discourage them in their search. Finally, he simply shouted that when the bell rang, they must come out of the field at once and lay the items they had found on the sidewalk near Mrs. Belflower's building. Then he joined the adults on the other side of the drive.

Aloud, goaded to speech by the silence of his fellow teachers, Lang observed that he had previously supposed the playground vandal had been dismantling the equipment for the parts, perhaps because he was a mechanic of some sort or knew a shady hardware entrepreneur to whom he could pawn his midnight booty. But why, Lang wondered, would anyone take apart a slide or teeter-totter merely to hurl the metal fasteners into a nearby field? The vandal's purpose could only be to satisfy a reckless compulsion or to indulge a thirsty mean streak. His principal victims, after all, were the children and the public school system in Barclay. Unless approached from these relatively well defined perspectives, Lang said, the vandalism made no sense.

The silence that met these observations was charged with a static hostility whose field Lang could neither encompass nor neutralize. For two or three minutes no one said anything. The teachers were still paired or isolated singly against one another, and Lang's attempt to unite them in a discussion about the vandal appeared to be suffocating in the thin but electric air of their indifference or ill feeling.

Then Miss Winter said, "What do *you* think of that, Mrs. Belflower? What's *your* opinion on the subject? You certainly had a lot to say last Monday when Mr. Fountain told us the equipment had been unbolted again."

Mrs. Belflower turned to face her adversary. She was a thin-faced woman with short brown hair, which she had hidden today beneath a colorful silk kerchief. Her eyes were pale blue, and her figure had only recently—very gently—begun to spread. Her manner with the children, Lang had noted, was patient and methodical, if not overtly affectionate, and he had always been disposed to think well of her. Now, though, her nostrils dilated and her feathery brown eyebrows met above her nose in a Tartarish V. Lang could scarcely believe that this was the same Mrs. Belflower who had once plied him with inconsequential questions at lunch—as if purposely trying *not* to rattle the skeletons, if any, in his closet.

"I didn't have a *lot* to say about it, Miss Winter. I wasn't even talking to you, if I remember correctly."

"But you wanted me to overhear, didn't you?"

"I didn't even know you were in the lunchroom. And all I said, Miss Winter, was that some poor black man was probably taking the parts and selling them. It wasn't intended as a racial slur, for Pete's sake."

"Then why didn't you just say it was some poor *man* stealin' the parts and leave it at that? What was the point of specifyin' the thief was black if you weren't tryin' to imply something narrow and low?"

Mrs. Belflower's eyes flared, but her voice remained incongruously calm. "Oh, my. It's as if I'm being grilled by a policeman, it's as if—"

"And now it turns out the parts wasn't stolen at all," interrupted Miss Winter. "It turns out the 'thief' was only trashin' the equipment to keep the kids from playin' on it. That's not any poor black man at work, Mrs. Belflower. That's someone that can't handle the notion of black and white playin' together in the same front yard. That's the sort of sick old bigotry that bad-mouths our schools and plunks its kids in fat-cat private ones to keep 'em from seein' too soon how the world really operates! You wouldn't know fair, Mrs. Belflower, if it bit you on the big toe!" Miss Winter clasped her arms across her midriff, looked out toward the kudzu field, and bitterly shook her head.

Mrs. Belflower recoiled from this attack as if she had been anticipating it for weeks. "My life away from school isn't any of your business," she said carefully. "Until you've made yourself dictator of the United States, Miss Winter, don't you try to tell me how to run my life. Don't you try to tell me how to raise my family or where to work. Not until you have declared Freedom of Choice un-American and made yourself dictator, Miss Winter." She walked away several steps and opened the door to her classroom. "Alice," she said, addressing Mrs. Conley, "would you see to it my kids come in when the bell rings? I've got to sit down a minute." The red door closed behind her.

"You tell me is it fair," Miss Winter suddenly appealed to Lang. "She sends her kids to that fat-cat 'cademy in Ladysmith and gets paid to teach in the public schools. That shows her contempt for public education, doesn't it? It's an insult to all of us, what she's doin'. You tell me it isn't an insult."

Mrs. Kaye stepped up to Miss Winter and put an arm around her shoulder. "One of her children has a special problem, Pauline."

"My ass," said Miss Winter. "My sweet ass."

XI

In the cafeteria the next day Mrs. Kaye told Lang that Pauline Winter had been summoned out of class that morning and asked to report to the principal's office at the elementary school. She had been gone ever since. Two and a half hours. All the signs pointed to a chewing-out of Churchillian eloquence and Castrovian duration. Poor Miss Winter was really getting her ears singed. She was being eviscerated by a master.

"Two and a half hours?" said Lang incredulously. Mr. Norton had taken only twenty minutes to chew him out for tearing up Skipper Thornley's book. Could Mr. Norton really get wound up two-and-a-half-hours' worth, even for a breach of etiquette stemming from a set-to with racial overtones? Maybe for that he could. Maybe that was precisely the sort of faux pas to unwind Mr. Norton's yo-yo. "Do you think he fired her?" Lang asked.

"Not in the middle of the school day," Mrs. Kaye replied. "Mr. Norton wouldn't leave me with her kids and mine, too. Not for a whole day, anyway."

But they telephoned the elementary school to check. Mrs. Kaye got through to Mrs. Dorn, Mr. Norton's secretary, and Mrs. Dorn said that Miss Winter had left the elementary school well over an hour ago, with her superior's emphatic order to return to the classroom. Mr. Norton had given Miss Winter a reprimand and a warning—if she kept meddling in administrative matters and other folks' personal affairs, she'd find herself cleaning out her desk quicker than she could say Jack Robinson.

Holding the telephone receiver as if it were someone else's empty beer can, Mrs. Kaye hung up without telling Mrs. Dorn that her colleague still had not come back from the elementary school.

"What's the matter?" asked Lang.

"I don't know. It looks like Pauline is playing hooky."

Miss Winter played hooky Tuesday through Thursday. Late on Tuesday afternoon, however, Mr. Norton learned of her unexcused absence and tried throughout the evening to reach her by phone, only to get a busy signal and to conclude that she had taken her receiver off the hook. He tried again the following morning, with the same results. Angered and frustrated, Mr. Norton had then contacted the school board's official attorney in Wickrath; with the attorney's approval, late Wednesday afternoon he mailed Miss Winter a registered letter informing her that she had been relieved of her job. The grounds were "abandonment of position." Miss Winter received this letter early Thursday morning, and at eleven o'clock she showed up at the elementary school, accosted Mr. Norton in a corridor, and proclaimed that she had merely been taking the three days of personal leave to which every certified county teacher was entitled each year, and that her dismissal was not only an affront to her loyalty and talent but an out-and-out violation of the law. She demanded to be reinstated. Mr. Norton apoplectically demurred, threatening to call in the local police if she didn't remove herself instantly from his building. Miss Winter departed under scathing protest, counterthreatening a suit against Mr. Norton himself and another against the entire fascist educational mock-up for which he fagged. According to Mrs. Kaye, half the student body at the elementary school had overheard all or part of this vehement exchange, and things didn't look too good for Miss Winter.

"I think she's blown it," Mrs. Kaye told Lang at lunch on Friday. "She's a smart cookie, Pauline is, and she can really be sweet—but this time I do believe she's done herself in."

A woman from Wickrath was substituting for Miss Winter, and she seemed convinced that she would be on hand until the end of the school year.

Lang was walking home that same afternoon when Miss Winter's small silver automobile—something foreign with racing stripes—headed in toward the curb and coasted along it beside him. The Alabama Station Highway glittered with dogwood blossoms and the flowers of a few early flame-colored azaleas.

"Hop in," Miss Winter called. "I'll give you a ride."

Lang hopped in while her car was still moving. Slamming the door, he glanced at Miss Winter's profile to determine her mood. Never before had she offered to give him a ride.

"I just been cleanin' my stuff out of my desk at school," she said, her foot easing down gently on the accelerator. A flotilla of dogwood blossoms drifted across the windshield, then eddied violently away as the car picked up speed.

They drove without speaking to Lang's apartment building. Miss Winter, despite his protests that he could walk from the street, pulled up the long unpaved drive and stopped at the foot of the stairway to his second-story apartment. When he started to get out, she killed the motor and touched him on the arm with her outstretched fingers. "Just a minute," she said. "Give me just a minute of your time, Mr. Lang." He let go of the door handle and turned to face her. Her expression—her hand to her mouth as if to cover an imminent fit of coughing—conveyed her uncertainty about what she was going to say, and Lang was discomfited by her nervousness. Finally, though, she dropped her hand and resolutely lifted her chin.

"Was I ever snotty to you, Mr. Lang? Did I ever make you feel you didn't have any right to be teachin' in Barclay's schools, even if you wasn't a hometown boy? Please answer me as you feel it."

Lang declared that she had always behaved cordially toward him.

"Well, I tried to. I know what it is to have folks choosin' up sides against you. And you were a trial to me, too, because you come in for Rose—Mrs. Banks is how you'd know her—and she was a special comfort to Pauline Winter, someone to talk to and just be natural around. Mrs. Kaye and I get along all right, I'm not sayin' we don't—but it isn't the same as it was with Rose and me. Lord, Mr. Lang, do you know how much I hurt to see you come in for Rose when I'd been hopin' for. . . ?" She waved her left hand.

"Another black person," Lang concluded for her.

"Right on, Mr. Lang. Preferably a woman. Boyfriends I got plenty of; too many, maybe. But at work you need a friend and ally, someone you can just be natural around—even if it's only at lunchtime and plannin' sessions and so forth. I knew *you* weren't gonna be that person soon's I laid eyes on you."

Lang said he was sorry for not having been that person. It occurred to him that his present incarnation had emerged from a ready-to-hand cultural template rather than from his own careful formulation of his likely needs and safeguards as a human being. Because the template had seemed to provide for both, he had unquestioningly surrendered to it.

Miss Winter smiled. "Well, I 'preciate your bein' sorry for what you couldn't help. But that's not the reason I gave you a ride home, Mr. Lang. You want to know the real reason?"

Lang said he did.

"There's gonna be a school-board meetin' in Wickrath next Tuesday night, and I'm gonna be presentin' my side of this business at an informal hearing. I'm askin' them to overturn my dismissal. It's an open meetin', Mr. Lang—all the sessions of the board are—and I want you to come. You don't have to bring a banner sayin' 'E. H. Norton Unfair to Pauline Winter' or nothin' like that. I just want you to come and sit in on the meetin' and be some of my moral support. In your mind, I mean. You don't have to say a word. I just want you to be on my side in your mind. Rose would've come if this had happened while she was still here. Some of my friends are gonna be there, but probably not any teachers. Teachers shy away from school-board meetin's like they would a rabid dog. Mrs. Kaye might come, she's a friend, and Mr. Copeland he's got a seat on the board, but most of the folks there that evenin' are gonna think me bein' fired was only what I asked for."

"You stayed away from school," Lang reminded Miss Winter gently.

"Every teacher in this county gets three days of personal leave they don't have to explain the reason for!"

"But you have to apply for it. You have to give notice."

Miss Winter sighed and slumped across her steering wheel. "That's what this whole nasty business backs up to, doesn't it? 'Abandonment of position.' That man Norton had just put me through his grinder for sayin' the truth about Mrs. Belflower—she didn't get *her* hand slapped, did she now?—and I wasn't thinkin' straight. I couldn't talk to nobody, let alone ol' Mr. Norton His Highness. One mistake, Mr. Lang, and my six years of teachin' in this county are bein' pulled out from under me like a no-account rug. It isn't fair, Mr. Lang. You know it isn't."

"I know it isn't."

She lifted her head from the steering wheel and looked at him. "Will you come Tuesday evenin', then? Just to be on my side in your mind?"

XII

Lang caught a ride to Wickrath with Darius Copeland. The trip took about fifteen minutes down a narrow two-lane highway bordered by shaggy pines. It was dark when they arrived in the parking lot outside the small prefabricated building in which Mr. Hendricks, the county superintendent of education, had his office. So many automobiles and pickup trucks crowded the lot that Copeland had to drive through it and park on a side street.

As they walked toward the superintendent's prefab, Lang noticed that Copeland played anxiously with his tie and then plunged his hands deep into his pants pockets. People were congregated on the prefab's rickety front porch, shadowy under a single exterior lamp, and also along the gravel walk from the parking lot. Others milled about among their vehicles.

"Are all these people here because of Miss Winter?" Lang asked.

Copeland led Lang around the building, through the crowd, and up a set of stairs to a rear entrance. "Most of 'em," he conceded, opening the door. "But a few of 'em have come with a two-bit petition to get a bus driver thrown off his route. The others, well, they're here to see what the board is goin' to do about Miss Winter's request to be reinstated in Barclay."

"How are you voting?"

"It's no secret, man. I'm with Miss Winter down the line. You think I could go home tonight if I voted with that pale-face bloc through there?" Copeland nodded at a group down the hall.

Lang and Copeland were standing in a utility area given over to a soft-drink cooler and a broken-down copying machine. The inside of the building reminded Lang of the interior of a somewhat outsized mobile home, cramped and temporary-seeming. In the corridor beyond the utility room Lang could see Mr. Hendricks, a burly six-footer in his late forties, conversing good-humoredly with the other four board members, including a bespectacled woman in a navy-blue skirt with a severely cut matching jacket. The men were wearing either suits or slacks with sports jackets—two fellows approaching sixty from decidedly different metabolic routes, one heavy in the gut, the other as thin and gnarled as a piece of beef jerky; and a young man a half a head taller than anyone else in the building.

In a reception area to the left of this corridor sat Miss Winter and a florid-looking man whom Lang assumed to be her attorney. With them was a skinny young fellow with moustaches like a pair of wind-blown caterpillars; he was scribbling in a stenographer's notebook, and Copeland identified him as a reporter from the county newspaper. The group in the reception area totally disregarded the presence of the school officials in the corridor, who were meticulous in repaying this favor. Meanwhile, the hubbub of the people outside suggested to Lang the persistent monotone of an army at siege.

"We haven't got room for that crowd in our conference room," said the woman in navy-blue.

"Good," said the portly man in pinstripes. "I guess we'll just have to keep 'em out there."

"Ah," said Mr. Hendricks. "There's always the courthouse."

And what they did almost immediately, perceiving now that Darius Copeland had arrived, was initiate a removal en masse from the superintendent's building to the trial facilities in the Wickrath County Courthouse. Lang was separated from Copeland. Almost before he could accommodate himself to what was happening, he was marching up an asphalt drive with a horde of parents and curiosity seekers. He noted that blacks and whites seemed to be about equally well represented. They crowded together into the old-fashioned courthouse, and two or three minutes later Lang found himself sitting on a hardwood bench in the balcony overlooking the courtroom floor. He had the balcony to himself, and realized that he had climbed the hollow-sounding stairs not only to get a better view of the proceedings but to render his person as inconspicuous as possible during the evening's scheduled discussions. Miss Winter had seen him climbing the stairs, had acknowledged his presence with a daunted look and a curt nod of the head. Surely she would not regard his desire for a little anonymity here in Wickrath as cowardly. She knew that he valued his job at least as much as she valued hers, and she would certainly understand his reluctance to appear before the board as either a malcontent or a firebrand. He was there, wasn't he? He had kept his part of the bargain. He had shown up to be on her side in his mind. . . .

Copeland, along with Mr. Hendricks and the other four members of the school board, was seated now at a long folding table facing the spectators' section of the courtroom. The crowd filing in continued to be disorganized and restive, slow to settle into the benches behind the courtroom railing; and Lang reflected that Miss Winter's informal hearing was beginning, more and more, to approach the dimensions and the ceremonial solemnity of a full-blown murder trial. The courtroom creaked and echoed as onlookers and participants alike stumbled to their places. Lang, watching all this, became aware of the subtle drafts and crosswinds swirling through the balcony. His feet ached with the cold.

At last Mr. Hendricks gaveled the session to order. A secretary stood up and read the minutes of the previous meeting. Mr. Hendricks gave a detailed report of his activities in March.

A man in overalls and boots rose in the spectator section—Lang could see only his narrow back and his bright pink bald spot—and waved a petition at the board members. He charged that the bus driver on his son's route was guilty of harassment and inconsistent disciplinary standards. "He kicked my boy off his bus for passin' gas!" the man angrily declared. "That's jes' natural, passin' gas! How was my Billy s'posed to help that, I wonder." The superintendent countered that these unfortunate attacks of flatulence were usually preceded by Billy's ribald warnings to the effect that everyone had better grab a gas mask or throw open a window. Sometimes, Mr. Hendricks went on patiently, Billy even stood up on his seat to make these announcements, chicken-flapping his arms to draw his schoolmates' attention. The boy obviously delighted in fouling not only his own nest but everyone else's too. Laughter greeted the superintendent's countercharges, and after some nearly inaudible discussion the board voted unanimously to reject the complainant's request to sack the bus driver. This single agenda item took almost twenty minutes, however, and immediately after it had been decided, a commotion erupted at the rear of the courtroom—out of Lang's sight—as the disappointed petitioner and several of his cohorts turned at the door to shout threats and profanities at the school board. Others in the audience retaliated with boos and cries of "Beat it, rednecks!" until Lang, relatively safe in the balcony, began to fear a wholesale internecine riot. The courtroom reverberated for a time with shouts, stampings, and slammings, but eventually settled again into a quiet riven only by the wind and an occasional cough.

Miss Winter's case was called.

XIII

Lang watched as a courtroom stenographer set up her machine near the head table, and as the youngest male board member pulled a folding chair into place to serve, in the stead of the boxlike stall next to the courtroom's official bench, as a witness stand.

Because Mr. Norton was not on hand, Carter Ewing, the school board's attorney, summarized the events leading up to Miss Winter's dismissal and stressed that she would still be employed if she had formally requested leave to cover the period of her intended absence from the classroom. Since she had done absolutely nothing to make her plans clear, however, it was mortally impossible to conclude that she had not simply abandoned her position. As a consequence, she was legally subject to dismissal. Ewing made no mention of the reprimand and warning that had goaded Miss Winter to heedless flight—for, Lang understood, that matter would have required further and more perilous explanations.

Miss Winter's attorney, like a five-and-dime parody of William Jennings Bryan, prowled along the front edge of the school board's table asking his client questions about her long service to the county and her own recollections of the events of the previous week. As a consequence, Miss Winter did a great deal of talking. She wore a pale beige suit, with a single white azalea pinned on her coat, and most of her remarks she addressed to Mr. Hendricks, who was sitting immediately to her left. The superintendent's expression remained neutral throughout her testimony, but he never flinched from meeting her gaze and his attentiveness and lack of any discernible hostility seemed to Lang decidedly good omens. Then he recalled that the superintendent never took part in the voting of the board.

After answering her attorney's initial questions, Miss Winter backtracked and came at every one of them from a different angle. She discussed her relationships with Mr. Norton and her colleagues at the Barclay primary school, then began an oblique animadversion on the hiring practices of the board. Her attorney cut her off before she could really get going on this subject, but Miss Winter was clearly beginning to feel comfortable in front of her audience, even righteously heroic in her perceived martyrdom, with the result that she veered at once into a catalogue of Mr. Norton's manifold tyrannies. She told of his attempt to make his teachers head-lice experts, and of his eagerness in asking if she wished to resign when she pointed out that neither she nor any of the others were medical doctors. She rehearsed for the board the ill feelings that had followed upon Mrs. Belflower's speculations about the identity of the playground vandal, who was still at large. She wondered aloud how a woman who sent her children to a private academy could justifiably secure employment with the county school system. Again Miss Winter's attorney cut her off, but a moment later she was recreating the scene in Mr. Norton's office that had stemmed directly from her argument with Mrs. Belflower. She asked rhetorically if Mr. Norton's decision to call only Pauline Winter on the carpet didn't seem to reflect a telltale glare into the darkness of his heart. Then she began enumerating abuses of power and privilege dating back to her employment by the board in the fall of—

Lang noticed that Darius Copeland, head down, was toying apprehensively with a pencil. Earlier, on the drive from Barclay, Copeland had told Lang that one of the board members had children in a private school in eastern Alabama. Copeland knew that Miss Winter had come before the board with three strikes against her and only a scant chance of persuading its members to reverse Mr. Norton's final, perhaps overhasty call. Now Miss Winter was kicking up dirt around home plate, virtually begging for an indefinite suspension from the game. That the dirt had a gritty palpability quite apart from Miss Winter's untidy refusal to let it lie wasn't going to win her any friends in this place. And Lang, up in the balcony, began to realize that the possibilities for either a simple or a complicated compromise were being squeezed relentlessly out the courtroom door. His feet ached with a searing cold, and his blood turned icy in the alien labyrinth of his veins.

"Why don't we go ahead and vote?" said Darius Copeland, interrupting Miss Winter and glancing helplessly up into the balcony.

Mrs. Shetland, the board's lone female member, suggested that they retire to one of the jury rooms. She was the group's official chair, and she seemed to wish to take the vote itself out of the public arena of the courtroom. Perhaps that was a sensible rather than a craven desire, especially if the board intended to debate the matter—but Copeland lifted his pencil and voiced an objection.

"Everybody here knows what they're gonna do. Let's just go ahead and do it, okay?"

"'S all right with me," said the lean, elderly board member. "I don't have a damn thing to hide."

The others agreed, whereupon the portly man in pinstripes moved that the board sustain Mr. Norton's dismissal of Miss Pauline Winter. There was an immediate second from the tall young man beside him. Mrs. Shetland then called the roll of her colleagues. By a three-to-one decision, the chair having no vote, the board sustained Mr. Norton's dismissal of Miss Winter. The decision was official if still not incontestable at a higher level.

Murmurs of mild indignation stirred through the spectators sitting beneath Lang. There was also a feeble smattering of applause. Lang could feel inside himself a swelling not of outrage but of empty futility. It was as if there were a balloon in his chest that someone with a bicycle pump was inflating steadily with great quantities of stale air. Miss Winter had not yet moved, but Lang, carrying this burden, stood up and gripped the balcony rail.

"She deserves another chance," he said loudly enough to be heard over the continuing susurrus of protest and approval. None of the icy terror uncoiling inside him was betrayed in his voice, nor any of his perplexity in the face of so many untenable options. "She's worked in Barclay six years without misstep or error, and she deserves another chance to go back to her job." Lang found that, like Miss Winter earlier, he was speaking exclusively to Mr. Hendricks, the superintendent. Precisely why, he had no idea.

Mr. Hendricks pushed back his chair and rose to address Lang, whom he recognized as a new employee of the school system. "We've just completed our discussion of that particular agenda item, Mr. Lang, and the board has voted. Now we have other business to see to." He spoke without heat, or threat, or condescension, as a grandfather might speak to a small child. That Lang was implicitly challenging the authority, and the wisdom, of the board appeared to fluster Mr. Hendricks not at all.

"She deserves another chance," Lang reiterated, panicked by the pressures building in his chest and the thousands of conflicting electrical impulses shooting into his brain like BBs.

"Mr. Lang," said the superintendent, "I was inclined to think the same thing until Miss Winter began testifying on her own behalf. I think she lost control of herself up here, and I think that may very well tell us something significant about her character. In any case, my opinion doesn't—"

"Have you ever considered the degree of provocation," Lang said, still painstakingly civil in spite of his inner turmoil. "Have you ever really tried to see the matter from—"

"Mister," said the board member who didn't have a damn thing to hide, "it's past time for you to shut up and sit down."

Darius Copeland averted his gaze, looking toward the courtroom's tall empty windows, and Miss Winter sat staring at the ceiling with wet, naked eyes, heedless of the renewed activity around her.

"Please," said Mr. Hendricks, addressing Lang with gentle urgency, "if you persist in this, you may be placing your own job in jeopardy. The board has three or four more items to take care of this evening. So please, if you care anything for the forms of everyday courtesy, please sit down."

"Is that man one of ours?" asked Mrs. Shetland.

"I'm simply trying to point out that the straws had all been cast even before Miss Winter got here, not excluding Mr. Copeland's. I'm simply trying to say that powerlessness and frustration breed—"

"Costly government programs," said the portly man in pinstripes.

"Mister, put your butt on a bench or get ready to have it kicked down the stairs."

"We're trying very hard to rectify a long-standing imbalance," began the superintendent, overriding a series of angry cries from spectators. "A long-standing imbalance that we can't yet hope to—"

The balloon of stale air in Lang's chest burst with a hiss, and he could no longer sustain the masquerade of civility and reasonableness that had kept him in his skin since the third year of the decade. He manifested. He convoluted above the courtroom floor, unfurling, with all the magnificent grace of a clipper ship spreading canvas, an armor of metallic blue and iridescent gold scales. His wings and his cold ethereal intelligence held him aloft. Eyes of hot implacable ruby surveyed the shambles of overturned furniture and fleeing human bodies his metamorphosis had made of the courtroom. He trod the air with regal impunity. His glinting jade talons, five to each foot, opened and closed on the invading night wind like those of a hawk in full expectation of its prey. From the enigma of his jaws shot a tongue of searching liquid fire. Neither the courthouse nor the whole of Wickrath County could contain him. In a nictitating eyeblink he recreated the surrounding Georgia countryside in the vivid chiaroscuro of the terrains of undying myth. Meanwhile, and afterwards, he rose like many raucous birds toward the mute simplicity of the moon.

But before the part of this manifestation that was Lang fell forever into eclipse, it acknowledged again how miserably unfulfilled were its good intentions and how tangled and strange were the ways of men.

Seasons of Belief

In the dead of winter, in a high-ceilinged room in a drafty, many-gabled house, a family had gathered to pass the twilight hour after supper. Father was reading a book, Mother was busy with thimble and needle at her quilting frame, and the children were stretched out in front of the room's copper-colored space heater with their crayons and several big yellow-grey sheets of newsprint.

It was not long before their bedtime. The silence in the room had grown as thick and muffling as the coverlets of snow on the house's gables and windowsills. In everyone's mind was the half-formed thought that the first word spoken into this stillness would seem as loud and unexpected as a Fourth of July firecracker.

In everyone's mind, that is, except Stefa's. Stefa was five. She had suddenly grown tired of drawing trees across her paper and of worrying about explaining to everyone else what her fine treelike trees were *really* supposed to be. Father would mistake them for people, Mother for tornadoes or big green bananas, and Jimbo, willfully, for scribbles. Stefa was also tired of sharing the crayons, even though the box contained at least a hundred of them. Only a few were good honest colors like red, yellow, blue, green, and orange.

All the rest were imposters like burnt sienna, aquamarine, raw umber, goldenrod, or colors equally shady; and what, exactly, were they *good* for?

Stefa threw her good honest green crayon on the floor and watched it roll under the space heater. "Tell us a story," she demanded.

Her brother, Jimbo, who was seven, jumped as if a Fourth of July firecracker had just exploded. But after looking disapprovingly at Stefa, he turned to his parents and repeated his sister's request: "Yes, tell us a story. We're tired of drawing."

"Your turn," said Mother, looking directly at her husband. "Last night I told them about rollerskating to the circus."

The children hurried across the room and crumpled the pages of Father's book climbing into his lap. When they were finally settled on either side of him in the big green chair, Stefa said:

"A scary story, please."

"All right," Father told them, finally adjusted to their presence. "This is a story about the grither—because Stefa wants a scary story."

"What's a grither?" Jimbo asked.

"A grither is a creature," began the children's father, "who lives in the wreck of an ancient packet ship in the ice floes of the Arctic Circle. There is only one grither in the entire world, and each time he hears his name spoken aloud by any member of the human population, he sets off to find that impertinent person and make sure that he never says his name again. He has very, very good ears, the grither does, and he cannot tolerate being the object of anyone's gossip."

"Don't tell *this* story," Stefa cautioned her father. "I don't want you to tell it."

Mother looked up from her quilting frame. "It may be too late to stop him, Stefa. Your father has already mentioned the grither's name, and the creature is probably on his way to our house right this very moment."

"He's only just started," the father said. "It'll take him a while to get here, of course, and if I'm careful to keep this story short, the grither may not be able to reach our house before I've finished. He depends on hearing his name several times to get to where he needs to go."

"Don't tell it," Stefa pleaded, hoping that her father would go on to the last possible moment before their safety was irrevocably compromised and the grither sprang into the room to devour them.

"Do you know why the grither is called a grither?" Father asked, looking first at Stefa and then at Jimbo.

"Why?" the children asked together.

"Because the grither has fists as big as basketballs and arms as long as boa constrictors. When he finally locates the human busybodies who have been tossing his lovely name around, he opens up his fists, reaches out his arms, and—*grithers'em in!* Just like that, Stefa and Jimbo, just as if he were hugging his cousins at a family reunion—he *grithers'em in!*"

Jimbo and Stefa shuddered and pressed themselves more tightly against their father.

"Is the grither a bigfoot?" the boy asked.

"No," Father responded. "The grither isn't a bigfoot, or an abominable snowman, or any of those other doubtful monsters that people sometimes think they've seen. The grither has never been seen by *anyone*—except, of course, by the people whom he grithers in and gobbles up. And those unfortunate folks are no longer around to tell us what he looks like."

"What does he look like?" asked Jimbo.

"Well, besides his basketball fists and boa-constrictor arms, the grither has a body as tall and supple as a poplar tree. You can see right through him, though, as if he were made of melting, colorless gelatin. He looks a little bit like a plastic road map because inside his legs and arms and chest and face you can see the tiny red-and-blue veins that twist through his body and help to hold him together. The blue's for fear, the red's for rage, and these feelings, flowing through his veins, help to keep him warm, too. As you may imagine, it's very chilly in the hold of a packet ship stuck in the pack ice—much chillier, my children, than it ever gets here."

"Then why doesn't he leave?" Stefa objected.

"He does," Father said. "Every time he hears anyone speaking his name aloud. When I first started telling this story, the grither snaked his way out of that shipwrecked vessel's hold, slithered over the gunwales, and began loping across the blue-white Arctic deserts toward the sound of our voices. He doesn't like gossip, as I've already told you, but he's always glad for the chance to go somewhere to stifle it. He's coming now. Listen."

"No!" shrieked Stefa, covering her ears and shutting her eyes. But even so she could hear the sighing of the wind in the naked oaks—a sound as sinister as a siren at midnight.

"Where is he now?" Jimbo asked. The boy peered at the room's solitary, icy window, sneaked a look at the door, and glanced suspiciously at the innocent ceiling.

"That's hard to say," Father replied. "But as he comes to get whoever's gossiping about him, he always sings this song." And, narrowing his eyes and doing something strange to his voice, Father showed them how the song was sung:

"I am the grither, gruesome and hungry.
Here I come, folks,
All the while grimacing.
You cannot escape me—it's simply impossible.
Don't even try.
I am the grither, crude and most grum.
Pleading is useless.
So are your prayers—also your rabbit's feet.
The grither is greedy
For only one thing:
To silence your gossip, folks.
That's why this song says
Your moments are numbered.
I'm quite sorry for you.
I'm quite sorry for you.
So please do accept
My most heartfelt apologies."

Scandalized, Stefa protested, "That doesn't even *rhyme!* There aren't no sound-alikes!"

"'Any,'" Mother interjected.

"There aren't *any* sound-alikes," Stefa corrected herself.

"That's true," Father admitted. "And the grither doesn't sing very well, either."

"But where is he now?" Jimbo asked.

Father tilted his head and listened to the sound of the grither's song as it was apparently borne to him on the sighing winter wind. "Maine," he said. "The grither's in Maine—but he's heading relentlessly south and taking all the shortcuts he knows."

"Stop!" cried Stefa. "Don't tell any more!"

"It's cheating," said Father, "if you don't finish the story. You just have to be sure to finish it before the grither arrives—that's the main thing. Now that the grither's on his way, it would be terribly unfair to leave him stranded in Bangor. He doesn't like short trips, you know."

"It isn't fair to the people in Maine, either," Mother pointed out. "He's always traipsing back and forth through their state, and we can't allow that revengeful critter to impose on their hospitality any more than he already manages to."

"No, we can't," Father agreed.

"Well, then," said Stefa impatiently, "please hurry up and finish telling the story."

"Yes," said Jimbo. "Maybe you can leave him stranded in New Jersey or Virginia. Virginia's a pretty state."

"That's an idea," said Father, contemplating this notion. "All right, then. I'll go on with my story. You may be wondering where the grither came from in the first place. Well, the fact is—"

Just then the telephone—which hung from a wall in the kitchen, right next to the pantry door—began to ring. Stefa thought that the burring noise it emitted was exactly the sort of sound you could expect a statue in the park to make, if only statues could come alive in the cold to shiver and suffer.

"Would you mind getting that?" Mother asked Father. "I've almost finished quilting this square."

"Oh, no!" cried Jimbo and Stefa in unison.

Father shrugged amiably, eased himself out of the big green chair, and disappeared into the kitchen to make the phone stop ringing. He caught it on the sixth or seventh burr.

Stefa and Jimbo, with a warm dent between them in the cushion, looked at each other and made worried faces. They lived in the South, but not *that* far south, and the grither was descending upon them like a ravenous avalanche. Stefa could not understand her parents' lack of concern—they were usually very sensible people.

"Where is he now?" she moaned. "Where is he now?"

"Boston, maybe," Mother said, without looking up from the quilting frame. "Or Philadelphia, if he's flying."

"Flying?" said Jimbo. "How?"

"Well," said Mother, briefly pursing her lips as she forced the needle through two layers of cloth and the cotton batting between them, "the grither's ears—which are invisibly small to start with—get bigger and bigger each time his name is spoken. By the time it's been spoken ten or twelve times, they're big enough to carry him wherever he's going; a pair of miraculous transparent wings." Mother took off her thimble, kissed her thumb, and tugged thoughtfully at her ear lobe. "I'd imagine our grither's over Philadelphia, or maybe Baltimore, by now. He ought to have an extremely nice pair of ear-wings—we've been gossiping about him for quite some time."

"Daddy!" Stefa screamed at the kitchen. *"Daddy!"*

Father came strolling back into the living room with his hands in his pockets. "Here I am," he said. He sat down between the children.

"Hurry," Stefa advised him. "Finish telling the story."

"Who was that?" Mother asked, nodding her head toward the kitchen and the telephone.

"I don't know," Father responded mysteriously. (Stefa was not sure if he had winked at Mother or not.) "Someone who knows who we are and who wondered if we were home. I said we were, of course."

"Was it the grither?" Jimbo asked, his face betraying both excitement and alarm.

"I don't know that, either. You see, Jimbo, the caller didn't say who he was and I've never heard the grither speak before. How do you suppose I ought to be able to recognize his voice?"

"You sang his silly song," Stefa reminded him.

"Right," Father said. "But that was from memory."

Neither Stefa nor Jimbo understood the precise meaning of this explanation, but it kept them from asking any more questions about the grither's voice. It didn't, however, keep them from worrying about the telephone call.

Pounding her kneecaps, Stefa urged Father to finish the story.

"Washington, D.C.," Mother noncommittally informed her family. "I believe he's over Washington."

"Please," said Stefa.

"Well," said Father, trying to take up where the telephone call had interrupted him, "the grither came into existence when a royal packet ship steaming between Boston, Massachusetts, and Portsmouth, England, was blown ridiculously off course by a storm and driven up Baffin Bay toward the Pole. Not a soul aboard that ship survived—but before they all drowned or froze to death, they lifted their voices into the storm to remind the heavens that they were under the King's protection. The grither was born from the fear, rage, and disappointment of those who died. And it has ever since been merciless to those who speak its name because the storm was merciless to those who had to die to give the grither life."

"Is that all?" asked Stefa.

"Richmond, Virginia," said Mother. "He's soaring over Richmond—on his way to Winston-Salem."

"No," said Father, looking at his little girl. "Not quite all. The story goes that the grither won't cease to exist until—"

There was a knock on the door. Mother looked at Father. Stefa and Jimbo looked at each other. The wind, as it curled around the gables of the house, set the walls and floorboards a-creaking. The light bulb hanging from its cord in the center of the room began to bob and dance.

And a voice beyond the door was singing:

"The grither is greedy
For only one thing:
To silence your gossip, folks.
That's why this song says
Your moments are numbered.
I'm quite sorry for you.
So please do accept
My most heartfelt apologies."

When the singing was finished, the knocking on the door grew louder and louder.

"Who's going to answer it?" asked Father.

Stefa and Jimbo shrank back against the big green chair's bolster cushion and gave their father disbelieving looks. When Mother saw their fear, she in turn gave Father a look of reproach and warning.

"I'm sorry," Father began contritely. "It's really just—"

But the door banged open with a crash, a huge furry figure leapt through the opening with a roar of Arctic air, and the double row of tiny blue flames in the space heater rippled and guttered as the same voice that had been singing the grither's song cried out in malevolent glee:

"GOTCHA!"

The entire family gasped as a single person. Father, indeed, jumped out of his chair.

Then they all saw that the figure who had sprung through the door was Stefa and Jimbo's grandfather, dressed for the season in a raccoon coat and a Russian hat. Coming into the high-ceilinged room behind him, Grandmother had the practicality and presence of mind to close the wide-thrown door.

"Grandfather sometimes gets carried away," she apologized.

"I telephoned to say we were coming," said Grandfather unrepentantly, winking at Mother. "Didn't this husband of yours tell the children?"

Father's mouth was still open. He had neither the practicality nor the presence of mind to close it.

"I've finished with this," said Mother, rising from her quilting frame. "Let's go into the kitchen for coffee and doughnuts." She led Grandmother and Grandfather, scolding each other and laughing, out of the dim and drafty living room to the comfort of the kitchen table.

"Where's the grither?" Stefa demanded of her father, wiping tears of fright from her eyes. "Where's the *real* grither?"

"Yes," said Jimbo. "What about the rest of the story?"

Father closed his mouth and put his hands in his pockets. Then he opened his mouth and said very slowly:

"I hope neither of you really believes in the grither. You don't, do you?"

"No-o-ohh," the children managed.

"Good," boomed Father jovially. "Because if you don't believe in what isn't, it can't do you any harm. Can it?"

Stefa and Jimbo looked at each other. In unison, each prompted by the other, they doubtfully shook their heads.

"It's almost bedtime. Come into the kitchen for milk and doughnuts, and then we'll go up to bed." Father paused before leaving and looked at the floor. "But first pick up your crayons, please."

Alone in the high-ceilinged living room, Stefa and Jimbo got down in front of the space heater to pick up their scattered crayons—the aquamarines and goldenrods as well as the reds and blues.

"Winston-Salem isn't too far from here," Jimbo said as they gathered up the crayons. "I've seen it on a map at school."

And Stefa whispered miserably, "I wonder where the grither is right now." For Stefa believed in the grither, and what she believed in could certainly do her harm, couldn't it?

"Look," said Jimbo, and he pointed at the rime-coated window across the room. In the final moments of dusk, with the electric glare of the light bulb glinting off the glass, the window was veined with slender threads of red and blue, and the glass itself seemed to be melting—just like leftover Jell-O when no one has put it back in the refrigerator.

But because they weren't a bit surprised, Stefa and Jimbo didn't even scream. . . .

Cold War Orphans

In late August, 1957, my father—who had just resigned his commission in the United States Air Force—drove me across country from Edwards Air Force Base in the Mojave Desert to the little community of Huerfano, Kansas, some thirty-five or forty miles due south of Wichita. Here he left me in the drafty Victorian house of my great-aunt, Theodosia Moyer, an apple-faced woman of a certain, almost stereotyped Midwestern craziness, and drove away toward Washington, D.C., his jumping-off place for a position with the National Advisory Committee for Aeronautics. All that he would tell either my great-aunt or me (Doozie was approaching sixty, and I had just turned twelve) was that he would be working out of Incirlik Air Force Base near Adana, Turkey; he would be flying weather reconnaissance missions from this base as part of NACA's contribution to the International Geophysical Year. Neither Theodosia nor I could understand why he had to resign his captaincy if he was still going to be flying government aircraft, but he dismissed our questions with some unconvincing talk about Congressional funding and "contractual domain." What most mattered to me, though, was that my father was abandoning me to the care of a woman I scarcely knew, in a community whose population and values were as alien to me as Adana, Turkey's, were likely to be to my father. I was a cosmopolitan Air Force brat, after all, and felt that I had been unceremoniously dumped among country people and small-town gossips.

Just before my father left, Theodosia took his arm and said to him, "I've figured out what you're really going to be doing, Wesley Ray." We were standing together near the driveway in front of her house, and the blunt, boxy, scarlet-and-white '55 Chevrolet convertible that had carried us from California was griddle-hot in the August sun.

"What am I 'really going to be doing'?" Wesley Ray Weir asked the sister of his dead mother.

"Working for the FBI," Doozie informed him. "That's why you're not in the Air Force anymore. That's why you can't take Malcolm with you."

It seemed to me that my father's eyes widened, that his jaw grew slack, but he abruptly broke my great-aunt's grip on his arm and began to laugh. Doozie's house was on the northeastern corner of Huerfano, a big isolated house on a treeless rise, and my father's laughter echoed out over the highway running down from Wichita toward Missouri and Arkansas.

"What's the matter?" Theodosia asked. "Did I earn my name?"

"Yes, ma'am," Wesley Ray Weir answered her, still chuckling. "You're nothing if not a doozie." Ten minutes later he had roared away down that highway above which the mirage of his laughter still shimmered. He was gone.

He stayed gone with a will. I started school in September, and by the middle of that month I had heard from him only once: a postcard of the Propylaea, the sacred gateway of the Acropolis, from Athens, Greece, where he had already gone for a recreational weekend. Three lines of inconsequential chatter ending, "When you get them, send me your grades."

At the beginning of October the Soviet Union sent up the first man-made satellite, Sputnik, and thereby shocked the entire Western world out of its delusions of technological superiority. But still my father did not write. In November the Russians followed Sputnik I with a dog act, sending aloft the doomed bitch Laika, bait to which animal lovers and antivivisectionists everywhere rose like hungry carp. The United States responded to this challenge by ballyhooing the minuscule Vanguard satellite that we intended to launch on December 6 and then failing publicly on our designated Day of Reckoning. We were an international laughingstock. But still my father did not write, and this, to me, was a profounder disappointment than our highly visible and apparently very funny "kaputnik."

I was unskillful at making friends, and by the middle of December I had grown bitter and uncommunicative.

During my Christmas break, Doozie caught me moping about her huge kitchen and dragged me to a wall-mounted telephone. "We'll call him," she said; "we'll call him long-distance, all the way from Huerfano to whatever-its-name-is in Turkey. Come on."

To establish any sort of overseas connection at all took better than thirty minutes, and the first European voice to thread its reedy way through the receiver spoke a language I could not identify; it wasn't French or German, that's all I knew. The transmission was prohibitively garbled and thin.

Somehow, after another ten minutes had passed, Theodosia found herself talking to a self-reputed Air Force noncom who said he'd never heard of either a Mr. or a Capt. Wesley R. Weir. Between Doozie's and my heads, the telephone receiver was a bone of black contention.

"Who am I talking to?" my great-aunt shouted into the phone.

A sea of whirrs and whizzes, in which floated an armada of random clicks, poured forth in response. At last the radioman said, *"This is Tech Sergeant Federico Seleno of the First Lunar Communications Detachment."* Even the broth of noise behind these words could not disguise the fact that our noncom was either drunk or crazy.

"Put on somebody else!" Theodosia shouted.

Static. The roar of the void. Finally: *"Ain't nobody else. I'm the only manjack up here. Scott never made it, and poor old Seleno's been marooned on the moon, good missus."*

"Get out of that radio room," Theodosia advised Sgt. Seleno. "Get out of that radio room and go to bed."

SMITH

"Bring me home," the man called out through the high thin roar of several intervening time zones. *"Dear sweet missus, bring me home. . . ."*

"This is not the party you wished?" interjected a nasal female voice, much closer to hand than the First Lunar Communications Detachment.

"No," responded Doozie; "no, it isn't."

"Then perhaps we'd better terminate this call. Try again at another time, please." The receiver clicked and regaled Theodosia and me with a protracted raspberry, a death-buzz and an insult at once. I reflected that I had never liked telephones; they sat on end tables like ebony Buddhas with clocks in their stomachs or hung from kitchen walls like plastic fire-alarm boxes. At best, they were useless; at worst, they were evil messengers.

"Nice try," I told my great-aunt without sarcasm and wandered into her bedroom to stare out her wide french windows at the creeping December twilight.

All of a sudden it was 1958. In January I was surprised to read in a copy of *Time* left lying on a table in the school library that the weather during the previous year had been warmer than usual. "The waves in the planetary wind," *Time* told me, "were feeble and lethargic. . . . New England had weather 15° to 18° above normal, and such notorious cold spots as Montana were mild." This made me believe that Huerfano's thick Christmas snowfall had been a completely local phenomenon, if not some sort of weird optical illusion. A mild autumn and winter? The autumn and winter of 1957 had been the coldest I had ever known, and now the article under my hands was saying that the planetary winds had grown active again and the nation was in for extracold temperatures.

Zero-at-the-bone my constant internal reading, zero-at-the-bone the most accurate measure of my impenetrable mental state, I sleepwalked through the first three weeks of the new year. . . .

On Thursday, January 23, along with a grocery circular and a sample tube of toothpaste, there arrived in Theodosia's mailbox a manila envelope from my father. Postmarked the 16th from Munich, Germany, and covered with a host of emphatically canceled foreign stamps, it was addressed exclusively to me. I carried this packet upstairs to my unheated room and, trembling from more than mere cold, tore it open. Then, from the envelope, I pulled page after page of letter, all of it fastidiously spelled and neatly hand-corrected with a fountain pen. It remains to this day the longest letter I have ever received; and, in spite of the instructions it contains for its disposal, I have saved my father's letter, hidden it, and guarded it for almost twenty years.

As you will soon see, my father's favorite punctuation mark was the dash, and he insisted on capitalizing every letter of dialogue in his letter—maybe because air-to-ground radio transmissions were often transcribed in this way in classified documents of the period; I don't really know. I mention the dashes and the capitalization, however, because my father was not ordinarily a meticulous person, and here, apparently as a kind of penance, he made himself adhere to a carefully worked-out and rigid epistolary form. Characteristically, that form was one of his own devising.

Dearest Son,

Belated greetings from *Türkiye.* I don't know how to begin, I don't know how to approach you. Down the road from Incirlik and Detachment 10-10—about 43 kilometers to be as exact as I can—is Tarsus, the birthplace of Saint Paul. It's almost Christmas as I begin this, and it was Saint Paul—they say—who first thought of Christianity as a universal religion. But I have never been an artist with my feelings and always a pretty poor one with words—I can't do what Rembrandt did and paint myself to look like Saint Paul, can I. I have not even been a very good father, much less any kind of saint, and I am sorry for this, Mal.

I don't think I have ever told you I am religious, but I am. All I have in my trailer here on base—I am typing this on a card table—is a book called *The Bible Designed To Be Read As Living Literature.* I checked it out from our base library, such as it is, but I know my mother would never have classified this book as a REAL Bible. Anyway, I have been so far from either a saint or a father to you that I want to type out a line or two from this pseudo-Bible I have beside me.Okay?

> The Spirit itself
> beareth witness with our spirit, that we are the children of God: and if children, then heirs; heirs of God, and joint

> heirs with Christ; if so be that we suffer with him, that we may be also glorified together. For I reckon that the sufferings of this present time are not worthy to be compared with the glory which shall be revealed in us.

And this too, Mal—

> For we are saved by hope: but hope that is seen is not hope: for what man seeth, why doth he yet hope for? But if we hope for that we see not, then do we with patience wait for it.

These are from the Epistles to the Romans. Paul was a better letter-writer than I am, wasn't he. But if you'd begun to think I'd forgotten about you, please read these passages a couple of times and think about them. You are a deep thinker, Mal—at least compared to me—and you will probably see what I am trying to say by stealing somebody else's words to say it. I hope you have had hope, you see. Hope is what saves you—faith and hope.

My excuse for revealing my religious feelings to you in a letter is that not too long ago I went to Tarsus and saw Sen Pol Kuyusu, the fountain from which the family of Saint Paul got its water. Sometimes it seems that the world's fountain of faith and hope is running dry, and I don't want you to feel that way, Mal.

Damn typewriter—look how muddy the *e*'s and *o*'s are and the *n* sticks too—

Besides *The Bible Designed To Be Read As Living Literature* I also have here a copy of a letter from my aunt—your great-aunt—my conscience. WRITE YOUR SON is basically what her letter says, but I will quote from it: "I am opposed to *paternalism* in just about every human endeavor, W.R., but *paternity* is something else again. I am afraid you have ceased to think of this last word except in conjunction with the legalism *suit.* This is wrong, W.R. Wake up, for shame, and write your son!!!" When the letter arrived it looked to me as if it had been opened in transit.

Almost all of the letters I have received here, Malcolm, have been tampered with. That's why I'm not going to mail this from the base post office. I am not going to put my APO number on the envelope either—just my name. For the sake of security I suppose it is possible that someone in our intelligence section is censoring both in-coming and out-going mail. (That is *one* of the reasons I have not written you before, although I know this is a poor excuse.) A person who would take such a job, I think, is a kind of human jackal, eating other people's guts and privates, and if that jackal was to read how I feel, he might well rip my whole letter up. I don't want that to happen, but I want to say what I want to say—that's why I'll mail my letter from somewhere else and then keep my fingers crossed.

To show my faith in you, Malcolm, I am going to tell you exactly what I am doing. You mustn't tell anyone else though—not even Doozie. If my letter's intercepted before it reaches you, I'll be canned and called a traitor and a few things worse than that. I'm willing to take this risk to show my faith and to make you a gift for Christmas from a bad Christian in a Moslem land. It'll be a late gift, I guess.

I'm working for the Central Intelligence Agency—that's why I resigned my commission, they made me give it up to take this job—and flying a new reconnaissance aircraft over the Soviet Union. The other pilots and I take aerial photographs of military and industrial centers—we also snap missile and rocket launches. Although none of us here saw the Sputniks go up, we have seen and taken pictures of a couple of the big fizzles at the Tyuratam Cosmodrome—which is where the Russians shoot most of their rockets off from. I feel a silly pride in saying that these folks aren't Superman anymore than Uncle Sam is. (We pilots are Superman, I guess, gliding untouched and unseen over the breast of Mother Russia.) What they are is a scared and prideful bunch of people—with zippers in their pants and vodka on their breaths—who know we're watching everything they do and counting down their every countdown as we watch. That's why their Fat Man rattles rockets. He's a scared bear, he thinks we're going to run him up a tree and shoot him—he really does.

I am being paid $30,000 a year, and I do not like my job. I'm supposed to be an employee of Lockheed—you knew this, I think—on loan to the National Advisory Committee for Aeronautics. I'm supposed to be a pilot in the Second Weather Observational Squadron (Provisional), and I'm supposed to be one of those studying turbulence and meteorological conditions in the Middle East. What I really am—as Doozie pretty near guessed last August—is a spy. I don't like being a spy, in spite of the $30,000. Being a spy makes me nervous and ill-tempered—I don't even enjoy flying the fragile aerodynamic beauty that seemed to me during my training at the Watertown Strip in Nevada such a magnificent piece of American flight-engineering. Sometimes I'm afraid I'm going to upchuck in my helmet and breathe vomit all the way back to base. (For 24 hours prior to each overflight I purposely do not eat—nausea will kill me before the cyanide capsules we're permitted to take along for "emergencies.")

There are six other pilots on duty here, Malcolm, although I'm presently without a trailermate. When I arrived, the man with whom I was assigned to share quarters—I'll call him G because I really don't want to put the finger on any of these fellows—was nearing the end of his 18-month contract and didn't know whether he'd re-up for another twelve months or not. G's wife had somehow managed to get a civil-service position at Wheelus Air Force Base in Tripoli—there aren't any jobs for American civilians around here—and in September they both went stateside on G's leave to discuss the situation. When the CIA finally agreed to permit dependents to come to Incirlik if all our short-termers extended their contracts, G extended. Just before Christmas—which was yesterday, by the way—G and his wife returned, but they have a house in Adana now—as do most of the other married pilots—and that means that most of the time I live in this trailer alone.

My trailer's not far from the airstrip. There's a fence around the Detachment 10-10 section of base with UNAUTHORIZED PERSONNEL PROHIBITED signs on the chain link and helmeted sentries at all the gates. Sometimes I feel that I'm in prison here, but most of the other pilots seem happy to be here and fond of their jobs. It's rumored that we'll soon have an Officers Club.

Christmas is past. An Asian-African Peoples' Solidarity Conference had been going on for several days in Cairo, and on Saturday a henchman of the Fat Man notified the conference that their country would support all "movements for independence" initiated there. I wish I was in Cairo—but I'm neither Asian nor African and guess I don't really belong.

I don't belong here, either.

Up there in the pages I wrote the day after Christmas I say that "most of the time I live in this trailer alone." But sometimes I don't. When G left Incirlik to straighten things out with his wife in the States, a Gung-Ho Pilot from two trailers over began to drop in on me every time he and his trailermate—whom I will call Q—had a falling-out. Q is a slovenly 36-year-old fellow with a great many human failings, whereas the Gung-Ho Pilot is a poker-straight 27-year-old model of American manhood. I am going to give the Gung-Ho Pilot's real name here because he is dead now and there is no way that I can compromise his life to the Enemy.

The Gung-Ho Pilot's real name was Lt. John Scott Brown. Technically he wasn't a lieutenant at all anymore—just as I am no longer a captain—but we still seem to think of ourselves as military personnel and John Scott Brown was a lieutenant before he was a CIA agent. He was a pilot before he was a lieutenant. He was a fanatic before he was a pilot. I don't believe he was a little boy before he was a fanatic because I'm unable to picture him as anything other than his 27-year-old self. He looked like a model for the Air Force formal mess-dress uniform—one of those plastic department-store dummies with perfect eyebrows and artificially rosy cheeks—but he was a real human being. At least I think he was. Q still swears that Scott slept in a hair net and a foundation of facial cream—without even the testimony of his own eyes for proof. Q also suspected Scott of wearing tiny colored lenses over his eyes to give him a startling blue-eyed stare and maybe to correct a vision problem. (None of us U-2 pilots are supposed to have vision problems, of course.)

I WOKE UP EARLY ONE MORNING WITH A BELLYACHE, Q told me late in August, AND WHEN I GOT TO THE BATHROOM, SCOTT WAS WASHING HIS FACE OVER THE SINK. HE LOOKED UP AT ME, RAY, AND

HE WAS AS CROSS-EYED AS A SIAMESE CAT, WITH IRISES THE COLOR OF FRESH-MADE POWDERED MILK. THEN HE DID SOMETHING WITH HIS HANDS, COVERING HIS FACE, AND HE WAS SUDDENLY HIS DAY-TIME SELF AGAIN—VIOLET-EYED AND MEAN-LOOKING. Q said that it was about five a.m. and that Scott was secretly washing off his cold cream. He said Scott's hair net was probably in his robe pocket.

DID YOU SEE THE HAIR NET, I asked Q. DID YOU SEE THE COLD CREAM ON HIS FACE. ARE YOU SURE YOU WEREN'T JUST WOOZY AND IMAGINING THINGS.

I WASN'T JUST WOOZY, RAY. THAT BASTARD ALWAYS WENT TO BED LATER THAN I DID AND GOT UP EARLIER. WHEN I WAS SLEEPING HE PUT ON HIS MAKEUP AND HIS HAIR NET AND TOOK OUT HIS EYES. THAT MORNING I WOKE UP SICK, RAY, I DAMN NEAR CAUGHT THE BASTARD AT HIS TRICKS. THE SONUVABITCH HAS WHITE IRISES I'M TELLING YOU!

HE GETS UP EARLIER THAN YOU, I said, BECAUSE HE DOESN'T WANT ANYBODY IN THE DETACHMENT TO BE MORE MILITARY THAN HIM, THAT'S ALL.

Q shook his head and mumbled that he was the only man on base in a position to really know Scott's "secrets." It was amazing, Q said, that Scott had been able to get past all the CIA's preliminary screenings back in the States. But this was when I was new to Incirlik, Malcolm—a replacement for a pilot whose plane had been caught in the turbulence of two Canadian Air Force jets over Giebelstadt in Germany—and my first impression was that Q had gone crazy sweating out the summer on Turkey's beaches and stumbling through the Hittite ruins at Karatepe. Also I had seen that he could drink more beer than me, and—reacting just as Doozie would have—I didn't trust his judgments.

Then I met John Scott Brown at closer quarters—my own. It was Saturday, early in October, and surprisingly hot. Someone started pounding on my trailer door like eight or ten battering rams, and I zigzagged over that way in my bathrobe to find John Scott Brown standing in the glare outside looking very neat, upright, and businesslike.

YOU'RE NOT STILL SLEEPING, ARE YOU. I told him that I wasn't still sleeping anymore, and he said, Q HAS FOULED OUR NEST, RAY,

AND I HAVE TO GET OUT OF THE STINK AND SMOKE. IT SHOULDN'T BOTHER YOU HAVING ME IN BECAUSE THIS IS A TWO-MAN TRAILER AND G ISN'T EVEN HERE. He came up the steps, looked at the clutter just like a man from the Inspector General's office, and sniffed the air to see if it was breathable.

Scott—I had already learned—made it a practice to go to the Detachment's personnel section to find out new arrivals' full names. Then he chose from that person's Christian, middle, and family names the one that he—Scott—liked best and proceeded to call the new arrival by that choice. He himself insisted on being called Scott, and many of us here, even after his disappearance and death, are called by our middle names simply because Scott happened to like that one above all the other possibilities. Since I have always been called by *two* names, it wasn't hard to adjust to hearing only the middle one—but Q doesn't like *his* middle name and resents its use.

WHAT HAS Q DONE, I asked Scott after he'd sniffed the air.

HE BOUGHT A BETTY CROCKER DEVIL'S-FOOD CAKE MIX AT THE BX YESTERDAY, AND THIS MORNING HE TRIED TO MAKE IT—THAT'S WHAT HE'S DONE!

BUT WHAT'S HE DOING NOW, SCOTT.

HE'S SITTING ON HIS BED IN HIS SHORTS DRINKING FALSTAFFS. HE'S GOT EMPTY CANS ALL OVER THE PLACE. I'M GOING TO SPEND THE DAY OVER HERE, RAY, AND THE NIGHT TOO IF HE DOESN'T GET THE MESS CLEANED UP. He asked me for some coffee and said he hadn't yet eaten breakfast. WE WERE GOING TO HAVE CAKE, BUT THE CAKE LOOKS LIKE AN EARLY-AMERICAN FLATIRON.

Scott sat down at the table in the living room and turned on my air-conditioner. He crossed his feet at the ankles and then began to play with his hands as if he was taking off a pair of white gloves finger by finger. He wasn't wearing any gloves though. I stayed in the "kitchen" the whole time our coffee water was boiling, and he kept taking off and putting on his invisible gloves. Then I brought two cups of Turkish coffee to the table and sat down across from him. (I'd bought the coffee in Adana's covered market, the Kapali Çarşi—it's the kind you have to boil in a kettle with lots of sugar.) The air-conditioner was blowing right across the tops of our cups.

YOU'RE FROM KANSAS, he said after sipping the stuff. YOU HAVE A WONDERFUL FUTURE AHEAD OF YOU.

WHY, I asked.

KANSAS IS THE HEART OF THE HEART OF THE COUNTRY.

THE ARMPIT, SOME PEOPLE SAY.

NOT AROUND ME THEY DON'T. I'M A KANSAN MYSELF. I'M FROM WICHITA. Then he said, THE FUTURE BELONGS TO THE NATION THAT CONTROLS THE EXOSPHERE AND INTERPLANETARY SPACE, AND WICHITA'S THE AIR CAPITAL OF THE WORLD. CESSNA, BEECH, AND BOEING FLOURISH THERE, NOT TO MENTION MCCONNELL AIR FORCE BASE.

NO ONE'S GOING INTO INTERPLANETARY SPACE IN A BEECH TWO-SEATER, I told him. AND IT'S THE RUSSIANS WHO'VE JUST PUT A SATELLITE UP.

He ignored this last. WHERE IN KANSAS ARE YOU FROM, RAY.

HUERFANO, I said.

NEVER HEARD OF IT.

I'VE HEARD OF WICHITA. I'VE ALSO HEARD OF ANOTHER KANSAN WHOSE NAME WAS JOHN BROWN.

A DISTANT RELATIVE OF MINE. HIS MIDDLE NAME WASN'T SCOTT THOUGH. HE WAS A CRAZY MAN—OFF HIS NUT. HE THOUGHT HEAVEN WAS THE FUTURE—THAT WAS HIS MISTAKE—AND HE SHED OTHER PEOPLE'S BLOOD SO THAT THEY COULD GO THERE CLEANSED. I'M NOT SO DELUDED.

We sipped at our cups, and the air-conditioner made a low humming noise as it cooled our coffee down. I thought Scott would come back to talking about how Kansans had a great future ahead of them, but he let me get him a fresh cup of coffee and changed the subject. He asked me if I was married and how many kids I had, so I told him about you. Then he wanted to know what kind of name Malcolm was, and I told him it was a name your mother and I had chosen together—that was all. He shook his head. He wanted to know what your middle name was, I think, but your records weren't available and he didn't like to ask. Finally he took his wallet out and showed me some photographs.

I HAVE TWO-POINT-THREE CHILDREN, he said. THAT'S THE NATIONAL AVERAGE. BEING KANSANS, MARY AND I LIKE TO THINK THAT OUR THIRD ONE IS ALWAYS UNDETECTED IN THE OVEN. AC-

TUALLY, I CAN BARELY STOMACH THE TWO HOUSE-APES WE'VE ALREADY GOT—BUT YOU'D NEVER GET ME TO ADMIT THAT, NOT EVEN WITH SPLINTERS UNDER MY FINGERNAILS AND HOT TONGS ON MY BALLS.

WHAT DID YOU SAY, I asked him. I'd let my mind wander a little, and his last words jolted me awake again.

NOTHING, he said, smiling at me with eyes as blue as the waters off Iskenderun. So of course I wondered if I had only imagined hearing him say what I have written above.

Scott's two children were named Curt and Cathy—not Curtis and Catherine, he warned me, for even their birth certificates said Curt and Cathy—and they appeared to be about six and four. They were photographed sitting on the hood of a 1957 Ford, and they were as towheaded as if they'd just crawled out of a stack of loose hay. Mary—Scott's wife—stood to one side of the automobile wearing a Wichita State letter sweater that was too big for her housewifely shoulders. She was pretty though.

YOU HAVE A LOVELY FAMILY.

YES, Scott said, THEY'RE MY CAREER ASSETS.

About a week later Scott, Q, and I went into Adana for dinner. The only really decent place to go is the roof-garden restaurant at the *Erciyas Palas* Hotel. Rich Turkish people, foreign businessmen, and American officers from Incirlik—sometimes wearing uniforms instead of mufti like us CIA "civilians"—go there to eat. You can hear street noises from the restaurant tables while you're picking apart your Circassian-style chicken or the meat and tomatoes on a *şiş kebabi* skewer—but it's usually cool up there in the evening and you've got lattice work overhead with colored lights suspended among the vines. (G took me there once right after my arrival, and back on base I developed a bad case of the GIs. It wasn't the food, G told me, it was me—you just have to get acclimated.) Anyway—on the evening we went to the *Erciyas Palas*—Q ordered for all three of us. A cucumber salad for starters, then Mediterranean swordfish cut in pieces and served on a spit, and white wine from Anatolia. This was about three days after Secretary Dulles warned Russia of the consequences of an attack on Turkey. Elections were coming up too. Scott and Q, over their food, were tossing around names like Menderes, Ismet Inonu, and Kasim Gulek. (Gulek is a Republican who was arrested for breaking a law against political meetings after shaking hands with a few of his peasant supporters in a village market.) No one on base would go downtown with Scott and Q—I found this out later, when it didn't do me any good—because they always argued Turkish politics in loud voices, without any regard for the sort of crowd they might be in. I ate my swordfish and drank my wine while Scott and Q argued.

MENDERES IS A PRICK, Q was saying loudly but calmly. HE'S A DEMOCRAT LIKE PRETTY BOY FLOYD WAS A MINISTER OF THE GOSPEL.

YOU'RE TALKING ABOUT THE SPIRITUAL HEIR OF ATATÜRK, Scott responded. MENDERES IS BRINGING THIS COUNTRY INTO THE 20TH CENTURY.

MY ASS. HE'S LEADING IT DOWN THE ROAD TO BANKRUPTCY.

NO, HE ISN'T. HE'S A BUILDER, HE'S A PHARAOH!

THE PHARAOH CAN'T EVEN GET A LOAN FROM HIS OWN NATIONAL BANK. HE'S A LOSER. DISAGREE WITH THE BASTARD AND IT'S THE TIGER-CAGE.

(Yes, I know, Malcolm, there is a lot of ugly talk here—but you have heard worse, even from me. I guess you're growing up very fast. That's okay because I've never seen anyone so young as you adjust so well to changes.)

People were looking at us, but Q and Scott kept arguing. Scott was the louder because—usually—whoever was arguing with him gave up when he started getting loud. Q didn't give up though—he made vulgar rebuttals and watched Scott's rosy cheeks grow redder and redder as the argument went on. Q liked to bait Scott and Scott could never see that he was being baited. I was grateful that the loud one at our table was arguing *for* the Menderes regime, even though his loudness implied that either Q or I was arguing against it. My *kilic şiş* didn't taste very good.

REPRESSIVE! Scott was shouting. IF HE'S REPRESSIVE IT'S BECAUSE THE HEAD OF THE ARMY IN SYRIA IS A COMMUNIST! IT'S BECAUSE HE KNOWS THE RUSSIANS COULD WALK FROM KARS TO IZMIR ON THE BODIES OF ALL THE LIBERALS WHO CRY REFORM IN THE FACE OF

THESE THREATS! THANK GOD FOR ADNAN MENDERES, I SAY! WE'D ALL BE EATING BORSCHT OTHERWISE!

MY ASS, said Q. IT'S A WONDER WE'RE NOT ALL EATING HOT DOGS.

A waiter was moving around among the tables—he kept glancing our way—and I had just spilled my wine fumbling with my glass. I put a napkin on the spill and watched the napkin darken—I didn't want to see if the waiter had decided to take any action about our loudness—Scott's loudness, I mean, and Q's. I wondered if I should try to start a conversation about Mickey Mantle or Johnny Unitas.

Then I heard the fourth chair at our table squeak across the floor. I glanced sideways and saw—instead of an angry waiter—a little boy in a coarse linen shirt and a pair of low-cut American sneakers that would have been only a size or two too small for me. He was also wearing a pair of baggy pants with calf-length trouser legs. He jostled the chair around and finally got it where he could sit down and put his elbows on the table.

YEŞAR! Scott said happily. WHERE'VE YOU BEEN KEEPING YOURSELF. The argument was over. RAY, THIS IS YEŞAR ATABÖY. YEŞAR, THIS IS RAY.

HELLO, I said. And the waiter hurried over with the intention of running the little Yeşar Ataböy out of the restaurant. Scott ordered another dinner though and sent the waiter back to the kitchen. The boy was about your age, Malcolm, but much smaller and darker. He had a small purple-pink mouth, like a violet bloom, and eyebrows that bridged his nose. If you looked at him just right—or maybe I should say "just wrong"—he seemed to be closer to sixty than to twelve. He was just a kid, but he had the kind of smooth baby face that some older men—like your grandfather, Malcolm—carry with them to the grave.

In halting English Yeşar told us that his older sister—with whom he'd been living—had just been "arrested a little." My first thought was that the girl must have been a prostitute, but the rest of the boy's story made it clear that she was a devotee of an outlawed dervish sect who had been discovered about two weeks before—on the day of the Russian satellite launch—whirling slowly and deliberately through one of Adana's markets, the *Bazar Hamam,* crooning heretical verses to herself. This was what she was "arrested a little" for. Worse, it is usually men who choose to invite arrest in this way—it's almost unheard of for a woman to do such a thing, for even the dervish sect to which his sister belonged, Yeşar told us, frowns on woman whirlers. All of us at the table expressed our regrets that such a thing should have happened.

DONUT WORRY, Yeşar Ataböy said. SHE CRAZY PERSON. MY MOST BAD NEWS IS THAT I BE KICKED FROM OUT MY DWELLING.

YOU DON'T HAVE A PLACE TO LIVE, Scott asked him. WHAT ABOUT YOUR BROTHER. DOESN'T HE SEND YOU MONEY.

Yeşar's brother was an infantryman stationed on the border between Russia and Turkey, not too far from the Black Sea. He was a *mehmetcik.* Nihad was his name, and Q told me later that Nihad had sent no money to pay for his and his sister's rent in Adana. Until she had been "arrested a little," Ömür—the sister—had worked for a bath catering to invalids and other sick persons. Yeşar's apartment had lately been rented out from under him. The past two weeks he had slept in a hiding place of his own discovery in one of the city's mosques—this place was comfortable, he said, because there was always a little piece of carpet under him.

THAT'S TERRIBLE! Scott shouted. THAT'S A DISGRACE! YOU'RE COMING OUT TO INCIRLIK WITH US!

OH NO, groaned Q.

Scott whirled on Q faster than any dervish could have. ALL YOUR PISSING AND MOANING FOR OTHER PEOPLE'S RIGHTS PETERS OUT WHEN YOU RUN INTO SOMEBODY WHO'S REALLY IN TROUBLE. YEŞAR NEEDS A PLACE TO STAY. WE'LL PUT HIM IN THE TRAILER WITH US.

WHOSE BED, asked Q.

I DON'T CARE—MINE, IF NEED BE!

Yeşar liked this idea, he said he wanted to visit the United States one day. The cities he most wanted to see were Wichita—which he had heard about from Scott—and California. When his dinner came, he gobbled it down while Q and I sat watching like ancient Chinamen. Q smoked a fat brown-green cigar and blew smoke over Yeşar's dinner plate, but this may not have been on purpose. Scott got happier the more

Yeşar ate—he tried to talk Turkey with the boy through Q's cigar smoke—he even had *baklava* for dessert while Q and I scraped our chairs around.

Scott and Q both owned motor scooters, and we returned to the air base on them, Yeşar behind Scott, your daddy hanging on to Q. It's a real rollercoaster ride taking a scooter through Adana's streets after dark—better than at Kiddie Land in Wichita—but the APs on duty wouldn't let Scott bring Yeşar into the Detachment 10-10 area and Scott went off his tracks like a runaway 'coaster car. He told the guards what regulation-bound egg-suckers they were for denying this boy—to whom he was a United Nations Foster Parent anyway—a bed for the night. Did they want Yeşar to sleep in an infidel place of worship. The APs were enlisted men, and Scott kept getting louder and louder until one of them said, GO ON IN, SIR—JUST GET HIM OUT OF HERE TOMORROW, OKAY. And Yeşar spent the night with me because I had an extra bed in my trailer and Scott and Q didn't.

The next day Scott went to the base infirmary and wangled several bottles of hydrogen peroxide from a medic. Then he bleached Yeşar Ataböy's hair. After that he took Yeşar around the compound with him introducing him as his son Curt—Curt has been flown in from the States via Athens as a reward to Scott for extending his contract. Riding on Scott's shoulders, the boy looked like a Barbary ape that Scott had picked up on an R&R trip to Gibraltar or Tripoli—a Barbary ape with a head of disheveled, sick-yellow hair.

Even Q thought that Scott had finally turned his rug over and flashed his hand. The General was sure to get wind of Scott's transparent lie, sure to see him carrying Yeşar around base pickaback. Then the masquerade would be over, and Scott would end up stateside with a medical discharge and a small disability pension. That didn't happen though. Curt—Yeşar—was accepted by everybody as Scott's son, even though nobody really believed he was, and depending on which of us had night missions to fly, the boy stayed in my trailer three or four nights a week and in Scott's and Q's the rest of the time.

That's another reason I haven't written before, Malcolm. Yeşar's frequent visits made it hard to sit down and write you. I can't explain this at all—but his presence in the trailer—his presence in the 10-10 compound—made me feel guilty about *wanting* to write you. In fact, because of that aged little boy with black caterpillar eyebrows and hoarjaundice hair, I felt guiltier about wanting to write you than I did for failing to write.

Yeşar Ataböy became the child of our Detachment. The other pilots and I were his father as much as Scott was, and only Q seemed actively to resent him. One morning when Q saw Scott riding Yeşar on his shoulders right out across the steaming flight-line, he raised a fuss and had them both removed.

THAT BOY'S A SPY! he shouted from the ladder next to his aircraft. HE'S AN ARMENIAN SOVIET SPY AND HE WANTS TO BOOBY-TRAP MY EJECTION SEAT! Since Q was wearing his cumbersome flight suit, the faceplate on his helmet open, all he could do was shout these accusations across the tarmac. Two APs in a jeep escorted Scott and Yeşar off the flight-line though, and as soon as they'd gone, I helped Q climb the rest of the way into the cockpit. (I was flying-safety officer that day.) Q mumbled and groused about how we'd let Incirlik's security be compromised. We were bounders, fools, and amateurs.

YOU'RE STARTING TO SOUND AS PARANOID AS SCOTT, I told him.

MY ASS, said Q.

NO, YOU REALLY ARE—LISTEN TO YOURSELF.

I AM LISTENING TO MYSELF. YOU'RE PROBABLY RIGHT. HE'S AFTER MY ASS IS WHAT I MEANT. HE KNOWS I DIDN'T WANT HIM FOR A TRAILERMATE, SO HE SNEAKS OUT HERE AT NIGHT AND TAMPERS WITH MY AIRPLANE—SCOTT TAMPERS TOO. JUST PRAY I NEVER NEED MY EJECTION SEAT, RAY, BECAUSE IF I EVER HAVE TO FIRE THE DAMN THING IT'S GOING TO BLOW ME RIGHT OUT THROUGH THE NOSE OF THIS BABY. THEY'VE BEEN TAMPERING WITH THE CHARGE.

NO, THEY HAVEN'T. LET ME SHOW YOU.

NO! DON'T TOUCH IT! LEAVE IT ALONE! Before beginning various preflight checks we're supposed to make with the canopy up, Q secured his faceplate and closed the canopy. Pretty soon his aircraft's engine whine was drilling into my inner ear, and I backed away holding the sides of my head—the sound is a little like a giant electric vacuum cleaner's and a little like a disaster siren. Standing there on the hot windy tarmac—I remember—I was afraid that Q wouldn't come back from this flight, I had a strange intuition. He did come back though, and I was sure from then on that Q was just as crazy as Scott. Maybe he's crazier.

The reason I like it, I think, is that you're alone and undetected—flying, I mean. You're alone and undetected and very powerful. It is even better than those dreams I always have about being able to fly unassisted just by willing myself into the air and stretching out my body. In these dreams, Malcolm, I am always indoors. I can fly from room to room—or down corridors—or around and about the light fixtures and chandeliers in somebody's anonymous mansion somewhere—but I can never fly outside. Outdoors there are trees, telephone wires, and—worst of all—wind currents that won't let me control my flight. So whenever I dream about flying I always see myself floating just under a ceiling—with my arms outstretched and my head hunched forward to keep from bumping it on the tiny upside-down dunes of plaster above me. I feel as the Wright Bros. must have felt at Kitty Hawk, powerful and happy but very aware of my aircraft's limitations.

People who dream that they can fly—I have heard—are supposed to be victims of "superiority complexes." I frequently dream that I can fly—indoors, anyway—but I have never truly felt that I was a superior *person.* It may be that I am a superior pilot, but I am by no means a superior human being or a superior Christian or a superior father. A person who dreams that he can only fly indoors must certainly have some doubts about his superiority, don't you think. I think that I am humble about the few things—actually, flying government aircraft is all that I can think of right now—at which I may possibly be superior. I know that this sounds funny, but it *is* true. I am not even prideful about being humble about those things—or that thing—at which I may be superior. The most superior thing about me, Malcolm, is probably you.

But flying this aircraft—we have been told that the Russians call it The Black Lady of Espionage, even though we have recently begun to paint the U-2 silver-blue instead of black—they don't know this, I guess—is better than dreaming. Flying the U-2 is better than changing into a cape and tights in a phone booth. Wearing a pressurized suit and a frail cross-shaped machine, you are as close to heaven as it seems possible to be. The earth is below you—exposed, naked, and vulnerable—and the sky keeps braiding itself around you like pale-blue spun sugar. You feel that God is your co-pilot—yes you do. You feel—as the pilots' poem has it—that you have often reached out and touched the face of God. But you also feel quite awed and humble about having these feelings. I do at least—this is the truth.

They do not pay me $30,000 a year to fly this airplane, Malcolm. They pay me $30,000 a year to fly this airplane *over Russia.*

Even on those nights that he slept in my trailer, Yeşar Ataböy managed to stay out of my way. Although his sneakers were too big for him—none of us ever thought to buy him a better-fitting pair—he walked about in them as quietly as a cockroach. Once a week—every Sunday morning—Scott helped Yeşar peroxide his hair for the purposes of their now needless conspiracy against base regulations. No one even saw the need to call the boy Curt anymore—he was Yeşar, Scott's son.

Q drank sixpack after sixpack though and slept with a .22 pistol under his pillow—but he didn't insist that the boy be returned to Adana. When he was feeling really low, Q would buy several different kinds of Betty Crocker cake mixes at the BX and—sometimes leaving them in their boxes—burn them in his and Scott's oven. By this means he was able to chase Scott & Son over to my trailer. Scott didn't care. With Yeşar around he did not rail so much against Q's slovenliness.

About two weeks after the second Soviet satellite launch—the one with the dog—Q came over one evening and told me a strange thing.

RAY, he said, SCOTT IS MAKING YEŞAR A U-2 PRESSURE SUIT. HE'S CUT ONE OF OUR BIG SUITS DOWN AND HE'S EVEN MAKING A HELMET TO FIT THE BOY. THE FACEPLATE'S PLEXIGLAS, I THINK, AND THE HELMET HAS THE ST. LOUIS CARDINAL FOOTBALL TEAM'S REDBIRD DECAL ON EACH SIDE.

IT'S PROBABLY JUST A GIFT, I said. IT PROBABLY DOESN'T MEAN ANYTHING—YOU KNOW, A TOY.

I'M SUSPICIOUS OF THAT BASTARD, RAY. I DON'T TRUST HIM. HE'S A WEIRDO.

HAVE YOU ASKED HIM ABOUT THE SUIT, WHY HE'S MAKING IT.

HE SAYS IT'S FOR A MONKEY.

A MONKEY.

YES. HE SAYS HE'S MAKING IT FOR A MONKEY. HE SAYS IF THAT RUSSIAN DOG HAD HAD A PRESSURE SUIT, THEY MIGHT'VE BEEN ABLE TO RECOVER IT. HE SAYS THAT ONE DAY THE U.S.'LL CERTAINLY SEND UP A MONKEY AND HE HOPES TO GET HIS FOOT IN THE DOOR BY HAVING ITS SUIT READY.

WHAT DOOR. WHAT DOOR IS HE TRYING TO GET HIS FOOT IN.

I DON'T KNOW. THE MAKING-SPACESUITS-FOR-MONKEYS DOOR, WHO KNOWS. BUT I SAY THE SUIT'S FOR YEŞAR AND I DON'T LIKE IT.

About three days after this talk with Q, I saw Yeşar on Scott's shoulders in the BX. The boy was wearing the same clothes he had come to base in, but on his head was a modified St. Louis Cardinal football helmet with a lifted Plexiglas faceplate. I could see the red-and-white cask of the helmet—and the boy's dark grinning face inside it—bobbing along above one of the toiletry and first-aid counters. Scott was probably buying peroxide—he was always buying or finagling peroxide—Q said their trailer was full of it. But neither Yeşar nor Scott saw me, and I didn't wave to them.

The weekend after Thanksgiving we had a mixer-and-poker-party in my trailer. The party was Scott's idea, and he sent us all invitations printed at a shop in Adana—to us U-2 pilots on base and to a couple of support personnel from other units. Not everybody came. Q was given an invitation, but he pleaded indigestion—I AM SICK OF AND FROM TOO MUCH TURKEY is what he told me the morning of the party. He was also sick of Yeşar Ataböy, who was to be one of the guests. That was why Scott shifted the party from his and Q's trailer to mine—even though he didn't have time to have corrections printed and so had to notify all his guests of the change in person. This did not spoil his mood though, for Q no longer had any power to upset him.

Scott brought all the refreshments—beer, booze, crackers, cheeses, chips, dips, sardines, cold cuts, ice. All I had to do was open up the trailer for the guests and put out a couple of folding tables, one of them borrowed. The guests included—I'm talking about the ones who actually came—four U-2 pilots in addition to Scott and me, Yeşar Ataböy in his football helmet, and Tech Sergeant Frederic Sereno from the base radio unit.

Sereno was invited, Scott said, because he's perpetually homesick. He showed up wearing fatigues, but even in that baggy outfit he was so wiry he looked as if he had been raised in a place where the laws of gravity have been repealed. Scott felt sorry for him because his eyes are always misted—he's been known to break down weeping while relaying flight information to airborne pilots. He won't take leave and usually volunteers to work weekends because he thinks he's accumulating enough leave-time to spend the last two years of his 20-year career at home. Nobody can convince him that leave must be used during the year in which it has accrued or else it is altogether forfeited—he says his dedication will exempt him from this rule. His dedication and his weepy looks have made him very unpopular on base. He's just 24 years old, but his voice sounds like the hiss of a cottonmouth—a cottonmouth holding its skinny head an inch or two out of the water in which it is swimming.

My trailer was crowded, Malcolm. The floor shook when anyone shifted his weight or wobbled down the "hall" to the bathroom. Of all the pilots, only Scott and I really wanted to play poker—so we had to recruit Yeşar and Sereno to sit down at my table with us. Our colleagues stood in the "kitchen" with drinks in their hands and swapped war stories. Scott is the only one of us who did not serve in the Korean Police Action—all of us others had been fighter-jocks then, flying the F-84F.

It was hard to concentrate on my cards because you cannot tell an F-84 war story without zooming your hands around and making engine and machine-gun noises. L kept spilling his drink, refilling it, and spilling it again—because of his right hand's superior maneuverability and his left hand's repeated failures to elude his right hand's guns. T showed everybody how he had flown beneath a nonexistent bridge on the Yalu River, while B and LK did thumb-to-thumb barrel rolls in precision formation. They did these things for a long time, getting louder and louder and more and more heroic. I have done the same thing myself, Malcolm—it's a tension-releasing camaraderie in which each man is almost as alone as he would be at 70,000 feet in a silver-blue U-2. But God doesn't intrude on this indoor zooming of hands, and you can sip liquor even while you're at the controls. (This is why we need an Officers Club more than a chapel.)

This talk of liquor and machine-guns reminds me that Doozie would not approve. When you are finished reading this letter, Mal, I want you to burn it. Read it again if you like—read it three or four times—but when you're finished, put this letter in the bottom of your metal wastebasket and set it afire. Once you have burned this letter, my treason will become—very nearly—only a conjectural matter.

Back at my folding card table, Yeşar had begun to YOK. He would YOK when he did not wish to be hit with a card. He would YOK when he did not wish to bid. He would YOK if you offered him something to eat or drink. YOK is a Turkish negative, Malcolm—it means NO, or THERE ISN'T ANY, or—the way Yeşar seemed to be using it— even I DON'T WANT TO. In order to YOK the boy would throw his head back, bark this word, and stare at us out of his football helmet with a fierce and contemptuous expression. Scott had taught him how to play poker—seven-card stud was the game of the moment—and now he was yokking and winning so often that I began to think that he had worn his helmet to protect himself from the angry losers at our table. But I was the only angry loser, really—Scott enjoyed seeing Yeşar win and Sereno was too busy being homesick to be angry at anyone.

I'M THE ONLY ENLISTED MANJACK AT THIS PARTY, he'd say occasionally. I OUGHT TO GO BACK TO THE RADIO ROOM.

DEAL, Yeşar Ataböy would command him.

The yokking and the zooming kept on around me for hours. My head hurt—I had drunk too much—and so much cigar and cigarette smoke was curling past our table that I half thought it was from the airplane crashes that my colleagues were describing to one another. A hundred

Chinese MiGs had crashed and burned at various places around my trailer, and now these imaginary heaps of metal were smogging up the air with their ropy death belches. To keep this smoke out of his lungs Yeşar lowered his faceplate. I threw down my lousy hand—a deuce, a trey, some other garbage—and leaned back on the rear two legs of my chair the way your mother and Doozie have told me never to do—and looked around at my poker partners just as mean and resentful as you could want. I sure felt nasty.

SCOTT, I said, WHY ARE YOU MAKING YOUR LITTLE MONKEY A PRESSURE SUIT.

WHAT LITTLE MONKEY, he asked.

THAT ONE, I said, and I nodded at Yeşar Ataböy. HE HAS NO BUSINESS WEARING U.S. GOVERNMENT PROPERTY AND YOU HAVE NO BUSINESS ALTERING THAT PROPERTY SO IT'LL FIT HIM.

I HAD MARY SEND ME THAT FOOTBALL HELMET, Scott said evenly. THAT'S NOT GOVERNMENT PROPERTY. NEITHER'S THE FACEPLATE—MARY SENT THAT TOO.

Q SAYS YOU'RE MAKING YEŞAR A U-2 PRESSURE SUIT.

Q IS MISINFORMED, RAY. I'M MAKING A SPACESUIT FOR THE FIRST RHESUS, CHIMPANZEE, OR SPIDER MONKEY THAT NACA CHOOSES TO SHOOT INTO ORBIT—I'M USING YEŞAR AS A MODEL, THAT'S ALL.

WHY.

BECAUSE HE SEEMS ABOUT THE RIGHT SIZE.

I MEAN WHY ARE YOU MAKING A SPACESUIT FOR A MONKEY. Scott just stared at me—he was smiling faintly. I said, WHAT DOOR IS IT YOU'RE TRYING TO GET YOUR FOOT IN. Q SAYS YOU'RE TRYING TO GET YOUR FOOT IN THE DOOR.

FOR ONCE, Q'S ON THE MONEY. THE DOOR IS ASTRONAUTICS, RAY. THE RUSSIANS HAVE PUT TWO SATELLITES UP AND THAT MEANS THAT THE GOOD OLE U.S.A. IS GOING TO HAVE TO DO THE SAME THING. AFTER THE PASSENGERLESS SATELLITES WE'LL SEND MONKEYS. THEN WE'LL SEND MEN. THERE'S GOING TO BE A NATIONAL SPACE PROGRAM, RAY, AND I INTEND TO BE ONE OF THE FIRST MEN WHO GOES UP—BY VIRTUE OF MY SPACESUITING THE FIRST MONKEY.

BUT WHAT IF WE SEND A DOG UP, LIKE THE RUSSIANS JUST DID.

IT'LL BE MONKEYS, RAY. AMERICANS THINK TOO MUCH OF THEIR DOGS TO SEND THEM INTO SPACE. MONKEYS ARE OKAY BECAUSE THEY'RE MORE LIKE PEOPLE.

BUT YOU'RE A U-2 PILOT, NOT A SPACEMAN.

THERE AREN'T ANY SPACEMEN YET—WE'RE THE CLOSEST THING. THAT JASPER IN THE BALLOON LAST SUMMER DOESN'T COUNT. He looked at me sharply. BUT ONCE THE SPACE ADMINISTRATION'S SET UP, IT'S GOING TO BE LOOKING FOR PEOPLE LIKE ME—I'M PERFECTLY SUITED TO THE NEEDS OF SUCH A PROGRAM, I'M EVERYTHING IT COULD WANT. YOU DON'T TAKE CHANCES THOUGH. IF YOU WANT TO GET IN ON THE GROUND FLOOR YOU HAVE TO CONTRIBUTE, DO A LITTLE PR. THAT'S WHY I'M USING YEŞAR AS A MODEL FOR MY MONKEY SUIT—THAT'S THE FIRST STEP, GAINING THEIR ATTENTION. ONCE THEY SEE ME, RAY, I'M A CINCH TO GET IN.

BECAUSE YOU'RE A MODEL PILOT AND A MODEL AMERICAN.

EXACTLY. I HAVE BOYISH GOOD LOOKS, A LOVELY WIFE, THREE-POINT-TWO CHILDREN (he'd been drinking a good deal, too), AND A KANSAS UPBRINGING. THAT'S WHY IT'S GOING TO BE JOHN SCOTT BROWN WHO FIRST PUTS HIS BOOTPRINTS IN THE LUNAR SNOW, RAY. I'LL SAY, "HOLY SHIT, I DID IT!" TO A WORLD-WIDE TELEVISION AUDIENCE, AND MY NAME WILL NEVER BE FORGOTTEN.

YOUR VOICE AIN'T GONNA GET THROUGH, Tech Sergeant Sereno put in. ALL THEY'LL HEAR IS STATIC AND THE SQUEALING OF HYDROGEN ATOMS. His eyes were more red-rimmed than usual, maybe because of the tobacco smoke drifting about, eddying each time anyone waved a hand or blew out another lungful.

THEY'LL HEAR THE SINGING OF THE HERO-ASTRONAUT, ALL RIGHT—THEY'LL SEE ME SHINING AGAINST THE MOON.

IS THAT WHY YOU WANT TO GO, I asked.

YEAH, SURE. AND TO GET AWAY. WHATEVER'S WORTH LIVING FOR HAS TO BE OUT THERE, RAY—IT'S SURE AS HELL NOT DOWN HERE. BUT YOU'D NEVER GET ME TO ADMIT THAT AGAIN, NOT EVEN WITH SPLINTERS UNDER MY FINGERNAILS AND HOT TONGS ON MY BALLS.

WHAT DID YOU SAY, I asked him, tilting my chair forward, surprised.

THIS GAME IS FIVE-CARD STUD, Scott responded. DEAL, SERENO, BEFORE YOU SOGGY UP THE ALLAH-DAMN DECK.

Yeşar flipped up his faceplate. NO ALLAH, he said, and he yokked Allah out of existence. GOOD REASON SERGEANT HAS TO CRY. WHO CARE, SOGGY CARDS—WHO CARE.

The boy won the next four hands, then Scott said it was Yeşar's bedtime. He put him on his shoulders, duckwalked around shaking hands with the other guests, promised to help me clean up in the morning, and went down into the dark with a little Turkish monkey on his back. I watched them wobble away toward their trailer—the cask on Yeşar's head gleaming spookily in the thin moonlight, Scott singing "Shine On, Harvest Moon" in his lovely drunken tenor.

A few days before I began this letter—a week or so after the failure of the Vanguard satellite launch—John Scott Brown and Yeşar Ataböy disappeared. They took a U-2 with them. They took the aircraft up as high as it would go, I guess—prodded by Scott's fear of the Air Force's nascent X-15 program, which he had only lately caught wind of. In radio contact with Sgt. Sereno, Scott reported that they were ten miles up—then twelve—then fourteen. They were close to the U-2's maximum altitude, but still Scott and Yeşar were taking their aircraft up up up.

WE'RE GOING TO THE MOON is what Sereno says Scott told him. THE EARTH'S LAID OUT UNDER US LIKE A WAR MAP. IT'S BEAUTIFUL BUT COLD—SO WE'RE GOING TO THE MOON.

THE MOON'S WORSE, Sereno says he answered them. AND YOU AIN'T A FRACTION OF THE WAY THERE. THE GENERAL ORDERS YOU BACK TO BASE.

TELL EVERYBODY WE'RE GOING. TELL EVERYBODY WHEN WE GET THERE. YEŞAR'S FLYING THIS THING THOUGH, AND HE'S NOT UNDER ORDERS TO ANY OFFICER OF THE UNITED STATES AIR FORCE. HE'S A TURKISH CITIZEN. I'M NOT A SELFISH SONUVABITCH, SERENO. I'M SHARING THE GLORY.

PLEASE, SIR, REQUEST THAT THE TURKISH CITIZEN BRING YOU BACK TO BASE.

NO CAN DO, Scott replied. IT'S THE MOON OR NOWHERE.

Sereno argued and pleaded. He told Scott that the U-2—as brilliantly designed and capable an aircraft as it was—had never been meant for travel on the fringes of outer space—much less in the vacuum between the earth and the moon. Even if by some fantastic extension of its altitudinal range it carried Scott and Yeşar into the stratosphere, the thermosphere, and the exosphere (!!!)—this was all so unlikely that Sereno wept as he outlined the irrationality of Scott's hope—the airplane would still be unable to *maneuver* at those giddy heights. It *was* an airplane, after all, not a spaceship, and the thinness of the atmosphere at 100-plus miles would render the ever-climbing and loudly shuddering U-2 nothing but an "unguided missile." Its wings would be death warrants and its engines about as useful as bicycle pedals. Yeşar would be floating above Scott's lap, and so would all the unsecured gear that a U-2 pilot carries with him in the event of a bailout or a forced landing. If the seat pack containing this gear were dislodged, in fact, it would not be hard to imagine the U-2's passenger and pilot—whichever was which—surrounded by swimming signal flares, rings and wristwatches, foreign currency (both paper and coin), water-purification tablets, and an assortment of foil-wrapped prophylactics. Pilot and passenger would pass into the outer reaches of the atmosphere amid a clutter so banal and earthly that all the romance of their dying would be gone. They didn't want that to happen, did they. Sereno hissed at them through the radio and tempted them back to base by describing the shame and indecorousness of the deaths they had in store—Sereno is not an unpersuasive man, I ought to add, when his tears and his pleading come together in a sincerely heartfelt appeal.

But John Scott Brown laughed at the radioman. They had brought none of that banal earthly trash with them, he said—none at all. Instead he and Yeşar had secretly modified their aircraft for a moon trip. They had done their work at night, right under Q's nose, and had made their last physical adjustments to the airplane with such split-second timing and professionalism that they had hoodwinked not only Q but the armed guards on the flight-line. Now the U-2 was equipped with six small vernier jets on its wing and tail, and these would take over the steering functions abdicated by airfoils, rudders, and ailerons in the mesosphere. Their plane was not an "unguided missile" at all—it was a rocketship. Scott, in fact, had stolen the idea for the wing and tail jets from the design of the X-15 rocketplane manufactured by North American Aviation.

FUEL, Sereno responded. WHAT ARE YOU USING FOR FUEL. A LOAD OF GASOLINE AIN'T GONNA GET YOU TO THE MOON AND BACK.

WE'VE TAKEN CARE OF THAT.

HOW, SIR. HOW HAVE YOU TAKEN CARE OF THAT.

FIRST OFF, SERENO, WE'RE NOT COMING BACK. THAT'S WHY WE DON'T NEED ANY WRISTWATCHES, RUBLES, OR RUBBERS. ALL WE

NEED'S FUEL FOR A ONE-WAY TRIP AND THAT'S WHAT WE'VE GOT. The transmission was getting messed up at this point, crackles and hissing and static.

A ONE-WAY TRIP, Sereno exclaimed.

A ONE-WAY TRIP TO GLORY, WE'VE GOT A CONVERTER IN THE FUSELAGE OF THIS BABY CHANGING HYDROGEN PEROXIDE TO BURNABLE GASES, SERENO, AND THERE'S ENOUGH PEROXIDE ABOARD TO GET US A LONG, LONG WAY—EVERY WAY BUT BACK. Then Scott's words dovetailed away and Sereno couldn't get anything more out of either him or Yeşar Ataböy. The U-2 was gone.

And Sereno has followed them in spirit to the moon—he's stopped trying to get home from the air base here, from Turkey, and started trying to get home from a communications outpost in the Sea of Fertility.

They don't allow condoms there, he says. Or need them.

Besides the things I quoted you earlier, Malcolm, Paul of Tarsus once wrote—

> All flesh is not the same flesh: but there is one kind of flesh of men, another flesh of beasts, another of fishes, and another of birds. There are also celestial bodies, and bodies terrestrial: but the glory of the celestial is one, and the glory of the terrestrial is another. There is one glory of the sun, and another glory of the moon, and another glory of the stars: for one star differeth from another star in glory. So also is the resurrection of the dead. It is sown in corruption, it is raised in incorruption; it is sown in dishonour, it is raised in glory; it is sown in weakness, it is raised in power; it is sown a natural body, it is raised a spiritual body.

This—so says my copy of *The Bible Designed To Be Read As Literature*—is from Paul's Epistles to the Corinthians. (Tarsus is only 43 kilometers from here.) I have a reason for quoting this passage—I really do—but I am having trouble thinking of it. A ONE-WAY TRIP TO GLORY, Scott told Sereno. Now he is dead without much hope of resurrection, especially since the Air Force and the CIA do not intend to allow his weird exploit to surface publicly. Mary, Curt, and Cathy will be bought off, and no one will know. What price glory. Well, the going rate here at Incirlik seems to be $30,000 a year. With his artificial eyes, his hair net, and his foundation of facial cream, Scott was sown a natural body—my reasons for quoting are beginning to come back, shabbily and tardily—but lately in me he has been raised a spiritual body. I think—I am not sure—I am having trouble with this—I hope you're trying to help me, Mal.

Christmas is long gone. The two weeks that have just passed could easily be 2,000 years—all the way back to the original birth—over the corpses of 200 brutal and beautiful centuries. I think I have flown a couple of missions during this time, but it's hard to be certain. Maybe neither John Scott Brown nor Yeşar Ataböy ever existed—evidence to the contrary is that Q has no trailermate these days and we do seem to be short an aircraft. I suppose these things could be explained by the frequent shuttling of our U-2s between here and Atsugi in Japan or between here and Lahore and Peshawar in Pakistan—maybe Scott has just been temporarily transferred to another Detachment. So they would like us to believe. I don't believe it. All that my frayed faith is hanging by these days is the silly conviction that Scott and Yeşar got Out There far enough for their substance to be transformed. I spend a lot of time looking at the moon.

So. This letter full of treasons and melancholy religion is my belated Christmas gift to you. I must tell you of my deep and painful love for you and urge you to look with hope toward your future. You are a Kansan, aren't you. Put yourself at the center without arrogance. Everything is woven together finally and you must believe that you are one of the threads in the tapestry—an important one, if only to yourself. Believe otherwise and you unravel more than just the warp and woof of who you are—you unravel patterns bigger than yourself. That is why—today—so many things seem to be unraveling.

Burn this letter. Tomorrow I am going to Germany. If children, then heirs. Don't forget to burn this.

Love,
PAPA

Shivering, I read this letter from my father a second, third, and fourth time. Then I dropped it into the metal wastebasket that we had taken from our quarters at Edwards Air Force Base and held a match above the basket. I couldn't let the match fall. I fetched the pages out of the trash can and hid them in my room.

On the last day of January, 1958, an Army Jupiter-C put the Explorer I into orbit, and the United States officially joined the Soviet Union in outer space. My excitement was genuine. Even though my father didn't write me again, this American success and the letter filed away in one of my desk drawers combined to temper my depressions and undercut my bitterness. I had no doubt that my father loved me and that justice would therefore prevail in international affairs.

It wasn't until summer, during Huerfano's annual Pioneer Days festivities, that a man came down from Wichita to tell Theodosia and me that my father was missing on a routine weather mission over the Middle East. Since he had been missing almost seventy-two hours, things didn't look very good. As it happened, Wesley Ray Weir never came home. None of this ever got in the papers, and my principal consolation has been the belief that he defected—not to a political body but to an incorruption that has nothing to do with this world.

And I have never been a religious man.

The Yukio Mishima Cultural Association of Kudzu Valley, Georgia

June 1, 1975

I am a new resident of Kudzu Valley, Georgia. After losing my teaching position at the state university, I came to Kudzu Valley to 1) steep myself in bitterness, 2) find solace in the rural life, 3) lead the local inhabitants out of their charming but dissolute provincialism, and 4) gain, during my exile, sufficient inner resolve and outside support to browbeat the villainous provost into reinstating me as an instructor in the comparative literature section of the English department, preferably with clauses in my contract granting me back pay, a private office in the *old,* and hence more prestigious, wing of Park Hall, and damages for "the untoward suffering wreaked upon Mr. M. by an unfeeling bureaucracy." That's how I envision it. Quite.

You see, I was turned out because my last highest degree—a master's with a thesis entitled "Mather Biles: His Role in the Introduction of the Heroic Couplet from England to the American Colonies"—is from the state university, and the provost has declared that, in the interests of catholicity and cosmopolitanism, not to mention that of upgrading the educational milieu of the campus, no one who has earned his last highest degree from our institution may hold forth in its lecture rooms. A taboo, if you like, against "intellectual incest." There are exceptions to this primitive ruling, of course, but *I* was not one of them.

Here in Kudzu Valley, then, I intend to devote myself to Purpose No. 1 (see above) for no less than two but no more than three months; to Purpose No. 2 for all that time from the end of my bitter steeping to my triumphant return to the comp. lit. division; to Purpose No. 3 whenever the occasion should present itself; and to Purpose No. 4 coterminously with my observance of each of the other three purposes hereinbefore noted. Since I am single and living in a house willed to me off the top of a distant cousin's cancerous skull ("This town's been dying even longer than I have," it's reported this old woman—one Clarabelle Musgrove Sims—told her physician toward the last; "I intend to transfuse it by my dying"), I should be able to devote myself to these various enterprises without significant let.

October 23

My self-imposed durance of bitter steeping has lasted four months rather than three, and, upon inquiry, I have passed off my solitariness as a period of meditative acclimatization. Then Mrs. Bernard Bligh Brumblelo—the foremost social lioness in town, and, as she has told me over the telephone, "a dear friend of your beloved, departed cousin Clarabelle"—invites me to an evening tea. I accept, not because I am overfond of either tea or Mrs. Bernard Bligh Brumblelo, but because attending this affair will offer me a nice possibility of fulfilling Purpose No. 3.

Others at the get-together in the old woman's starkly modern, all-electric home are Ruby and Clarence Unfug (of Unfug's Electric), the groceryman Spurgeon Creed, Lisbeth and Q. B. Meacham (of Kudzu Valley Drugs), the plumber and electrician Augustus Houseriser, the kindergarten teacher Lonnie Pederson and her husband Tom, who works for Valley Poultry Processing, and, surprisingly, at least to me, the black woman preacher Fontessa Boddie. We are perfunctorily introduced. Tea and hot apple cider are served.

An insufficient number of chairs forces us to stand on Mrs.

Brumblelo's pepper-and-salt shag carpet shifting our tea cups and canapés from hand to hand and getting in, I'm afraid, nary a bite. We discuss, in turn, these four topics while our hostess putters in the kitchen: 1) The ill health of Kudzu Valley businesses, 2) flagging attendance at the community's two churches, 3) the almost inevitable prospect of the valley's inundation when the state legislature approves the construction, above us, of a new dam, and 4) public apathy in the face of these several threats to the general welfare.

"But," says Mrs. Brumblelo when she at last emerges from the kitchen, "I asked you here not simply to rehash Kudzu Valley's problems—since our mayor and police department will do nothing—but to acquaint you all with Clarabelle's young cousin Mr. M., who has only recently moved among us."

At last we put behind us the wearying catalogue of topics (see above) that has preempted all other discussion the last thirty or forty minutes, and I am paid heed to. "What do you do," Augustus Houseriser wants to know. "Nothing," I say, "at present." Everyone considers this. "What *did* you do?" Fontessa Boddie asks, savioress of the untenable moment. I tell them about the comp. lit. section of the English department at the state university. Says Clarence Unfug, "What—exactly, you know—is this *comp. lit.* business?" I chuckle appreciatively at the way he has made the abbreviation—all inadvertently, of course—sound like a footnote in Latin. Then I say, "It's a discipline whose purpose is to discover significant relationships among different works of literature, across the barriers of both language and time." Petite Lonnie Pederson, whose husband Tom's dewlaps are wagging (I suppose) much in the manner of his preprocessed turkeys', says with a hint of endearing pique, "For instance, Mr. M.?" "Well," I oblige, "one of the graduate students in our section has just composed a paper detailing the similarities between the works of the French writer Proust and the Japanese novelist Yukio Mishima." "Oh, I just *love* Proust," says Mrs. Brumblelo, who is a female littérateur manqué as well as a lioness long since manifest (one wall is lined with Reader's Digest Condensed Books); "he's so *soporific.*" But neither she nor anyone else there has heard of Yukio Mishima, and Mrs. Brumblelo asks me to write the name down for her on the back of a napkin. In the meantime, I tell the group about Mishima's melodramatic suicide in 1970, discoursing a bit on the meaning and the various techniques of *seppuku* and explaining as best I can—most of this, really, is out of my field of greatest expertise, Early American Literature—why a writer at the height of his powers would do such a repellent thing. Even the laconic Spurgeon Creed is subtly animated during my lecture: both erubescent earlobes, obscenely pink pendulums, begin to tick. The Unfugs are openmouthed, the Meachams quietly stupefied. How rewarding it is to fulfill Purpose No. 3.

Fontessa Boddie says, "He died that horrible way to protest the road his country was goin' down?"

I incline my head in assent.

"That's very interesting," says Mrs. Bernard Bligh Brumblelo; "that's very interesting." While saying goodnight to us at the very stroke of ten (I am the last one out the door), she now and again mumbles, as if to fix the words in her memory, "*Yukio Mishima, Yukio Mishima, Yukio. . . .*" A foreboding follows me outside, sniveling to itself as forebodings are wont to do.

October 25

Two days later I receive this note from the lioness:

> *Kudzu Valley is committing suicide by default, Mr. M., and the old saviors of private pride, religion, community spirit, and free enterprise have failed us. In telephone consultations with the Unfugs, Fontessa Boddie, the Meachams, the Pedersons, Spurgeon Creed, and Augustus Houseriser I put forth the idea of a Yukio Mishima Cultural Association to help us draw back from the abyss. Everyone agreed that this was a wonderful idea, and I now have the pleasure of informing you, dear Mr. M., that we have unanimously appointed you our chairperson.*

November 9

I am *not* delighted. Nevertheless, I have complied with the unanimous request of the social "elite" of Kudzu Valley. If not I, who would have undertaken the chairing of this association, ill-conceived and incongruous as it may well be? One must accept his responsibilities and run with the ball—even if the ball comes, so to speak, from out of left field. This is a sentiment that national leaders from Valley Forge to Chappaquiddick and beyond have frequently endorsed, because of its soundness. It *was* I, after all, who put Mrs. Brumblelo on to Mishima, and palpable good may yet derive from a society devoted to the life and works of a foreign author.

As Fontessa Boddie put it in an organizational assembly in the gymnasium of the Kudzu Valley Elementary School two nights ago, "We been kickin' aroun' ole Joel Chandler Harris for too long, folks."

Present at this assembly, somewhat amazingly, were 110 people, only two hundred or so short of the population of the entire town and surrounding community.

My first official acts as chairperson were to gavel this assembly to order and to preside over the ensuing discussions. The most heated of these involved the name of our society, since Berle Maunder, the owner of the builders' supply store on East Broadway, expressed some concern that our acronym might spawn confusion among outsiders. He even suggested that we follow the Japanese practice of placing the surname first, the given name second, in order to avoid any possible confusion.

Seated to my right at the head of the table, Mrs. Brumblelo had the final word: "There is no chapter of that *other* group in Kudzu Valley, Mr. Maunder, and since this one is solely for residents of our immediate area, I see no reason to yield up our original choice. In any case, think how much better we will be able to remember the initials of our *own* association."

November 12 to December 2

I have been putting up "Who is Yukio Mishima?" posters in public places. These are expensive black-light posters, ordered from Atlanta. In them Yukio Mishima is naked but for a loin cloth, his hands and feet are bound, and his body is pierced with many cruel-looking arrows. This is the pose of a Western saint, I am told, in whom the Oriental novelist was interested; I don't know which saint, however, since none of this falls within my area of greatest expertise. The posters are eye-catching, in a shoddy sensationalist way. I have put them up in the post office, the laundromat, the Greyhound stopover depot, two service station garages, and the lobby of the Farmers and Merchants Bank of Kudzu Valley.

There are no bookstores or newsstands in Kudzu Valley. The Variety Five and Dime has a solitary spin-around rack with a number of books in it, but most of these titles are by either Dale Evans or Pat Boone.

From the proper New York distributor I order copies of Mishima's final work, the tetralogy that he called *The Sea of Fertility*. In a mere three weeks the books have arrived, and Clarence and Ruby Unfug agree to display the novels in the window of Unfug's Electric. Ruby and Clarence are true to their word. One fine rural Monday morning I go by their shop and see copies of *Spring Snow, Runaway Horses, The Temple of Dawn,* and *The Decay of the Angel* in the front window—right there among the propane space heaters, the air conditioners, the gas and electric water heaters, the portable fans, the toasters, the microwave ovens, and the automatic can openers.

The Unfugs, inside, wave at me enthusiastically. Business is brisk. As I stand on the sidewalk wondering what has happened to derail so thoroughly the fulfillment of Purpose No. 4 on my list of top-priority endeavors, a black teenager comes out of Unfug's with an armful of books. "Hey, man," he says and goes on up the street. Kudzu Valley overflows with goodwill these days, and I realize that Mrs. Bernard Brumblelo and the other intellectually, if not otherwise, disadvantaged inhabitants of this backwater community *like* me. Such an illumination is unnerving: I put one hand on the Unfugs' well-scrubbed plate glass window.

How am I going to tell these people that never in my life have I read an entire work by Yukio Mishima? How am I going to impress upon them that I don't intend to, either?

December 14
In the Atlanta *Constitution* one morning I read,

> *The legislature has approved funds to complete construction of the Cusseta Dam above Kudzu Valley. Little resistance to this plan is expected from residents of the area.*

> *"Those affected will be generously and swiftly reimbursed," said state senator Ira Weems late yesterday, "and the recreational opportunities which will be available after the dam has been built may reverse the economic slump they've been experiencing down there."*

This means I will be paid for Clarabelle Musgrove Sims's house. This means I will inherit, indirectly, to a cash legacy. Go back to square one, I tell myself, in order that you may fulfill Purpose No. 4; all the others are behind you, after all, and in Purpose No. 3 you have succeeded too well, too well. . . .

January 3, 1976

Yukio Mishima to Donald Keene, as quoted in the "About the Author" section of each of the four volumes of his tetralogy: "The title, *The Sea of Fertility,* is intended to suggest the arid sea of the moon that belies its name. Or I might say that it superimposes the image of cosmic nihilism on that of the fertile sea."

Fontessa Boddie has been canvassing Kudzu Valley, taking subscriptions for the construction of a new church. At the moment, Kudzu Valley has a Baptist church and a Methodist church; it does not have a church of Cosmic Nihilism. Fontessa Boddie has been collecting funds in order that we may build a First Cosmic Nihilist Church right here in the Valley—this she does in the face of adverse and probably prohibitive news out of the capital. Fontessa Boddie, formerly a freelancer, intends to be the more-or-less permanent minister of this new church.

I gave her two dollars.

March 26

It has got out of hand, this business; it has got monstrously out of hand. When I go by the elementary school during recess periods, the children in the schoolyard are dueling with bamboo staves, practicing karate, or meditating like Hosso Buddhists in front of the teeter-totters and monkey bars. Black and white alike, they all cry *kendo!* or they all say their ineffable Buddhist prayers.

Construction on Fontessa Boddie's First Cosmic Nihilist Church is nearing completion, and the Methodist and Baptist ministers have publicly abjured their respective Protestant denominations in favor of membership in Miss Boddie's fold.

At night it is possible to go to the elementary school and hear both children and adults read reports on Mishima-related topics. One evening, when I could no longer abide the haunted silence of Clarabelle Musgrove Sims's wallpapered parlor, I took me to this school and heard these papers:

1. "Takamori Saigo: The Last Samurai?"
2. "Ichikawa's *Enjo:* Mishima into Film"
3. "The Influence of Lady Murasaki on Yukio Mishima"
4. "Masculinity and Homosexuality in Mishima's *Forbidden Colors*"
5. "The Meiji Era and Contemporary Japan"
6. "*Spring Snow:* Kiyoaki Matsugae as a Romantic Analogue of the Author"
7. "*Seppuku:* The Death of an Honorable Man"

Most of these papers, I am certain, were improperly footnoted, and the children did not project their voices well.

Yesterday, in the bank, a complete stranger asked me if I knew that both Mishima and Proust had been influenced by Ruskin; this stranger was a farmer in a railroadman's striped coveralls, and he gave me to understand that he had recently written the comp. lit. section of the English department at the state university for "any additional, you know, information you got on ole Mishima." I left without cashing my check. But for the cornucopian goodwill of the citizenry, I could almost believe myself once again in an academic environment. No, that overstates the case—but clearly the advent of the Yukio Mishima Cultural Association has led these people into unbecoming extremes of behavior.

It has all got out of hand, this business; it has all got monstrously out of hand.

Last night, for instance, that paradigmatic observer of the proprieties, Mrs. Bernard Bligh Brumblelo, drops in on me at 10:17 P.M. without so much as a telephone call for warning. First, still clad in my Edgar Allan Poe dressing gown, I must make tea for her. Then in the parlor I have to entertain her while trying, in the interests of modesty, to keep my knees together. Mrs. Brumblelo notices nothing amiss; she does not even recognize the indecorousness of her own untimely visit, so far has the general insanity progressed.

"Did you know that before he actually committed *seppuku,*" Mrs. Brumblelo says, her thin face elongating into a distorted oval, "Yukio"—of late she has taken to calling him Yukio—"told an American friend that he didn't know what he would write upon the completion of his tetralogy, and that he was afraid. Did you know that, Mr. M.?"

"No," I say.

"Oh, let me read it to you. I have it right here." Mrs. Brumblelo takes a magazine clipping out of her purse. It trembles in her hands. "'What are you afraid of?'" she read. "'It's just a big book, after all.' That's his American friend asking him, you see, Mr. M., and this is what Yukio replied: 'Yes, I don't know. I'm afraid, and I really don't know why.' So touching, so touching, it's an absolute revelation to me, Mr. M., it truly, truly is." Mrs. Brumblelo's transparently violet eyes fill up with tears; with an embroidered handkerchief she daubs at these tears, and the veins in her haggard old face open up to me an appalling anatomy primer.

To make matters even more unpleasant, after Mrs. Brumblelo has left, I have a dream in which Clarabelle Musgrove Sims slips into my bedchamber—the room she insisted on dying in, by the way—and urges me to drink water from the top of a human skull. "Quite rejuvenating," she says, "if you put your mind to it." I have always been put off by non sequiturs, and for this reason I awake in either a tepid or a moderately coolish sweat, my confusion permits no accurate discrimination. This whole business, I must reiterate, has got monstrously out of hand.

April 3

I receive a formal invitation bearing upon it a monogram resembling a golden butterfly afloat: a large *B* with two smaller *B*'s overlapping each other inside it.

Dear Mr. M.:

The members of the Yukio Mishima Cultural Association of Kudzu Valley, Georgia, and environs, herewith invite you to commit seppuku *with us on the last day of*

April, at two o'clock in the afternoon, on the lawn of the U.S. Post Office building. This event will serve as 1) quite a dramatic protest against the unfeeling pragmatism of our state bureaucracy, 2) an irrevocable farewell to our conciliatory and apathetic pasts, 3) a fulfillment of your cousin Clarabelle Musgrove Sims's dying wishes (indirectly, you know), and 4) a heartfelt homage to Yukio Mishima, who has saved us by his example.

We have also agreed among ourselves that as chairperson of our association you, Mr. M., ought by rights to have the opportunity to precede the remainder of us in the commission of these several purposes. That honor, should you desire it, is yours.

Yours in Yukio,
Mrs. Bernard Bligh Brumblelo

RSVP

I am enraged. The fools. The country simpletons. The redneck louts aspiring to be literary. Across my dead cousin's parlor I hurl a decorative china plate, which breaks on the fireplace grating and shatters into a diversified population of accusatory shards.

Later, more calm, I send regrets.

June 1

Yesterday afternoon everybody in Kudzu Valley, Georgia, with the exception only of children under the age of six and a single responsible adult, committed *seppuku* on the lawn of the U.S. Post Office building. This morning's Atlanta *Constitution,* in a story run under the by-line of Sybyl Celeste, reports that the ceremony was "lovely."

My hands tremble. The trembling surface of my coffee, in a hand-painted china cup, returns to me a disconcerting image of a man whose purposes are unfulfilled. By this premeditated treachery, you see, Mrs. Bernard Bligh Brumblelo and all the conspiring others have made me the sole adult inhabitant of their anemic, tumbledown, backwater community.

I have become Kudzu Valley, Georgia. Dear, dear God, what am I supposed to *do*?

Out of the Mouths of Olympus

For the past year my father had been tuning the volcano. His work was in preparation for the decennial Day of Diapason, when we who have made a home of the once-desolate mojaves and himalayas of Mars salute the long-dead planet where our species was born.

I had just turned eight, but our patriot population observes a double year, counting by the 687-day period in which Mars revolves around the sun. A colonist on Titan or Ganymede, harking back to Earth-style dating, would say I was fifteen and a half.

Though fast approaching adulthood, I had never heard my father or anyone else play the mountain. The Vox Olympica (as devout Krystic Harmonists generally call it) is not truly duplicable by any human-scale recording system, and I was eager for firsthand experience of the ancient volcano's voice. I was also eager to see my father again.

While supervising the tuning of the several hundred painstakingly cored-out calderas and vents of Olympus Mons, my father had come home for only brief visits. These obligatory "rests," mandated by the church, he had spent poring over computer diagrams of the great mountain's bowels, collating and memorizing the chromatic readouts of its glassy flues. As a result, he had made no real fuss over my improving grades in history and hydraulic science; he had shown only polite interest in my collection of preadapted insects from the Tharsis Steppe; and, although he had listened dutifully to three of my melodeon compositions (at my mother's dogged bidding), afterwards he had dispensed rote praise rather than incisive criticism. His mind had been elsewhere.

Vanora, my mother, resented the Day of Diapason as much as Theon, my father, revered it. To her it represented not only a disaster for the continuity of our family life but also a perverse wallowing in the fabled destruction of Earth. Why must we carry on so about what was lost forever? Beginning only a year after their bond-covenant, my father's first stint as Memorialist had almost destroyed their marriage. Somehow, though, they had survived the separations, the misunderstandings, the arguments. Finally my birth in Spaulding, West Tithonia, where Vanora headed one of the Northern Hemisphere's ground-based divisions of OSAS (Orbital Solar Amplification System), had confirmed their faith in the benefits of reconciliation. I was the tie that binds.

Seven years later the church had again selected my father to oversee the preparations at Olympus Mons, and Theon, despite his many intervening promises to my mother, had accepted the commission.

I was on my father's side, and I told Vanora so.

To me Theon's selection by the Harmonists seemed a signal honor, and I was prepared to forgive him a hundred humiliating slights if only I could sit beside him in the mountain organ room on the day he made even distant Hellas ring. When he played, the whole planet was supposed to teeter in its orbit. I wanted to be with him, booming out a diapasonal lament for long-dead Earth. He had hinted that this might be possible. Perhaps he would even let the volcano give prodigious voice to one of my melodeon sonatinas. I had written an especially good one since his last visit to Spaulding.

"Gayle," my mother said, after listening to this feverish recitation of my hopes, "you shame yourself with every word."

"Why do you say that?"

"Because you're older now, child, but scarcely any wiser."

I was sitting at my melodeon, a gift from Theon on my seventh birthday. I had been filling our bunker with frisky runs and grace notes. Now I turned the melodeon off and covered its keyboard.

"Listen, Gayle, the ceremony's tradition-bound. The Memorialist plays what every other Memorialist since Zivu, the first, has played. Zivu established the program. Your father isn't going to squeeze in a little Gaylean ditty as a sop to your vanity."

"I know that, Mother. I was only talking."

"Well, your talk of joining him under the mountain is nonsense, too."

"He said I might."

"Gayle, he probably wasn't even listening." Vanora's voice conveyed her concern as well as her exasperation. "Did you know that the Memorialist hears only the ghost of his own performance?"

"The ghost?"

"It's true. The keyboard room is soundproofed. Everyone entering it—traditionally, the Memorialist and a single technician—must wear absorbent plugs and a pair of padded earphones. Zivu went deaf hymning Earth's lost glory. Knowing full well what the result would be, he performed the entire day's program without protection."

"Father's not deaf."

"No, but his hearing's impaired. Sometimes I think he accepted this second commission not for the honor of it but because he wants to be able to hear music again in the only way he really can—through his bones."

"Then why do you begrudge him?"

Stung, Vanora leveled an appraising glance at me. Then her expression softened. "First, because he told me this would never happen again. And second, Gayle, because the Day of Diapason's a Harmonist anachronism. It's disruptive of the new order we've established, and it's morbid in its celebration of the poisoning and death of our homeworld."

"It doesn't celebrate, Mother. It memorializes."

Vanora dismissed my view of the matter by picking a thread from her tunic and dropping it to the floor. I was lucky that she was talking at all. Ordinarily, except when arguing with Theon and allowing her feelings to run away with her, she avoided discussing the topic in my presence. That she had *initiated* a conversation about the Day of Diapason with me—well, that was a breakthrough akin to faster-than-light travel. I tried to press my advantage before it fled at that speed.

"What was Father's first performance like?"

My mother looked at me, then let her gaze swing past the redwood statue of Ares guarding the corridor to her night chamber. "I'm afraid I didn't hear it, Gayle. I didn't want to hear it."

"You didn't hear it?"

"I *felt* it," Vanora said, intercepting my stare. "Or at least I think I did. OSAS held a training program for executive candidates in Stanleyville, Northwest Hellas, two weeks before the Day, and I stayed there, using my leave time, even after our training sessions were over. I was in the bunker of a government hospice in the Southern Hemisphere when your father played the mountain. I felt the music he was making, and an officer at the nearby OSAS facility recorded it on a seismograph."

"You could have got back in time to hear him, and you didn't even make the effort?"

"That's right."

I shook my head. "That's astonishing, Mother." Vanora did not reply. "Are you going to listen to him this time?"

"Spaulding's much closer to Olympus than Stanleyville is. I suppose I'll hear your father's performance. I'm going to spend the day down here, though, with our sound units turned up and my ears plugged."

"That's spiteful, Mother! Sheer irreligious spite!"

"Your father's the religionist in this family, Gayle, though he's pulled you that way, too. I just don't have any desire to hear the music he makes for a foolish memorial ceremony."

Controlling my outrage, I said, "I do."

"I know you do. Step aboveground on the Day of Diapason and you'll hear it everywhere—hour upon hour of merciless unending bombast. But legislation in the Parliament at Chryse promises to make this year's ceremony the Harmonists' swan song, at least so far as that ogreish mountain is concerned. So listen well, Gayle, and remember what you hear."

"Goodnight, Vanora." I stood up, brushed the wrinkles from my clothes, and strode past the tutelary statue of Ares to my tiny room. My own mother was a skeptic and an enemy.

"Goodnight, child," she said, resigned to my sharpness. "Sleep well."

A week before the Day of Diapason I ran away from home. I carried with me an Isidian silver harmonica, a printout of my sonatina "If I Forget Thee, O Elysian Earth of Yore," an enameled box in which to house captured insects, and a satchel for my clothes. I left at night when the OSAS veils throw a bronze dusk over Tithonia's giant redwood groves, for then a brown-clad figure among the trees blends with the antique shadows like an otter or a deer.

As for Spaulding, a government town where the door to every buried house resembles an upright marble grave marker—well, no one there saw me take my leave.

My destination, of course, was Olympus Mons, the enormous shield volcano in the Martian province informally known as Blackshale. The mountain's chief city is a well-to-do vacation community, incongruously called Hardscrabble, on the eastern flank, high above the Olympus Palisades, which front the Tharsis Steppe. My father received mail and occasionally slept in Hardscrabble, which lay more than twenty-one hundred kilometers northwest of our home in Spaulding.

To get there, I was going to have to pass through several government redwood groves, dairy farms, winter-wheat collectives, and mining hamlets. My course pointed me straight through the famous Wilder Plains, separating the two northernmost volcanoes of the Tharsis Ridge, Ascra and Pavo. If I made it through that pass by my second day of travel, I would be doing well. Everything depended on my catching rides. In only a week not even a towering three-legged war machine could walk to Olympus.

That first night, though, I deliberately avoided people. I ran through the oxygen-exhaling redwoods like a two-year-old, my heart bursting with unwritten melodeon music. I was free. If anyone stopped me, I could show him my birth card, which confirmed me to be old enough for freelancing, and explain that I was a Harmonist novitiate on my first solo pilgrimage to the Holy Mountain. That was true, pretty much. It fell short of total truthfulness only in that I had not registered my intentions with the church.

Toward dawn I sat down beneath a redwood, emptied my pockets, and played "If I Forget Thee" on my harmonica. It sounded tinny and pitiful there in the woods, despite the sterling quality of my instrument, another gift from Theon, and I stopped before finishing the sonatina and returned both the mouth organ and my clumsy score to my satchel. I ate a dried beef cake and a seedless tangerine from Coprates, then stretched out to sleep. Around noon I was awakened by cricket song.

Instantly alert, I searched for my self-appointed alarm clock. Most crickets do not chirp during the day, but perpetual dusk has superseded night on Mars and a few cricket species have so far accommodated to this pattern that even full daylight does not inhibit them. I found my minstrel in a patch of white moss on the south side of a nearby redwood, caught it between my cupped palms, and eased it into my perforated box. It was white, my cricket—not a pink-eyed albino but an emerald-eyed mutant of a species I had never seen before. I took it with me.

Early that afternoon I left the forest and labored to a hilltop overlooking the Wilder Valley. Beneath me was a kilometer-wide tributary of the Canal Irrigation System (CIS), carrying water from the northern polar cap to Blackshale, Tithonia, Isidis, and other equatorial regions. This particular canal was the Wilder Interprovincial Tributary: CIS-WIT, to acronym lovers.

Gazing down, I was stunned by the amount of activity, both mercantile and recreational, along the broad concrete aprons of the locks. Like an immense liquid python, a strip of silver water curled away to the northwest and into a forest of dark green conifers. Up and down the middle of the canal moved colorful barges, while bathers and holiday anglers made use of the peripheral areas specifically set aside for them. Dock workers and freight vehicles labored noisily on the quays, and hundreds of gaily dressed people from nearby townships mingled among the wooden booths and striped canvas tents of the canalside markets. Spaulding, by comparison, was a drowsy memorial garden. I ran down the hill. It seemed unlikely that anyone in this busy festive place would know or care that I was a runaway.

After buying a cup of milk and a shell sandwich with some of last year's emergency scrip (it was worthless at home, but negotiable on the canals), I sauntered along the quays, looking for up-channel transportation. No one paid me any mind. I spilled most of the granulated beef from my shell sandwich, but a black dog and a pair of cheeky fulmars cleaned up after me. No reprimand from angry authority figures.

But no advice about how to catch a ride into Blackshale, either. It seemed that three quarters of the water traffic was coming *down* the canal. I despaired of reaching my father before D-Day. Surely, though, there had to be other pilgrims journeying up the CIS-WIT to hear the Holy Mountain hymn the planet of our origins. I would join them.

Unfortunately, I could not find them. Everyone along this lock of the Wilder Tributary was pursuing secular matters—trade, water games, day labor, holiday courtships, and eating. A haggard veteran of the expedition against the Argyre Separatist Army was hawking tickets for the Recompense Lottery from her powered wheelchair. I bought a ticket with five pieces of my tattered scrip.

"Isn't there any way to get up-channel, Sergeant?"

She folded the scrip into a deerskin sporran in her lap, then pointed into the crowd north of me. "Go to Quay Number Twelve, ask for Harbin, and tell him old Oona's calling in a favor."

"I don't need a favor. I need a ride."

"If all you have is scrip, child, you need a favor. Go on. Find Harbin and tell him what I've said."

Backing away, I thanked the crippled sergeant repeatedly. She waved me on. I reoriented myself among the streaming pedestrians and counted off every quay until I had found Number Twelve. There, beside a ladder, sat a short, burly man in a dirty blue pea jacket. Older than my father, he was also wearing stained coveralls and boots. I approached and told him what the sergeant had instructed me to tell him. Out of the corner of my eye I saw a dilapidated airboat gently breasting the swells that broke against the canal wall.

"I'll give you a ride," Harbin said. "What's for pay?"

"Wait a minute. Oona said she was calling in a favor, remember?"

"The favor's letting you aboard, upstart. What's for pay?"

My heart sinking, I showed Harbin the last of my scrip.

"That won't do. What else have you got?"

I searched my pockets. My harmonica came into my hand. I turned it out so that the airboat owner could see it.

"Silver?"

"From Isidis," I boasted. "The best."

"It's small, though." He took the harmonica from me and examined it closely. "All right, Gayle, here's your fare. I'm assuming you play this thing. You do? Good. All right, then. You play for me whenever I ask you to, and when we get to WIT's End—you know, the beginning of the Blackshale Tributary—you give up the harmonica and go your own way. Agreed?"

Although I thought about it for a minute, I finally agreed.

Harbin's airboat sprinted northwest on a cushion of downblasting air. Water spewed up beside us from the vessel's sculpted hydrofoils, and the battery-powered fans roared like miniature cyclones. So long as we were on the move, there was no question of my playing the mouth organ, nor could we really talk.

Holding the sides of my chair, I watched the lethargic barges and canal tugs flash by us in the glitter of the airboat's ceaseless spray. Harbin slowed down only when we had arrived at another lock level.

Here, as if piloting a helicraft rather than a water vessel, he would adjust the controls to power us up and over the wall. This stunning maneuver, he later told me, would have been impossible on Earth, where gravity had exerted a significantly stronger force.

The sky turned bronze, and the lights of the other mercantile craft looked like gems floating in amber syrup. We continued to skim along. In fact, we traveled for nearly ten hours, with only two brief breaks, neither of which gave me enough time to serenade Harbin on the harmonica. The conifer forests on our left gave way to the sprawling irrigated pastures of government dairy farms as we passed through the Wilder Plains. On the far horizon the peak of Olympus Mons, where even native Martians dare not venture without oxygen gear, grew dimly visible.

The peak was naked, wavery brown in the twilight, for several weeks ago the Harmonists had paid OSAS to melt the summit snow. The runoff, I knew, would have turned the mountain's lower skirts a stunning deep green and replenished most of the minor tributaries of the local canal system. But we were still not close enough to see below the mountain's timberline.

Around midnight we docked at an outpost called Parkhill, a trading center built of logs and sod, with latex calking in the chinks and prefabricated plastic shutters on the double-paned windows.

The owner, who knew Harbin, gave us a late supper of beer and fried squirrel, which we consumed on a wooded hillside overlooking both the trading post and the canal. My body was vibrating from the long noisy ride, and I ate greedily to overcome my fatigue. When I had finished, Harbin demanded that I play. Willingly enough, my hands shaking, I complied. Bittersweet ballads, lively jigs, and familiar Harmonist hymns—music that I accurately surmised would appeal to an uneducated but independent soul like my airboat pilot.

"Not too shoddy for an upstart," he commented afterwards.

"My father's Theon the Memorialist."

"Ah, so *that's* why you're heading for the mountain." (It had not occurred to him to doubt my story.) "Well, maybe you'd better not tell *every* traveler along the way who your daddy is."

"Why not?"

"Harmonists—mouthy ones, anyhow—are none too popular in Blackshale this year. The hospice keepers in Hardscrabble would like to send Theon on a half-round trip to the bottom of the CISBIT."

"Why?"

"Because the government's ordered a three-day evacuation of the communities around the volcano. Everyone's got to withdraw at least two hundred kilometers from the Olympus Palisades. Some have already started pulling out. That's a dandy fuss for those folks, just so the church can turn the tallest mountain in the solar system into a wind-spittin' calliope. Me, I'm rapstatic this is probably the last decennial it's ever gonna blow."

Bitterly I pointed out that Harbin would not be alive for the next Day of Diapason, anyway.

"Don't be so sure. My mother, without genetic reconditioning or the usual butt-minded immortalist diets—my mother lived to be sixty-one. Why, on Earth, she would have been well over a century old. These days lots of folks get older than she did."

"Most of the ones who do are Harmonists."

"Maybe."

I nodded at the trading post below us. "Ask Parkhill's terminal for an actuarial readout. What I say is true, Harbin."

"Well, upstart, I've never understood that."

"Whosoever is harmonically composed delights in harmony," I quoted.

"Nor that, either."

I explained that the basic ordering of the physical universe is essentially crystalline. Because music also has a crystalline structure, it constitutes an important *seam* between the spiritual and the material worlds. Spiritually hungry human beings (I lectured the old man) have a deep-seated urge to bridge the two realities through music, and talented adepts like my father must mediate between these realms for the many people who lack his gift. Through either their own devout efforts or the salvific talent of a mediator like Theon, a longer or a more vital life comes to those who search for and find the crystalline harmonies undergirding the *whole* of Nature. Such is my credo, and I outlined it enthusiastically.

"You talk even fancier than you play," Harbin noted.

I was not finished yet. "The volcanoes surrounding us—Olympus ahead, Ascra behind, Pavo and Ars to the south—they're *frozen music,* Harbin. The entire physical universe is God's dream of creation inscribed as a secret crystalline music. You and I are parts of the dream that have awakened. We must awaken the rest. We must draw the music of God's thought out of the physical substances embodying it. That's what the colonizing—the warming, the watering, the seeding—of half-frozen planets like precolonial Mars is all about, Pilot. That's why we're here."

"Theology's never been my strong suit, upstart. I'm here because after the Punitive Expedition to the Argyre I saved enough to buy an airboat. Beats doing butt work in a government bunker, wouldn't you say?"

"Operating an airboat is what you do to accommodate to physical reality, Harbin. Too often we let that side of Nature get the upper hand. Earth was blooming, unfreezing, awakening, but people unaware or uncaring that the implicit harmonies of God's thought were finally manifesting themselves killed the planet before its music was fully audible. We betrayed ourselves. The result was not simply death for our world but a lingering"—I searched for a word—"a lingering *dissonance* in the lives of those who escaped the catastrophe. At all costs, we must save Mars from that kind of betrayal, in order to save ourselves, too."

I was preaching. Although the look on Harbin's face conveyed a wry regard for my precocious eloquence, he obviously thought it both misplaced and haughty. I promptly shut up.

The pilot reached over and rumpled my hair. "Go ahead. Get it all out, upstart. I've got plenty of time. Just don't expect a contribution when you've wound down for good."

Pulling away, I drained a last drop of beer from my stein.

"Surely you must have a *moral,* upstart. Most preachers—Harmonists, Syncretists, whatever other mouthy kind—most of 'em end up with a moral."

I stared at the pilot defiantly. "Just this, Harbin: The entire universe, the whole staff of God's harmonic thought, sings through the consciousness of every human being, but few of us train ourselves to hear the melodies. And some of us," I added pointedly, "are more deaf than others."

"Well, I'm not deaf to that singing in your pocket. What have you got there, upstart?"

Stunned, I realized that the cricket in my box had begun, quite faintly, to chirp. I had forgotten about the creature. Folding back my pocket, I turned the perforated box out onto the hillside. Then I picked it up and began stuffing grass blades and sprigs of clover through the tiny holes. It was a wonder the insect had not suffocated. As soon as the box had fallen from my pocket, of course, the cricket had stopped singing, but it appeared little worse for close confinement, and I was relieved.

"You're not planning to keep it, are you?"

"Well, I found it this morning when—"

"Let it go."

I looked uncertainly at the airboat pilot.

"Let it go," he repeated more forcibly. "What do you want to keep the little fiddler for, anyway?"

"I collect singing insects. Cicadas, crickets, grasshoppers. It's a hobby of mine. I've been doing it since—"

"Collect 'em! Caterwauling Krystos, upstart, *what for?* Are you

afraid you're missing a note or two of God's great hidden symphony? Do you think you have to pick 'em up secondhand? Where's your faith, upstart? *Where's your faith?*"

"Listen, it's not—"

"If you want a ride to WIT's End with me, upstart, you're going to have to let that pale little fiddler loose."

I tried to stare Harbin down, but that was impossible. Finally I pulled the top from the capture box and bumped the white cricket gently into a patch of clover, where it was conspicuous against the green.

"Now give me the box," Harbin said.

"What for?"

"To pay for your ride."

"I thought you wanted the harmonica."

"I do. I want the box, too. I always charge more for well-tuned hypocrites than for live-and-let-live folks with tin ears."

"Oh, I see. You've found out my father's Theon the Memorialist, and you're going to gouge me for having a well-known father."

"You don't see anything. And you don't hear so good, either, even if it's not because you're deaf."

He strode down the slope to Parkhill's trading post, to surrender his stein and wooden bowl and to scribble a farewell to the owner on the slate hanging beside the door. After seeing to our provisioning, Parkhill had gone back to bed. Reluctantly I followed Harbin, for without his airboat I would never reach Olympus.

We reached the end of the Wilder Interprovincial Tributary a little before dawn. Traffic here was nonexistent; we had the canal locks and the countryside all to ourselves.

Harbin made me disembark on a lock apron from which the volcanic surface of the ancient Tharsis Steppe was visible. Unredeemed basalt and jumbled rocks rich in iron oxide. A primeval desert in the midst of irrigated pastures and lovely evergreen groves. In fact, the naked area—known today as the Tharsis Precolonial Preserve—had been set aside by the government as a commemorative park. Because few latter-day Martians care to remember what our world looked like before the Warming, however, no one was about to give me transportation farther west into Blackshale Province. I saw no prospect of continuing my journey other than by foot.

"What am I supposed to do now?" I asked Harbin.

"Take a hike through the park"—the desert, he meant—"and if you keep bearing toward the mountain, you'll soon run up on Volcano Flats. It's too big to miss. You should be able to get help there. Just don't tell 'em you're a caterwauling Harmonist."

Harbin had dry goods from New Tithonia to deliver to a crater community called Lower Alba. He saluted me, leaped his airboat over the lock wall, and sprinted off north over the water. His was still the only vessel on the canal, and I stood on the vast blank apron of the automated lock and watched it go cycloning out of my life.

Then I turned and walked westward into the antique desolation of the Tharsis Precolonial Preserve.

Lizards, birds, and rodents live among the rocks of this prehistoric landscape. They do not contribute to the precolonial authenticity of the park, but they made my passage through its barrens less lonely and therefore more endurable.

I hiked for nearly six hours along a well-marked trail and at last emerged into the stony sprawl of Volcano Flats, a lively city with an aerodrome, dozens of wide pedestrian thoroughfares, and a host of carven-looking beige buildings whose windows winked in the sunlight like murals of hammered copper. The city was full of people. Many of them, it became clear, were affluent evacuees from Olympus Mons, tourists who had come out well ahead of D-Day.

I told no one on the streets that my father was Theon the Memorialist. Nor did I say that I was a pilgrim to the Holy Mountain. Instead, after asking directions to the aerodrome, I swung along past the Volcano Flats Carnival Grounds and the Blackshale Livestock Emporia as if frivolity and commerce were my birthrights and I a native of this boisterous frontier town. No one looked at me twice.

At the aerodrome I engaged in some imaginative haggling and suffered several discouraging setbacks. However, I finally connived my way aboard one of the skyliner dirigibles that cruised back and forth between Volcano Flats and the East Olympus Palisades. My story was that my parents, trade representatives from Epur, on the

Jovian satellite Ganymede, had left me in town in order to take a three-day holiday by themselves in Hardscrabble. But they had been gone a week now, the money they had given me to get by in Volcano Flats had run out, and I feared that some terrible mishap had befallen them. The manager at the hospice where they had planned to stay had recently told me by tellaser transmission that they had never even arrived. Frantic, almost weeping, I begged the agents of the dirigible service to give me passage to Olympus Mons to find out what had happened. Although these people tried to refer me to local government authorities for help, a woman going back to Hardscrabble for an entertainment contractor overheard my pitiful tale and bought me a ticket for the next flight.

The woman's name was Ardath. She sat beside me in the dirigible's passenger gondola and plied me with questions that made me stammer, blush, and finally, full of remorse, confess my true identity. The surprising upshot of my confession was that Ardath found the truth harder to swallow than the lie I had told at the aerodrome. Disappointed, she patted my knee and folded several pieces of planetary currency into my hand, not scrip but money, nearly a hundred legitimate marsnotes.

"Gayle, maybe you won't feel compelled to counterfeit identities for yourself if you have a little money ready to hand."

"Please, Elder, it's not—"

"I don't know what it is, Gayle. Never mind, though. I think I understand. I was young once, too."

Ardath rose and went aft into the dirigible's library. Miserable, I looked out the window at the deep green landscape rolling by beneath us. Because of the impending Diapason, the gondola was virtually empty, and Ardath did not return to her seat beside me.

At dusk we tethered at an aerodrome below the Olympus Palisades, above which lighter-than-air craft may not venture without special permit. I disembarked on a marshy pasture below the great volcano. The iodine of twilight bronzed the entire world. Beneath the cliffs, two kilometers high, you could see neither the mountain's cloud-ringed summit nor its lava-coated skirts, but the distant din of running water attested to the success of the snowcap's carefully channeled melt.

While the other dirigible passengers straggled across the landing field to a village of A-frame lodges, I made for the cog-lift depot. There I used a little of Ardath's money to purchase a ride to the top of the Palisades.

An hour later I was in Hardscrabble, a ghost town of glass chalets and pueblo-style apartments built of rock and extruded foam. I sought out the Harmonist cloister above the village. My knowledge of *The Lore of Krystos* got me past the cenobite guards stationed outside the gate, and when I showed them my birth card, I suddenly became an honored guest.

Inside, I told a youthful cenobite named Doloro what I had come for. Like Ardath, he did not believe my father was Theon, in spite of my birth card and my facile grasp of Harmonist dogma. However, his training and his natural courtesy did not permit him to dispute my claim. He merely mentioned that most of those at the Olympus Cloister had abandoned the mountain last week. They would not return until after the Diapason. He and the other cenobites still present would depart in another three days. Meanwhile they were carrying out their traditional duties and guarding the cloister against vandalism. Theon might or might not be my father, Doloro's remarks implied, but I would not be permitted to remain on the Holy Mountain any longer than bona fide servants of the church.

"I want to hear my father play."

"Very well, but you don't warm your hands by sticking them into the fire."

Wind chimes hung in the red-glass towers of the cloister, and the quiet sawings of stringed instruments knitted its various rooms together as surely as did the crystal statues lining its corridors. In the communication center Doloro put through a tellase to my father in the keyboard room deep in the bowels of the mountain. On the third try, one of Theon's technicians answered, and a few minutes later an image of my father's face was floating in the projection cylinder.

"Gayle!"

"You said I could come."

"Vanora was through to me yesterday. She was afraid something terrible had happened to you. Gayle, you can't stay. You just can't!"

We argued, and Doloro discreetly left the communication center. Theon adduced reasons for my returning to Spaulding, and I either countered these or attacked the general thrust of my father's argument, whichever seemed the more promising course. Finally, weary of our exchange, my father threatened to abdicate the responsibilities of Memorialist in order to discipline me. Someone else—Eldora, say, or Kiernan—could earn the glory for which he had spent the last six hundred days laying the groundwork. This threat frightened me, and even in his air-conditioned cage under the mountain he could see the cold fear in my eyes.

"I wrote a sonatina for you," I pleaded.

"For me?"

"For Earth, Father."

"Leave it with Doloro, and go back to Spaulding. Tellase your mother, and let her know you're coming. Otherwise, Gayle, I'll inform the Ecclesiarchal Council I'm resigning and take you home myself."

"In Spaulding I'll hear nothing!"

"What is loud and cacophonous close to hand acquires, with distance, a mellow harmony."

I parried the epigram: "I'll retreat to Volcano Flats with the other evacuees, but I'll remain there until after the Diapason. I want to hear it, Father! I want to hear it!"

For some minutes Theon's face floated expressionless in the translucent cylinder. Then it said, "Leave your sonatina with Doloro," and it faded from view. By making a concession, I had called my father's bluff.

Doloro returned and helped me reach my mother in Spaulding. We awakened her, and she spent a few minutes trying to shake the sleep from her head. I explained what had passed between Theon and me, then told her that I would meet her not in Volcano Flats but on an artificial hill several kilometers north of the city. This was a Harmonist retreat where many cenobites and pilgrims, according to Doloro, would gather to hear my father's performance.

Vanora protested. She wanted me to come home at once, and she had no intention of meeting me at a Harmonist gathering place.

But I had just learned a deceitful debating technique from Theon, and I explained that if she wished to see me again, she must make the journey to Harmony Knoll and meet me there on Diapason Eve. Otherwise I would ride the canals to some faraway plain or canyon and never again set foot in West Tithonia except by a vagrant whim. Unlike my father's, this threat was one that the threatener felt capable of carrying out.

"I'll be there, Gayle, but I'll remember this."

Doloro led me to a night chamber. Later, dreaming, I heard several harsh thudding sounds, and in the morning a cenobite named Talitha told me that a small gang of adolescents from Hardscrabble had come up to the cloister and stoned its unbreakable towers of rose glass. Doloro, Risa, and two constables from the village had routed the troublemakers. The protests this decennial were mild, primarily because everyone understood that there would never be another.

The church could no longer afford to finance the attendant evacuation, and local law-enforcement units no longer wanted to organize and police the withdrawal. Those who opposed the Day of Diapason were finally inclined to be tolerant of those who cherished it. The Parliament had written their objections into law.

Two days before D-Day, I accompanied most of the Hardscrabble cenobites to Harmony Knoll. We floated back across the volcanic plains in the gondola of the same dirigible that I had boarded with Ardath. We spent the entire flight playing ceramic flutes and singing Harmonist rounds.

My reunion with Vanora was chilly. An old ecclesiarch had given us a tent in the city of tents facing Olympus Mons, and my mother and I shared this diaphanous chapel—it seemed to have been made of lavender scarves and oiled rice paper—like strangers who do not understand each other's language. I slept on one side, she on the other, and when I tried to apologize for my blackmail by bringing her tea or apples from the fellowship center, she accepted these gifts without speaking.

"Are you sure you still want me to come home with you?"

Vanora smiled, for the first time. "Of course I do. It's going to be lonely without your father."

"He'll come home, too, Mother."

"That remains to be seen."

"Whose fault will it be if he doesn't?"

"His. Mine. Who knows, Gayle?"

We did not talk about the matter again, and on Diapason Eve every cenobite and pilgrim on Harmony Knoll stood on the hillside keeping vigil with chants and musical prayer candles. Vanora and I kept vigil, too, gazing westward at the colossal blue-black silhouette of Olympus Mons. Near dawn she allowed her hand to creep into mine, and we waited together. There were more than a thousand of us waiting for the universe to sing through our individual consciousnesses, a chorus of sympathetically vibrating minds, each brain a crystal.

The sun rose at our backs, and the first deep utterance of the Vox Olympica sounded across the land.

Our feet trembled. A murmur of awe ran through our ranks like a ripple of wind over a field of wheat. A second note sounded, and the sky seemed to scintillate the way a spill of whiskey enlivens a shallow pan of water. A third, a fourth, a fifth, a dozen more notes boomed out over the plains of Blackshale, and the power of this stately melody forced people to their knees. The ground was quaking. The solar-amplification veils high above the planet seemed to ricochet sound as well as light.

It went on for twenty minutes, this first ringing hymn. The silence after the polyphonic caroling of the mountain was like a drought, a famine, an extinction. I was afraid to look up. If I did, I would find that the atmosphere of Mars had peeled back to reveal a blackness in which the crystalline arrangements of the stars shadowed forth God's primal thought. If I looked up, I would hear as well as see that thought.

So I did not look up, and no one on the hillside moved. Then my father began playing the second movement of the requiem. The sun continued to rise and our adoptive planet to stagger in its orbit.

Or so I imagined.

Later the manifold vents and calderas of the volcano gave out recognizable paraphrases of "If I Forget Thee, O Elysian Earth of Yore." Theon worked them into the various movements of Zivu's original program and played them back and forth through the laments, the paeans, and the hallelujahs. On the winds howling so sweetly from the mountain, clouds broke apart, and like a mantle of audible fallout my sonatina traveled ever outward.

I looked at Vanora. Her face was wet, radiant. She squeezed my hand, and we stood together in the ocean of sound, listening to its cunning surges and imagining unknown or half-forgotten referents for its themes. Neither of us had ever heard the sea before, not really, but now, thanks to Theon and the Vox Olympica, we had.

Three evenings later, after Vanora and I had returned to Spaulding, a flickering of household lights indicated that visitors stood outside the upright cenotaph of our door. Expecting only the evening post or perhaps one of my mother's OSAS colleagues, I rode the entry platform to ground level and opened to our callers.

"Father!"

Supported by a young believer unfamiliar to me, Theon gave me a wan smile and touched my lower lip with a trembling finger. His face was horribly bruised. A gash in his right cheek had not reacted well to its first subcutaneous treatments, for the lips of the wound were livid.

"This is Corydon," my father said, nodding in the direction of the young man. "He's brought me home."

Too shocked to speak, I wrapped my arm about my father's waist and led him onto the platform. He was strong enough to stand without my help, but I insisted on lending my hip and shoulder. Meanwhile, wearing a half-angry, half-bereft expression, Corydon remained outside.

"A small band of anti-Harmonist fanatics met our dirigible at the Volcano Flats aerodrome," he explained, his voice deliberately loud. "Had several of us not fought back fiercely, they might have killed your father."

"The authorities intervened," Theon reminded Corydon.

"Only when they saw that *we* might inflict a few injuries, too. I have only contempt for the so-called authorities, Master Theon."

My father invited the young man in, urging him to rest a little before journeying back to Harmony Knoll.

"Now is a time to be with believers," Corydon said pointedly. "For an entire day, Master Theon, you knitted all the patterns together, revealed the latticework behind Creation. You did this magnificently, sir, but the deaf and the indifferent have pulled the patterns asunder again, and today—forgive me, sir—today I am unable to face even one more such person."

Before my father could reply, Corydon turned and strode off down the green hillside toward the silver tracking discs and relay towers of the OSAS facility.

Theon and I descended into the house. A moment later, in the center of the music room, he and Vanora were silently embracing. They seemed to take no notice of me.

"I thought you wouldn't come home," my mother whispered.

Theon stepped back and tugged on one earlobe to suggest that he had not really heard her, and Vanora repeated her last words aloud.

"Why would you think that?" he asked her, still gripping her shoulders.

"Years of argument, years of hostility, years of trying to accommodate ourselves to each other's belief." Though on the edge of tears, my mother did not ease herself back into Theon's arms. "Or lack of belief, I should probably add. Finally the connectives snap, and everything disintegrates."

Theon shook his head. "And years of loving each other, Vanora. You can't leave that out. It's unheard music—sweeter, far sweeter, than all the desperate clangor of those other things. You know that, don't you?"

This response appeared to embarrass my mother. She glanced at me, then pulled gently away from Theon's hands.

A moment later she said, "Everyone at the OSAS facility—everyone old enough to have heard the Vox Olympica two or three times before—well, they're all convinced that no performance in memory can rival this last one. They're sorry there's never going to be another. They're *genuinely* sorry, Theon, and I suppose I am, too."

"After people have succeeded in murdering something important," I blurted, "it becomes fashionable to mourn what they've killed. That's the way it always is."

"Hush," my father admonished me.

"It makes me sick—angry and sick."

"Just as it does Corydon and all the other young ones," Theon replied. "Go aboveground, Gayle. Give your mother and me a chance to lay our ghosts to rest without—"

"Without my interference," I bitterly concluded.

But Theon merely looked me toward the entry well, and I followed his meaning look onto the platform and from there upward and into the lonely memorial gardens of the dusk. Here, cursing both my parents, I wandered about among the tombstone doorways like a spirit seeking its body's grave. Predictably I soon tired of this game and sat down in the grass bordering an orchard of flowering apple trees.

Somewhat later Theon emerged from our doorway and climbed the vast communal lawn to the orchard. He took up a sentry position only a couple of meters away. Lifting his bruised face to the sky, he surveyed the dim, almost invisible scatter of stars beyond the canted solar veils. Although I tried not to, I found myself sneaking glimpses of his dark heavy-jowled profile.

"There's Phobos," he said presently.

I looked up and saw the inner moon come floating by. It always reminds me of a pitted hominid skull, and so of Earth, and I shuddered to see that tiny lunar death's-head passing over our township. Another emblem, it seemed that night, of our failure to deflect Martian institutions and mores from the self-destructive course taken by the majority of our homeworld forebears. Another word for fear, Phobos; another word for failure.

"I'm not going to let it end this way," I told my father, loudly enough to penetrate his incipient deafness.

"Let what end this way?"

"What we believe in. I'm a Harmonist. Three days ago you played the mountain, but tonight you seem to have given up."

Theon turned toward me. "I've given up trying to badger a good woman into putting on a belief system that doesn't fit her."

"But everyone's got to—"

"Everyone's got to nothing, Gayle. For anyone past puberty intolerance is an unaffordable luxury. I'm not giving up. I'm merely passing the baton to you. If you don't try to beat everybody over the head with it, you may be able to coax some singular music from your own spiritual resources. Do you understand me? Your *own,* not this or that other poor beggar's."

Suddenly, as if palsy-stricken, my hands were shaking.

"That's where it starts, Gayle. Do you understand what I'm telling you?"

"Yes, sir." A chorus of crickets had begun singing in the grass beneath the apple trees. Weeping, I went to Theon for warmth and reassurance. I was weeping, I realized, not merely in filial gratitude but in the painful knowledge that Theon could no longer hear the crickets' faint, stridulous music. My heirloom. And my charge.

SMITH

Patriots

"Settle down, Denny," Hugo Monegal told the young lieutenant striding grimly barefoot down the beach ahead of him. "Everything's going to be okay, kid."

"*If* I go back."

"Well, of course. You've got to go back."

"I'm through, Sergeant Monegal. I don't give a damn if the General himself orders me back up."

"But this way, kid, you'll get your ass court-martialed."

Denny Rojas stopped, put his hands on his hips, and stared out across the dawnlit swells of the Pacific. The sun was rising on Guam. It was the Fourth of July, 1973, but the disadvantaged populations of Hawaii, Alaska, and the continental United States would not be able to celebrate Independence Day for another twenty-four hours. They were trapped behind the International Date Line, an invisible barrier over two thousand miles to the east.

"I'm already being fined six hundred and fifty bucks," Denny said. "Did you know that, Monegal?"

"For refusing to fly? You're lucky it's not four or five years in a federal prison."

"I haven't formally refused to fly yet. Only this morning did I make my mind up. The fine's for something else, Monegal—something that's being kept hushed up."

"What?"

Denny hurled a piece of coral out toward the reef and began lurching southward away from the base again. *"Madre de Dios,"* he said, "I really, really goofed."

"How?" the sergeant pursued him. "How did you goof?"

"I'm a fuck-up and a murderer," the young man said without stopping. Fragments of coral were shredding the soles of his feet the way a vegetable grater curls away the skin of a carrot.

"Denny, look at your goddamn feet, will you?"

"You think I give a shit?"

He did not seem to. Deliberately scourging himself, he stepped on every shard of coral he could find. Dribbles of blood punctuated the last fifty or sixty feet of sand the two men had plodded through.

Taken by a sudden impulse, Monegal grabbed Denny by the shoulder and thrust into his face the microphone of the cassette recorder riding on the sergeant's hip. The recorder was a recent BX purchase. Monegal's family back in Wyoming had begun sending him taped messages instead of letters, and he had brought the machine with him on this impromptu trip down the beach in hopes of eventually taping a reply to their latest one. Denny recoiled from the microphone.

"What the hell, Monegal!"

"Tell your story to the machine, Denny. A kind of confession. Then we'll throw the cassette into the ocean—wash your sins away."

"Ha!" the younger man said, resuming his single-minded march. "And probably right back up onto the beach."

Monegal shouted, "You've got to get this out of your system, Denny!"

Suddenly the lieutenant halted. Monegal caught up with him. On a beach blanket the size of Costa Rica, there a few yards ahead of them, a man and a woman were embracing on their knees. The young woman's naked back shone brown and supple; her buttocks, cradled in a pink-and-scarlet bikini bottom, were cleft as poignantly as any peach. The man was kissing her neck.

"We're just what they need, aren't we?" Denny whispered. "Come on, Monegal, let's get out of here."

They started to retreat, but a male voice hailed them: "American airmen! A minute, please, American airmen!"

When the two soldiers turned back, the man from the big green blanket was trotting toward them in a black Olympic-style bathing suit and a pair of expensive Adidas jogging shoes. He appeared to be a Japanese gentleman in his late forties or early fifties, very lithe and muscular in spite of his years.

"Let me congratulate you," he said, reaching Monegal and Denny and shaking their hands in turn. "Today's a glorious day in the history of your country, and it's fortunate we've met."

"It is?" Denny said. He had spent the night returning from a B-52 sortie over western Cambodia, and his subjective time sense was still muddled from the flight. Nor did either he or Monegal understand why interrupting the gentleman's dalliance with the young woman was so auspicious.

"Of course," said the Japanese gentleman. "It's the Fourth of July. I know because it's also my birthday."

"Happy birthday," Denny said, and they all shook hands again.

The newcomer introduced himself as Jinsai Fujita, an Osaka businessman specializing in industrial explosives and tourist-related enterprises. He invited the Americans to join his companion and him. Together they would celebrate not only his birthday but the independence of the United States of America. He was delighted they had come along.

Monegal gestured vaguely at the young woman, who was pulling on a man's summer dress shirt and knotting its tail at her midriff.

"No, no," Fujita said, as if reading the sergeant's mind. "We're finished for the morning. In fact, I'm probably spent until noon or after." He tapped the sleeve of Denny's flight suit and led the Americans away from the water to where the beach blanket lay. Smiling faintly, his companion inclined her head as they approached.

"This is Rebecca Facpi," Fujita said. "She's a Guamanian of Chamorro descent."

"I've got a little American blood, too," she told them.

"She's a member of the choir at the University of Guam in

Agana," Fujita bragged. "She's pursuing a *double* major. Tell them in what subjects, Becky—I'm sure they'd like to know."

"Business administration and philosophy." This brief recital seemed to embarrass her. Crossing her arms, she hugged her shoulders.

Denny was staring absently out to sea instead of at this lovely young woman. Monegal began to worry about him again. He was a twenty-four-year-old bachelor whom the sergeant had befriended because they both came from Spanish-speaking cultures alien to most of their comrades.

Jabbering nonstop, Fujita folded up the beach blanket and gathered together the items that had just fallen from it: a package of Kools, a pair of Foster Grant sunglasses, a Ronson lighter, a bottle of Johnson's Baby Oil, an Italian billfold, and some odd-looking ivory paraphernalia that Monegal thought might be Oriental aids to potency. Fujita stuffed these various things into a canvas carry-all.

"My firm's developing a three-hundred-room resort hotel on Tumon Bay," he was saying. "Guam is a paradise for honeymooners, vacationers, world-travelers. If you'll come with us, Lieutenant Rojas, Sergeant Monegal, Becky and I will conduct you on a holiday tour of the interior. We were planning a picnic at a secluded spot, but Becky would probably enjoy the company of people who aren't always talking about economic indices and international exchange rates."

"Denny can't take a tour of the interior," Monegal protested. "Look at his feet."

"I'm sure we have something to put on them," Fujita said. "Besides, he needn't even employ them. Becky and I have mounts." He pointed over sand and grey volcanic tuff to a grassy area beyond the palms where two grazing horses were tethered. "Their names are Tokyo Rose and Admiral Halsey. They belong to the Jinsai Fujita Equestrian Academy for Tourists, just north of the village of Talofofo. No rental fee for you gentlemen today, however. This is my pleasure and my treat." He gestured with the canvas bag. "Come on, then."

Monegal helped Denny up the beach to the horses. Bridled but saddleless, the animals did not even lift their heads at the company's approach.

"Tokyo Rose is Honey's horse," Rebecca Facpi said. "Admiral Halsey's mine. Who wants to ride with whom?"

Grinning amiably, Fujita said, "Honey's her spooning sort of nickname for me, I'm afraid."

"I'll ride with Mr. Fujita," Denny abruptly declared.

"Why?" Monegal whispered, passing close to his friend. "Why ride with the old man when you could climb up behind that luscious *señorita?*"

Denny spoke curtly under his breath: "Because I don't deserve to ride with the girl. Any other questions?"

And so the lieutenant mounted behind Fujita, and the sergeant positioned himself on Admiral Halsey behind the young woman in the bikini bottoms and the nearly transparent silk shirt. Soon they were bound westward through mango and papaya trees, ragged palms, and bowers of wild orchids. Rebecca Facpi smelled as good as their surroundings, and Monegal could not help thinking that back home in Cheyenne a certain tough, talented woman probably believed him hard at work chiefing a maintenance crew on the sweltering flight-line at Andersen Air Force Base. Well, it was a holiday. . . .

Tokyo Rose led Admiral Halsey farther and farther inland, through thicker and steeper vegetation. Once, through a gap overlooking a distant clearing, the sergeant spied a cluster of quonset huts painted in subdued pastel colors, a different washed-out pastel for each tumbledown hut. Later, a mile or more from that colorful enclave, their horses began descending a narrow path into a wooded ravine with a half-hidden fresh-water pool at its bottom. The sea and the tinted huts were altogether lost to the riders.

Looking down, Monegal saw that on the other side of the pool rested an abandoned army tank, of World War II vintage, twined about with creepers and gutted with rust. At first he had mistaken it for part of the jungle, a geological outcropping. The tank was treadless and hatchless, except for a solitary circular cover that stood open like the lid of a waffle iron. Fujita pulled up the reins on Tokyo Rose and turned the hefty filly about.

"I've never seen that before," he said.

"Does that mean you're lost?" Becky asked him.

"I hope not. I think not."

"Weren't you taking us back toward Talofofo?"

"Roundabout, roundabout," Fujita replied. Although Tokyo Rose stutter-stepped precariously on the narrow path, Denny Rojas sat behind Fujita as calmly as any zombie, listless and unperturbed. "Let's explore this beautiful place."

Fujita prodded their horse down the path toward the pool and the bright crystal rope of the waterfall splashing softly into it from a sequence of small stone ledges. Becky and Monegal followed on their mount, and at the bottom of the ravine the riders all climbed down to stretch their legs and drink. The horses also waded in.

Squatting on his haunches, Denny lifted water to his mouth in his cupped hands. Suddenly, though, he stood bolt upright and stared up the far side of the ravine at something none of the rest of them could see. *"Madre de Dios,"* he said.

"What is it?" Monegal asked him. All the sergeant could perceive was greenery and a single swiftly flying bird.

Ka-pow! Ka-chiiing!

Gunshots and wayward ricochets.

"Jesus!" Monegal cried, flopping down on his belly in the shallow pool, but Denny had been staggered by one of the bullets and driven backward to the water's verge, where he collapsed screaming. Becky lurched through the water to take shelter in the lee of the abandoned tank, and Fujita, who had been holding Tokyo Rose by her bridle, lost control of the animal. She and Admiral Halsey plunged through the pool to a jumble of mossy boulders several yards to the north. Denny stopped screaming, and Fujita hurried to see what was wrong with him. Monegal pushed his cassette recorder to the small of his back and crawled toward them to check on Denny, too. As suddenly as it had begun, the fusillade from the farther slope had ceased.

"Father, I thank you for supplying me an assassin," Denny was saying. "You've taken my death out of my hands and given me hope of heaven."

"You're wounded in the shoulder," Monegal told him. "You're not going to die. Not today, anyway."

Two more shots rang out, the first throwing up a spray of water behind them, the second chuttering away through the trees.

"Let's get him to the cover of the tank," Fujita suggested.

With Denny suspended between them, then, Fujita and Monegal scrambled through the pool to the barnacled ironclad. It occurred to the sergeant that they might have been smarter to go the other way. Now, along with Becky, they were pinned down without much hope of reinforcement or relief. The group crouched together on the moist ground behind the tank, breathing like winded sprinters.

"You saw the *cabrón* shooting at us," Monegal told Denny. "Who was it?"

"An angel in a tree," Denny said, his head lolling against the treadless side of the tank. "An angel or an ape."

"I know who it is," Becky vowed, easing herself alongside Denny and slipping her arm behind his neck.

"Who?" Monegal asked her.

"The Samurai Straggler."

Fujita's face took on a cold, malignant look none of them had seen before. "The Samurai Straggler doesn't exist."

"He sure as hell does," Becky countered. "He's been sighted around this island on and off for thirty years. Once he set fire to an airplane on the flight-line at Andersen."

"Rumor!" Fujita scoffed. "The last Japanese stragglers were taken off Guam in the early sixties. This is probably an escapee from an American military hospital, someone addled by his service in Vietnam."

"Someone like me," Denny declared, closing his eyes.

At the sound of another rifle report Fujita ducked his head beneath the tank's scaly fender. Monegal squatted in front of Denny, fiddling with a zipper on the upper arm of his flight suit, trying to get at the wound. It was not a fatal injury, properly cared for; the bullet had entered and exited cleanly. The sergeant used his pocketknife to strip away the nylon sleeve.

"It *is* the Samurai Straggler," Becky hissed. "He makes occasional raids on our villages for food and weapons."

"Nonsense."

"Nonsense your stinkin' self, Honey. Stick your head up and shout something in Japanese. I bet that turkey gobbles right back at you."

Fujita appeared to consider this proposition.

"What are you waiting for? Tell him the war's over. Tell him to stop shooting at us."

Without moving, Fujita shouted several phrases in Japanese.

The sniper responded at some length in the same language. Then he loosed another barrage of bullets.

"Becky, I'm sorry. You're right. He's definitely Japanese."

"What did he say, Honey?"

"That I must be a traitor, a collaborator with the enemy. That his commander's last orders to him were to continue guerrilla warfare. That he's not going to quit the jungle until the forces of the Emperor return."

"If I die without confessing my sins, I'll be damned," Denny whispered. "Damned to eternal hellfire, Monegal."

The sergeant took off his T-shirt, tore it into strips, and began knotting a makeshift cotton bandage around the lieutenant's upper arm. "Denny, you're not going to die. I've already told you that."

Somewhere above them the Samurai Straggler rattled off another torrent of words and yet another angry enfilade of gunfire. Thirty years in the jungle had taken none of the edge off his hatred of the enemy. His would-be targets huddled together like people cowering in a tornado shelter.

"Translate," Becky urged Fujita.

"He says he has no intention of surrendering to three shameless beachcombers and a man in a juggler's costume."

This last was undoubtedly a reference to Denny's flight suit. An almost iridescent Day-Glo orange, it had so many zippers that it appeared to be held together by hundreds of gleaming metal teeth.

"We're liable to be here awhile," Becky said.

"I need a priest," Denny murmured, rolling his head. "Merciful God, you've killed me, but you haven't provided a priest."

"What about the cassette recorder, Denny? If you die, I'll play it back for the chaplain and he can absolve you *in absentia.*"

"Don't mock him," Becky scolded Monegal.

"It's a superficial wound. He's not going to die. Besides, I'm not mocking him. There's something he needs to get off his chest."

"Great idea, the cassette recorder. Let me talk into it before . . . before I black out, Monegal."

The Samurai Straggler opened fire again. Shouting more unintelligible abuse, he raked the tank, the pool, the waxy fronds surrounding the pinned-down party. Tokyo Rose, Monegal noticed, had prudently trotted three quarters of the way back up the hillside that they had just descended.

"Is the recorder on, Monegal?"

"Go ahead," the sergeant said, laying the microphone on his chest and depressing a plastic lever.

Denny looked at Fujita and then at the young Guamanian woman. "I'm a navigator, you see. Last month, on a mission over Cambodia, I was"—he grimaced— "navigating. In Cambodia we plot our bombing coordinates by taking fixes on radar beacons installed in towns friendly to Lon Nol's government. There aren't any ground radar sites to help us target, not like there are in Vietnam."

"I don't follow you," Fujita said.

"I was using a beacon in a village called Luong Phom, or Phong Luom, or—hell, something gookish." Denny's exasperation with himself got the better of him. "I can't even remember the goddamn place's goddamn name, can I? No, sir. That goddamn place's goddamn name seems to have escaped me." He winced as Monegal tightened the bandage on his arm. "Ain't that just like me, Sergeant? Forgettin' a name as goddamn important as that one?"

"Just tell your story," the older man urged him.

"Yeah. My story. The true and faithful history of my fuck-up." He looked off past Monegal into the glittering trees. "You see, Mr. Fujita, I was supposed to throw an offset switch on my radar scope. That's how it's done. If you don't flip the goddamn switch, your B-52 goes growlin' over the village with the beacon instead of over the bombing site you've plotted beforehand."

"Yes," said Fujita, comprehension dawning.

"Let me finish. It won't count if I don't finish. God forgive me, I forgot to throw that switch. And God forgive me, too, for all the times I *did* flip it—for all the times I sat up there in my monkey suit with all the other star-spangled glory-boys." He winced again, either from the sergeant's nervous fumbling or from the hot excruciations of memory. "*Christ!*"

More rant and gibberish from the Samurai Straggler. Although the sniper did not follow this verbal outburst with another hail of shots, Monegal dropped down beside Becky to keep his head from being blown away.

"He's glad to have human enemies again," Fujita translated. "He says that for many years now his most terrible enemy has been Time. American aircraft get bigger and bigger while his own body shrivels and his youthful strength ebbs. By killing us he hopes to make partial atonement for failing to retake the island single-handedly."

"Tell him the Japanese have already retaken the island, Honey. The American bombers he's seen are now on the Japanese side."

Denny was not listening to either the Straggler or the Honey and Becky Show. "And so I murdered"—another painful grimace—"yeah, I murdered the very people whose lives and property we were supposed to be protecting. I was responsible for walking thirty tons of deadly ordnance right down the middle of Luong Phom, or Phong Luom, or whatever the fuckin' hell they call that fuckin' backwater." His voice was getting feebler. "Knocked out a goddamn hospital, Monegal. Wasted a sixth of the population, wounded another third, bereaved every-fuckin'-body else. It's all in the report. All in the classified report."

More shots, perhaps a dozen.

Denny licked his lips and continued: "Our ambassador in Phnom Penh went in there later and promised the survivors money to rebuild with—plus a hundred dollars for every fuckin' casualty. That's a little over a grand, the casualty money. Me, now, they fined six hundred and fifty smackers. For failure to take elementary precautions during targeting procedures. Pretty stiff, huh?"

The weakness of the young man's voice was beginning to alarm Monegal. "Denny, are you shot somewhere besides your arm?"

"I'm dying, Sergeant. That's all I know." He gagged on these words, and a tiny geyser of blood burst from his mouth.

"He's gut-shot," the sergeant told Fujita and Becky, leaning over Becky to examine the belly of Denny's flight suit. "Right here in the fold of this goddamn zipper. Jesus, he's been gut-shot all along."

"Shut off the fuckin' machine," Denny whispered. "You don't have to get my death rattle, too."

Monegal removed the microphone, sat back on his haunches, and mashed the recorder's Stop button.

"'Send My Body Home to Mama, COD,'" Denny said. That was the title of an apocryphal country-and-western song and a long-standing joke among the airmen at Andersen. Spittle and blood made a vampirish froth on the young man's lips. "Ha, ha."

The Samurai Straggler began firing again, and Becky told Fujita he had better get busy if he was going to save them all from the same miserable fate Denny was suffering. She suggested that Honey try to convince the sniper not only that World War II was over, but also that Japan had won. The Straggler would find proof of this victory on Tumon Bay, where honeymooners from his homeland spent their nights together in luxury hotels and dined in elegant restaurants run by Japanese. Toyota, Honda, and Datsun automobiles would help corroborate Fujita's argument. All Honey had to do was entice the Straggler out of the jungle.

"Tell him he can have me as a hostage until he's completely sure we're speaking the truth," Becky said.

"I can't do that, Becky."

"Tell him," she insisted.

Fujita sighed and gave in. Shouting forcefully, he relayed the gist of Becky's message to the sniper.

Meanwhile Denny's head clunked against the fender of the tank, and his eyes filmed over. Fujita and the Samurai Straggler were still pursuing their friendly chat. To Monegal's amazement, Becky reached over and closed Denny's eyes with the tips of her fingers.

"I'm afraid he's dead," she whispered. "Your sad young friend."

"Dead," the sergeant echoed her. Reflexively, not really believing in the usefulness of the gesture, not really knowing what else to do, he crossed himself. "Dead?"

"You've seen this before," Becky replied. "Surely it can't surprise you."

"It surprises the hell out of me!" Monegal snapped. "It always surprises the hell out of me!"

"I'm sorry," the young Guamanian woman said.

"*Tan tonto no puedo creerlo,*" the sergeant told her. "So stupid I can't even believe it."

"At least you confessed him, Sergeant. At least you gave him a kind of absolution."

"Absolution for another stupidity! Where does it stop? How does it all begin, and where does the stupidity stop?"

Rebecca Facpi said nothing.

"'*Morir! Tremenda cosa!*' That's from an opera my wife loves. 'To die is a tremendous thing.' It's bullshit, though. Verdi should have lived long enough to see for himself." The sergeant put two questioning fingers on Denny Rojas's chin. "Beautiful bullshit."

"You don't know," Becky said. "Your perspective's too narrow."

Fujita interrupted this whispered argument: "He wants you to go up there to him. He says taking a hostage is a fine idea."

Scarcely hesitating, Becky scrambled to her feet, put her hands behind her head, and strode up the dappled hillside to the sniper's leaf-veiled redoubt. Fujita kept up the reassuring patter that Becky had programmed into him, and when she returned to them, five or six minutes later, she returned with the barrel of a rifle in her back and a wizened Oriental face peering over her shoulder. This was the man who had just murdered Denny Rojas.

Hate rose up in Monegal like vomit. "You cowardly little shit!" he raged, spilling a little.

The barrel of the Straggler's rifle shifted from Becky's back to the sergeant's sweat-streaked belly—whereupon, bowing and smiling, Fujita intervened to dispel the mounting tension.

To the American he said, "I've just told our friend that you greeted him with a fierce Yankee epithet much used between veteran warriors. Don't make him think otherwise, Sergeant Monegal, or we'll all pay for your rashness."

The sergeant fought to control both his anger and his chagrin. The sniper was a man in his early fifties, a contemporary of Fujita's, but with eyes so deep-set they looked as if they had been fired into his head with a slingshot. Sallow-skinned and cadaverous, he had gone bald on Guam. The clothes he wore—although obviously not his original uniform—had almost rotted away, and he stank of a vivid salt-sweat musk. Somehow his cartridge belt had withstood the inroads of mildew and constant use, and his rifle—a .30-06 Remington with a cross-hair scope—seemed to have come fresh from the factory crate. His name was Imai or Inukai or something ending with a long anguished vowel sound. Monegal made no real effort to get it straight. Everything about the little man was hateful to him.

After parleying a few more minutes, Fujita and his countryman fell into each other's arms. The latter was weeping. His ordeal on Guam was over. His ordeal back in Tokyo—reporters, photographers, politicians, hucksters—had not yet begun. A little man rescued from duty by its fanatic fulfillment at the expense of Dennis Rojas, who had not even been born when the Emperor signed formal surrender terms aboard the USS *Missouri* in Tokyo Bay.

Becky fetched Admiral Halsey back to the tank, and Monegal slung his friend's body over the horse's broad rump. Then the four survivors trudged up the western slope of the ravine and eventually into a tiny meadow with a magnificent view of the ocean. Tokyo Rose was grazing there, and Monegal thought he heard the sound of gunshots drifting down the coast from the air base. The Samurai Straggler cast an apprehensive look at Fujita, who rattled off an explanation that apparently allayed his fears. Monegal was still in the dark, though. The continuing noise made no sense.

"Firecrackers," Fujita said. "A few of your friends are already celebrating the Fourth."

The American felt hopelessly stupid not to have guessed.

Later, on the beach itself, Fujita pulled the sergeant aside, found his Italian wallet in his carryall, and counted into Monegal's hand several American bills of large denomination. Benjamin Franklin's face flashed past the sergeant's eyes at least six times.

"The authorities have probably already docked this sum from the young lieutenant's salary, Sergeant Monegal, but maybe you wouldn't mind sending these bills to his family."

"I don't want your money, Fujita, and Denny wouldn't want you to pay his lousy fine, either."

"I'm not giving this to *you,* I'm afraid. Nor do I think you know what the lieutenant would or would not have wanted me to do."

Rebecca Facpi, hearing their argument, came to them from the water's edge and touched the American's arm. "Money's the only sort of spiritual gift Honey knows how to make, Sergeant, but it's sincere, it's utterly sincere. Don't refuse it."

Monegal let his fingers close on the bills.

Fujita bowed. Then he and his graceful companion walked back to the weary Japanese infantryman waiting for them beside the horses and the vast indigo serenity of the sea. Bereft of everything but Fujita's money and his own festering hate, the surviving American stood transfixed, listening to the faraway firecrackers bursting, bursting in air. . . .

Collaborating

How does it feel to be a two-headed man? Better, how does it feel to be two men with one body? Maybe we can tell you. We're writing this—though it's I, Robert, who am up at the moment—because we've been commissioned to tell you what it's like living inside the same skin another human being inhabits and because we have to have our say.

I'm Robert. My brother's name is James. Our adoptive surname is Self—without contrivance on our part, even if this name seems to mock the circumstances of our life. James and I call our body The Monster. Who owns The Monster is a question that has occupied a good deal of our time, by virtue of a straitjacketing necessity. On more than one occasion The Monster has nearly killed us, but now we have pretty much domesticated it.

James Self. Robert Self. And The Monster.

It's quite late. James, who sits on the right side of our shoulders, has long since nodded away, giving control to me. My brother has subdued The Monster more effectively than I, however. When he's up, we move with a catlike agility I can never manage. Although our muscle tone and stamina are excellent, when I'm up The Mon-

SMITH

ster shudders under my steering, and shambles, and shifts anatomical gears I didn't even know we possessed. At six foot three I am a hulking man, whereas James at six foot four—he's taller through the temples than I—is a graceful one. And we share the same body.

As a result, James often overmasters me during the day: I feel, then, like a sharp-witted invalid going the rounds in the arms of a kindly quarterback. Late at night, though, with James down in sleep and The Monster arranged propitiatingly on a leather lounge chair, even I can savor the animal potential of our limbs, the warmth of a good wine in our maw, the tingle of a privately resolvable sexual stirring. The Monster can be lived with.

But I'm leaping ahead. Let me tell you how we got this way, and what we look forward to, and why we persevere.

James and I were born in a southeastern state in 1951. (Gemini is our birth sign, though neither of us credits astrology.) A breech delivery, we've been told. I suppose we aligned ourselves buttocks first because we didn't know how to determine precedence at the opposite end. We were taken with forceps, and the emergence of James and Robert together, two perfect infant heads groggy from the general anesthetic they'd given our mother, made the obstetrics team draw back into a white huddle from which it regarded us with fear, skepticism, awe, incredulity. How could anyone have expected this? A two-headed infant has only one heartbeat to measure, and there'd been no X-rays.

We were spirited away from the delivery room before our mother could recover and ask about us. The presiding physician, Dr. Larimer Self, then decreed that she would be told her child was stillborn. Self destroyed hospital records of the birth, swore his staff to silence, and gave my biological father, an itinerant laborer following the peach and cotton crops, a recommendation for a job in Texas. Thus, our obstetrician became our father. And our real parents were lost to us forever.

Larimer Self was an autocrat—but a sentimental one. He raised James and me in virtual isolation in a small community seventeen miles from the tricounty hospital where we'd been born. He gave us into the daytime care of a black woman named Velma Bymer. We grew up in a two-story house surrounded by holly bushes, crape myrtle, nandin, and pecan trees. Two or three months ago, after attaining a notoriety or infamy you may already be aware of, we severed all connections with the outside world and returned to this big eighty-year-old house. Neither Robert nor I know when we will choose to leave it again; it's the only real home we've ever had.

Velma was too old to wet-nurse us, and a bachelor woman besides, but she bottle-fed us in her arms, careful to alternate feedings between Robert's head and mine, since we could not both take formula at once. She was forty-six when we came into her care, and from the beginning she looked upon us not as a snakish curse for her own barrenness, but as a holy charge. A guerdon for her piety. My memories of her focus on her raw-boned purple hands and a voice like sweet water flowing over rocks. James says he remembers her instead for a smell like damp cotton mixed up with the odor of slowly baking bran rolls. Today Velma drives to Wilson & Cathet's for her groceries in a little blue Fiat and sits evenings in her tiny one-room house with the Bible open on her lap. She won't move from that house—but she does come over on Thursday afternoons to play checkers with James.

Larimer Self taught us how to read, do mathematics, and reconcile our disagreements through rapid, on-the-spot bargaining. Now and again he took a strop to The Monster.

Most children have no real concept of "sharing" until well after three. James and I, with help from our stepfather, reached an earlier accommodation. We had to. If we wanted The Monster to work for us at all we had to subordinate self and cooperate in the manipulation of legs, arms, hands. Otherwise we did a Vitus dance, or spasmed like an epileptic, or crumpled into trembling stillness. Although I wrote earlier that James often "overmasters" me, I didn't mean to imply that his motor control is stronger than mine, merely better, and that I sometimes voluntarily give him my up time for activities like walking, lifting, toting, anything primarily physical. As children we were the same. We could neutralize each other's strengths, but we couldn't—except in rare instances of fatigue or inattention—impose our will on the other. And so at six or seven months, maybe even earlier, we began to learn how to share our first toy: the baby animal under our necks. We became that organizational anomaly, a team with two captains.

Let me emphasize this: James and I don't have a psychic link, or a telepathic hookup, or even a wholly trustworthy line to each other's emotions. It's true that when I'm depressed James is frequently depressed, too; that when I'm exhilarated or euphoric James is the same. And why not? A number of feelings have biochemical determinants as well as psychological ones, and the biochemical state of Robert Self is pretty much the biochemical state of James Self. When James drinks, I get drunk. When I take smoke into our lungs, after a moment's delay James may well do the coughing. But we can't read each other's thoughts, and my brother—as I believe he could well say of me, too—can be as unpredictable as an utter stranger. By design or necessity we share many things, but our personalities and our thoughts are our own.

It's probably a little like being married, even down to the matter of sex. Usually our purely physical urges coincide, but one can put himself in a mental frame either welcoming or denying the satisfaction of that urge, whereupon, like husband and wife, James and Robert must negotiate. Of course, in our case the matter can be incredibly more complex than this. Legislation before congress, I suppose you could call some of our floor fights. But on this subject I yield to James, whose province the complexities are.

All right. What does being "up" mean if neither James nor I happen to be strong enough to seize The Monster's instrument panel and march it around to a goose step of our own? It means that whoever's up has almost absolute motor control, that whoever's down has willingly relinquished this power. Both James and I can give up motor control and remain fully aware of the world; we can—and do—engage in cognitive activity and, since our speech centers aren't affected, communicate our ideas. This ability has something Eastern and yogic about it, I'm sure, but we have developed it without recourse to gurus or meditation.

How, then, do we decide who's to be up, who's to be down? Well, it's a "you first, Alphonse" / "after you, Gaston" matter, I'm afraid, and the only thing to be said in its favor is that it works. Finally, if either of us is sleeping, the other is automatically up.*

* This state can be complicated, however. James dreams with such intensity that The Monster thrashes out with barely restrainable, subterranean vehemence. Not always, but often enough.

The Monster gets only three or four hours of uninterrupted rest a night, but that, we have decided, is the price a monster must pay to preserve the sanity of its masters.

Of course there are always those who think that James and I are the monster. Many feel this way. Except for nearly two years in the national limelight, when we didn't know what the hell we were doing, we have spent our life trying to prove these people wrong. We are human beings, James and I, despite the unconscionable trick played on us in our mother's womb, and we want everybody to know it.

Come, Monster. Come under my hand. Goodbrother's asleep, it's seven o'clock in the A.M., and you've had at least three long hours of shut-eye, all four lids fluttering like window shades in gusty May! Three hours! So come under my hand, Monster, and let's see what we can add to this.

There are those who think that James and I are the monster.

O considerate brother, stopping where I can take off with a tail wind, even if The Monster is a little sluggish on the runway this morning. Robert is the man to be up, though; he's the one who taps this tipritter with the most authority, even if I am the high-hurdle man on our team. (He certainly wouldn't be mixing metaphors like this, goodbrother Robert.) Our editor wants both of us to contribute, however, and dissecting our monsterhood might be a good place for James to begin. Just let Robert snooze while you take my dictation, Monster, that's all I ask.

Yes. Many do see us as a monster. And somewhere in his introductory notes my goodbrother puts his hand to his mouth and whispers in an aside, "James is taller than me." Well, that's true—I am. You see, Robert and I aren't identical twins. (I'm better looking than Robert.) (And taller.) This means that a different genetic template was responsible for each goodbrother's face and features, and, in the words of a local shopkeeper, "That Just Don't Happen." The chromosomes must have got twisted, the genes multiplied and scrambled, and a monster set loose on the helical stairway of the nucleotides. What we are, I'm afraid, is a sort of double mutant. . . . That's right, you hear me clearly: a mutant.

M.U.T.A.N.T.

I hope you haven't panicked and run off to Bolivia. Mutants are scary, yes—but usually because they don't work very well or fit together like they ought. A lot of mutations, whether fruit flies or sheep, are stillborn, dead to begin with. Others die later. The odds don't favor creatures with abbreviated limbs and heads without skullcaps. Should your code get bollixed, about the best you can hope for is an aristocratic sixth finger, one more pinky to lift away from your teacup. And everybody's seen those movies where radiation has turned picnicking ants or happy-go-lucky grasshoppers into ogres as big as frigates. Those are *mutants,* you know.

And two-headed men?

Well, in the popular media they're usually a step below your bona fide mutant, surgical freaks skulking through swamps, ax at the ready, both bottom lips adrool. Or, if the culprit *is* radiation—an after-the-bomb comeuppance for mankind's vanity—one of the heads is a lump capable only of going "la la, la la" and repeating whatever the supposedly normal head says. Or else the two heads are equally dumb and carry on like an Abbott and Costello comedy team, bumping noggins and singing duets. Capital crimes, all these gambits. Ha ha.

No one identifies with a two-headed man.

If you dare suggest that the subject has its serious side, bingo, the word they drop on you is—"morbid." Others in the avoidance arsenal? Try "Grotesque." "Diseased." "Gruesome." "Pathological." "Perverse." Or even this: "*poly*perverse." But "morbid" is the mortar shell they lob in to break off serious discussion and the fragments corkscrew through you until even you are aghast at your depravity. People wonder why you don't kill yourselves at first awareness of your hideousness. And you can only wince and slink away, a morbid silver trail behind you. Like snail slime.

Can you imagine, then, what it's like being a (so-called) two-headed man in Monocephalic America? Robert and I may well be the ultimate minority. Robert and I and The Monster, the three of us together.

Last year in St. Augustine, Florida, at the Ripley's museum, on tour with an Atlanta publicist, my brother and I saw a two-headed calf.

Stuffed. One head blind and misshapen, lolling away from the sighted head. A mutant, preserved for the delight and edification of tourists to the Oldest City in the USA. Huzza huzza.

In the crowded display room in front of this specimen our party halted. Silence snapped down like a guillotine blade. What were the Selfs going to do now, everyone wondered. Do you suppose we've offended them? Aw, don't worry about it, they knew what they were getting into. Yeah, but—

Sez I to brother, "This is a Bolshevik calf, Robert. The calf is undoubtedly no marcher in the procession of natural creatures. It's a Soviet sew-up. They did it to Man's Best Friend and now they've done it to a potential bearer of Nature's Most Perfect Food. Here's the proof of it, goodbrother, right here in America's Oldest City."

"Tsk, tsk," sez Robert. He sez that rather well.

"And how many Social Security numbers do you suppose our officialdom gave this calf before it succumbed? How many times did they let this moo-cow manqué inscribe in the local voting register?"

"This *commie* calf?"

"Affirmative."

"Oh, two, certainly. If it's a Soviet sew-up, James, it probably weaseled its rights from both the Social Security apparatus and the voting registrar. Whereas we—"

"Upright American citizens."

"Aye," sez Robert. "Whereas we are but a single person in the eyes of the State."

"Except for purposes of taxation," sez I.

"Except for purposes of taxation," Robert echoes. "Though it is given to us to file a joint return."

We can do Abbott and Costello, too, you see. Larry Blackman, the writer, publicist, and "talent handler," wheezed significantly, moved in, and herded our party to a glass case full of partially addressed envelopes that—believe it or not—had nevertheless been delivered to the Ripley museum. One envelope had arrived safely with only a rip (!) in its cover as a clue to its intended destination.

"From rip to Zip," sez I, "and service has gotten worse."

Blackman coughed, chuckled, and tried to keep Robert from glancing over our shoulder at that goddamn calf. I still don't know if he ever understood just how bad he'd screwed up.

That night in our motel room Robert hung his head forward and wept. We were racked with sobs. Pretty soon The Monster had ole smartass Jamebo doing it, too, just as if we were nine years old again and crying for Velma after burning a strawberry on our knobbly knee. James and Robert Self, in a Howard Johnson's outside St. Augustine, sobbing in an anvil chorus of bafflement . . . I only bring this up because the episode occurred toward the end of our association with Blackman and because our editor wanted a bit of "psychology" in this collaborative effort.

There it is, then: a little psychology. Make of it what you will.

Up, Monster! Get ye from this desk without awakening Robert and I'll feed ye cold peaches from the Frigidaire. Upon our shared life and my own particular palate, I will.

People wonder why you didn't kill yourselves at first awareness of your hideousness.

(James is reading over our chest as I write, happy that I've begun by quoting him. Quid pro quo, I say: tit for tat.)

Sex and death. Death and sex. Our contract calls upon us to write about these things, but James has merely touched on the one while altogether avoiding the other. Maybe he wishes to leave the harvesting of morbidities to me. Could that possibly be it?

("You've seen right through me, goodbrother," replies James.)

Leaving aside the weighty matter of taxes, then, let's talk about death and sex. . . . No, let's narrow our subject to death. I still have hopes that James will spare me a recounting of a side of our life I've allowed him, by default, to direct. James?

("Okay, Robert. Done.")

Very well. The case is this: When James dies, I will die. When I die, James will die. Coronary thrombosis. Cancer of the lungs. Starvation. Food poisoning. Electrocution. Snakebite. Defenestration. Anything fatally injurious to the body does us both in—two personalities are blotted out at one blow. The Monster dies, taking us with it. The last convulsion, the final laugh, belongs to the creature we will have spent our lives training to our wills. Well, maybe we owe it that much.

You may, however, be wondering: Isn't it possible that James or Robert could suffer a lethal blow without causing his brother's death? A tumor? An embolism? An aneurysm? A bullet wound? Yes, that might happen. But the physical shock to The Monster, the poisoning of our bloodstream, the emotional and psychological repercussions for the surviving Self, would probably bring about the other's death as a matter of course. We are not Siamese twins, James and I, to be separated with a scalpel or a medical laser and then sent on our individual ways, each of us less a man than before. Our ways have never been separate, and never will be, and yet we don't find ourselves hideous simply because the fact of our interdependence has been cast in an inescapable anatomical metaphor. Just the opposite, perhaps.

At the beginning of our assault on the World of Entertainment two years ago (and, yes, we still receive daily inquiries from carnivals and circuses, both American and European), we made an appearance on the *Midnight Chatter*. This was Blackman's doing, a means of introducing us to the public without resorting to loudspeakers and illustrated posters. We were very lucky to get the booking, he told us, and it was easy to see that Blackman felt he'd pulled off a major show-business coup.

James and I came on at the tail end of a Wednesday's evening show, behind segments featuring the psychologist Dr. Irving Brothers, the playwright Kentucky Mann, and the actress Victoria Pate. When we finally came out from the backstage dressing rooms, to no musical accompaniment at all, the audience boggled and then timidly began to applaud. (James says he heard someone exclaim "Holy cow!" over the less than robust clapping, but I can't confirm this.) *Midnight Chatter*'s host, Tommy Carver, greeted us with boyish innocence, as if we were the Pope.

"I know you must, uh, turn heads where you go, Mr. Self," he began, gulping theatrically and tapping an unsharpened pencil on his desk. "Uh, *Misters* Self, that is. But what is it—I mean, what question really disturbs you the most, turns you off to the attention you must attract?"

"That one," James said. "That's the one."

The audience boggled again, not so much at this lame witticism as at the fact that we'd actually spoken. A woman in the front row snickered.

"Okay," Carver said, doing a shaking-off-the-roundhouse bit with his head, "I deserved that. What's your biggest personal worry, then? I mean, is it something common to all of us or something, uh, peculiar to just you?" That *peculiar* drew a few more snickers.

"My biggest worry," James said, "is that Robert will try to murder me by committing suicide."

The audience, catching on, laughed at this. Carver was looking amused and startled at once—the studio monitor had him isolated in a close-up and he kept throwing coy glances at the camera.

"Why would Robert here—that's not a criminal face, after all—want to murder you?"

"He thinks I've been beating his time with his girl."

Over renewed studio laughter Carver continued to play his straight-man's role. "Now is *that* true, Robert?" I must have been looking fidgety or distraught—he wanted to pull me into the exchange.

"Of course it isn't," James said. "If he's got a date, I keep my eyes closed. I don't want to embarrass anybody."

It went like that right up to a commercial for dog food. Larry Blackman had written the routine for us, and James had practiced it so that he could drop in the laugh-lines even if the right questions weren't asked. It was all a matter, said Blackman, of manipulating the material. *Midnight Chatter*'s booking agent had expected us to be a "people guest" rather than a performer—one whose appeal lies in what he is rather than the image he projects. But Blackman said we could be both, James the comedian, me the sincere human expert on our predicament. Blackman's casting was adequate, I suppose; it was the script that was at heart gangrenous. Each head a half. The audience liked the half it had seen.

("He's coming back to the subject now, folks," James says. "See if he doesn't.")

After the English sheepdog had wolfed down his rations, I said, "Earlier James told you he was afraid I'd murder him by committing suicide—"

"Yeah. That took us all back a bit."

"Well, the truth is, James and I *have* discussed killing ourselves."

"Seriously?" Carver leaned back in his chair and opened his jacket.

"Very seriously. Because it's impossible for us to operate independently of each other. If I were to take an overdose of amphetamines, for instance, it would be *our* stomach they pumped."

Carver gazed over his desk at our midsection. "Yeah. I see what you mean."

"Or if James grew despondent and took advantage of his up time to slash our wrists, it would be both of us who bled to death. One's suicide is the other's murder, you see."

"The perfect crime," offered Victoria Pate.

"No," I replied, "because the act is its own punishment. James and I understand that very well. That's why we've made a pact to the effect that neither of us will attempt suicide until we've made a pact to do it together."

"You've made a pact to make a suicide pact?"

"Right," James said. "We're blood brothers that way. And that's how we expect to die."

Carver buttoned his jacket and ran a finger around the inside of his collar. "Not terribly soon, I hope. I don't believe this crowd is up for that sort of *Midnight Chatter* first."

"Oh, no," I assured him. "We're not expecting to take any action for several more years yet. But who knows? Circumstances will certainly dictate what we do, eventually."

Afterwards viewers inundated the studio switchboard with calls. Negative reaction to our remarks on suicide ran higher than questions about how the cameramen had "done it." Although Blackman congratulated us both heartily, The Monster didn't sleep very well that night.

"He thinks I've been beating his time with his girl."

Well, strange types scuttled after us while Blackman was running interference for Robert and James Self. The Monster devoured them, just as if they were dog food. When it wasn't exhausted. We gave them stereophonic sweet nothings and the nightmares they couldn't have by themselves. Robert, for my and The Monster's sakes, didn't say nay. He indulged us. He never carped. Which has led to resentments on both sides, the right and the left. We've talked about these.

Before leaving town for parts north, west, and glittering, Robert and I were briefly engaged to be married. And not to each other. She was four years older than us. She worked in the front office of the local power company, at a desk you could reach only by weaving through a staggered lot of electric ranges, dishwashers, and hot-water heaters, most of them white, a few avocado.

We usually mail in our bill payments, or ask Velma to take them if she's going uptown—but this time, since our monthly charges had been fluctuating unpredictably and we couldn't ring through on the phone, I drove us across the two-lane into our business district. (Robert doesn't have a license.) Our future fiancée—I'm going to call her X—was patiently explaining to a group of housewives and day laborers the rate hike recently approved by the Public Service Commission, the consumer rebates ordered by the PSC for the previous year's disallowed fuel tax, and the summer rates soon to go into effect. Her voice was quavering a little. Through the door behind her desk we could see two grown men huddling out of harm's way, the storeroom light off.

(Robert wants to know, "Are you going to turn this into a How-We-Rescued-the-Maiden-from-the-Dragon story?")

("Fuck off," I tell him.)

(Robert would probably like The Monster to shrug his indifference to my rebuke—but I'm the one who's up now and I'm going to finish this bloodsucking reminiscence.)

Our appearance in the power company office had its usual impact. We, uh, turned heads. Three or four people moved away from the payments desk, a couple of others pretended—not very successfully—that we weren't there at all, and an old man in overalls stared. A woman we'd met once in Wilson & Cathet's said, "Good morning, Mr. Self," and dragged a child of indeterminate sex into the street behind her.

X pushed herself up from her chair and stood at her desk with her head hanging between her rigid supporting arms. "Oh, shit," she whispered. "This is too much."

"We'll come back when you're feeling better," a biddy in curlers said stiffly. The whole crew ambled out, even the man in overalls, his cheeks a shiny knot because of the chewing tobacco hidden there. Nobody used the aisle we were standing in to exit by.

The telephone rang. X took it off the hook, hefted it as if it were a truncheon, and looked at Robert and me without a jot of surprise.

"This number isn't working," she said into the receiver. "It's out of order." And she hung up.

On her desk beside the telephone I saw a battered paperback copy of *The Thorn Birds*. But X hadn't been able to read much that morning.

"Don't be alarmed," I said. X didn't look alarmed. "We're a lion tamer," I went on. "That's the head I stick into their mouths."

"Ha ha," Robert said.

A beginning. The game didn't last long, though. After we first invited her, X came over to Larimer Self's old house—*our* old house—nearly every night for a month, and she proved to be interested in us, both Robert and me, in ways that our little freak-show groupies never had any conception of. They came later, though, and maybe Robert and I didn't then recognize what an uncommon woman this hip and straightforward X really was. She regarded us as people, X did.

We would sit in our candle-lit living room listening to the Incredible String Band sing "Douglas Traherne Harding," among others, and talking about old movies. (The candles weren't for romance; they were to spite, with X's full approval, the power company.) In the kitchen, The Monster, mindless, baked us chocolate-chip cookies and gave its burned fingers to Robert or me to suck. Back in the living room, all of us chewing cookies, we talked like a cage full of gibbering monkeys, and laughed giddily, and finally ended up getting serious enough to discuss serious things like jobs and goals and long-dreamt-of tomorrows. But Robert and I let X do most of the talking and watched her in rapt mystification and surrender.

One evening, aware of our silence, she suddenly stopped and came over to us and kissed us both on our foreheads. Then, having led The Monster gently up the stairs, she showed it how to coordinate its untutored mechanical rhythms with those of a different but complementary sort of creature. Until then, it had been a virgin.

And the sentient Selfs? Well, Robert, as he put it, was "charmed, really charmed." Me, I was glazed over and strung out with a whole complex of feelings that most people regard as symptomatic of romantic love. How the hell could Robert be merely—I think I'm going to be sick—"charmed"?

("The bitterness again?")

("Well, goodbrother, we knew it would happen. Didn't we?")

We discussed X, rationally and otherwise. She was from Ohio, and she had come to our town by way of a coastal resort where she had worked as a night-clerk in a motel. The Arab oil embargo had taken that job away from her, she figured, but she had come inland with true resilience and captured another with our power company —on the basis of a college diploma, a folder of recommendations, and the snow job she'd done on old Grey Bates, her boss. She flattered Robert and me, though, by telling us that we were the only people in town she could be herself with. I think she meant it, too, and I'm pretty certain that Robert also believed her. If he's changed his mind of late, it's only because he has to justify his own subsequent vacillation and sabotage.

("James, damn you—!")

("All right. All right.")

About two weeks after X first started coming to our house in the evenings Robert and I reached an agreement. We asked her to marry us. Both of us. All three of us. There was no other way.

She didn't say yes. She didn't say no. She said she'd have to think about it, and both Robert and I backed off to keep from crowding her. Later, after we'd somehow managed to get past the awkwardness of the marriage proposal, X leaned forward and asked us how we supported ourselves. It was something we'd never talked about before.

"Why do you ask?" Robert snapped. He began to grind his molars—that kind of sound gets conducted through the bones.

"It's Larimer's money," I interjected. "So much a month from the bank. And the house and grounds are paid for."

"Why do you ask?" Robert again demanded.

"I'm worred about you," X said. "Is Larimer's money going to last forever? Because you two don't *do* anything that I'm aware of, and I've always been uptight about people who don't make their own way. I've always supported myself, you see, and that's how I am. And I don't want to be uptight about my—well, my husbands."

Robert had flushed. It was affecting me, too—I could feel the heat rising in my face. "No," Robert said. "Larimer's legacy to us won't last forever."

X was wearing flowered shorts and a halter. She had her clean bare feet on the dirty upholstery of our divan. The flesh around her navel was pleated enticingly.

"Do you think I want your money, Rob? I don't want your money. I'm just afraid you may be regarding marriage to me as a panacea for all your problems. It's not, you know. There's a world that has to be lived in. You have to make your own way in it for yourselves, married or not. Otherwise it's impossible to be happy. Don't you see? Marriage isn't just a string of party evenings, fellows."

"We know," I said.

"I suppose you do," X acknowledged readily enough. "Well, I do, too. I was married in Dayton. For six years."

"That doesn't matter to us. Does it, goodbrother?"

Robert swallowed. It was pretty clear he wished that business about Dayton had come out before, if only between the clicks of our record changer. "No," he said gamely. "It doesn't matter."

"One light," the Incredible String Band sang: *"the light that is one though the lamps be many."*

"Listen," X said earnestly. "If you have any idea what I'm talking about, maybe I *will* marry you. And I'll go anywhere you want to go to find the other keys to your happiness. I just need a little time to think."

I forget who was up just then, Robert or me. Maybe neither of us. Who cares? The Monster trucked us across the room with the clear intention of devouring X on the dirty divan. The moment seemed sweet, even if the setting wasn't, and I was close to tears thinking that Robert and I were practically *engaged* to this decent and compassionate woman.

But The Monster failed us that night. Even though X received the three of us as her lover. The Monster wasn't able to perform, and I knew with absolute certainty that its failure was Robert's fault.

"I'll marry you," X whispered consolingly. "There'll be other nights, other times. Sometimes this happens."

We *were* engaged! This fact, that evening, didn't rouse The Monster to a fever pitch of gentle passion—but me, at least, it greatly comforted. And on several successive evenings, as Robert apparently tried to acquiesce in our mutual good fortune, The Monster was as good as new again: I began to envision a home in the country, a job as a power company lineman, and, God help me, children in whose childish features it might be possible to see something of all three of us.

("A bevy of bicephalic urchins? Or were you going to shoot for a Cerberus at every single birth?")

("Robert, damn you, *shut up!*")

And then, without warning, Robert once again began sabotaging The Monster's poignant attempts to make it with X. Although capable of regarding its malfunctioning as a temporary phenomenon, X was also smart enough to realize that something serious underlay it. Sex? For the last week that Robert and I knew her, there wasn't any. I didn't mind that. What I minded was the knowledge that my own brother was using his power—a purely *negative* sort of power—to betray the both of us. I don't really believe that I've gotten over his betrayal yet. Maybe I never will.

So that's the sex part, goodbrother. As far as I'm concerned, that's the sex part. You did the death. I did the sex. And we were both undone by what you did and didn't do in both arenas. At least that's how I see it. . . . I had intended to finish this—but to hell with it, Robert. You finish it. It's your baby. Take it.

All right. We've engaged in so many recriminations over this matter that our every argument and counterargument is annotated. That we didn't marry X is probably my fault. Put aside the wisdom or the folly of our even hoping to marry—for in the end we didn't. We haven't. And the fault is mine.

You can strike that "probably" I use up there.

James once joked—he hasn't joked much about this affair—that I got "cold foot." After all, he was willing, The Monster was amenable, it was only goodbrother Robert who was weak. Perhaps. I only know that after our proposal I could never summon the same enthusiasm for X's visits as I had before. I can remember her saying, "You two don't *do* anything that I'm aware of, and I've always been uptight about people who don't make their own way." I'll always believe there was something smug and condescending—not to say downright insensitive—in this observation. And, in her desire to know how we had managed to support ourselves, something grasping and feral. She had a surface frankness under which her ulteriority bobbed like a tethered mine, and James never could see the danger.

("Bullshit. Utter bullshit.")

("Do you want this back, Mr. Self? It's yours if you want it.")

(James stares out of the window at our Japanese yew.)

X was alerted to my disenchantment by The Monster's failure to perform. Even though she persevered for a time in the apparent hope that James would eventually win me over, she was as alert as a finch. She knew that I had gone sour on our relationship. Our conversations began to turn on questions like "Want another drink?" and "How'd it go today?" The Monster sweated.

Finally, on the last evening, X looked at me and said: "You don't really want us to marry, do you, Robert? You're afraid of what might happen. Even in the cause of your own possible happiness, you don't want to take any risks."

It was put up or shut up. "No," I told her: "I don't want us to marry. And the only thing I'm afraid of is what you might do to James and me by trying to impose your inequitable love on us in an opportunistic marriage."

"*Opportunistic?*" She made her voice sound properly disbelieving.

"James and I are going to make a great deal of money. We don't have to depend on Larimer's legacy. And you knew that the moment you saw us, didn't you?"

X shook her head. "Do you really think, Rob, that I'd marry"—here she chose her words very carefully—"two-men-with-one-body in order to improve my own financial situation?"

"People have undergone sex changes for no better reason."

"That's speculation," she said. "I don't believe it."

James, his head averted from mine, was absolutely silent. I couldn't even hear him breathing.

X shifted on the divan. She looked at me piercingly, as if conspicuous directness would persuade me of her sincerity: "Rob, aren't you simply afraid that somehow I'll come between you and James?"

"That's impossible," I answered.

"I know it is. That's why you're being unreasonable to even assume it could happen."

"Who assumed such a thing?" I demanded. "But I do know this—you'll never be able to love us both equally, will you? You'll never be able to bestow your heart's affection on me as you bestow it on James."

She looked at the ceiling, exhaled showily, then stood up and crossed to the chair in which The Monster was sitting. She kissed me on the bridge of my nose, turned immediately to James and favored him with a similar benediction.

"I would have tried," she said. "Bye, fellas."

James kept his head averted, and The Monster shook with a vehemence that would have bewildered me had I not understood how sorely I had disappointed my brother—even in attempting to save us both from a situation that had very nearly exploded in our faces.

X didn't come back again, and I wouldn't let James phone her. Three days after our final goodbye, clouds rolled in from the Gulf and it rained as if in memory of Noah. During the thunderstorm our electricity went out. It didn't come back on all that day. A day later it was still out. The freezer compartment in our refrigerator began to defrost.

James called the power company. X wasn't there, much to my relief. Bates told us that she had given notice the day before and walked out into the rain without her paycheck. He couldn't understand why our power should be off if we had paid our bills as conscientiously as we said. Never mind, though, he'd see to it that we got our lights back. The whole episode was tangible confirmation of X's pettiness.

It wasn't long after she had left that I finally persuaded James to let me write to Larry Blackman in Atlanta. We came out of seclusion. As X might have cattily put it, we finally got around to *doing* something. With a hokey comedy routine and the magic of our inborn uniqueness we threw ourselves into the national spotlight and made money hand over fist. James was so clever and cooperative that I allowed him to feed The Monster whenever the opportunity arose, and there were times, I have to admit, when I thought that neither it nor James was capable of being sated. But not once did I fail to indulge them. Not once—

All right. That's enough, goodbrother. I know you have some feelings. I saw you in that Howard Johnson's in St. Augustine. I remember how you cried when Charles Laughton fell off the cathedral of Notre Dame. And when King Kong plummeted from the Empire State Building. And when the creature from twenty thousand fathoms was electrocuted under the roller coaster on Coney Island. And when I suggested to you at the end of our last road tour that maybe it was time to make the pact that we had so long ago agreed to make one day. You weren't ready, you said. And I am unable by the rules of both love and decency to make that pact and carry out its articles without your approval. Have I unilaterally rejected your veto? No. No, I haven't.

So have a little pity.

Midnight. James has long since nodded away, giving control to me. Velma called this afternoon. She says she'll be over tomorrow afternoon for checkers. That seemed to perk James up a little. But I'm hoping to get him back on the road before this month is out. Activity's the best thing for him now—the best thing for both of us. I'm sure he'll eventually realize that.

Lights out.

I brush my lips against my brother's sleeping cheek.

Within the Walls of Tyre

As she eased her Nova into the lane permitting access to the perimeter highway, Marilyn Odau reflected that the hardest time of year for her was the Christmas season. From late November to well into January her nerves were invariably as taut as harp strings. The traffic on the expressway—lane-jumping vans and pickups, sleek sports cars, tailgating semis, and all the blurred, indistinguishable others—was no help, either. Even though she could see her hands on the wheel, trembling inside beige leather-tooled gloves, her Nova seemed hardly to be under her control; instead, it was a piece of machinery given all its impetus and direction by an invisible slot in the concrete beneath it. Her illusion of control was exactly that—an illusion.

Looking quickly over her left shoulder, Marilyn Odau had to laugh at herself as she yanked the automobile around a bearded young man on a motorcycle. If your car's in someone else's control, why is it so damn hard to steer?

Nerves; balky Yuletide nerves.

Marilyn Odau was fifty-five; she had lived in this city—*her* city—ever since leaving Greenville during the first days of World War II to begin her own life and to take a job clerking at Satterwhite's. Ten minutes ago, before reaching the perimeter highway, she had passed through the heart of the city and driven beneath the great, grey cracking backside of Satterwhite's (which was now a temporary warehouse for an electronics firm located in a suburban industrial complex). Like the heart of the city itself, Satterwhite's was dead—its great silver escalators, its pneumatic message tubes, its elevator bell tones, and its perfume-scented mezzanines as surely things of the past as . . . well, as Tojo, Tarawa Atoll, and a young marine named Jordan Burk. That was why, particularly at this time of year, Marilyn never glanced at the old department store as she drove beneath it on her way to Summerstone.

For the past two years she had been the manager of the Creighton's Corner Boutique at Summerstone Mall, the largest self-contained shopping facility in the five-county metropolitan area. Business had been shifting steadily, for well over a decade, from downtown to suburban and even quasi-rural commercial centers. And when a position had opened up for her at the new trilevel mecca bewilderingly dubbed Summerstone, Marilyn had shifted too, moving from Creighton's original franchise near Capitol Square to a second-level shop in an acre-square monolith sixteen miles to the city's northwest—a building more like a starship hangar than a shopping center.

Soon, she supposed, she ought also to shift residences. There were town houses closer to Summerstone, after all, with names just as ersatz-elegant as that of the Brookmist complex in which she now lived: Château Royale, Springhaven, Tivoli, Smoke Glade, Eden Manor, Sussex Wood. . . . *There,* she told herself, glancing sidelong at the Matterhorn Heights complex nestled below the highway to her left, its cheesebox-and-cardboard-shingle chalets distorted by a teepee of glaring windowpanes on a glass truck cruising abreast of her.

Living at Matterhorn Heights would have put Marilyn fifteen minutes closer to her job, but it would have meant enduring a gaudier lapse of taste than she had opted for at Brookmist. There were degrees of artificiality, she knew, and each person found his own level. . . . Above her, a green-and-white highway sign indicated the Willowglen and Summerstone exits. Surprised as always by its sudden appearance, she wrestled the Nova into an off-ramp lane and heard behind her the inevitable blaring of horns.

Pack it in, she told the driver on her bumper—an expression she had learned from Jane Sidney, one of her employees at the boutique. Pack it in, laddie.

Intent on the traffic light at the end of the off-ramp, conscious too of the wetness under the arms of her pantsuit jacket, Marilyn managed to giggle at the incongruous *feel* of these words. In her rearview mirror she could see the angry features of a modishly long-haired young man squinting at her over the hood of a Le Mans—and it was impossible to imagine herself confronting him, outside their automobiles, with the imperative, "Pack it in, laddie!" Absolutely impossible. All she could do was giggle at the thought and jab nervously at her clutch and brake pedals. Morning traffic—Christmas traffic—was bearable only if you remembered that impatience was a self-punishing sin.

At 8:50 she reached Summerstone and found a parking place near a battery of army-green trash bins. A security guard was passing in mall employees through a second-tier entrance near Montgomery-Ward's; and when Marilyn showed him her ID card, he said almost by way of ritual shibboleth, "Have a good day, Miss Odau." Then, with a host of people to whom she never spoke, she was on the enclosed promenade of machined wooden beams and open carpeted shops. As always, the hour could have been high noon or twelve midnight—there was no way to tell. The season was identifiable only because of the winter merchandise on display and the Christmas decorations suspended overhead or twining like tinfoil helixes through the central shaft of the mall. The smells of ammonia, confectionary goods, and perfumes commingled piquantly, even at this early hour, but Marilyn scarcely noticed.

Managing Creighton's Corner had become her life, the enterprise for which she lived; and because Summerstone contained Creighton's Corner, she went into it daily with less philosophical scrutiny than a coal miner gives his mine. Such speculation, Marilyn knew from thirty-five years on her own, was worse than useless—it imprisoned you in doubts and misapprehensions largely of your own devising. She was glad to be but a few short steps from Creighton's, glad to feel her funk disintegrating beneath the prospect of an efficient day at work. . . .

"Good morning, Ms. Odau," Jane Sidney said as she entered Creighton's.

"Good morning. You look nice today."

The girl was wearing a green-and-gold jersey, a kind of gaucho skirt of imitation leather, and suede boots. Her hair was not much longer than a military cadet's. She always pronounced "Ms." as a muted buzz—either out of feminist conviction or, more likely, her fear that "Miss" would betray her more-than-middle-aged superior as unmarried . . . as if that were a shameful thing in one of Marilyn's generation. Only Cissy Campbell of the three girls who worked in the boutique could address her as "Miss Odau" without looking flustered. Or maybe Marilyn imagined this. She didn't try to plumb the personal feelings of her employees, and they in turn didn't try to cast her in the role of a mother confessor. They liked her well enough, though. Everyone got along.

"I'm working for Cissy until three, Ms. Odau. We've traded shifts. Is that all right?" Jane followed her toward her office.

"Of course it is. What about Terri?"

The walls were mercury-colored mirrors; there were mirrors overhead. Racks of swirl-patterned jerseys, erotically tailored jumpsuits, and flamboyant scarves were reiterated around them like the refrain of a toothpaste or cola jingle. Macramé baskets with plastic flowers and exotic bath soaps hung from the ceiling. Black-light and pop-art posters went in and out on the walls, even though they never moved—and looking up at one of them, Marilyn had a vision of Satterwhite's during the austere days of 1942–43, when the war had begun to put money in people's pockets for the first time since the twenties but it was unpatriotic to spend it. She remembered the Office of Price Administration and ration-stamp booklets. Because of leather shortages, you couldn't have more than two pairs of shoes a year. . . .

Jane was looking at her fixedly.

"I'm sorry, Jane. I didn't hear you."

"I said Terri'll be here at twelve, but she wants to work all day tomorrow too, if that's okay. There aren't any Tuesday classes at

City College, and she wants to get in as many hours as she can before final exams come up." Terri was still relatively new to the boutique.

"Of course, that's fine. Won't you be here too?"

"Yes, ma'am. In the afternoon."

"Okay, good . . . I've got some order forms to look over and a letter or two to write." She excused herself and went behind a tie-dyed curtain into an office as plain and practical as Creighton's decor was peacockish and orgiastic. She sat down to a small metal filing cabinet with an audible moan—a moan at odds with the satisfaction she felt in getting down to work. What was wrong with her? She knew, she knew, dear God wasn't she perfectly aware. . . . Marilyn pulled her gloves off. As her fingers went to the onion-skin order forms and bills of lading in her files, she was surprised by the deep oxblood color of her nails. Why? She had worn this polish for a week, since well before Thanksgiving. . . .

The answer of course was Maggie Hood. During the war Marilyn and Maggie had roomed together in a clapboard house not far from Satterwhite's, a house with two poplars in the small front yard but not a single blade of grass. Maggie had worked for the telephone company (an irony, since they had no phone in their house), and she always wore oxblood nail polish. Several months before the Axis surrender, Maggie married a 4-F telephone-company official and moved to Mobile. The little house on Greenbriar Street was torn down during the midfifties to make way for an office building. Maggie Hood and oxblood nail polish—

Recollections that skirted the heart of the matter, Marilyn knew. She shook them off and got down to business.

Tasteful rock was playing in the boutique, something from Stevie Wonder's *Songs in the Key of Life*—Jane had flipped the music on. Through it, Marilyn could hear the morning herds passing along the concourses and interior bridges of Summerstone. Sometimes it seemed that half the population of the state was out there. Twice the previous Christmas season the structural vibrations had become so worrisome that security guards were ordered to keep new shoppers out until enough people had left to avert the danger of collapse. That was the rumor, anyway, and Marilyn almost believed it. Summerstone's several owners, on the other hand, claimed that the doors had been locked simply to minimize crowding. But how many times did sane business people turn away customers solely to "minimize crowding"?

Marilyn helped Jane wait on shoppers until noon. Then Terri Bready arrived, and she went back to her office. Instead of eating she checked outstanding accounts and sought to square away records. She kept her mind wholly occupied with the minutiae of running her business for its semiretired owners, Charlie and Agnes Creighton. It didn't bother her at all that they were ten years younger than she, absentee landlords with a condominium apartment on the Gulf Coast. She did a good job for them, working evenings as well as lunch hours, and the Creightons were smart enough to realize her worth. They trusted her completely and paid her well.

At one o'clock Terri Bready stepped through Marilyn's curtain and made an apologetic noise in her throat.

"Hey, Terri. What is it?"

"There's a salesman out here who'd like to see you." Bending a business card between her thumb and forefinger, the girl gave an odd baritone chuckle. Tawny-haired and lean, she was a freshman drama major who made the most fashionable clothes look like off-the-racks from a Salvation Army outlet. But she was sweet—so sweet that Marilyn had been embarrassed to hear her discussing with Cissy Campbell the boy she was living with.

"Is he someone we regularly buy from, Terri?"

"I don't know. I don't know who we buy from."

"Is that his card?"

"Yeah, it is."

"Why don't you let me see it, then?"

"Oh. Okay. Sorry, Ms. Odau. Here." Trying to hand it over, the girl popped the card out of her fingers; it struck Marilyn's chest and fluttered into her lap. "Sorry again. Sheesh, I really am." Terri chuckled her baritone chuckle, and Marilyn, smiling briefly, retrieved the card.

It said: *Nicholas Anson / Products Consultant & Sales Representative / Latter-Day Novelties / Los Angeles, California.* Also on the card were two telephone numbers and a zip code.

Terri Bready wet her lips with her tongue. "He's a hunk, Ms. Odau, I'm not kidding you—he's as pretty as a naked Swede."

"Is that right? How old?"

"Oh, he's too old for me. He's got to be in his thirties at least."

"The poor decrepit dear."

"Oh, he's not decrepit, any. But I'm out of the market. You know."

"Off the auction block?"

"Yes, ma'am. Yeah."

"What's he selling? We don't often work through independent dealers—the Creightons don't, that is—and I've never heard of this firm."

"Jane says she thinks he's been hitting the stores up and down the mall for the last couple of days. Don't know what he's pushing. He's got a samples case, though—and really the most incredible kiss-me eyes."

"If he's been here two days, I'm surprised he hasn't already sold those."

"Do you want me to send him back? He's too polite to burst in. He's been calling Jane and me Ms. Sidney and Ms. Bready, like that."

"Don't send him back yet." Marilyn had a premonition, almost a fear. "Let me take a look at him first."

Terri Bready barked a laugh and had to cover her mouth. "Hey, Ms. Odau, I wouldn't talk him up like Robert Redford and then send you a bald frog. I mean, why would I?"

"Go on, Terri. I'll talk to him in a couple of minutes."

"Yeah. Okay." The girl was quickly gone, and at the curtain's edge Marilyn looked out. Jane was waiting on a heavy-set woman in a fire-engine-red pantsuit, and just inside the boutique's open threshold the man named Nicholas Anson was watching the crowds and countercrowds work through each other like grim armies.

Anson's hair was modishly long, and he reminded Marilyn a bit of the man who had grimaced at her on the off-ramp. Then, however, the sun had been ricocheting off windshields, grilles, and hood ornaments, and any real identification of the man in the Le Mans with this composed sales representative was impossible, if not downright pointless. A person in an automobile was not the same person you met on common ground. . . . Now Terri was approaching this Anson fellow, and he was turning toward the girl.

Marilyn Odau felt her fingers tighten on the curtain. Already she had taken in the man's navy-blue leisure jacket and, beneath it, his silky shirt the color and pattern of a cumulus-filled sky. Already she had noted the length and the sun-flecked blondness of his hair, the etched-out quality of his profile. . . . But when he turned, the only thing apparent to her was Anson's resemblance to a dead marine named Jordan Burk, even though he was older than Jordan had lived to be. Ten or twelve years older, at the very least. Jordan Burk had died at twenty-four taking an amphibious tractor ashore at Betio, a tiny island near Tarawa Atoll in the Gilbert Islands. Nicholas Anson, however, had crow's-feet at the corners of his eyes and glints of silver in his sideburns. These things didn't matter much—the resemblance was still a heartbreaking one, and Marilyn found that she was staring at Anson like a star-struck teenager. She let the curtain fall.

This has happened before, she told herself. In a world of four billion people, over a period of thirty-five years, it isn't surprising that you should encounter two or more young men who look like each other. For God's sake, Odau, don't go to pieces over the sight of still another man who reminds you of Jordan—a stranger from Los Angeles who in just a couple of years is going to be old enough to be the *father* of your forever-twenty-four Jordan darling.

It's the season, Marilyn protested, answering her relentlessly rational self. It's especially cruel that this should happen now.

It happens all the time. You're just more susceptible at this time of year. Odau, you haven't outgrown what amounts to a basically childish syndrome, and it's beginning to look as if you never will.

Old enough in just a couple of years to be Jordan's father? He's old enough right now to be Jordan's and my child. *Our* child.

Marilyn could feel tears welling up from some ancient spring; susceptible, she had an unexpected mental glimpse of the upstairs bedroom in her Brookmist townhouse, the bedroom next to hers, the bedroom she had made a sort of shrine. In its corner, a white wicker bassinet—

That's enough, Odau!

"That's enough!" she said aloud, clenching a fist at her throat.

The curtain drew back, and she was again face to face with Terri Bready. "I'm sorry, Ms. Odau. You talkin' to me?"

"No, Terri. To myself."

"He's a neat fella, really. Says he played drums for a rock band in Haight-Ashbury once upon a time. Says he was one of the original hippies. He's been straight since Nixon resigned, he says—his faith was restored— Whyn't you talk to him, Ms. Odau? Even if you don't place an order with him, he's an interesting person to talk to. Really. He says he's heard good things about you from the other managers on the mall. He thinks our place is just the sort of place to handle one of his products."

"I bet he does. You certainly got a lot out of him in the short time he's been here."

"Yeah. All my doing, too. I thought maybe, being from Los Angeles, he knew somebody in Hollywood. I sorta told him I was a drama major. You know. . . . Let me send him back, okay?"

"All right. Send him back."

Marilyn sat down at her desk. Almost immediately Nicholas Anson came through the curtain with his samples case. They exchanged polite greetings, and she was struck again by his resemblance to Jordan. Seeing him at close range didn't dispel the illusion of an older Jordan Burk, but intensified it. This was the reverse of the way it usually happened, and when he put his case on her desk, she had to resist a real urge to reach out and touch his hand.

No wonder Terri had been snowed. Anson's presence was a mature and amiable one, faintly sexual in its undertones. Haight-Ashbury? No, that was wrong. Marilyn couldn't imagine this man among Jesus freaks and flower children, begging small change, the ankles of his grubby blue jeans frayed above a pair of falling-to-pieces sandals. Altogether wrong. Thank God, he had found his calling. He seemed born to move gracefully among boutiques and front-line department stores, making recommendations, giving of his smile. Was it possible that he had once turned his gaunt young face upward to the beacon of a strobe and howled his heart out to the rhythms of his own acid drumming? Probably. A great many things had changed since the sixties. . . .

"You're quite far afield," Marilyn said, to be saying something. "I've never heard of Latter-Day Novelties."

"It's a consortium of independent business people and manufacturers," Anson responded. "We're trying to expand our markets, go nationwide. I'm not really used to acting as—what does it say on my card?—a sales representative. My first job—my real love—is being a products consultant. If your company is a novelties company, it has to have novelties, products that are new and appealing and unusual. Prior to coming East on this trip, my principal responsibility was making product suggestions. That seems to be my forte, and that's what I really like to do."

"Well, I think you'll be an able enough sales representative too."

"Thank you, Miss Odau. Still, I always feel a little hesitation opening this case and going to bat for what it contains. There's an element of egotism in going out and pushing your own brainchildren on the world."

"There's an element of egotism in almost every human enterprise. I don't think you need to worry."

"I suppose not."

"Why don't you show me what you have?"

Nicholas Anson undid the catches on his case. "I've only brought you a single product. It was my judgment you wouldn't be interested in celebrity T-shirts, cartoon-character paperweights—products of that nature. Have I judged fairly, Miss Odau?"

"We've sold novelty T-shirts and jerseys, Mr. Anson, but the others sound like gift-shop gimcracks and we don't ordinarily stock that sort of thing. Clothing, cosmetics, toiletries, a few handicraft or decorator items if they correlate well with the Creightons' image of their franchise."

"Okay." Anson removed a glossy cardboard package from his case and handed it across the desk to Marilyn. The kit was blue and white, with two triangular windows in the cardboard. Elegant longhand lettering on the package spelled out the words *Liquid Sheers.* Through one of the triangular windows she could see a bottle of mahogany-colored liquid, a small foil tray, and a short-bristled brush with a grip on its back; through the other window was visible an array of colored pencils.

"'Liquid Sheers'?"

"Yes, ma'am. The idea struck me only about a month ago, I drew up a marketing prospectus, and the Latter-Day consortium rushed the concept into production so quickly that the product's already selling quite well in a number of West Coast boutiques. Speed is one of the keynotes of our company's early success. By cutting down the elasped time between concept-visualization and actual manufacture of the product, we've been able to stay ahead of most of our California competitors. . . . If you like Liquid Sheers, we have the means to keep you in a good supply."

Marilyn was reading the instructions on the kit. Her attention refused to stay fixed on the words, and they kept slipping away from her. Anson's matter-of-fact monologue about his company's business practices didn't help her concentration. She gave up and set the package down.

"But what are they? These Liquid Sheers?"

"They're a novel substitute—a decorator substitute—for pantyhose or nylons, Miss Odau. A woman mixes a small amount of the Liquid Sheer solution with water and rubs or paints it on her legs. The pencils can be used to draw on seams or color in some of the applicator designs we've included with the kit—butterflies, flowers, that sort of thing. Placement's up to the individual. . . . We have kits for dark- as well as light-complexioned women, and the application process takes much less time than you might expect. It's fun too, some of our products-testers have told us. Several boutiques have even reported increased sales of shorts, abbreviated skirts, and short culotte outfits once they began stocking Liquid Sheers. This, I ought to add, right here at the beginning of winter." Anson stopped, his spiel dutifully completed and his smile expectant.

"They're bottled stockings," Marilyn said.

"Yes, ma'am. I suppose you could phrase it that way."

"We sold something very like this at Satterwhite's during the war," Marilyn went on, careful not to look at Anson. "Without the design doodads and the different colored pencils, at any rate. Women painted on their stockings and set the seams with mascara pencils."

Anson laughed. "To tell you the truth, Miss Odau, that's where I got part of my original idea. I rummage old mail-order catalogues and the ads in old magazines. Of course, Liquid Sheers also derive a little from the body-painting fad of the sixties—but in our advertising we plan to lay heavy stress on their affinity to the World War era."

"Why?"

"Nostalgia sells. Girls who don't know World War II from the Peloponnesian War—girls who've worn seamless stockings all their lives, if they've worn stockings at all—are painting on Liquid Sheers and setting grease-pencil seams because they've seen Lauren Bacall and Ann Sheridan in Bogart film revivals and it makes them feel vaguely heroic. It's amazing, Miss Odau. In the last few years we've had sales and entertainment booms featuring nostalgia for the twenties, the thirties, the fifties, and the sixties. The forties—if you except Bogart—have been pretty much bypassed, and Liquid Sheers purposely play to that era while recalling some of the art-deco creations of the Beatles period too."

Marilyn met Anson's gaze and refused to fall back from it. "Maybe the forties have been 'pretty much bypassed' because it's hard to recall World War II with unfettered joy."

"I don't really buy that," Anson replied, earnest and undismayed. "The twenties gave us Harding and Coolidge, the thirties the Great Depression, the fifties the Cold War, and the sixties Vietnam. There's no accounting what people are going to remember with fondness—but I can assure you that Liquid Sheers are doing well in California."

Marilyn pushed her chair back on its coasters and stood up. "I sold bottled stockings, Mr. Anson. I painted them on my legs. You couldn't *pay* me to use a product like that again—even with colored pencils and butterflies thrown in gratis."

Seemingly out of deference to her Anson also stood. "Oh, no, Miss Odau—I wouldn't expect you to. This is a product aimed at adolescent girls and postadolescent young women. We fully realize it's a fad product. We expect booming sales for a year and then a rapid tapering off. But it won't matter—our overhead on Liquid Sheers is low and when sales have bottomed out we'll drop 'em and move on to something else. You understand the transience of items like this."

"Mr. Anson, do you know why bottled stockings existed at all during the Second World War?"

"Yes, ma'am. There was a nylon shortage."

"The nylon went into the war effort—parachutes, I don't know what else." She shook her head, trying to remember. "All I know is that you didn't see them as often as you'd been used to. They were an important commodity on the domestic black market, just like alcohol and gasoline and shoes."

Anson's smile was sympathetic, but he seemed to know he was defeated. "I guess you're not interested in Liquid Sheers?"

"I don't see how I could have them on my shelves, Mr. Anson."

He reached across her desk, picked up the kit he had given her, and dropped it in his samples case. When he snapped its lid down, the reports of the catches were like distant gunshots. "Maybe you'll let me try you with something else, another time."

"You don't have anything else with you?"

"To tell you the truth, I was so certain you'd like these I didn't bring another product along. I've placed Liquid Sheers with another boutique on the first level, though, and sold a few things to gift and novelty stores. Not a complete loss, this trip." He paused at the curtain. "Nice doing business with you, Miss Odau."

"I'll walk you to the front."

Together they strolled through an aisleway of clothes racks and toiletry shelves over a mulberry carpet. Jane and Terri were busy with customers. . . . Why am I being so solicitous? Marilyn asked herself. Anson didn't look a bit broken by her refusal, and Liquid Sheers were definitely offensive to her—she wanted nothing to do with them. Still, any rejection was an intimation of failure, and Marilyn knew how this young man must feel. It was a shame her visitor would have to plunge himself back into the mall's motivelessly surging bodies on a note, however small, of defeat. He would be lost to her, borne to oblivion on the tide. . . .

"I'm sorry, Jordan," she said. "Please do try us again with something else."

The man beside her flinched and cocked his head. "You called me Jordan, Miss Odau."

Marilyn covered the lower portion of her face with her hand. She spread her fingers and spoke through them. "Forgive me." She dropped her hand. "Actually, I'm surprised it didn't happen before now. You look very much like someone I once knew. The resemblance is uncanny."

"You did say Jordan, didn't you?"

"Yes, I guess I did—that was his name."

"Ah." Anson seemed on the verge of some further comment, but all he came out with was, "Goodbye, Miss Odau. Hope you have a good Christmas season," after which he set himself adrift and disappeared in the crowd.

The tinfoil decorations in the mall's central shaft were like columns of a strange scarlet coral, and Marilyn studied them intently until Terri Bready spoke her name and returned her to the present. She didn't leave the boutique until ten that evening.

Tuesday, ten minutes before noon.

He wore the same navy-blue leisure jacket, with an open collar shirt of gentle beige and bold indigo. He carried no samples case, and speaking with Cissy Campbell and then Terri, he seemed from the vantage of Marilyn's office, her curtain partially drawn back, less certain of his ground. Marilyn knew a similar uncertainty—Anson's presence seemed ominous, a challenge. She put a hand to her hair, then rose and went through the shop to meet him.

"You didn't bring me something else to look at, did you?"

"No, no, I didn't." He revealed his empty hands. "I didn't come on business at all . . . unless . . ." He let his voice trail away. "You haven't changed your mind about Liquid Sheers, have you?"

This surprised her. Marilyn could hear the stiffness in her voice. "I'm afraid I haven't."

Anson waved a hand. "Please forget that. I shouldn't have brought it up—because I *didn't* come on business." He raised his palm, like a Boy Scout pledging his honor. "I was hoping you'd have lunch with me."

"Why?"

"Because you seem *simpático*—that's the Spanish word for the quality you have. And it would be nice to sit down and talk with someone congenial about something other than Latter-Day Novelties. I've been on the road a week."

Out of the corner of her eye she could see Terri Bready straining to interpret her response to this proposal. Cissy Campbell, Marilyn's black clerk, had stopped racking a new supply of puff-sleeved blouses, and Marilyn had a glimpse of orange eyeliner and iridescent lipstick—the girl's face was that of an alert and self-confident panther.

"I don't usually eat lunch, Mr. Anson."

"Make an exception today. Not a word about business, I promise you."

"Go with him," Terri urged from the cash computer. "Cissy and I can take care of things here, Ms. Odau." Then she chuckled.

"Excellent advice," Anson said. "If I were you, I'd take it."

"Okay," Marilyn agreed. "So long as we don't leave Summerstone and don't stay gone too long. Let me get my bag."

Inevitably, they ended up at the McDonald's downstairs—yellow-and-orange wall paneling, trash bins covered with woodgrained contact paper, rows of people six and seven deep at the shiny metal counters. Marilyn found a two-person table and eased herself into one of the attached, scoop-shaped plastic chairs. It took Anson almost fifteen minutes to return with two cheeseburgers and a couple of softdrinks, which he nearly spilled squeezing his way out of the crowd to their tiny table.

"Thank God for plastic tops. Is it always like this?"

"Worse at Christmas. Aren't there any McDonald's in Los Angeles?"

"Nothing but. But it's three whole weeks till Christmas. Have these people no piety?"

"None."

"It's the same in Los Angeles."

They ate. While they were eating, Anson asked that she use his first name and she in turn felt obligated to tell him hers. Now they were Marilyn and Nicholas, mother and son on an outing to McDonald's. Except that his attention to her wasn't filial—it was warm and direct, with a wooer's deliberately restrained urgency. His manner reminded her again of Jordan Burk, and at one point she realized that she had heard nothing at all he'd said for the last several minutes. Listen to this man, she cautioned herself. Come back to the here and now. After that, she managed better.

He told her that he'd been born in the East, raised singlehandedly by his mother until her remarriage in the late forties, and, after his new family's removal to Encino, educated entirely on the West Coast. He told her of his abortive career as a rock drummer, his early resistance to the war in Southeast Asia, and his difficulties with the United States military.

"I had no direction at all until my thirty-second birthday, Marilyn. Then I discovered where my talent lay and I haven't looked back since. I tell you, if I had the sixties to do over again—well, I'd gladly do them. I'd finagle myself a place in an Army reserve unit, be a weekend soldier, and get right down to products-consulting on a full-time basis. If I'd done that in '65 I'd probably be retired by now."

"You have plenty of time. You're still young."

"I've just turned thirty-six."

"You look less."

"But not much. Thanks anyway, though—it's nice to hear."

"Did you fight in Vietnam?" Marilyn asked on impulse.

"I *went* there in '68. I don't think you could say I fought. I was one of the oldest enlisted men in my unit, with a history of antiwar activity and draft-card burning. I'm going to tell you something, though—once I got home and turned myself around, I wept when Saigon fell. That's the truth—I wept. Saigon was some city, if you looked at it right."

Mentally counting back, Marilyn realized that Nicholas was the right age to be her and Jordan's child. Exactly. In early December, 1942, she and Jordan had made their last farewells in the little house on Greenbriar Street. . . . She attached no shame to this memory, had no regrets about it. The shame had come twenty-six years later—the same year, strangely enough, that Nicholas Anson was reluctantly pulling a tour of duty in Vietnam. The white wicker bassinet in her upstairs shrine was a perpetual reminder of this shame, of her secret monstrousness, and yet she could not dispose of the evidence branding her a freak, if only to herself, for the simple reason that she loved it. She loved it because she had once loved Jordan Burk. . . . Marilyn put her cheeseburger down. There was no way—no way at all—that she was going to be able to finish eating.

"Are you all right?"

"I need to get back to the boutique."

"Let me take you out to dinner this evening. You can hardly call this a relaxed and unhurried get-together. I'd like to take you somewhere nice. I'd like to buy you a snifter of brandy and a nice rare cut of prime rib."

"Why?"

"You use that word like a stiletto, Marilyn. Why not?"

"Because I don't go out. My work keeps me busy. And there's a discrepancy in our ages that embarrasses me. I don't know whether your motives are commercial, innocently social, or. . . . Go ahead, then—laugh." She was wadding up the wrapper from her cheeseburger, squeezing the paper tighter and tighter, and she could tell that her face was crimsoning.

"I'm not laughing," Nicholas said. "I don't either—know what my motives are, I mean. Except that they're not blameworthy or unnatural."

"I'd better go." She eased herself out of the underslung plastic chair and draped her bag over her shoulder.

"When can I see you?" His eyes were full of remonstrance and appeal. "The company wants me here another week or so—problems with a delivery. I don't know anyone in this city. I'm living out of a suitcase. And I've never in my life been married, if that's worrying you."

"Maybe I should worry because you haven't."

Nicholas smiled at her, a self-effacing charmer's smile. "When?"

"Wednesdays and Sundays are the only nights I don't work. And tomorrow's Wednesday."

"What time?"

"I don't know," she said distractedly. "Call me. Or come by the boutique. Or don't. Whatever you want."

She stepped into the aisle beside their table and quickly worked her way through the crowd to the capsule-lift outside McDonald's. Her thoughts were jumbled, and she hoped feebly—willing the hope—that Nicholas Anson would simply disappear from her life.

The next morning, before any customers had been admitted to the mall, Marilyn Odau went down to Summerstone's first level and walked past the boutique whose owner had elected to sell Nicholas's Liquid Sheers. The kits were on display in two colorful pyramids just inside the shop's entrance.

That afternoon a leggy, dark-haired girl came into Creighton's Corner to browse, and when she let her fur-trimmed coat fall open Marilyn saw a small magenta rose above her right knee. The girl's winter tan had been rubbed or brushed on, and there were magenta seams going up the backs of her legs. Marilyn didn't like the effect, but she understood that others might not find it unattractive.

At six o'clock Nicholas Anson showed up in sports clothes and an expensive deerskin coat. Jane Sidney and Cissy Campbell left, and Marilyn had a mall attendant draw the shop's movable grating across its entrance. Despite the early Wednesday closing time, people were still milling about as shopkeepers transacted last-minute business or sought to shoo away their final heel-dragging customers. This was the last Wednesday evening before Christmas that Summerstone would be closed.

Marilyn began walking, and Nicholas fell in beside her like an assigned escort at a military ball. "Did you think I wasn't coming?"

"I didn't know. What now?"

"Dinner."

"I'd like to go home first. To freshen up."

"I'll drive you."

"I have a car."

"Lock it and let it sit. This place is about as well guarded as Fort Knox. I've rented a car from the service at the airport."

Marilyn didn't want to see Nicholas Anson's rental car. "Let *yours* sit. You can drive me home in mine." He started to protest. "It's either that or an early goodbye. I worry about my car."

So he drove her to Brookmist in her '68 Nova. The perimeter highway was yellow-grey under its ghostly lamps, and the traffic was bewilderingly swift. Twilight had already edged over into the evening—a drear winter evening. The Nova's gears rattled even when Nicholas wasn't touching the stick on the steering column.

"I'm surprised you don't have a newer car. Surely you can afford one."

"I could, I suppose, but I like this one. It's easy on gas, and during the oil embargo I felt quite smart. . . . What's the matter with it?"

"Nothing. It's just that I'd imagined you in a bigger or a sportier one. I shouldn't have said anything." He banged his temple with the heel of his right hand. "I'm sorry, Marilyn."

"Don't apologize. Jane Sidney asked me the same thing one day. I told her that my parents were dirt-poor during the Depression and that as soon as I was able to sock any money away for them, that's what I did. It's a habit I haven't been able to break—even today, with my family dead and no real financial worries."

They rode in silence beneath the haloed lamps on the overpass and the looming grey shadow of Satterwhite's.

"A girl came into the boutique this afternoon wearing Liquid Sheers," Marilyn said. "It does seem your product's selling."

"Hooo," Nicholas replied, laughing mirthlessly. "Just remember that *I* didn't bring that up, okay?"

They left the expressway and drove down several elm-lined residential streets. The Brookmist complex of townhouses came into the Nova's headlights like a photographic image emerging from a wash of chemicals, everything gauzy and indistinct at first. Marilyn directed Nicholas to the community carport against a brick wall behind one of the rows of houses, and he parked the car. They walked hunch-shouldered in the cold to a tall redwood fence enclosing a concrete patio not much bigger than a phone booth. Marilyn pushed the gate aside, let the latch fall behind them, and put her key into the lock on the kitchen door. Two or three flower pots with drooping, unrecognizable plants in them sat on a peeling windowsill beside the door.

"I suppose you think I could afford a nicer place to live, too."

"No, but you do give yourself a long drive to work."

"This place is paid for, Nicholas. It's mine."

She left him sitting under a table lamp with several old copies of *McCall's* and *Cosmopolitan* in front of him on her stonework coffee table and went upstairs to change clothes. She came back down wearing a long-sleeved black jumpsuit with a peach-colored sweater and a single polished-stone pendant at her throat. The heat had kicked on, and the downstairs was cozily warm.

Nicholas stood up. "You've set things up so that I'm going to have to drive your car and you're going to have to navigate. I hope you'll let me buy the gas."

"Why couldn't I drive and you just sit back and enjoy the ride?" Her voice was tight again, with uneasiness and mild disdain. For a products consultant Nicholas didn't seem quite as imaginative as he ought. Liquid Sheers were a rip-off of an idea born out of necessity during World War II, and the "novelties" he'd mentioned in his spiel on Monday were for the most part variations on the standard fare of gift shops and bookstores. He wasn't even able to envision her doing the driving while he relaxed and played the role of a passenger. And *he* was the one who'd come to maturity during the sixties, that fabled decade of egalitarian upheaval and heightened social awareness. . . .

"The real point, Marilyn, is that I wanted to do something for *you.* But you've taken the evening out of my hands."

All right, she could see that. She relented. "Nicholas, I'm not trying to stage-manage this—this *date,* if that's what it is. I was surprised that you came by the shop. I wasn't ready. And I'm not ready to go out this evening, either—I'm cold and I'm tired. I have a pair of steaks and a bottle of Cold Duck in the refrigerator, and enough fixings for a salad. Let me make dinner."

"A *pair* of steaks?"

"There's a grocery store off the perimeter highway that stays open night and day. I stopped there last night after work."

"But you didn't think I'd come by today?"

"No. Not really. And despite buying the steaks, I'm not sure I really wanted you to. I know that sounds backwards somehow, but it's the truth."

Nicholas ignored this. "But you'll have to cook. I wanted to spare you that. I wanted to do something *for* you."

"Spare me another trip down the highway in my car and the agony of waiting for service in one of this city's snooty night spots."

He gave in, and she felt kindlier toward him. They ate at the coffee table in the living room, sitting on the floor in their stocking feet and listening to an FM radio station. They talked cursorily about sports and politics and movies, which neither of them was particularly interested in anymore; and then, because they had both staked their lives to it, Marilyn lifted the taboo that Nicholas had promised to observe and they talked business. They didn't talk about Liquid Sheers or profit margins or tax shelters, they talked about the involvement of their feelings with what they were doing and the sense of satisfaction that they derived from their work. That was common ground, and the evening passed—as Jane Sidney might have put it—"like sixty."

They were finishing the bottle of Cold Duck. Nicholas shifted positions, catching his knees with his right arm and rocking back a little.

"Marilyn?"

"Mmm?"

"You would never have let me drive you over here if I hadn't reminded you of this fellow you once knew, would you? This fellow named Jordan? Tell me the truth. No bet-hedging."

Her uneasiness returned. "I don't know."

"Yes, you do. Your answer won't hurt my feelings. I'd like to think that now that you know me a little better my resemblance to this person doesn't matter anymore—that you like me for myself." He waited.

"Okay, then. You're right."

"I'm right," he echoed her dubiously.

"I wouldn't have let you bring me home if you hadn't looked like Jordan. But now that I know you a little better it doesn't make any difference."

Not much, Marilyn told herself. At least I've stopped putting you in a marine uniform and trimming back the hair over your ears. . . . She felt a quiet tenderness for both men, the dead Jordan and the boyish Nicholas Anson who in many ways seemed younger than Jordan ever had. . . . That's because Jordan was almost three years older than you, Odau, and Nicholas is almost twenty years younger. Think a little.

The young man who resembled Jordan Burk drained his glass and hoisted himself nimbly off the floor.

"I'm staying at the Holiday Inn near the airport," he said. "Let me call a cab so you won't have to get out again."

"Cabs aren't very good about answering night calls anymore. The drivers are afraid to come."

"I hate for you to have to drive me, Marilyn." His look was expectant, and she hated to disappoint him.

"Why don't you just spend the night here?" she said.

They went upstairs together, and she was careful to close the door to the bedroom containing the wicker bassinet before following him into her own. They undressed in the greenish light sifting through her curtains from the arc lamp in the elm trees. Her heart raced. Then his body covered its beating, and afterwards she lay staring wide-eyed and bemused at her acoustic ceiling panels as he slept beside her with a hand on her hip. Then she fell asleep too, and woke when her sleeping mind noted that his hand was gone, and sat up to discover that Nicholas was no longer there. The wind in the leafless elms was making a noise like angry surf.

"Nick!" she called.

He didn't answer.

She swung her feet to the carpet, put on her gown, and found him standing in a pair of plaid boxer shorts beside the wicker bassinet. He had put on a desk lamp, and its glow made a pool of light that contained and illuminated everything in that corner of the room. There was no doubt that he had discovered the proof of her monstrousness there, even if he didn't know what it meant.

Instead of screaming or flying at him like a drunken doxy, she sank to the floor in the billow of her dressing gown, shamefully conscious of her restraint and too well satisfied by Nicholas's snooping to be shocked by it. If she hadn't wanted this to happen, she would never have let him come. Or she would have locked the door to her shrine. Or she would have murdered Nicholas in the numb sleep of his fulfillment. Any number of things. But this was what she had wanted.

Confession and surcease.

"I was looking for the bathroom," Nicholas said. "I didn't know where the upstairs bathroom was. But when I saw the baby bed . . . well, I didn't know why you'd have a baby bed and—" He broke off.

"Don't explain, Nicholas." She gave him an up-from-under look and wondered what her own appearance must suggest. Age, promiscuousness, dissolution? You grew old, that you couldn't stop. But the others . . . those were lies. She wanted confession and surcease, that was all, and he was too intent on the bassinet to escape giving them to her, too intent to see how downright *old* she could look at two in the morning. Consumed by years. Consumed by that which life itself is nourished by. Just one of a world of consumer goods.

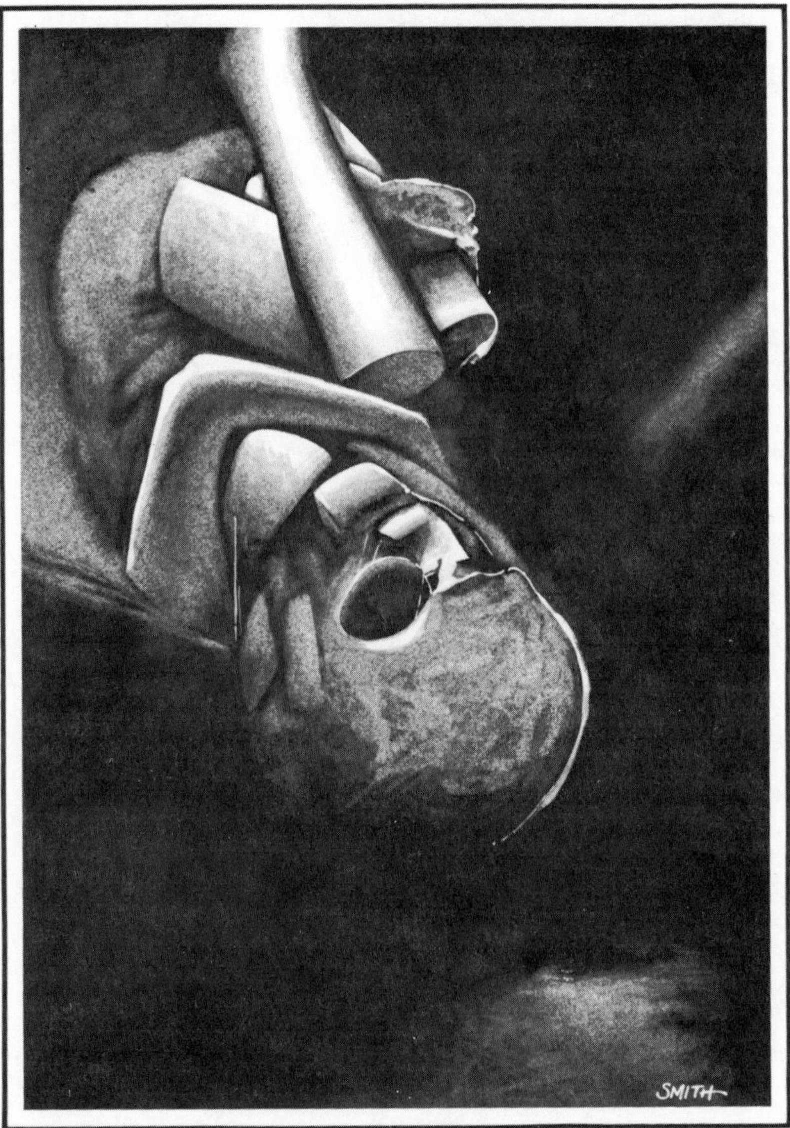
SMITH

Nicholas lifted something from the bassinet. He held it in the palm of one hand. "What it this?" he asked. "Marilyn . . . ?"

"Lithopedion," she said numbly. "The medical term is lithopedion. And lithopedion is the word I use when I want to put myself at a distance from it. With you here, that's what I think I want to do—put myself at a distance from it. I don't know. Do you understand?"

He stared at her blankly.

"It means stone child, Nicholas. I was delivered of it during the first week of December, 1968. A petrified fetus."

"Delivered of it?"

"That's wrong. I don't know why I said that. It was removed surgically, cut from my abdominal cavity. Lithopedion." Finally she began to cry. "Bring him to me."

The unfamiliar man across from her didn't move. He held the stone child questioningly on his naked palm.

"Damn it, Nicholas, I asked you to bring him to me! He's mine! Bring him here!"

She put a fist to one of her eyes and drew it away to find black makeup on the back of her hand. Anson brought her the lithopedion, and she cradled it against the flimsy bodice of her dressing gown. A male child, calcified, with a tiny hand to the side of its face and its eyes forever shut; a fossil before it had ever really begun to live.

"This is Jordan's son," Marilyn told Anson, who was still standing over her. "Jordan's and mine."

"But how could that be? He died during the Pacific campaign."

Marilyn took no notice of either the disbelief in Anson's voice or his unaccountable knowledge of the circumstances of Jordan's death. "We had a honeymoon in the house on Greenbriar while Maggie was off for Christmas," she said, cradling her son. "Then Jordan had to return to his Division. In late March of '43 I collapsed while I was clerking at Satterwhite's. I was stricken with terrible cramps and I collapsed. Maggie drove me home to Greenville, and I was treated for intestinal flu. That was the diagnosis of a local doctor. I was in a coma for a while. I had to be forcibly fed. But after a while I got well again, and the manager of the notions department at Satterwhite's let me have my job back. I came back to the city."

"And twenty-five years later you had your baby?"

Even the nastiness that Anson imparted to this question failed to dismay her. "Yes. It was an ectopic pregnancy. The fetus grew not in my womb, you see, but in the right Fallopian tube—where there isn't much room for it to grow. I didn't know, I didn't suspect anything. There were no signs."

"Until you collapsed at Satterwhite's?"

"Dr. Rule says that was the fetus bursting the Fallopian tube and escaping into the abdominal cavity. I didn't know. I was twenty years old. It was diagnosed as flu, and they put me to bed. I had a terrible time. I almost died. Later in the year, just before Thanksgiving, Jordan was killed at Tarawa, and I wished that I had died before him."

"He never lived to see his son," Anson said bitterly.

"No. I was frightened of doctors. I'm still frightened by them. But in 1965 I went to work for the Creightons at Capitol Square, and when I began having severe pains in my side a couple of years later, they *made* me go to Dr. Rule. They told me I'd have to give up my job if I didn't go." Marilyn brought a fold of her nightgown around the calcified infant in her arms. "He discovered what was wrong. He delivered my baby. A lithopedion, he said. . . . Do you know that there've been only a few hundred of them in all recorded history? That makes me a freak, all my love at the beck and call of a father and son who'll never be able to hear me." Marilyn's shoulders began to heave, and her mouth fell slack to let the sounds of her grief work clear. "A freak," she repeated, sobbing.

"No more a freak than that thing's father."

She caught Anson's tone and turned her eyes up to see his face through a blur of tears.

"Its father was Jordan Burk," Anson told her. "My father was Jordan Burk. He even went so far as to *marry* my mother, Miss Odau. But when he discovered she was pregnant, he deserted her to enlist in a Division bound for combat. But he came here first and found another pretty piece to slip it to before he left. You."

"No," Marilyn said, her sobs suddenly stilled.

"Yes. My mother found Burk in this city and asked him to come back to her. He pleaded his overmastering love for another woman and refused. *I* was no enticement at all—I was an argument for remaining with you. Once during her futile visit here Burk took my mother into Satterwhite's by a side-street entrance and pointed you out to her from one of the mezzanines. The 'other woman' was prettier than she was, my mother said. She gave up and returned home. She permitted Burk to divorce her without alimony while he was in the Pacific. Don't ask me why. I don't know. Later my mother married a man named Samuel Anson and we moved with him to California. . . . That thing in your arms, Miss Odau, is my half-brother."

It was impossible to cry now. Marilyn could hear her voice growing shrill and accusative. "That's why you asked me to lunch yesterday, isn't it? And why you asked me to dinner this evening. A chance for revenge. A chance to defile a memory you could have easily left untouched." She slapped Anson across the thigh, harmlessly. "I didn't know anything about your mother or you! I never suspected and I wasn't responsible! I'm not that kind of freak! Why have you set out to destroy both me and one of the few things in my life I've truly been able to cherish? Why do you turn on me with a nasty 'truth' that doesn't have any significance for me and never can? What kind of vindictive jackal are you?"

Anson looked bewildered. He dropped onto his knees in front of her and tried to grip her shoulders. She shook his hands away.

"Marilyn, I'm sorry. I asked you out because you called me Jordan, just like you let me drive you home because I resembled him."

" 'Marilyn'? What happened to 'Miss Odau'?"

"Never mind that." He tried to grip her shoulders again, and she shook him off. "Is my crime greater than yours? If I've spoiled your memory of the man who fathered me, it's because of the bitterness I've carried against him for as long as I can remember. My intention wasn't to hurt you. The 'other woman' that my mother always used to talk about, even after she married Anson, has always been an abstract to me. Revenge wasn't my motive. Curiosity, maybe. But not revenge. Please believe me."

"You have no imagination, Nicholas."

He looked at her searchingly. "What does that mean?"

"It means that if you'd only . . . Why should I explain this to you? I want you to get dressed and take my car and drive back to your motel. You can drop it off at Summerstone tomorrow when you come to get your rental car. Give the keys to one of the girls. I don't want to see you."

"Out into the cold, huh?"

"Please go, Nicholas. I might resort to screaming if you don't."

He rose, went into the other bedroom, and a few minutes later descended the carpeted stairs without saying a word. Marilyn heard the flaring of her Nova's engine and a faint grinding of gears. After that, she heard nothing but the wind in the skeletal elm trees.

Without rising from the floor in her second upstairs bedroom, she sang a lullaby to the fossil child in her arms. "Dapples and greys," she crooned. "Pintos and bays, / All the pretty little horses . . ."

It was almost seven o'clock of the following evening before Anson returned her key case to Cissy Campbell at the cash computer up front. Marilyn didn't hear him or see him, and she was happy that she had been in her office when he at last came by. The episode was over. She hoped that she never saw Anson again, even if he was truly Jordan's son—and she believed that Anson understood her wishes.

Four hours later she pulled into the carport at Brookmist and crossed the parking lot to her small patio. The redwood gate was standing open. She pulled it shut behind her and set its latch. Then, inside, she felt briefly on the verge of swooning because there was an odor in the air like that of a man's cologne, a fragrance Anson had worn. For a moment she considered running back onto the patio and shouting for assistance. If Anson was upstairs waiting for her, she'd be a fool to go up there alone. She'd be a fool to go up there at all. Who could read the mind of an enigma like Anson?

He's not up there waiting for you, Marilyn told herself. He's been here and gone.

But why?

Your baby, Marilyn—see to your baby. Who knows what Anson might have done for spite? Who knows what sick destruction he might have—

"Oh, God!" Marilyn cried aloud. She ran up the stairs unmindful of the intensifying smell of cologne and threw the door to her second bedroom open. The wicker bassinet was not in its corner but in the very center of the room. She ran to it and clutched its side, very nearly tipping it over.

Unharmed, her and Jordan's tiny child lay on the satin bolster she had made for him.

Marilyn stood over the baby trying to catch her breath. Then she moved his bed back into the corner where it belonged. Not until the following morning was the smell of that musky cologne dissipated enough for her to forget that Anson—or someone—had been in her house. Because she had no evidence of theft, she rationalized that the odor had drifted into her apartment through the ventilation system from the townhouse next to hers.

The fact that the bassinet had been moved she conveniently put out of her mind.

Two weeks passed. Business at Creighton's Corner Boutique was brisk, and if Marilyn thought of Nicholas Anson at all, it was to console herself with the thought that by now he was back in Los Angeles. A continent away. But on the last weekend before Christmas, Jane Sidney told Marilyn that she thought she had seen Anson going through the center of one of Summerstone's largest department stores carrying his samples case. He looked tan and happy, Jane said.

"Good. But if he shows up here, I'm not in. If I'm waiting on a customer and he comes by, you or Terri will have to take over for me. Do you understand?"

"Yes, ma'am."

But later that afternoon the telephone in her office rang, and when she answered it, the voice coming through the receiver was Anson's.

"Don't hang up, Miss Odau. I knew you wouldn't see me in person, so I've been reduced to telephoning."

"What do you want?"

"Take a walk down the mall toward Davner's. Take a walk down the mall and meet me there."

"Why should I do that? I thought that's why you phoned."

Anson hung up.

You can wait forever, then, she told him. The phone didn't ring again, and she busied herself with the onion-skin order forms and bills of lading. It was hard to pay attention to them, though.

At last she got up and told Jane she was going to stroll down the mall to stretch her legs. The crowd was shoulder to shoulder. She saw old people being pushed along in wheelchairs and, as if they were dogs or monkeys, small children in leather harnesses. There were girls whose legs had been painted with Liquid Sheers, and young men in Russian hats and low-heeled shoes who made no secret of their appreciation of these girls' legs. The benches lining the shaft at the center of the promenade were all occupied, and the people sitting on them looked fatigued and irritable.

A hundred or so yards ahead of her, in front of the jewelry store called Davner's, there was a Santa Claus and live reindeer.

She kept walking.

An odd display caught Marilyn's eye. She did a double-take and halted amid the traffic surging in both directions around her.

"Hey," a man said. He shoved past.

The shop window to her right was lined with eight or ten chalk-white effigies not much longer than her hand. They were eyeless. A small light played on them like the revolving blue strobe on a police vehicle. A sign in the window said *Stone Children for Christmas, from Latter-Day Novelties.* Marilyn put a hand to her mouth and made a gagging sound that no one else on the mall paid any mind. She spun around. It seemed that Summerstone itself was swaying under her. Across from the gift shop, on one of the display cases of the bookstore located there, were a dozen more of these minute statuettes. Tiny fingers, tiny feet, tiny eyeless faces. She looked down the collapsing mall and saw still another window displaying replicas of her and Jordan's baby. And in the windows that they weren't displayed, they were endlessly reflected.

Tiny fingers, tiny feet, tiny eyeless faces.

"Anson!" Marilyn shouted hoarsely, trying to find someone to hang on to. "Anson, God damn you! God *damn* you!" She rushed on the gift-shop window and broke it with her fists. Then, not knowing what else to do, she withdrew her hands—with their worn oxblood nail polish—and held them bleeding above her head. A woman screamed, and the crowd fell back from her aghast.

In front of Davner's, only three or four stores away now, Nicholas Anson was stroking the head of the live reindeer. When he saw Marilyn, he gave her a friendly boyish smile.

The Monkey's Bride

Born of noble parents in a far northern country where summer lasts an eyeblink, and winter goes on and on like rheumatism, Cathinka was a formidable young woman nearly six feet tall. In mid-July of her eighteenth year, with the snows in grudging retreat, she passed her time roaming the upland meadows in the company of a stocky, fair-haired young man named Waldemar, whose diffident suit she encouraged because his parents were well situated in the village, and also because a startling flare-up of inspiration or temper would sometimes transfigure the dull serenity of his pale eyes. Cathinka nevertheless believed that in any important conflict between Waldemar and her, she would inevitably prevail. If she did not prevail, it would be by choice, as a secret means of persuading her future husband that she did *not* triumph in every decision or argument.

Fate dismantled Cathinka's plans in the same indifferent way that the fingers of a child mutilate a milkweed pod.

Arriving home one evening from her customary outing with Waldemar, Cathinka found her mother and father awaiting her in the great drafty library where her father kept his accounts and desultorily scribbled at his memoirs. Once complete, the young woman reflected, these memoirs must assuredly take their place among the dullest documents ever perpetrated by human conceit. What had her father ever done but oversee his vast holdings, engage in stupid lawsuits, and so shamefully coddle Cathinka's mother that the poor woman had begun to regard each blast of winter wind as an unjustifiable assault on her personal comfort?

That both the Count and the Countess appeared flustered by her arrival annoyed, as well as surprised, Cathinka. Then she saw that they had a guest. Wrapped from head to foot in rich white silk, a hood cloaking his features, a cape covering his hands, this personage stood between two of the black-marble pillars supporting her father's gallery of incunabula. Although several inches shorter than Cathinka, the visitor commanded her awe not only because of his outlandish appearance, but also because of his bearing and odor. He slouched within his elegant garments, and the smell coming from him, although not offensive, suggested an exotic ripeness just this side of rot. Stammering, Cathinka's father introduced their visitor as Ignacio de la Selva, her betrothed. She and the newcomer would be married in this very hall in a special ceremony one week hence.

"I am Waldemar's, and he is mine!" Cathinka raged, storming back and forth like a Valkyrie. She cowed her father and reduced the shrewish Countess to a stingy sprinkle of tears. Out of the corner of her eye, however, Cathinka could see that Don Ignacio had neither fallen back nor flinched. He was peering out of his concealing hood as if enjoying the spectacle of an elemental maiden defending the romantic Republicanism of her young life. "Never have I heard of this man, Father! Not once have either of you mentioned him before, and suddenly, your selection of the moment an irony too bitter to be laughable, you announce that I am to be this stranger's bride! No!" she concluded, clenching her hands into fists. "No, I think not!"

Don Ignacio strode forward from the alcove and threw back his silken cowl. This gesture elicited a sharp cry from Cathinka's mother and prompted the abashed Count to turn sadly aside. For a moment Cathinka thought that their visitor was wearing a mask, a head stocking of white wool or velvet. However, it quickly became clear that Ignacio de la Selva bore on his scrunched shoulders the face and features of a monkey, albeit a man-sized monkey. Indeed, his abrupt gesture of unveiling had also disclosed simian hands, wrists, and forearms, along with an ascot of white fur at his throat. Her betrothed—God have mercy!—was not a man like Waldemar, but a beast whose diminutive cousins were sometimes seen with gypsies and tawdry traveling circuses.

Cathinka barked a sardonic laugh. Seldom, however, did she disobey her parents, preferring to browbeat them by daughterly degrees to her own point of view. Tonight they would not be browbeaten; they deflected her rage with silence. Recognizing, at last, the hopelessness of converting them, Cathinka fell weeping to the flagstones. To escape marrying the monkey-faced stranger, she might kill herself or flee across the austere desert of a glacier—but, without the Count's blessing, she would not marry Waldemar, either. Even as she wept, then, Cathinka began to adjust her sentiments into painful alignment with her parents'.

Perhaps her intended one (whose white whiskers and hideously sunken eyes must surely betray his great age) would not long outlive their wedding day. After all, his face reminded her of those chiseled icons of Death so common to the Lutheran churchyards of her country; and if Don Ignacio died within two or three years, or even if he persisted as many as five, she could take to Waldemar the amplified dowry, and experience, of a young widow. If she could tolerate for a while the unwanted affections of her father's choice, perhaps she could increase her value and desirability to her own. Rather histrionically, however, Cathinka continued to weep and wring her hands.

"Come," said the Count, rebuking his daughter without yet looking at her; "Don Ignacio deserves better than this. When I was a young man, a foreigner in a land of jaguars, snakes, and other tropical peculiarities, I stumbled into circumstances that nearly proved fatal. For trespassing upon an arcane local custom, the chief of an Amazonian Indian tribe wished to deprive me of various parts of my body—but the timely intercession of Ignacio de la Selva spared me these sacrifices, Cathinka, and in gratitude I promised to grant him any single boon within my power, either at that moment or at some future moment when my fortunes had conspicuously improved. 'Twenty years from now,' said Don Ignacio, 'is soon enough.' Until this noontide I had forgotten my promise, but my friend—" nodding at the monkey-man— "arrived today to remind me of it, and the boon he demanded above all others, darling Cathinka, was my only daughter's hand in marriage. I have broken a Commandment or two, but never a promise, and you must surrender to this arrangement without any further complaints or accusations."

Said Don Ignacio, stepping forward, "I am a former member of the Cancerian Order of Friars Minor Capuchins, the white-throated branch. I renounced my vows many years ago, when my fellow monks abandoned me to take part in either the latest leftist uprising or the most recent rain-forest gold rush (I forget which), and you will live with me, Cathinka, in the deserted jungle monastery that I have made my castle. We will raise our children unencumbered by either political or religious dogma, and you will find freedom in the expansive prison of my devotion."

Gazing up from the floor into her betrothed's deep-set eyes, the unwilling bride-to-be replied, "But you're a papist, while I am a devotee of Danton and the Abbé Sieyès."

"Indeed, lovely one, we are from different times as well as different worlds. However, I am no longer what you accuse me of being, a papist, and you are only a hypothetical revolutionary. Why, you cannot even bring yourself to rebel against the benign tyranny of your father and mother."

At these words the Countess swooned. Cathinka revived her with smelling salts while the Count and Don Ignacio looked on with unequal measures of interest. The matter was settled.

Because of Don Ignacio's adamant prohibitions against displays of either piety or politics, the wedding went forward without benefit of Lutheran clergy or any guests but a few befuddled family retainers. The Countess wept not only to see her daughter taken from her, but also to sanctify the bitterness with which the ceremony's want of pomp imbued her. She had expected nobility from every corner of the land to pack the village cathedral. Instead she must listen to her own husband lead the couple in an exchange of vows that Don Ignacio had composed himself, and she heard in the Count's feeble voice the pitiful piping of a sea gull on a forsaken strand.

Don Ignacio's vows placed great emphasis on fidelity. Cathinka was certain that the erstwhile Capuchin had written them with her passion for Waldemar firmly in mind.

As for Waldemar himself, earlier that afternoon Cathinka had parted from him without once intimating that she was shortly to be married to another. With difficulty (for Waldemar did not enjoy those games in which lovers rehearse their steadfastness in the face of various conjectural hindrances to their love), she had induced the young man to declare that, should she vanish from his life without warning, he would preserve himself a bachelor for at least ten years before losing faith in her intention to return to him. As she affirmed the last of her vows to Don Ignacio, Cathinka was pondering the rigorous pledge she had extracted from her true lover. Perhaps she had been too stringent. Perhaps, in speaking to the elegant but ugly Don Ignacio words she could never mean in her heart, she had committed a mortal sin. . . .

To seal their vows, the wedding couple did not kiss (a departure from tradition for which Cathinka was deeply thankful), but grasped hands and stared into each other's eyes. This ritual had its own unwelcome astonishments, however, for Don Ignacio's gaze seemed to propel the young woman through a maelstrom of memories to some unfathomable part of herself, while his clawlike hands sent through her palms a force like rushing water or channeled wind.

The journey to Cathinka's new home took many weeks. She and Don Ignacio shared carriages and ship cabins, but never the same bed. The former friar wore his white silk cloak and cowl whenever they ventured into teeming thoroughfares or the hard-bitten company of deck hands, but he was careless of these garments in the privacy of their makeshift quarters, whether a dusty inn room or the cramped cabin of a sailing vessel. Although he had no shame of his befurred and gnarled body, Cathinka would not even let down her hair in his presence; she invariably slept in her clothes, washing and changing only when her husband resignedly absented himself so that she could do so. Their enforced proximity had made Cathinka more critically conscious of the fact that Don Ignacio was a monkey; his distinctive smell had begun to pluck at her nerves as if it were a personality trait akin to sucking his teeth or drumming his claws on a tabletop. She was the bride of an animal!

Let a drunken sailor put a knife in his back, Cathinka profanely prayed. Let him fall overboard during a storm.

God disdained these pleas.

At last, by pirogue through the narrows of a rain-forest river, the newlyweds arrived at the crumbling monastery in the Tropic of Cancer where Don Ignacio had made his home. In pressing his case before Cathinka's parents he had described this rambling edifice as his castle, but to his horrified bride it more closely resembled a series of rotting stables tied together by thatched breezeways and tangled over with lianas and languid, copper-colored boa constrictors. Satan had gift-wrapped this castle. The heat was unbearable, the fetor of decay ubiquitous, and the garden inside the cloister was a small jungle surrounded by a much bigger one. Don Ignacio called the former monastery Alcázar de Cáncer, or Cancer Keep. His retainers were cockatoos and capuchin monkeys, salamanders and snakes, ant bears and armadillos. Cathinka wept.

Over the next several days, however, she sufficiently composed herself to explore her husband's holdings. If she must live here, she would try to make, from shriveled grapes, a potable champagne. But what most surprised her was that, in spite of Cancer Keep's outward disrepair, its dark and humid apartments housed a wonderful variety of magic apparatus, all of which Don Ignacio could awaken by a spoken word or a sorcerous wave of the hand. One machine lifted the contrapuntal melodies of Bach or Telemann into the torpid air; another disclosed the enigmatic behavior of strange human beings by projecting talking pictures of their activities against the otherwise opaque window of a wooden box; yet another contraption permitted Don Ignacio to converse with disembodied spirits that he said were thousands upon thousands of miles away. Cathinka was certain his communicants were demons.

The apparatus that most fascinated the young woman, however, was an unprepossessing machine that enabled Don Ignacio to translate his thoughts into neatly printed words, like those in a bona fide book. Cathinka liked this machine because she did not fear it. Its appearance was comprehensible, its parts had recognizable purposes, and the person sitting before it could direct its activities much in the way that a flautist controls a flute. Don Ignacio called the apparatus an electromanuscriber, and he taught his bride how to use it. She repaid him by continuing to spurn his tender invitations to consummate their union and by employing the machine to chronicle her ever-mounting aversion to both Cancer

Keep and the autocratic simian lord who kept her there. She poured her heart out through her fingertips and cached the humidity-proofed pages proclaiming her hatred and homesickness in a teakwood manuscript box.

On errands myriad and mysterious Don Ignacio was often away in the jungle. Although he sometimes offered to take Cathinka, she refused to go. His enterprises were undoubtedly horrid, and she had retained her sanity only by committing to paper through the agency of the electromanuscriber each of her darkest fears and desires. She could not safely interrupt this activity. Occasionally in her husband's absence, however, she would stop beneath a tree riotous with his retainers—birds of emerald plumage and ruby eye, monkeys in brown-velvet livery—to harangue them about their suzerain's despotism and possible ways of ending it. The cockatoos clucked at her, the capuchins only yawned. Oddly, she was grateful for their want of ardor. She did not really wish Don Ignacio to be borne off violently.

One evening the lord of Cancer Keep came to Cathinka's bedchamber, where she lay in rough clothes beneath a veil of mosquito netting, and dumped the contents of her teakwood box on the laterite floor. They had been monkey and wife for nearly a year. Although she had never warmed to him or spoken kindly to him except by accident, this ostentatious petty vandalism was his first display of temper. Chalk-white in the cloistered gloom, his face contorted fiendishly, a Gothic image so paradigmatic it was almost risible. Cathinka could not accept Don Ignacio, but neither could she fear him. She responded to his anger by chuckling derisively, for she, too, was angry; he had violated the small wooden stronghold of her secret life.

"I despair of ever winning you," her husband said. "You insist on regarding your marriage to me as a prison term, which you must stoically endure until your release. There *is* no release, Cathinka."

She glared at him pitilessly.

"However, I love you for your willfulness. In a last effort to conquer your repugnance to me, and to a union that must persist even should my effort fail, I am going to grant you three wishes, lady."

"As in a fairy tale?" Cathinka scoffed.

Don Ignacio ignored this riposte. "You must swear that you will use them all, one wish a year beginning on the first anniversary of our wedding day, which is not far off. Do you swear?"

"Do you swear that my wishes will come true?" She did not care for the stipulated waiting period between wishes, for she must remain at Cancer Keep at least another two full years, presumably even if Don Ignacio were to die during this time. However, one of her wishes might repeal or satisfactorily amend this strange proviso, and she would be a fool to refuse her husband's offer solely on its account.

"Cathinka, I do not intend to toy with your expectations. The wishes I grant you will indeed come true, but they are subject to several other conditions. Perhaps you should hear them before agreeing to accept my offer. I do not wish to deceive you."

"Granted," said Cathinka sardonically. "State your niggling conditions. They must certainly outnumber the wishes, for if you are anything like my father, your litigiousness surpasses your charity."

A large hairy spider tottered among the scattered sheets of paper on the floor, and Don Ignacio paced precariously near it reciting his litany of stipulations.

"Let me backtrack, Cathinka. First, you may not set aside our wedding vows. Second, you may not wish any physical harm upon either yourself or me. Third, you may not presume to transform either of us into any other human being or, indeed, into any other variety of matter, animate or inanimate—even if I would be more attractive to you as a butterfly, an exquisite crystal, or a perfect double of Waldemar. Fourth, you may not try to remove yourself or me to any other place in the entire universe. And, fifth, as I have told you, a year must pass between wishes."

"Very good, my husband. Two more provisos than wishes. Your magnanimity reminds me of the late French king's."

"Although you obviously do not realize it, Cathinka, these are modern times. Whoever bestows wishes without qualification must reap the dreadful rewards of such folly. To our credit, lady, neither of us is a fool. Think of what remains to you, not on what I have wisely proscribed."

Cathinka yielded, sullenly, to Don Ignacio's logic. She then bade him retire so that she could consider among the many bewildering alternatives. She had several days, and she fretted the question for three of them before hitting upon a wish that promised to deliver her from the former Capuchin's tyranny, even as it paved the way for an end to her loneliness. What her third wish might be, however, she still did not know; but, in the fatalistic words of the old Count, time would tell, time would most assuredly tell.

The first anniversary of the couple's wedding day arrived, and Don Ignacio summoned Cathinka to his small, oppressive study to state her wish. He had been working at an electromanuscriber, but, as soon as he heard her tread on the hard-packed laterite, he swiveled to face her, extending to her his crippled-looking hands. He asked her to take them as she had done at the conclusion of their wedding ceremony in her father's library, but she shuddered and placed her hands behind her.

"You must obey me if you desire your wish to come true."

"A sixth stipulation," the young woman remarked pointedly.

"By no means. You swore a willing oath to observe the five stipulations I outlined. You may break that oath if falseness is any part of your makeup. However, unless you grasp my hands, lady, you forfeit your wish even before you utter it—for our touching effects its fulfillment, and only our touching, and so our touching is a prerequisite rather than a mere proviso. Do you understand me, Cathinka?"

"I do," she said, stepping forward and taking Don Ignacio's hands.

"Then wish."

"Aloud?"

"I am not a psychic, child."

Cathinka had not bargained on holding her husband's hands and staring into his wizened face while making her wish.

"I w-w-wish . . . f-f-for D-d-don Ignacio t-t-to . . ."

"Stop stammering, Cathinka. Out with whatever treachery you may have contrived."

"I-wish-for-Don-Ignacio-to-fall-into-a-ten-year-slumber-during-which-he-continues-healthy-and-all-his-dreams-are-pleasant," Cathinka chanted almost ritually.

A feeling of relief, even serenity, began to descend upon her—but this feeling shattered when Don Ignacio's hands jumped a foot into the air without yet releasing their grip on her own. A galvanic force seemed to flow through Cathinka's body, altering the microscopic alignment of her constituent atoms. Meanwhile the monkey-man's eyes flashed like tiny mirrors.

A moment later his fingers slid away from hers, and she crossed her arms in front of her abdomen, concealing her hands. Don Ignacio was still awake, still alert, and he swiveled back to his electromanuscriber to record her first wish on the treated foolscap in his machine. It seemed that he had set up this huge formlike page for just that purpose.

"You are a clever young woman, Cathinka. By modifying an important noun and subordinating a compound clause to your main one, you have managed to squeeze all three wishes into your first. Did you *mean* to exhaust your allotment?"

"I did not."

Don Ignacio operated the machine. "Then I must note here that your first wish is for me to fall into a ten-year slumber, period. The adjective is permissible because it specifies the duration of my slumber, a matter undoubtedly crucial to your wish-making strategy. I am also noting, lady, that you have come perilously close to abrogating the stipulation forbidding any harm to befall either of us. . . . However, I admire the way you attempt to skirt the problem with a pair of sweet but inadmissible subordinate clauses. You leaven your deviousness with the yeast of old-fashioned conscience."

"Will you fall asleep, then?"

"Tomorrow, Cathinka. Give each wish a day to begin taking effect. I go to prepare a place for my slumber." Reproachfully dignified, Don Ignacio strode from the room, leaving his wife to contemplate the degree to which she had cheated the letter of one of his explicit stipulations. Certainly she had not meant to.

Outside Cancer Keep jaguars prowled and capuchins chittered strident admonitions.

The following morning Cathinka found, in the very center of the cloister's overgrown garden, the pirogue in which she and her husband had floated through the jungle to the monastery. Don Ignacio was lying inside the pirogue with his hands crossed on his chest and the fur at his throat reminiscent of a cluster of white lilies. He lay beneath a transparent canopy that his little cousins must have obediently worried into place; while a cockatoo the color of new snow kept vigil on a perch at the head of the coffinlike dugout. Even in slumber Don Ignacio was master of Cancer Keep. However, unless he arose before a decade had passed, Cathinka's first wish seemed to be fulfilling itself. Free of the monkey-faced tyrant, she spent that entire day singing.

The succeeding year was not so joyful. She could not leave Cancer Keep, for she had promised not to, and she could not converse with her retainers, as Don Ignacio had been able to do. They kept her fed and guarded the monastery as watchfully as ever, for their lord lay slumbering at its heart, but Cathinka had no real rapport with them and sometimes felt that they regarded her as inferior to themselves.

Some of her time Cathinka passed with the picture- and music-making apparatus in the various rooms, but the music intensified her loneliness and the activities of the people in the illuminated windows of the wooden boxes seemed either silly or cruel. Moreover, she refused to activate these machines herself and so had to depend on the sullen cooperation of the capuchins to make them work. Presently, without regret, she ceased to rely on these tiresome wonders at all. As for the apparatus through which Don Ignacio had communicated with demons, Cathinka continued to leave it strictly alone.

If not for the electromanuscriber, the year would have been unbearable. Even with the machine's assistance, its marvelous ability to make palpable the most subtle nuances of her mental life, Cathinka often felt like a traveler on the edge of an endless desert. She would die before she reached the other side. She did not die, however. She made two more teakwood boxes to hold her manuscript pages, and she survived that interminable twelvemonth by concocting philosophies, fantasies, strategies, and lies. The inside of her head was more capacious than either Cancer Keep or the vast encroaching jungle.

The second anniversary of Don Ignacio and Cathinka's exchange of vows dawned bright and cloudless, as had every preceding day for a month. It was time for her second wish.

Cathinka signaled a crew of monkeys to lift the canopy from her husband's unorthodox bedstead. When they had departed, she knelt beside the pirogue to make her wish, but hesitated to clasp Don Ignacio's hands because his body looked so shrunken and frail. He slept, but he had not continued especially robust, and the pained expression on his face suggested that the dreams he endured were far from pleasant. The sight surprised Cathinka because for a year she had purposely walked on the periphery of the garden. It also served to remind her that she must not try to squeeze too many qualifiers into the wording of her next two wishes. Magic was a conservative science.

Soon, though, she overcame her reluctance and took her husband's hands. "I wish that Waldemar were here," she said. What could be more elegant or simple? She had observed all of Don Ignacio's conditions—for surely the arrival of a male visitor did not constitute, in itself, a breach of fidelity—and she had conscientiously pruned her wish of all ambiguity and excess.

Then Don Ignacio's hands leapt, nearly throwing Cathinka off balance, and for a split instant she believed that he intended to pull her into the pirogue atop him. She caught herself, however, electrified by the force that had flowed from his small body into her big-boned one. Trembling with both expectation and power, she fitted the clumsy canopy back into place with no help from the estancia's retainers.

That night she began to fear that her wish would rebound upon her in an ugly or a mocking way. The ancient gods had invented wishes to ensnare and frustrate people, as in the case of the Phrygian king Midas. If Don Ignacio were a vassal of Satan, this tradition would eventually undo her, too.

Suppose that Waldemar had died during the past year. Tomorrow a corpse would arrive at Cancer Keep. Or suppose that when he set foot within the cloister, she was invisible to him because they no longer existed within the same time frame or because Don Ignacio had maliciously deprived her of her own corporality. Perhaps she had become a ghost who could not live in the world beyond Alcázar de Cáncer. Pinching her flank and tweaking her nose seemed to disprove this last hypothesis (both experiments produced genuine twinges), but Cathinka could not stop worrying.

Late the following afternoon Waldemar dropped from the sky into Cancer Keep. Cathinka saw him fall. He dangled from a dozen or more lines beneath a billowing parti-colored tent, like a puppet trying to escape being smothered by a floating pillow case. What a weird and beautiful advent!

Waldemar landed not far from Don Ignacio's bier, in a small shrub from which it took him almost thirty minutes to disentangle himself. Although clearly astonished to see Cathinka in the garden, while cutting himself free of the shrub he responded perfunctorily to both her cries of welcome and her many excited questions. At one point he grudgingly vouchsafed the information that some "varlets" in a flying machine, jealous of his moiety of their cargo of "magic plants," had thrust him into the air with only this colorful silken bag as a sop to their consciences. Waldemar cursed these anonymous personages. Bag or no bag, they had not expected him to outlive his terrible drop.

"Then your arrival is not the culmination of a deliberate search?" Cathinka asked.

"I never had any idea where you were," Waldemar replied, at last addressing her as if she were a genuine human being rather than a ghost. "The Count would not tell me, and several months ago I left our homeland to make my fortune. The world has changed spectacularly in that brief time, Cathinka. Assassinations plague every capital, societies subordinate ancient wisdom to youthful bravado, and one upstart nation even bruits about the news that it has sent visitors to the Moon." All his lines cut, Waldemar fell to the garden floor. Sitting there in a heap, he said, "Peril, pomp, and enterprise abound. At last, Cathinka, I am truly alive."

"No thanks to your ungrateful, greedy cohorts."

"No thanks, indeed."

Thus began the year subsequent to Cathinka's second wish. It had come true, this wish. Her lover was with her again, and in a series of chaste interviews at various places around the estancia she recounted for Waldemar the events preceding their unlikely reunion. As they stood gazing down on the crippled figure in the pirogue, she also told him of the conditions under which she had pledged to make her three wishes, of which the important final wish still remained.

Waldemar's pale eyes flamed up like coals under the revivifying breath of a bellows. Must an entire year go by, he wondered aloud, before she could wish again? Cathinka assured him that it must. He squinted at the scrunched form of Don Ignacio as if her husband were an unappetizing entrée on a glass-covered platter. His distaste for the monkey-man seemed as thoroughgoing as her own, an observation that occasioned Cathinka a surprising pang of resentment. This passed.

Like the world, Waldemar had changed. He was still taciturn—indeed, he spoke more sentences cutting loose his bag of silk than he did in the entire week subsequent—but his diffidence in regard to their courtship had utterly disappeared. He took every opportunity to kiss her hand. He brought her jungle flowers in the mornings. He paced the corridor outside her apartment at night. Once having learned how to use Don Ignacio's electromanuscriber, he prepared faultless copies of lovely *carpe diem* poems, which he then slid under her door or folded under the silver fruit bowl of her breakfast tray. Two of these later poems were his own compositions; they had neither meter nor rhyme to recommend them, but they burst within Cathinka's heart like Roman candles, owing primarily to the incandescent violence of their predominant sentiment. Had Waldemar's translation from an arctic to a tropic clime so enflamed him? The man had begun to behave like a Tupian buccaneer.

Cathinka did not know how to respond. She remembered that Don Ignacio's cardinal stipulation about her wishes was that none of them violate her wedding vows. She could not succumb to Waldemar's blandishments without breaking her word, for her lover had come to her as a direct consequence of her second wish. To lie with him would be to lie in an even more significant respect.

Yet she wished to surrender to him. The Tropic of Cancer had worked its amorous metastasis in her blood, and Waldemar's every breath was a provocation as lyrical as a poem. Cathinka began to think, to think, to think. She and Don Ignacio had never consummated their marriage. That being so, perhaps she could not be unfaithful to him by disporting her still unfulfilled flesh. . . .

Someone knocked on her door. Waldemar, of course. The monkeys never came to her of their own accord. She bade him enter. His pale eyes were blazing like fractured diamonds. He took her by the shoulders and pressed his case with his body rather than with a flurry of passionate arguments. Cathinka broke away, and he stared at her panting like a water spaniel. She was panting herself. A comatose monkey in a canoe was denying her the one boon she most desired, a commingling of essences, both spiritual and carnal, with Waldemar. What an absurd and demoralizing standoff the little beast had accomplished.

"Today, Cathinka," Waldemar told her, "chastity does not warrant so rigorous a defense."

"My chastity is not the question," she replied, bracing herself against her writing stand. Not to mock Waldemar's intelligence, she refrained from stating the true question. He repaid this courtesy by pulling a sheaf of yellowed pages from his bosom and unfolding them in his hands. Cathinka nodded at the papers. "What do you have?" she asked him.

"One of Don Ignacio's logs. In it he details the events that led him, so many years ago, to save your father's life. The Count, it seems, had been apprehended by a band of savage *indios* while attempting to force his affections on one of their maidens. Don Ignacio bartered with the band to spare him. If you wish to adhere to the principles of your worthy sire, Cathinka, your present behavior far exceeds that lenient standard."

"Depart," said Cathinka imperiously.

Waldemar bowed, but before taking his leave he tossed to the floor of her apartment the pages of Don Ignacio's log. When he was gone, Cathinka gathered these together and read them. Afterwards, she wept. By disillusioning her about her father's past, her lover had also disillusioned her about the nature of his own character. Two birds with one stone. The pithiness of this adage struck Cathinka for the first time, and she passed a restless, melancholy night.

Now, she believed, Waldemar would abandon Cancer Keep. He was not constrained by promises or provisos, and she rued the lovelorn folly of her second wish. The sooner he absented himself from her life the sooner she would be able to marshal her wits toward a purpose in which he had no part.

Waldemar, however, chose to remain. He ceased picking flowers and writing poems, but he attended her at mealtimes and spoke pleasantly of their youth together in the distant north. Cathinka reflected that she had made mistakes in her life; perhaps she owed her former suitor a mistake or two of his own.

These fluctuations of opinion and mood she continued to record on a daily basis with the electromanuscriber. Sometimes, at night, she could hear Waldemar operating Don Ignacio's other perplexing machines; he did not require the monkeys' aid to make them run. His familiarity with the apparatus disturbed her. Perhaps those playthings—rather than a concern for her welfare—had induced him to stay. She wrote and wrote, but the matter never did become clear.

On moonlit nights Cathinka visited the garden and brooded upon the twisted face and body of her husband. An irresistible impulse drew her. He seemed to be wasting away in his slumber. His bones revealed an angular girdering beneath the skimpy fringes of his fur. Like a chunk of bleached stone, his skull appeared to be emerging from his eroding lineaments. The moonlight hallowed this process. It was eerie and beautiful. It was ordinary and repulsive. It was very confusing. Cathinka found herself compulsively robing Don Ignacio's quasi-cadaver in memories of his tenderness and patience. As his body deteriorated and his face screwed up like a pale raisin, the intelligence that had animated the monkey-man lived again in her imagination. She likewise recalled the mystic force in his hands, the terrifying urgency of his gaze.

For months, however, his hands had been fisted and his eyes tightly closed. What if he died before their third anniversary? She had specified a ten-year slumber, and Don Ignacio had acceded to this adjective without apparent misgivings, but what if that feeble qualifier could not infallibly enforce a ten-year sleep? The premature death of her husband would deprive her of her third wish.

Fool! Cathinka scolded herself. The death of your husband would free you to embrace Waldemar without recourse to wishes.

This realization did not comfort her.

Walking back to her apartment that night, she thought she heard her electromanuscriber clattering disjointedly. Then this sound stopped. Bewildered, she proceeded to her room. Inside she found Waldemar tinkering with the device. Seeing her, the young man pulled a piece of foolscap from the apparatus and attempted to crumple it in his hands. Cathinka wrested the sheet from him and read the brief document in an outraged instant. It bore on its face an unfinished story in which she, Cathinka, employed her third wish to bestow great wealth and power on the penniless prodigal, Waldemar. His parents (the document attested) had disinherited him for his many conspicuous debaucheries, but with the wealth and power accruing from her third wish he intended to revenge himself upon them. Waldemar hastily explained that this narrative was only a fiction spun out to test the efficacy of his repairs upon the electromanuscriber—which, when Cathinka put her hands to it, no longer worked at all.

"You wrote that on *my* apparatus in the hope that doing so would influence my third wish," Cathinka accused the young man. "However, the unseemliness of your desires has caused the machine to break, exposing your villainy. Waldemar, I ask you to go away from here forever."

"Not until you have made your final wish."

"Months remain before that is possible, and I hardly intend to heed your recommendations about what my last wish should be."

Waldemar, his eyes flaring, exclaimed that tonight would serve as well as her anniversary day. If she did not agree, Waldemar pursued, he would slay the unnatural Don Ignacio in his ready-made coffin and thereby eliminate the possibility of her making any wish at all. To carry out this threat, he rushed from Cathinka's room and down the open corridor toward the garden. Despite the tropic heat, Cathinka was wearing a short-sleeved frock with a long embroidered train. She could not hope to catch or struggle successfully with Waldemar in such a cumbersome garment. Without a moment's hesitation she shed it. Then, wearing only an ivory-colored chemise and matching pantalettes, her long hair flying, she sprinted from the room in pursuit of the duplicitous young man.

In the garden she found Waldemar in a posture of resolute strain, his back bent and his fingers curled to prise the canopy from the pirogue. His arms came up, and the transparent cover flipped into the knotted weeds as if it weighed no more than a jellyfish. In later years Cathinka recalled that instead of daunting her, this sight sent a thrill of imminent combat surging through her, an energy that may have sprung from the heroic suppression of her natural longings. Or perhaps this energy was the force of righteousness asserting itself at the dare of bald-faced iniquity.

As Waldemar reached for Don Ignacio, then, Cathinka plunged through the snaky vines and obscene-looking equatorial flowers, seized the traitor by his hair, and hurled him aside as easily as he had flung away the dugout's crystal carapace. He did not go down, but caught himself against the thorny bole of a small tree, whirled about, and charged Cathinka like a grunting boar.

They grappled, Waldemar and Cathinka, standing upright and moving so little to either side that an uninformed observer might have thought them spooning. Their individual strengths were isometric. Monkeys gathered on the tiled roofs and thatched breezeways to watch the combat. The combatants, however, merely swayed in each other's arms. Puzzled by this behavior, the Moon (upon which people had lately walked) looked down with its mouth open. A bird screamed, and the hush of the jungle became the bated breath of Cathinka's own briefly recurring uncertainty. Did she love this man or hate him?

She hated him.

Summoning the resources of outrage, Cathinka shoved Waldemar away. As he sought to reinsinuate himself into her arms, there to squeeze her ribs until they cracked like brittle reeds, she struck him in the mouth with her elbow. He reeled away, his lip bleeding. She butted him in the shoulder with her head, stepped aside, cuffed his ear with her fist and forearm, received an answering blow to the temple, staggered, delivered an uppercut to his abdomen from her crouch, stood upright, ducked a battalion of knuckles behind which his angry face shone almost as bright as the Moon's, shot both hands through his routed defenses, levered her thumbs into his Adam's apple, and tightened the tourniquet of her fingers around his throbbing neck. He retaliated by kneeing her between the legs as if she were a man. A host of capuchin spectators scampered from roof to roof, lifting a babel of ambiguous encouragement above the compound, or falling eerily silent whenever one of the combatants seemed to be on the verge of dispatching the other.

The fight lasted hours. It swung from this side of the garden to that, in favor of Cathinka now, Waldemar next, and neither of

SMITH

them in the gasp-punctuated intervals. Don Ignacio slept through it all as a baby sleeps through family arguments, thunderstorms, air-raid sirens. Cathinka had done no horseback riding or archery exercises since her departure from her father's estates, but she had substituted walks about the monastery maze and the juggling of small weights to maintain her muscle tone, and she had had more time to adjust to the élan-sapping mugginess of the tropics than had Waldemar—with the consequence that, toward morning, the grunting young man had utterly exhausted himself. His masculine pride had offset his imperceptible pudginess for as long as it could. Cathinka, clasping her hands and swinging them into his chin like the prickly head of a mace, put period to their monomachy. Among the needles of a flattened succulent Waldemar lay bruised and torn, still marginally conscious but unable to rise. Cathinka stood over him in the tattered white banners of her chemise; she greatly resembled the central figure in Delacroix's painting, *Liberty Leading the People.*

Disappointed that the fight had concluded, the capuchins took no interest in the stark symbology of Cathinka's appearance. They returned to the jungle or to the more dilapidated cloisters of Alcázar de Cáncer to rest. It would take them a day or two to recuperate from what they had witnessed.

Later Cathinka provisioned Waldemar and sent him away in the company of those of Don Ignacio's cousins who had not slunk off to sleep. She and the young man exchanged no words either during the preparations for his trek or at the final moment of his sullen decampment. Parrots and cockatoos flew aerial reconnaissance missions to insure that Waldemar did not attempt to double back. Cathinka was alone again.

A transcendent peacefulness descended on her spirit. She took off her ruined chemise and stepped out of her pantalettes. She bathed her wounds in well water. She replenished her strength with fruits. She did not dress herself again, but slept naked in her apartment under the gaze of a blue-wattled lizard. That night, and the night after, and so on for every night until the third anniversary of her marriage to Don Ignacio, she visited her husband's bier in this prelapsarian attire. His scrunched body appeared to straighten, his scrunched features to unwrinkle. He slept on, of course, but a modicum of health was his again and the dreams that flickered through his slumber softened his monkeyish face without making it a whit more human. Cathinka did not care. She attended Don Ignacio as regularly as an experimental animal visits its food tray. Far from dulling the sensibilities of their prisoners, some habits are vital and sustaining. Or so Cathinka told herself, and so she slowly came to believe. Now that nakedness was her habitual raiment she felt herself an inalienable part of Cancer Keep.

During the last few days before the third anniversary, a tuft of beautiful white hair began to sprout on Cathinka's breastbone. It ran by degrees from her throat to her cleavage, spreading out over her breasts the way frost furs the sun-bleached boulders in a winter stream. This fur gleamed on her opalescent body, and, curling a forefinger in the tuft at her throat, Cathinka sat gazing on the magical creature in the pirogue. Finally, on the day Don Ignacio had told her to make her remaining wish, Cathinka clasped her husband's paws and softly spoke it. . . .

Vernalfest Morning

Priesman calls the place us kids live Little Camp Fuji. Fuji is short for refugee, and Priesman is—was—a lieutenant with the guerrillas on the rampart side of City. Since most of our mothers and daddies were sympathizers, one of Priesman's jobs is seeing after the kids in our camp. Already he's shown us how to keep the juveniles from Deeland, Viperhole, Poohburgh, and the other nearby kiddie camps out of our gardens and barracks, and twice in the last month he's been through Fuji with a side of wild greyhound.

I like Priesman. I like the way he takes care of us, and I like the way he looks. He always wears dappled fatigues, creased combat boots, an automatic carbine slung over his shoulder, and a pair of bristly 'rilla burns that sweep down from his ears and out across his cheeks like wings. My father (I have a photograph of him with his last bullet wound showing on his left temple) had 'rilla burns just like Priesman's.

A little over a week ago, four days before Vernalfest, Priesman came into Little Camp Fuji's central barracks, no. 3, and dropped a bloody side of greyhound on the floor. I was sitting on Little Mick's winter thermals playing a game of bodycount with Lajosipha

Joiner, our twelve-year-old self-appointed witchwoman. Lajosipha had made the bodycount markers out of spent machine-gun shells and several old rampart-side safe-passage tokens. A bunch of kids got up to look at the meat Priesman had just dropped, but the lieutenant turned my way.

"You're the oldest one here, aren't you, Neddie?"

"I'm fifteen."

Hands on hips, Priesman twisted at the waist to stare all the other kids right in the eye. "Anyone older than Neddie?" When no one fessed to being older, the lieutenant swaggered toward me, hooked a finger inside my shirt, and led me out onto the porch. While his big hands were squeezing my shoulders together, all I could see was the broken button just below the X of his cartridge belts.

"Fifteen, huh? If you weren't so damn puny, Neddie, you'd've probably been promoted out of Fuji by now."

I didn't say anything; I didn't look into Priesman's face. He already knew that in the last six months his own unit had run me back to camp half a dozen times. Finally, Priesman's beetle-browed colonel, Simpson, had said, "Don't come back before you're asked, little boy, or I'll have your scrotum for a dice bag. . . . "

"Listen, Neddie," Priesman was saying, "do you know who Maud Turska is? Ever heard her name?"

"She's in your unit. She's the Poohburgher proctor."

"That's right. Well, Simpson thinks she's passing holdfast locations and potential bomb targets to the airport-siders. He thinks she's using some of her kids as runners."

I looked up, wrinkling my forehead.

"Listen, now. We can't give you any metal, Neddie—no hard ammo, you understand—but on Vernalfest morning we want you to him 'em. Hit Poohburgh, I mean. Do it right, and you'll have your promotion out of Fuji, I can tell you that."

When I went back inside to tell the others, most of the kids had rumbled down the rear steps to spit Priesman's gift and build a fire under it. Lajosipha was still there, though, hunched over the shells and tokens, and when I told her about racking through Poohburgh she jumped up and paced all over the barracks like a stork on stilts.

Her legs were so long I sometimes used to think her head sat right on top of them.

"It don't matter, them not giving us any metal. Other ways will do; beautiful ways. We need cardboard, Neddie. We need cardboard. And lumber. And rags. And eight or ten old automobile tires. I think Lieutenant Priesman's asked the right folks to get this done, Neddie, I really do."

The next day, three days before Vernalfest, I led Little Mick, Awkward Alice Gomez, and a couple of other Fujiniles from barracks no. 4 through the rampart-side ruins to the old trucking warehouses under the expressway. Little Mick had a wagon, a noisy one with wheels that we'd wrapped with torn bedding, and it bumped along, going clink-clank-clatter, and slowing us up.

Over the drooping expressway bridges, drifting up from City's burnt-out heart, oily plumes of smoke wriggled on the sky, and I could imagine Lajosipha trying to conjure with them, voodooing the airport-siders but blessing us rampart 'rillas with magical gobbledygook. She wasn't worth a poot on a scavenger hunt, though, and I was glad we hadn't brought her.

As it was, Little Mick nearly did us in while we were flattening pasteboard crates near the warehouse incinerator and laying them out in our wagon. He got punchy with success, I guess, and started jigging around the parking lot each time we flattened and stacked a box. Just as a huge grey-green copter with rocket launchers under its carriage was tilting over the expressway toward the ack-ack emplacements on the mountain, Alice tripped Little Mick and hauled him up against the dumpster. That probably saved our bums. Priesman says the airport-siders like to go frog-gigging.

But we got back to Little Camp Fuji okay, and the next day while two other dog-parties were out for paint and lumber, Brian Rabbek took the wagon and a couple of thirteen-year-olds over toward the Pits. They were going to dig inner tubes and tires out of the sand. They ended up being gone 'till way past dark. Lajosipha, in fact, started muttering about death and weaving her arms around in front of her face like two black geese trying to knot a double hitch with their necks. The littler kids got spooked, and I told her to go do her witchwomaning in a closet somewhere. She ignored me and kept it up. Brian and the others eventually got back okay, though, and that pretty well undid the spookiness of her mumbling and jerking about. Damn good thing.

The day before Vernalfest broke clean and clear. Awkward Alice, just as if she was old enough to know, said that the smoke hanging over the airport across town and among the trees on the mountainside looked laundered. It *was* white, white and fluffy.

That was the day everyone in Little Camp Fuji really worked. We sat cross-legged out in the yard between barracks and worked at cutting the tires and inner tubes into long pieces. We made breastplates, helmets, and shields out of cardboard. We painted designs on the shields and cuirasses we'd finished. The plans for all this getup and for the coats-of-arms and mottoes we painted on it were all Lajosipha Joiner's; she told us what everything was supposed to be called, showed us how to use strips of rubber as flexings on our shin- and arm-guards, and insisted that every flimsy lance have a banner tied to it somewhere along its length. A few of us made broadswords out of scrap lumber, and Little Mick found a number of odd-sized tins that he cobbled together on a board for a set of marching drums. Lajosipha supervised everything. Her hands were streaked with three different colors of paint right up to her elbows. We were really busy.

Priesman came by in the afternoon. He was sweaty and crotchety, he had grey circles under his eyes. "What the hell is this, Neddie? You think you're going on a goddamn *crusade?*"

"No metal, you said. We've made our own stuff."

"Listen, the first Children's Crusade was a fiasco. If I know anything at all about first-strike advantage, Neddie, this one isn't going to go a bit better. They'll hear you coming. They'll *see* you coming. It'll all turn out a botch, and Simpson'll have my neck."

"He'll have your scrotum for a dice bag," I corrected Priesman.

"That's all right," Lajosipha said, answering the lieutenant instead of me. "We don't sneak." She was wearing a cardboard breastplate with a drippy red eagle outlined a little off-center against it. A white handprint lay on her left cheek like Indian war paint.

Priesman turned to me. "Neddie—"

"It'll be okay," I assured him. "We don't have to sneak to hit 'em right. We really don't."

Not looking at anybody, the lieutenant said, "Shit!" Then he unslung his carbine, fired three quick, pinging shots at the weather vane on the no. 4 barracks, and stalked to the entrance of Little Camp Fuji. Here he turned around and spoke only to me: "*Our* scrotums, Neddie. Yours and mine. Simpson wants Turska taken down and out, but her daddy was a field commander with the original rampart force, fifteen years ago, and it's got to be done obliquely." He let his eyes rove disgustedly over our medieval getups. "Obliquely doesn't mean backasswardly, Neddie, I swear, you just don't seem to understand."

He wiped his forehead with his sleeve, sent a blob of spittle into the dust, and disappeared up the hillside between an ashy-black automobile and a row of trashed phone booths.

On Vernalfest morning Lajosipha was the first one off the floor. And the first one to get down on it again in order to pray. Keening, moaning low, coughing from the spring cold, she woke the rest of us up. The barracks were dark, and when some of the kids in no. 3 started slamming doors to the dormitories next to us, it was hard not to think of gunshots.

With Little Mick's thermals under me for a mattress I lay staring at the ribbed ceiling and remembering how until I was four I had lived in the lobby of the International Hotel. Then the airportsiders had collapsed the building with mortars, and it was almost two years—I got real good at looting and grubbing, even as a little kid—before the first kiddie camps were "bilaterally organized." Priesman says there's a six-year-old treaty outlawing military activity in or around the camps, but Fuji's been strafed before and so have Viperhole and Mouse Town. Maybe the kids on airport side have caught it, too, I don't know. But if you just look up, you can see the colander holes, above the rafters. . . .

"Come on, Neddie," Brian Rabbek said. "If we don't get started, it'll be light soon."

Everyone dressed. Everyone pulled on their cuirasses, casques, and greaves, old Lajosipha right there to say which was which and to help lace you in if you couldn't do it yourself. Outside, as the aspens on the mountain ridge began to twinkle, we grabbed our lances and formed up in two columns. Little Mick started bongoing his peppermint and tobacco tins, but someone knocked him on his ass, and the stillness got thick and nerve-tweaking again. Pretty soon, we were all shuffling out of Little Camp Fuji like the pallbearers at a propaganda funeral. It was eerie, marching in front of them before first light.

I wasn't really in front, though. Lajosipha Joiner marched ahead of even me, wearing a long white dress that had once been her mother's and not an ounce of cardboard armoring. Her gooseneck arms weaved back and forth as she walked, as if she was spelling the sun to come up. I didn't mind her going ahead of me, because I kept waiting for a 'rilla unit—ours or theirs—to spring out of the rubble into our path and mow everybody down with words or rifle fire. In the cool, spooky morning rifle fire didn't seem much worse than words. Also, it was okay by me if Lajosipha wanted to lead us to Poohburgh, because it sits about two miles off the perimeter expressway in an area of rocks called Sand Spire and I felt like she knew where we were going maybe even better than I did. She had a sense for that kind of thing. So all I had to do that morning was wonder why, except for the flapping of our banners, it was so still and quiet.

"Truce today," Brian Rabbek whispered. "Vernalfest truce. We're breaking it, Neddie."

I guess we were, going against a rampart-side camp on the first Sunday after the spring's first full moon—but what mattered to me was doing what Priesman had asked and getting promoted into an adult unit bivouacked on the mountain face overlooking City. I was too old for Little Camp Fuji. Only a couple of the kids had ever really seemed like family to me, which was how Priesman said I ought to think of *all* of them. Anyhow, I've heard Simpson say truces are made to be broken, that's what they're for. . . .

"Play, Little Mick," Lajosipha commanded loudly as we straggled into Sand Spire toward the quonsets of Poohburgh. "Give us a tat-and-a-too to march to."

So Little Mick, with permission this time, began bongoing his tins, and all us Fujiniles flapped and fluttered along, holding our lances high and squinting against the pale light seeping across the eastern plains and through the ruins of City to the rock garden surrounding Poohburgh.

A sentry heard or saw us coming. He raised a piping, echoing shout to rouse his barracksmates. They got up in a hurry, too. They got up a lot faster that we had, in fact, so that whatever "first-strike advantage" Priesman had wished for us was lost by our fluttering and drumming. That didn't seem to matter, though. Our getups—our visors, our shields, our other cardboard whatnots—put even the older Poohburghers in a panic, and Lajosipha led us right up their main avenue before any of them thought of picking up a rock and flinging it at our funny-looking heads.

By this time our lances had come down and we were spreading out across the camp like iodine seeping through a bucket of water, scuffling along beside each other with our broadswords and lances pricking at whoever not from Fuji got in our way. I don't remember a whole lot of what happened, except that it didn't seem cool after we'd tramped into the Sand Spire area. I remember that a lot of the younger kids on the other side came out of their quonsets without many clothes on, and a couple of little boys were stiff from the dawn shock. When we chased them up against a porch railing or a boulder of sandstone, their bellies gave way as easily as a wet sponge would. What I remember mostly, I guess, is scuffling and screaming and myself feeling sick because everything seemed to take so long. It all just went on and on, and in the midst of it all I remember Lajosipha Joiner weaving spells with her arms and charming us invincible.

Finally, someone thought of picking up a rock. The first one thrown struck Lajosipha in the eye, and she crumpled down into her tattered white dress like a wilting flower. Then more rocks came, and while I was trying to pull Lajosipha out of camp I could hear the rocks bouncing off shields and breastplates with sickening *thwumps.* On one side of me I saw Brian Rabbek retrieving stones from the ground and chunking them back at the kids who had thrown them. Awkward Alice Gomez was doing the same thing on the other side. Pulling Lajosipha along, I noticed that the dust was clotted and sticky, but didn't really think about anything but getting her home. Throwing rocks and jabbing with our lances, we retreated. We backed out of the Poohburgh kiddie camp, tore our armor off, and tossed aside our weapons, and, after regrouping on the far side of the Sand Spire overpass, helped each other get home to Fuji.

Lajosipha was dead. We buried her in her mother's dress in the trough of dirt where we used to spit and roast the greyhounds Priesman brought us. Little Mick and a couple of kids from the no. 2 barracks never came back at all. Not counting one kid's mild concussion and some really-nothing scrapes and bruises, though, these were the only casualties we suffered. Brian Rabbek says we were gone only an hour and twenty minutes, and most of that time was used getting down to Sand Spire for the attack and then returning home. Three days later, in spite of how bad my memory is concerning what we did down there, I feel like we spent the whole day in Poohburgh. The rest of Vernalfest is just a shadow thrown by the morning, even poor Lajosipha's burial. We just dug her down and covered her up. I don't think a single one of us thought about carrying her in a prop-procession through the main streets here on rampart side, and that's too bad.

That's why I say that the rest of Vernalfest was just a shadow thrown by the morning.

It wasn't until yesterday that Priesman got by to see us again. I had myself so worked up waiting for him that two or three times I nearly went out looking for his unit's bivouac, just to ask him how us Fujiniles had done. When he finally came strolling in, though, Priesman was wearing *two* carbines and a smile that made his 'rilla burns stand out.

"Turska broke, tough old Maud herself. Her daughter by an airport-sider was in Poohburgh Vernalfest morning, and that just wiped her out. She fessed the whole schmeer under sedation, and Simpson's higher than a migrating goose." Priesman tossed a rifle at me. "Here's your carbine, Theodore. Let's get the hell out of Little Camp Fuji."

"I've been promoted?"

"Sure." He bent his fatigue collar down so that I could see the new insignia on it. "And so have I, Theodore, so have I."

Saving Face

"Get back," Rakestraw told his children, who were eyeing him curiously as he tried to chop the thick pruned branches of a holly tree into pieces small enough for the fireplace. "I don't want you to get hit."

He waited until the five-year-old girl and her slightly smaller twin brother backed hand in hand toward the mulch pile and the edge of the winter garden. Then, to demonstrate his strength to them, he swung the ax in a high arc and brought the blade down viciously on the propped-up holly branch. One half of it flew upward like a knotted boomerang, its grey-white bark coruscating silver in the December sunlight. After windmilling a good distance through the air, the severed piece landed with a thud at Gayle and Gabe's feet.

"Damn it!" Rakestraw bellowed, dropping the ax. "I told you to get back! Your mother'd kill me if I killed you!"

The boy retreated into the muddy turnip bed, but Gayle picked up the holly log and carried it to her father. Rakestraw knelt to accept it, and she reached toward his face with her small, damnably knowing fingers.

"You diddn shave," Gayle told him.

He started to catch her hand in order to rub his coarse chin in its palm, but the holly log impeded him and Gabe was running forward from the garden.

"Look, Daddy!" the boy cried. "Looka the truck!"

Rakestraw stood up and saw, not the truck, but some sort of fancily decorated imported van coming cautiously along the gravel road from town. He tossed the log among several others he had cut that morning and pulled his children to him. "Wait a minute," he said as they squirmed under his hands; "you don't know who that is. Hold still." He didn't recognize the vehicle as belonging to anyone in the county, and since the road it was traveling dead-ended only a stone's throw away, Rakestraw was as curious as the twins.

The van halted abreast of them, and a man wearing a neck scarf as big, red, and silky as a champion American Beauty rose stuck his head out the window and squinted at them. He had on a pair of sunglasses, but the lenses were nestled in his hair.

"Tom Rakestraw?" he asked.

"That's right," Rakestraw responded.

The man in the American Beauty cravat stuck his head back in the window, flipped his glasses down, and maneuvered the rear end of his van into the yard, running over several of the uncut holly branches Rakestraw had earlier dragged to the woodpile. He made a parking space between the garden and the house, where there'd never been a parking space. Another man sat in the front seat beside him, but the driver's clumsy maneuver delayed recognition until the van stopped and Sheriff Harrison had opened his door and climbed out.

Benny Harrison, wearing a khaki shirt with his badge half-hidden in one of its greasy folds, was a head shorter than the newcomer and a good deal less at ease. Even though he kept his thumbs in his belt, at unexpected moments his elbows flapped like poorly hung storm shutters. He introduced the man who had backed into the yard as Edgar Macmillan, an attorney from California.

Rakestraw said, "Gayle, Gabe, go play with Nickie." Nickie was the dog, a lethargic brown mongrel visible now as a furry lump in the grass below the kitchen window. The twins went reluctantly off in the dog's direction, and Rakestraw looked at Macmillan.

"I represent Craig Tiernan, Mr. Rakestraw."

"Who?"

"Craig Tiernan. Surely you've heard the name." Macmillan had his hands deep in the pockets of his blazer. The lenses of his sunglasses glinted like miniature hub caps. "Craig Tiernan."

"An actor," Benny Harrison put in. "A movie actor."

"He's placed first among male performers in three consecutive box-office polls, Mr. Rakestraw, and this year he's nominated for an Academy Award."

"We don't go to the movies."

"You read, don't you? You watch television?"

"We don't watch much television. But I read now and again."

"Then you've seen his name in the newspaper. In the amusement section, where the movie ads are. In 'people' news, in feature stories."

Benny Harrison flapped his elbows. "Tom gets the Dachies County *Journal,*" he told Macmillan by way of defending his friend. "And you've got a little library of history and farming books, don't you? And Nora's magazines. Nora subscribes to magazines."

"Tiernan's always in the women's magazines," Macmillan said almost accusingly. "He's always being featured. Sometimes he gets a cover."

"I don't read those," Rakestraw confessed. "Nora gets them for recipes and pictures of furniture. She shows me the pictures sometimes."

"Has she ever told you you look like Craig Tiernan?"

Rakestraw shook his head.

"That's why I've come out here," Macmillan said. "That's why I stopped at Caracal's sheriff's office and asked Sheriff Harrison to ride out here with me." He took a piece of paper from an inside blazer pocket, unfolded it, and shook it out so that Rakestraw could see the matter printed on it.

Rakestraw recognized it as the poster he had sat for when Harrison and two or three other people on the Caracal city council persuaded him to run for mayor against the sharp-spoken, doddering incumbent. He had lost by only ten or twelve votes, primarily because he had been unable to convince the ladies of the local women's club that he wasn't too young and inexperienced for the job, which in reality was little more than a sinecure. Mayor Birkett was pushing seventy, and Rakestraw had just turned thirty-two.

"Is this you?" Macmillan wanted to know. He paced toward the woodpile, then waved off his own question. "Of course it is. Otherwise I wouldn't be here." He turned around. "Somebody in Caracal sent this to the studio. The studio forwarded it to Tiernan, and Tiernan sent it to me, along with instructions and air fare to your state capital. A friend of mine up there loaned me this van, and here I am." A sudden gust of wind rattled the pecan tree towering over the woodpile, and the smoothed-out election poster in Macmillan's hand fluttered distractingly.

"Why?" Rakestraw asked.

"To take care of the matter."

"*What* matter, Mr. Macmillan?" Rakestraw heard the twins shouting and laughing in another part of the yard. He also heard the bewilderment and impatience of his own voice.

"Your trespass on Tiernan's physiognomic rights which he now has on file in Washington, D.C. Your state legislature approved local compliance with the Physiognomic Protection Act last May, Mr. Rakestraw, and that makes you subject to every statute of the otherwise provisional federal act."

"Benny," Rakestraw asked, "what the hell does that mean?"

"It means your face don't belong to you anymore," said Benny Harrison, flapping his elbows. "Sounds crazy, don't it?"

Rakestraw let his gaze drift from the perturbed, disheveled sheriff to the attorney with the crimson scarf at his throat, who was standing among the holly logs Rakestraw had already cut.

"Let me finish these," Rakestraw said. "I'm almost finished." He retrieved his ax and began hacking at a smooth grey-white holly limb only a small distance from Macmillan's foot. The attorney backed up to his borrowed van and watched the other man chopping wood as if witness to a performance as rare and exotic as ember-walking or lion-taming.

"Craig Tiernan?" Nora said. "Tom doesn't look like Craig Tiernan." She dug an old magazine out of the wall rack in the den and flipped it open to a double-page color layout.

"He does to me," Macmillan countered. "I've seen Tiernan up close, oh, a thousand times, and your husband looks like him. An amazing likeness, really amazing." He stubbed his cigarette out on the canning lid Nora had given him for an ashtray. "At least you know who Tiernan is, though. That's more than I can say for your husband. I wouldn't've believed anybody *that* uninformed or isolated, Mrs. Rakestraw. I mean, the boondocks just aren't the boondocks anymore—the media's everywhere. Everybody touches everybody else. That's why it's necessary to have a law like the Physiognomic Protection Act."

"Tom isn't interested in movies." Nora examined the photograph in the magazine. "And I don't think he looks like Craig Tiernan, either. I don't see what you see."

"That's why I'm going to drive him to the capital—so we can do a point-by-point match-up of features. This procedure isn't hit-or-miss, Mrs. Rakestraw—it's very scientific." Macmillan shook out another cigarette. "Okay. So he isn't interested in movies. But how can he be unaware? That's what I don't understand, how he can be so unaware."

"Do you know who the head of the government of Kenya is, Mr. Macmillan?" Nora asked the attorney.

"Hell, Mrs. Rakestraw, I don't even know who the President of Canada is."

"Prime Minister."

"Okay, Prime Minister. But the Prime Ministers of Canada and Kenya don't happen to be up for Academy Awards this year, either."

"Maybe they should be," Benny Harrison said. "The President, too." He stood by the double windows fronting the road to Caracal and, when a noise overhead reminded them all of Tom's activity upstairs, lifted his eyes to the ceiling.

"How long are you going to keep him?" Nora asked.

"I don't know," Macmillan replied, exhaling smoke. "He might get back tomorrow. It might be three or four days. Or a week. Depends on what the examiners report after the match-up of features."

"Well, what happens if—if they *match up*."

"There are options, Mrs. Rakestraw. Nobody gets thrown in jail or caught out for damages for looking like somebody else. —Listen, if the test's positive, you'll be able to talk to him by telephone at our expense. It's nothing to worry about. You may even make some money."

"I don't care about that. However much it is, it won't be worth going through all this. I don't even see why he has to go. It's ridiculous." There was more noise from upstairs. "Listen to that. He's upset with me for not helping him pack."

"Nora," Benny Harrison said, turning around, "Mr. Macmillan's got a legal summons for this test. That's why Tom's going."

"What am I supposed to tell Gayle and Gabe? This is working out just as if Tom's done something wrong. And he hasn't—not a thing."

Neither the attorney nor the sheriff answered her. Sunlight fell across the hardwood floor through the double windows, and Nora tilted her head to catch the subtly frantic inflection of Nickie's barking.

After a time, Tom came into the room with his overnight case and asked if there was an extra tube of toothpaste anywhere. As a concession to the legality, if not the reasonableness, of Macmillan's visit, Nora went looking for one. The men straggled out to the van while she looked, and when she found the extra tube of toothpaste, she carried it outside and handed it to her husband with a sense of vague disappointment. Nevertheless, she kissed him and touched him affectionately on the nose.

"Take care," Rakestraw said. "I'll call you."

Back inside the house, Nora found a check for a thousand dollars on the kitchen table. Macmillan's lazy signature was at the bottom, twisted like a section of line in Tom's tackle box. Nora wanted to tear the check up and scatter the pieces across the floor; instead, she left it lying on the table and returned thoughtfully to the den.

The drive from Caracal to the state capital took four hours. Rakestraw asked Macmillan no questions, and Macmillan volunteered nothing beyond ecstatic but obtuse comments about the scenery.

"Look at those blackbirds," he exclaimed as they sped by a harvested cornfield in which a host of grackles was strutting. "There must be a thousand of 'em!" He drummed his fingers on the dashboard in time to the disco music on the radio. He filled the van's ashtray with cigarette butts.

But he was subdued and solicitous checking Rakestraw into the private sanitarium where the testing was to be performed. He kept his voice down in the gloomy but spacious lobby where potted plants were reflected doubtfully in the streaked marble flooring, and he gave the black teenager who insisted on carrying Rakestraw's bag to his first-floor room a generous but far from flashy tip. Then he left and let Rakestraw get a nap.

Surprisingly, the testing itself began that same evening. A young man named Hurd and a young woman named Arberry—dressed, but for their name tags, as if for the street—came into Rakestraw's room with photographic equipment, a scale on removable coasters, a notebook of laminated superimpositions of Craig Tiernan's features, and various kinds of stainless-steel calibrating instruments, most of which looked sophisticated enough to induce envy in a physical anthropologist. Rakestraw reflected that these two young people *were* physical anthropologists of a kind—they wanted to determine, scientifically, whether or not he looked like Craig Tiernan.

"Do I look like Craig Tiernan?" Rakestraw asked Arberry as, after weighing him and noting down his height in centimeters, she posed him for a series of photographs.

"There's a real resemblance," Arberry said genially. She smiled at him and made him point his chin for a portrait of his left profile. "Don't people you've never met before do double takes when they first see you?"

"Not that I've noticed."

"Her next question," Hurd put in, fiddling with a calibrating tool, "is whether you're married or not."

"Married," Rakestraw managed between his teeth.

"Don't move," Arberry cautioned him mildly. In the same low-key tone she added, "Shut up, Hurd, and get your own act together."

There was a surprisingly silent flash from her camera, and then Arberry was posing him face on. Like a tailor, Hurd was using a tape measure across his shoulders. Rakestraw found their finicky probing more interesting now than annoying, and he cooperated with his examiners as he was always urging Gabe and Gayle to co-operate with Dr. Meade when he took them for checkups back in Caracal. Chin up, face on, no bickering; child or adult, that was how you were supposed to do things. . . .

Arberry and Hurd were in the room with him for most of the evening, but they did give him a few odd minutes to himself as they conferred over the notebook of plastic superimpositions, flipping pages and matching features.

Rakestraw began to feel like a pretender to the name, title, and person of the Grand Duchess Anastasia. Those fervid women had tried to prove their claims by a variety of methods, including the assertion that their ears had twelve or thirteen or fourteen positive points of identity—out of a possible seventeen—with the ears of the infant Anastasia, as revealed by photographs. The difference, of course, was that he didn't wish to establish himself as Craig Tiernan; he certainly didn't want his examiners to find enough points of similarity to make his resemblance to the actor a trespass against the Physiognomic Protection Act. Where had such legislation come from, anyway?

But Rakestraw was fascinated by the procedures Hurd and Arberry were using to determine the extent of his resemblance. Even when they weren't touching his jaw or forehead with cold metal instruments or trigonometrically surveying the pyramid of his nose, he hovered behind them, looking over their shoulders and eavesdropping on the cryptic verbal shorthand they used to communicate their findings to each other. Toward what decision were their measurements leading them?

Rakestraw's powerful curiosity was not strong enough to overcome his natural reticence, though, and he sat down on the old-fashioned tufted bedspread to wait them out. As he waited, indignation seeped back into him, and a painful sense of separation from everything that was important to him.

At last Arberry said, "Mr. Macmillan will be in to see you in the morning, Mr. Rakestraw. Jeff and I are going to report to him now."

Rubbing his frighteningly cold hands, Rakestraw stood up. He refrained from asking the question that even they expected him to ask. He was sure that the pressure of his self-control had to be visible in his face—the face they had clinically savaged for almost three hours.

Two polite, well-groomed, amiable technicians . . .

"Mr. Macmillan will give you the results in the morning," Arberry said, opening the door to his room.

Hurd pushed the scales through the door. "Goodnight, Mr. Rakestraw—hope you get a good night's sleep." He had an equipment bag over one shoulder. Arberry smiled pleasantly and followed her colleague into the long darkened palm-lined corridor.

They were gone.

An hour or two later the telephone beside Rakestraw's bed made a faint buzzing noise. Rakestraw picked it up.

"Turn on your TV," Macmillan said through the line. "They've got cable here, and there's a Craig Tiernan movie on channel twelve. A good one, too. Tiernan plays Robert Pirsig in *Phaedrus*. It got great reviews five years ago but bombed out at the box office—strange how those things happen."

"Did you talk with the examiners?"

"Yeah. I'll tell you about it in the morning. Turn on the boob tube, Mr. Rakestraw, and catch the flick." Macmillan hung up.

It took Rakestraw a good thirty or forty seconds to find the television set, even though it was in full view and he had been in the same room with it since late afternoon. The set rested on a gilded stand in the corner beyond the dressing table, and a large potted rose geranium obscured most of the stand. The eye of the television set was cold and empty, camouflaged mysteriously by its own nakedness. Rakestraw crossed the room and turned it on.

Opening titles rolled up and over a barren early-morning landscape of cattails and marsh water; a pair of motorcycles moved silently along the highway bordering the marsh. Rakestraw sat down on the bed.

The film turned out to be full of flashbacks and flashforwards, as well as several wrenching exchanges about metaphysical matters that Rakestraw had trouble keeping straight in his head. *Phaedrus* was beautifully photographed, however, and he felt a grudging but genuine sympathy for the complex personality Tiernan was recreating. Everybody in the film was suffering, everybody was on the edge of madness, and Rakestraw *felt* for them. An hour later he could take no more of their suffering—he got up and turned the set off.

"I don't look like that man," he said aloud. "I don't think we resemble each other at all."

Macmillan came for him in the morning and escorted him down the corridor to a dining room furnished with huge rattan chairs and tables with wrought-iron legs. They took coffee and Danish pastries from a serving board at one end of the room and found a table of their own.

"Your face belongs to Craig Tiernan," the attorney said a few minutes after they had sat down. "That's the verdict of the data that Hurd and Arberry came up with."

Rakestraw laughed humorlessly.

"It's true, I'm afraid. The resemblance is acute and actionable."

"If I've got Craig Tiernan's face, Mr. Macmillan, then he must be walking around California with all the expression of a hard-boiled egg."

"He lives in Oregon. When he isn't working."

"Then why the hell is he worried about Tom Rakestraw's face? I'm not going to Oregon. Who the hell does he think he is?"

"He may live in Oregon, Mr. Rakestraw, but he's a personality in every state of the union and more than a dozen foreign countries. Your infringement on those rights whereby his recognition is—"

"Please, Mr. Macmillan. No more legal double-talk. Just tell me what 'actionable' means if Tiernan can't win damages from me."

"It just means he can press suit, which is what he's doing. Don't worry about that, though. Here are your options under the law."

Macmillan took an envelope from his blazer pocket and began to write on it with a disposable plastic pen. Finally he pushed the envelope across the table to Rakestraw, who picked it up and hastily scanned what the attorney had listed as his options.

1. Co-ownership of the rights in question, through either purchase or grant.

2. Authorization as a legal impersonator of the licensed owner, 10 percent of income derived from this source to accrue to plaintiff and his appointed agents.

3. Voluntary self-sequestration, with the owner of the rights in question retaining to himself and his agents the means of checking and ensuring compliance.

4. Immigration to a country to which legal distribution of the public works of the owner of the rights in question has either not yet been approved or not been taken advantage of.

5. Permanent alteration of those features trespassing most conspicuously on the proprietary rights of the plaintiff, to be accomplished without appeal or delay.

"Six," Rakestraw added, placing the envelope in the middle of the table. "Voluntary self-annihilation of the offending party."

Macmillan laughed. "Oh, come on, it isn't as bad as that. The thing you forget is that in the case of suits under the Physiognomic Protection Act, it's the plaintiff who's responsible for court costs and all the financial obligations arising from the defendant's choice of an option. This is the only law on the books, Mr. Rakestraw, dictating that a victorious plaintiff must compensate his defeated court opponent for emotional suffering and any expenses following upon the action."

"But I haven't been in court, Mr. Macmillan!"

"You're there now, in a manner of speaking. Hurd and Arberry are testifying for both you and Craig Tiernan—or their data is, I should say. And the verdict of the data will be the verdict of the court. Our case seems to be a solid one, Mr. Rakestraw."

Rakestraw picked up the envelope again. "Let me see if I understand this," he said, glancing over it at the attorney. "Number one means that I can buy my face from Tiernan if he'll agree to sell. Or that he can give me part interest in it if he wants to be . . . generous."

"That's right. He won't do either, though."

"Okay. What's number two about?"

"The law permits three legal impersonators. Tiernan already has three, I'm afraid. Two perform movie stunts for him and one's a double at functions he doesn't wish to attend."

"Like the Academy Awards?"

"Oh, no—he'll be there in person this year. He's got a good chance to win."

"I've got my fingers crossed." Rakestraw took a sip of coffee, which by now was cold and scummy-tasting. "Three means that I can become a hermit and that Tiernan's lackeys have the right to make sure I'm staying indoors in my hair shirt and sandals."

Macmillan nodded. "More or less."

"Isn't Caracal hermitage enough for Craig Tiernan's purposes?"

"I'm afraid not. Your election poster went up all over Dachies County, the sheriff told me, on telephone poles and fence posts. That's an infringement of Tiernan's—"

"Number four seems pretty clear. What countries might Nora, the twins, and I hope to immigrate to, Mr. Macmillan?"

"I'd have to look that up. Great Britain and Western Europe are pretty much out, though. Tiernan has big followings in those places. —Not many people choose this option, I'm told. Once you get a job and get settled, the plaintiff's financial obligations to you begin to taper off really drastically."

"Which brings us to number five?"

"Plastic surgery," Macmillan said.

"Plastic surgery," Rakestraw hollowly echoed the man.

"Right. On the house. We've got the facilities for it right here in this lovely sanitarium, they tell me."

A week later, Rakestraw rode home on a bus. Benny Harrison met him at the little town's only grocery store, which also served as its bus depot, and drove him out to his house in the Caracal sheriff's car.

"Do you want me to go in with you?" Benny Harrison asked.

"No, thanks. Go on back to town. I appreciate the ride."

Rakestraw watched the car float away from him in a backboil of thrown gravel and drifting dust. Then he saw the door to the house open and Nora and the twins come out.

Nora was carrying a wreath of holly leaves. The berries on the wreath were like excruciatingly crimson drops of blood. Rakestraw's face tightened in reminiscence.

Gayle and Gabe looked toward him, and when Nora said, "Tom?" in surprise and evident doubt, the twins heard only the name and started to rush to him—as they had always done when he came in from the fields or back from a solitary trip to Caracal.

At that moment Nickie came banging out the kitchen door, loped madly past the children, and halted at the edge of the road in front

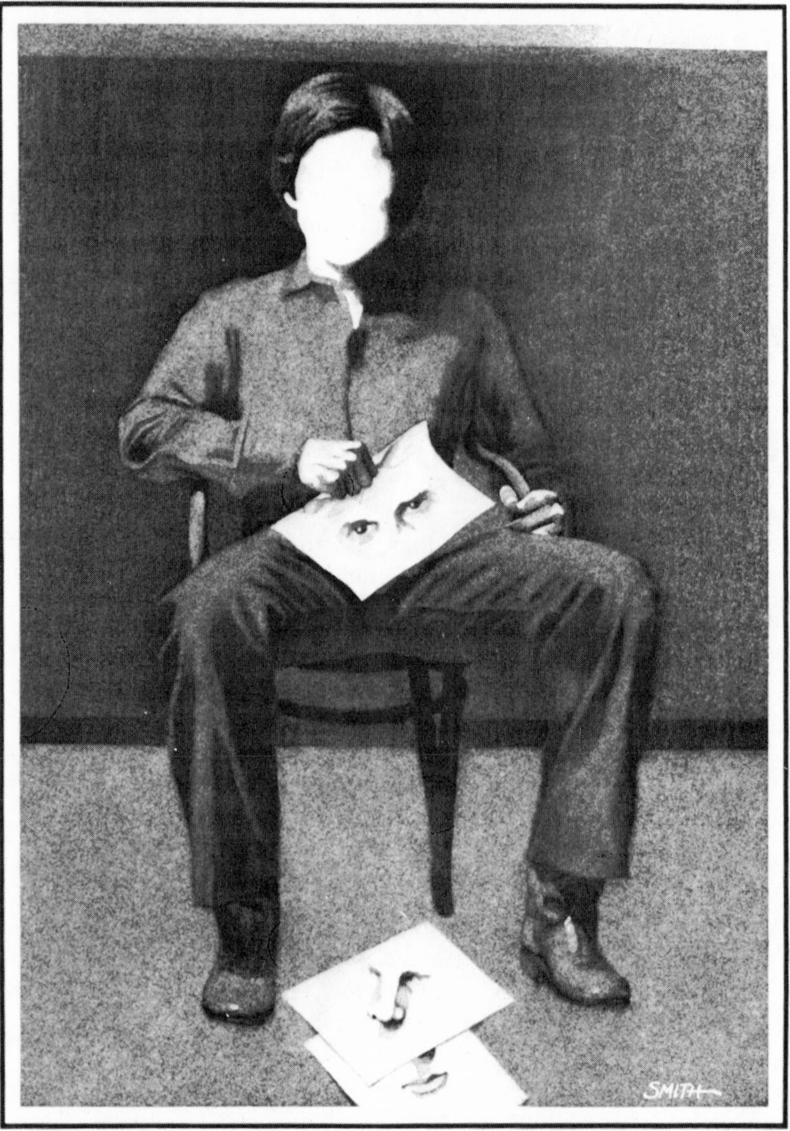
SMITH

of Rakestraw. Wagging its tail dubiously, the dog soon began to bark—a sonorous and violent heaving from deep within its chest. The hair on the dog's back stood up like a fan of porcupine quills, but it was clearly of two minds.

"Goddamn it, Nickie! It's me! Shut up, you dumb cur!"

Nickie kept barking, and when Rakestraw looked over the dog's ugly, persistently jerking head, he saw that Gayle and Gabe had retreated toward Nora and the house. How often, after all, had he warned them against taking up unquestioningly with strangers?

In the kitchen Rakestraw spoke to and embraced his children. By picking up his suitcase again, he avoided allowing Nora to put her arms around him, for he was alert to the fact that she wished to do so not only to welcome him home but to prove to him that the change didn't matter. It hurt to realize how fully Nora understood the trauma of his homecoming. It hurt even more to realize that he was not yet ready to accept the simple *kindness* embodied in her love.

"I'm going up to the guest room," he said abruptly.

As he swung out of the kitchen and began climbing the stairs, Gabe began to cry and Gayle to expostulate with her mother in bewildered, high-pitched tones. Rakestraw could hear Nora patiently declaring that she had told them their father would look a little different and wasn't it shameful to be making such a fuss when inside where it counted Daddy was exactly the same person and couldn't they understand that he was probably even more confused and uncertain than they were.

Upstairs, Rakestraw threw his suitcase into the guest room, angrily followed it in, and slammed and locked the door.

Long after the children had gone to bed, Nora knocked lightly and spoke his name. Knowing that she would be surprised to find him naked in the dark, he nevertheless opened to her, oddly indifferent to the pathos of his own behavior. This was not Tom Rakestraw acting in this unmanly, self-pitying way but an amazing, if imperfect, duplicate. Only the faces had been changed, to protect . . . well, some self-obsessed S.O.B. he had never even met.

Nora closed the door and embraced him. "Aren't you cold? It's not even spring yet, and here you are walking around in your birthday suit." Her hands moved gently up and down his back, as if to warm him, and Rakestraw surrendered to the extent of placing his chin on her head and embracing her chastely in return.

"I don't feel naked before you, Nora."

"You're not supposed to. Clothed or not, we're naked to each other almost all the time. We're married."

After a long silence Rakestraw said, "What I meant, Nora, is that I don't feel naked *at all.* I think I could walk through Caracal like this without feeling any shame. It wouldn't be me, anyway."

"Because your face is different?"

"Exactly."

"You're still the same person, Tom."

"I heard you tell Gabe and Gayle that, Nora—but it isn't true. I'm becoming someone else. It started the moment I saw myself in the mirror after surgery. And it's continuing even now."

Nora's fingers caressed the hair in the small of his back. "Maybe we'd better hurry, then."

"Hurry?"

"Before our lovemaking becomes adulterous."

Rakestraw kissed his wife, disengaged from her embrace, and walked to the bed to turn back its coverlet. This was a kindness for which they were both ready, and he could deny neither himself nor Nora.

"I don't care if they do have school tomorrow," Rakestraw told Nora at dinner several evenings later.

"But they need their sleep, Tom, and you really don't care who wins what. At least, you never have before."

"This year I care."

"Because of—"

"That's right. Because of Tiernan."

Gayle and Gabe were observing this exchange like spectators at a heated Ping-Pong match. The victor would determine their destinies between the approaching hours of nine and midnight.

"But it's everything you used to despise," Nora persisted, "if you thought about it at all. Is this Tiernan business enough to make you want to expose your children to the whole gaudy rigamarole?"

"They know what we think of that rigamarole. That's our parental guidance, their knowledge that we disapprove."

"They're first-graders, Tom. *First*-graders."

Rakestraw put his fork down and looked at each of the twins in turn. He had even more authority with them than he had had before. They listened to him now as if he were a policeman or a school principal.

"Do you think you can stay awake for the Academy Awards program?" he asked. "You certainly don't have to stay up if you don't want to."

"We want to," Gayle said.

"Yeah," said Gabe, wide-eyed and anxious.

"Lord, Tom—"

But Rakestraw, as he had known he would, prevailed. Nora did win a concession of sorts: she made pallets on the floor in front of the television for the twins.

By ten-thirty Gabe had fallen asleep with his stuffed paisley dog and Gayle was staring bravely, glassily, at a group of gowned women and bearded, tuxedoed men holding Oscars aloft for the polite approval of a Hollywood audience of celebrities and other film industry people. But because no camera had yet picked Craig Tiernan out of the crowd, even Rakestraw was growing impatient with the program.

Nora said, "Are you sure he's even there? I think I've read that he usually boycotts these things."

"He's nominated this year. Macmillan, the attorney, said he'd be on hand. He was in a film called *Yeardance*. Yesterday's paper listed him as the favorite for Best Actor."

"Can't we at least put the kids to bed?"

But the orchestra began playing a well-known movie theme and Rakestraw saw Tiernan, a lanky black starlet on his arm, descending a monumental tier of steps to the presenters' lectern.

"There he is, Nora. Wake up Gabe."

Nora shook her head in simultaneous refusal and exasperation.

"Wake him up, Nora!" Rakestraw got down on the floor, shook the boy by the shoulders, and pulled him to a precarious sitting position. "Who is that, kids? Tell me who that is!"

On the tiny television screen Tiernan was all glittering teeth and windswept coiffure. The young black woman at his side exuded a sultriness that seemed almost to mock his innocent good looks and bearing. Applause filled the auditorium. Then the couple went immediately into their clumsy, ghost-written repartee.

Gabe was jolted fully awake by the novelty of seeing his lost father in the company of a half-naked woman. Gayle, meanwhile, looked back and forth between the television set and the man who had just eased himself back onto the couch beside her mother.

"That used to be you," the girl said.

"That was never me," Rakestraw responded.

Tiernan and his sultry companion presented two awards for documentaries. The Rakestraws watched both presentations without speaking, fascinated by the eerie spectacle. Daddy was—or had been—a famous movie star.

"All right," Nora said. "They've seen him. Can't they go to bed now? Upstairs, I mean."

Rakestraw insisted that the twins stay for the Best Actor presentation, and Gayle and Gabe importuned their mother so enthusiastically that she had to relent. Tiernan's appearance on the program had dislodged the sleep from their eyes.

Another forty minutes passed before the Best Actor nominations were read, at which time a camera located Tiernan in the crowd and focused on him for almost half a minute. Then the screen was filled with that scene from *Yeardance* in which the title character comes face to face for the first time with the "lepers" under his care. It was a gruesome bit of film, but quickly over with. Tiernan, spotlighted again among his applauding colleagues, suddenly looked tense and uncertain. His smile was a rictus of counterfeit calm. Rakestraw could not recall ever having exercised the facial muscles that would produce such an expression.

"He really wants it."

"They all do," Nora said. "It's natural that they should."

The other nominees were shown, along with clips from their films. But the winner was not Tiernan. The winner was an eccentric Hollywood leading man who had made his first film during the early years of World War II. The auditorium rang with shouts and applause, and a television camera dollied in on Tiernan, cruelly, as he feigned a self-effacing grimace and then waved heartily at the victor threading his way to the stage.

"There's the Academy Award performance," Rakestraw said.

"Are you happy now?" Nora asked.

"Not yet," Rakestraw confessed. "Not yet."

The next day he drove to Ladysmith, a good-sized textile town about thirty-five miles south of Caracal, and purchased a videocassette recorder. In several different record and television shops he informed the clerks or sales managers that he wanted to buy videocassettes of all Craig Tiernan's movies.

"All of 'em?" asked a young woman with an unattractive blonde Afro who was clerking in a shop at the Ladysmith Mall.

"That's right—all of 'em."

"Well, you can buy some of the early films legit, but the most recent ones—you know, *Yeardance* and the remake of *Dark Passage*—well, you're not likely to find those anywhere but on the black market."

"I don't mind. Can you help me?"

"Hey, are you a cop?"

"No, I'm just a Craig Tiernan fancier."

The girl tilted her head and gave him an appraising look. "I might be able to help you if . . ."

"If what?"

"Take out your wallet and let me go through it," the clerk challenged him.

Rakestraw took out his wallet and laid it on the counter. Surprised, the girl picked it up, glanced at Rakestraw, and then began folding out the laminated cards and photographs until she came to his driver's license.

"Cripes," the girl said under her breath. "You've got Craig Tiernan's picture on your driver's license. You *ain't* a cop, are you? How in holy Christmas did you manage that?"

"I've got a friend at the Highway Patrol station." The lie made Rakestraw infinitely happy. Three or four weeks ago he had taken an intense private pride in his truthfulness, even in situations where a small distortion of the truth would have saved him either time or embarrassment.

"All right, mister. I guess it also looks like you can pay for what you want."

The clerk sold him the two black-market cassettes at steep prices, found five or six old Tiernan films in inventory, and helped him fill out an order for seven other Craig Tiernan vehicles. That was the whole shebang. Tiernan was still a young actor, and, Rakestraw had learned, he was notoriously picky about the roles he accepted.

"That's the third time today you've watched *Dark Passage,"* Nora told Rakestraw one midnight shortly after his visit to Ladysmith. "Bogart was twice as good in that part, too. What do you think you're accomplishing?"

"I never saw Bogart in the part. I think Tiernan does a pretty fair job, really."

"It's a pretentious and outdated movie, Tom. Using the camera as a character was fine the first time around, but in this remake it just seems silly. Self-conscious. The girl isn't as good as Bacall, either."

"How come you know so much about it?"

"I used to watch all the late movies on TV . . . until you started asking me out. Come to bed, Tom."

Rakestraw leaned forward, propped his chin on his fists, and continued to stare at the low-quality tape he had bought in Ladysmith. "You've got both critics and moviegoers on your side, Nora. Everything I've read about this one says it was a bomb. Tiernan and what's-her-face got panned, and no one went to see it until *Yeardance* was released a couple of months later. Then, they say, *Dark Passage* suddenly got hot at the box office."

Nora, standing in the doorway, looked with angry compassion at her transfigured husband. "The story fascinates you, doesn't it?"

Alerted by the cryptic tone of her voice, Rakestraw looked toward her. "A man with a past he has to overcome has plastic surgery and takes off to make a new life. Sure it fascinates me. It doesn't take a genius to figure out why, either."

"I'm going to bed, Tom. Do you want me to turn on your half of the electric blanket?"

When he shook his head, Nora left him in the den and walked through the dining room to the staircase.

Later, Rakestraw also went upstairs. But he strode down the hall to the guest room, turned on the light, locked the door, sat down at the antique vanity, and removed a small tape recorder from its drawer. Then he began contorting his altered features back toward the shapes he had known them to have only a few short weeks ago. Silently, hunching his shoulders and then straightening them again, he mimed the gestures that were Tiernan's hallmark as an actor. After a time he began to speak as Tiernan had spoken in *Dark Passage*. It astonished Rakestraw how easily and successfully the impersonation came to him, but he kept his voice down in order not to awaken Nora.

Two days later, Nora was surprised to look out the kitchen window and see parked on the edge of the yard an automobile bearing on its left-hand door the insignia of one of the state capital's major newspapers. Then a young woman with a camera case slung over her shoulder and a notebook in her hand knocked for admittance. Daffodils were growing in the grass between the kitchen door and the dirt road, and the young woman, her dark hair pulled back and tied in a navy-blue scarf, looked sunny and efficient.

"Is this the Rakestraws' residence?" she asked when Nora had opened the heavy Dutch door. "I'm Michelle Boyer, with the *World-Ledger*. I've got an appointment to talk with your husband."

Nora led Michelle Boyer into the den, where Rakestraw was intently watching Craig Tiernan in *Good Country People,* one of his early major films. Rakestraw turned off the videocassette and shook hands with the reporter, whereupon Nora, angry that her husband had said nothing to her about expecting a visitor, prepared to leave the two of them to whatever business they might have.

"Stay," Rakestraw said. "I think she'd like to hear what you have to say too, Nora. It's very important that she hear it, in fact." Finally Nora permitted herself to be persuaded.

Over the next two hours Rakestraw submitted to several photographs, and he and Nora detailed for Michelle Boyer the changes that had occurred in their lives because Craig Tiernan had invoked the Physiognomic Protection Act against him.

"I was the first defendant in this state," Rakestraw said, "and I lost on the basis of physical measurements of my skull and facial features. The data went to court, but I didn't."

"You're being compensated handsomely for the trauma, aren't you?" asked Boyer, taking the devil's-advocate role and writing in her notebook.

"Five hundred dollars a month. Which Tiernan, out in Oregon, writes off his income tax as a business expense."

"Are you looking for a larger settlement?"

"I'm not," Nora put in. "I don't know what Tom's looking for. The monthly check from Tiernan has turned him around. He spends all his waking hours doing what you found him doing when you came in. Two months ago he would have been chopping wood, preparing the ground, ordering seed."

"And now he obsessively watches Craig Tiernan movies?"

"He's a changed person, and I'm not just talking about his face. He's different inside. He admits it himself."

"What do you want," Boyer asked Rakestraw pointedly, lowering her notebook, "if it isn't more money?"

"Do you think this is fair?" Rakestraw asked her in turn. "Giving up a portion of myself because of another man's vanity?"

"You didn't have to opt for surgery, did you?"

"Not if I didn't mind moving to a war zone in Africa or an A-bomb test site in the Marshall Islands."

"What's been the effect on your children?"

"They're distant. They don't really believe I'm their father. They obey me without question." Rakestraw laughed.

"You don't sound like Craig Tiernan," Michelle Boyer observed. "How closely did you resemble him? Do you have any photographs?"

Nora took a padded leather photo album from one of the bookshelves and also found the infamous election poster. These she gave to the reporter, who glanced at the poster and then began turning the pages of the album.

"I think the resemblance is uncanny," she said after a while. "I can understand why Tiernan would have been alarmed. The danger of exploitation and overexposure is a real one to a celebrity who's worked his or her entire professional life to create a viable public image. Do you remember the Presley imitators? In those days death put Presley in the public domain, but then came the impersonators of *living* celebrities. Those exploiters didn't merely *imitate* their famous victims, Mr. Rakestraw, they had their faces surgically altered to resemble the President's or Bob Dylan's or Barbra Streisand's—while those people were still alive. Often they could libel and rip off their victims at the same time. Court cases proliferated, and a great deal of time and money was wasted. Hence, in states like New York and California, the Physiognomic Protection Act. It was probably overdue getting *here,* if you want my opinion."

"But Tom didn't surgically alter his face to resemble Tiernan's," Nora said. "It was his to begin with."

"That may be, Mrs. Rakestraw—but your husband's face wasn't essential to him in his livelihood. Tiernan was only trying to protect his livelihood."

"Tom Rakestraw was never a threat to Craig Tiernan's livelihood," Rakestraw said. "Never."

"Your voice isn't at all like his," Michelle Boyer observed again.

"No, it isn't," Nora said.

As if trying to make out the lineaments of the face that underlay his old one, the reporter looked at Rakestraw. "Why exactly did you call me down here?" she asked. "What did you want me to do for you?"

Rakestraw went to the VCR unit, turned it back on, and wound it forward to the loft sequence in *Good Country People.* The three of them watched as Craig Tiernan, playing the Bible-selling mountebank Manley Pointer, seduced Lisette Corley as Joy-Hulga Hopewell in the scene that not only solidified Tiernan's status as a rising beefcake star but earned him his present reputation as a formidable actor. It was impossible to watch Tiernan in this role, a piece of brilliant against-type casting, without laughing helplessly. As Nora and Michelle Boyer laughed, Rakestraw stepped forward and froze the motion picture on the screen at the precise point where Tiernan scrambled out of the loft with Corley's artificial leg in his Bible case.

"Is that why you had me come to Caracal?" the reporter asked. "To give me a private screening of the Great Leg Heist?"

"Partly." Rakestraw, facing the two women, set his feet apart, hunched his shoulders, and magically transformed himself into Craig Tiernan as Manley Pointer. When he spoke, the voice was Tiernan's Manley Pointer voice; and when he moved, the illusion of Tiernan as a callow but caustic redneck salesman was overwhelming. That illusion obliterated the commonplace reality of the den and its homely furniture.

"'I may sell Bibles,'" ranted Rakestraw in his Tiernan-Pointer voice, "'but I know which end is up and I wasn't born yesterday and I know where I'm going!'"

"Incredible," said Michelle Boyer, applauding him enthusiastically when he was finished. "No props, either. Very, very good."

Nora was staring at him as if he had just stripped naked at a Methodist covered-dish dinner. She was almost beginning to wonder if Macmillan had sent home to her from the sanitarium the same man he had taken.

Then the younger reporter's eyes narrowed suspiciously. "That's it, isn't it? You're going to try to milk your connection with Tiernan. You want notoriety, and you think the *World-Ledger* can give it to you."

Rakestraw let himself slump back into his own persona, which, over the past several days, had grown more and more protean and tenuous. Nora was conscious of a firm purpose somewhere inside him, but also of the fact that this purpose was one of the few phenomenological constants remaining to him. Twice recently he had wakened at night and sleepily asked her what his name was. Sometimes, when they had looked through the photographs she had just been showing Boyer, Rakestraw had failed to recognize himself. And although he always recognized Nora's features in the faces of their children, he said he could never—anymore—discern the imprint of his own. . . .

"That's right," Rakestraw said. "Don't you think there's a story here?"

"Oh, undoubtedly," Boyer acknowledged. "But you may not like the one I'm formulating."

"Balance it, or unbalance it, any way you like—but get in the violence done to both me and my family."

"Not to mention your burgeoning talents as an impersonator?"

"Why not? I think they're pretty goddamn pertinent."

"Tom!"

"Goodbye, Ms. Boyer. I appreciate your driving down." Rakestraw shoved his hands in his pockets and stalked out of the den.

Nora led Michelle Boyer back through the kitchen and then walked with her out to her car. Daffodils fluttered alongside the gravel road, and the breeze was silken.

"Try to remember," Nora told the reporter, "that he was never like this before. That means something, I think. It definitely means something. I hope you're smart enough to figure out what."

Under the headline CARACAL MAN LOSES FACE TO CRAIG TIERNAN, / MASKS HURT WITH RARE IMPERSONATIONS, the story appeared in the Sunday *World-Ledger.* The Rakestraws were surprised to find themselves reading a sympathetic human-interest feature, for, despite Michelle Boyer's sunny good looks and her short-lived delight in Rakestraw's impromptu performance, she had seemed something of an apologist for the Physiognomic Protection Act and Rakestraw had ended up swearing at her. But the story—complete with side-by-side photographs of Tiernan and the "new" Thomas Rakestraw—was a virtual paean to the Rakestraws and a forthright assault on the arrogance of legislation expressly designed to protect the privileged.

"I'm proud of her," said Nora. "I'm really proud of her."

"The sympathies of the thing aren't as important as the fact that my story made the paper," Rakestraw said. "This just makes it a little nicer, a little easier."

The following morning the telephone began to ring.

Rakestraw spoke to the editor of the Ladysmith *Times,* to news personnel from three different television stations in the state, and to a man with a booking agency in Nashville, Tennessee. Although he discouraged this man on the grounds that he wasn't yet ready to leave Caracal, he made appointments with several others; and over the next three days just that many television camera crews invaded the Rakestraw house to film him doing, sans props or makeup, the loft scene in *Good Country People,* the metamorphosis of Karst in *Singularity,* and the self-blinding of the title character in *Yeardance.* A different scene for each camera crew. These mini-performances were shown on evening news programs in Ladysmith, Fort

Lanier, and the state capital, each with an adulatory commentary and a brief interview with Rakestraw in his obsolescent persona as a wronged country boy.

A wire service picked up Michelle Boyer's story from the *World-Ledger,* and it was reprinted in newspapers nationwide.

In the wake of these events, a clip of Rakestraw's Tiernan-Pointer performance, originally filmed by the CBS affiliate in Fort Lanier, appeared the following Friday evening on network news, after which a rash of new telephone calls struck the house. Nora, after talking briefly with a woman in Lebanon, Kansas, who said she wanted to touch Rakestraw's perfect body with her mind, unplugged the telephone jack in the den and then went upstairs to lift the phone in the bedroom out of its cradle.

"This is certainly the week of Thomas Rakestraw," she said disgustedly, coming back down the steps.

Rakestraw was standing in the foyer beneath the staircase. "I've plugged the phone in the den back in."

"Why?"

Assuming a languid Craig Tiernan posture, Rakestraw aped the actor's gesture and voice. "Because," he said insouciantly, "it's more than a tad likely we're going to be getting a very important call, m'lady."

"Tom," Nora said softly.

"What?"

"Knock it off, all right? Please just knock it off."

As well as he was able, Rakestraw knocked it off. "It's just that I'm pretty sure Tiernan is going to try to get in touch," he said. "That's all."

"To let you have your face back?"

"Probably to threaten to cut off our monthly compensation."

"That might be almost as good as the other." Nora turned clumsily and went back up the stairs.

Four calls and two and a half hours later, Rakestraw reached over from his easy chair and uncradled the telephone in response to its renewed ringing.

"Thomas Rakestraw?" said a voice through the wire.

"Yo." Was this old army slang or Spanish? Rakestraw didn't

know. The word gave him a comfortable degree of distance from the apprehension he had begun to feel.

"This is Edgar Macmillan. Am I speaking to the same Thomas Rakestraw whom I met several weeks ago?"

"No."

"I'm sorry. I—"

"You're speaking with a different Thomas Rakestraw—whom, however, you did indeed meet several weeks ago."

Macmillan, after a silence, said, "You probably know why I'm calling, Mr. Rakestraw. Craig Tiernan has directed me to get in touch with you to point out that because you're presently in violation of the terms of our settlement, we intend to—"

"Halt my compensation payments."

Macmillan chuckled, maybe in surprise. "Of course."

"Well, Mr. Macmillan"—Rakestraw spoke into the phone with the authority of a prosecutor—"it's my opinion that you're just trying to steamroller me. I've had occasion to read the Physiognomic Protection Act very carefully, as well as the terms of our settlement, and nowhere in either is there any mention of the illegality of my impersonating the former plaintiff if I don't happen to resemble him facially. I no longer resemble him facially. My impersonations arise from an innate talent for mimicry that is exclusively my own, and Craig Tiernan has no lawful right to attempt to restrain the expression of that talent. Impersonators have long been a part of this business. Craig Tiernan himself is an impersonator, and if he denies my right to practice, he also denies his own."

Macmillan's subsequent silence led Rakestraw to believe that Tiernan was perhaps in the same room with his attorney. Were the two conferring because he had put a hitch in their assessment of his likely response? He hoped so.

"Mr. Rakestraw," Macmillan tentatively resumed, "it still remains the case that you're exploiting the talent, the work, and the personality of Craig Tiernan, and this infringement on his career is an actionable matter which may result in your having to *pay* damages rather than simply receiving them."

"Well, Mr. Macmillan, my 'infringement' on the career of Mr. Tiernan is a direct consequence of his infringement upon my life. I'd never even heard of the bastard before you came to Caracal. It's an accident of his own making that I'm impersonating anyone. Please tell him that I started with Craig Tiernan for pretty straightforward reasons, and that if I wanted to, I could do just about anybody I damn well choose, including his own most recent mother-in-law."

"We intend to sue for—"

"And I intend to countersue for unconscionable harassment after the indignity of having to forfeit the face I was born with."

"Mr. Rakestraw—"

"And when I press suit, you might remind Mr. Tiernan, he'll have to come to court. His plastic overlay photographs and my cranial measurements won't be able to speak for him. Craig Tiernan and Tom Rakestraw will occupy the same courtroom, and the publicity generated will be more than he bargained for and quite distinctive in its thrust as far as he and I are concerned."

"Mr. Rakestraw, you're . . . you're whistling in the dark."

"How much hate mail has Tiernan received this week?"

"Hate mail?"

"How many people have written to tell him what a jerk he is for depriving an innocent man of his own face?"

"I don't read Craig Tiernan's mail, Mr. Rakestraw."

"But it hasn't all been sympathetic gushings this week, has it?"

"No, it hasn't," Macmillan confessed. "But that's neither here nor there when—"

"It's there, Mr. Macmillan. Here the mail and telephone calls are mostly favorable. That's how I know what kind of communications your employer's been receiving."

"What exactly do you want?" Macmillan asked, a trace of desperation in his voice. Michelle Boyer had asked very nearly the same question more than a week ago, but the only honest reply Rakestraw could frame was one he could not bring himself to voice.

"I want to speak to Tiernan," he said instead.

"On the telephone?"

"In person."

"Do you propose to fly here for that purpose?"

"Why doesn't he come here? It's all tax-deductible, after all. For him, anyway."

A silence, during which Rakestraw felt sure that Macmillan and

Tiernan were discussing this turn of events. Maybe the attorney had a long-distance hookup with the actor, too, and maybe his, Rakestraw's, voice was being broadcast to Tiernan over a speaker in the attorney's office. If they were in the same room together, Rakestraw could hear none of their conversation.

Finally Macmillan said, "Mr. Tiernan has directed me to tell you he'll be happy to meet you at a neutral location within your own state. Maybe in a nearby community, if that's all right."

"Neutral location? Are he and I football franchises? Why can't he come here? We've got plenty of room."

"Think about that one a sec. or so, Mr. Rakestraw. You just might be able to come up with an answer."

"My family," Rakestraw said suddenly. "The effect on my family—Tiernan's worried about that."

Macmillan didn't reply.

"I'll make the preparations for his visit," Rakestraw said.

The owner of a theater complex in Ladysmith agreed to open one of his auditoriums at ten-thirty on a weekday morning so that Tiernan and Rakestraw could meet in a setting both private and apropos. Having these two people in his establishment, one of them an up-and-coming local boy, was incentive enough for the owner, but Tiernan had also consented to kick in an honorarium.

Rakestraw was the first to arrive. When he entered the drapery-lined theater, he found that *Phaedrus* was unraveling silently against the high, canted screen. The owner, ensconced in the projection booth, was paying homage to Tiernan with a showing of the most acclaimed and probably most neglected motion picture of the actor's career. Perhaps this homage encompassed Rakestraw as well, for the film—the first of Tiernan's that Rakestraw had ever seen—bore strangely on the terrible change in his life.

Even without the aid of the soundtrack Rakestraw could recall every word of Tiernan's voice-over narration for the dream sequence now unfolding. Halted midway down the left-hand aisle of the theater, he allowed himself to repeat these words under his breath: "'My hands sink into something soft. . . . It writhes, and I tighten the grip, as one holds a serpent. And now, holding it tighter and tighter, we'll get it into the light. Here it comes!'"

Aloud, at the dream sequence's climactic moment, Rakestraw cried, "'*Now we'll see its face!*'"

Whereupon he heard the real Craig Tiernan say quietly, from the aisle opposite his, "'A mind divided against itself . . . me . . . I'm the evil figure in the shadows. I'm the loathsome one. . . .'"

Rakestraw turned to face the double whom he no longer resembled. Craig Tiernan was dressed from head to foot in white; a fine gold chain circled his neck and glinted in the diffuse illumination thrown by the movie projector. He hardly seemed real.

"That's been your basic assumption from the beginning, hasn't it? That I'm the loathsome one."

His heart thudding wetly, Rakestraw stared across a row of shadowy seats into a face he had often seen in his own bathroom mirror.

"Here I am, then. Direct to you from Oregon via Southern California. And this little tête-à-tête is holding up the production of a thirty-million-dollar epic. I'm supposed to be in Nairobi. Or Cairo. What do you have to say to me, Rakestraw?"

Rakestraw continued to stare.

"This is petty and self-indulgent," Tiernan said. "But the surgery's reversible. It's designed to be that way in case anything happens to the owner of the physiognomic rights in question. If you'll return to your own home and agree to stay there without any further infringement on me or my work, I'm prepared to grant you co-ownership of those rights. Macmillan will take care of the details. We'll even continue your emotional-hardship compensation."

"What happened to me is irreversible," Rakestraw finally said.

Tiernan took a step down the aisle toward Rakestraw. "You'll be all right when you get your face back. Some people just don't adjust very well to that sort of surgery. Even money doesn't help much. You're one of those people, I guess."

"I don't want my face back."

Almost as if dumbstruck, Tiernan halted. On the movie screen, Rakestraw noted peripherally, a man and a boy on motorcycles were climbing toward a stunning mountain lake. Crater Lake, probably. The man on the motorcycle was Craig Tiernan.

"What, then?" the actor himself said. "*Is* it more money?"

Rakestraw didn't respond.

"I'll up the payments if that's really the problem. Lord knows, I've brought this on myself. Just don't push me too far, Mr. Rakestraw. You're treading dangerous ground with these publicity-seeking impersonations."

"But I'm not breaking any law." Rakestraw was conscious of a shift of settings on the screen. Now Tiernan and another actor in a coat and tie were arguing mutely in a university classroom. Outdoors, indoors. The film was schizophrenic. "And, it isn't money," Rakestraw added distractedly. "Not entirely, anyway."

"Goddamn it, man!" Tiernan suddenly raged. "What am I doing here, then? Did you have me come all this way just to show yourself you could do it? Just to prove you could get me in the same building with you?"

Rakestraw returned his eyes to the real Tiernan. "I thought you ought to see me," he said. "And vice versa."

"Why?"

"Listen, when Macmillan arrived to tell me I was violating your rights, we had nothing in common. Absolutely nothing, despite your long-distance concern about my face. Well, now that I no longer resemble you facially, we have a great deal in common. I find that I like that. If I took my old face back, people outside of Caracal wouldn't know who I was. They'd think I was you, and I'm not. We're more alike today than we were before you had me altered, and although there remains a difference that's important, I'd just like to . . ."

Tiernan, gripping the back of a theater seat, waited for him to conclude.

"I'd just like to thank you for opening up my life."

That night, in bed, he rehearsed for Nora for the fourth or fifth time the details of his meeting with Tiernan. Moonlight came into their bedroom from a dormer window, and Gabe, across the hall, moaned and twisted audibly in his bedding. The nights were growing warmer.

"It frightens me," Nora said when he was finished.

"It should," Rakestraw said, stroking his wife's hair. "It's always a little frightening, a new life. You never know where it's going."

"Where *is* it going, Tom?"

Rakestraw lay back and stared at the ceiling. When he closed his eyes, he seemed to see the ganglia of his own feverish brain, like roads branching in a hundred different directions.

"Nora," he said, without opening his eyes, "I feel filled with power. It came on me slowly, opening up inside me after the surrender that took my face. It's been like climbing out of a well into the light. I still don't recognize myself, but what I see isn't displeasing."

There was a small hitch in Nora's otherwise regular breathing.

Turning toward her, Rakestraw said, "What would you think about leaving Caracal? About selling the farm and going somewhere else?"

"This is all I've ever wanted, Tom."

"It was all I ever wanted, too—until Macmillan showed up and I surrendered to him. But I'm different now, for good or for ill. Something that was pent up has been set free, and I don't think it's going to go willingly back to where it came from."

"I'd have to think about it," Nora said evenly, turning her own eyes to the ceiling. "Where do you want us to go?"

"That's something *I* still have to think about, I guess."

Conversation failed. They lay side by side in the familiar bed, their hands touching, thinking toward tomorrow.

The Quickening

I

Lawson came out of his sleep feeling drugged and disoriented. Instead of the susurrus of traffic on Rivermont and the early-morning barking of dogs, he heard running feet and an unsettling orchestration of moans and cries. No curtains screened or softened the sun that beat down on his face, and an incandescent blueness had replaced their ceiling. "Marlena," Lawson said doubtfully. He wondered if one of the children was sick and told himself that he ought to get up to help.

But when he tried to rise, scraping the back of his hand on a stone set firmly in mortar, he found that his bed had become a parapet beside a river flowing through an unfamiliar city. He was wearing, instead of the green Chinese-peasant pajamas that Marlena had given him for Christmas, a suit of khaki 1505s from his days in the Air Force and a pair of ragged Converse sneakers. Clumsily, as if deserting a mortuary slab, Lawson leapt away from the wall. In his sleep, the world had turned over. The forms of a bewildered anarchy had begun to assert themselves.

The city—and Lawson knew that it sure as hell wasn't Lynchburg, that the river running through it wasn't the James—was full of people. A few, their expressions terrified and their postures defensive, were padding past Lawson on the boulevard beside the parapet. Many shrieked or babbled as they ran. Other human shapes, dressed not even remotely alike, were lifting themselves bemusedly from paving stones, or riverside benches, or the gutter beyond the sidewalk. Their grogginess and their swiftly congealing fear, Lawson realized, mirrored his own: like him, these people were awakening to nightmare.

Because the terrible fact of his displacement seemed more important than the myriad physical details confronting him, it was hard to take in everything at once—but Lawson tried to balance and integrate what he saw.

The city was foreign. Its architecture was a clash of the Gothic and the sterile, pseudoadobe Modern, one style to each side of the river. On this side, palm trees waved their dreamy fronds at precise intervals along the boulevard, and toward the city's interior an intricate cathedral tower defined by its great height nearly everything beneath it. Already the sun crackled off the rose-colored tower with an arid fierceness that struck Lawson, who had never been abroad, as Mediterranean. . . . Off to his left was a bridge leading into a more modern quarter of the city, where beige and brick-red high-rises clustered like tombstones. On both sides of the bridge buses, taxicabs, and other sorts of motorized vehicles were stalled or abandoned in the thoroughfares.

Unfamiliar, Lawson reflected, but not unearthly—he recognized things, saw the imprint of a culture somewhat akin to his own. And, for a moment, he let the inanimate bulk of the city and the languor of its palms and bougainvillea crowd out of his vision the human horror show taking place in the streets.

A dark woman in a sari hurried past. Lawson lifted his hand to her. Dredging up a remnant of a high-school language course, he shouted, "*¿Habla Español?*" The woman quickened her pace, crossed the street, recrossed it, crossed it again; her movements were random, motivated, it seemed, by panic and the complicated need to *do* something.

At a black man in loincloth farther down the parapet, Lawson

SMITH

shouted, "This is Spain! We're somewhere in Spain! That's all I know! Do you speak English? Spanish? Do you know what's happened to us?"

The black man, grimacing so that his skin went taut across his cheekbones, flattened himself atop the wall like a lizard. His elbows jutted, his eyes narrowed to slits. Watching him, Lawson perceived that the man was listening intently to a sound that had been steadily rising in volume ever since Lawson had opened his eyes: the city was wailing. From courtyards, apartment buildings, taverns, and plazas, an eerie and discordant wail was rising into the bland blue indifference of the day. It consisted of many strains. The Negro in the loincloth seemed determined to separate these and pick out the ones that spoke most directly to him. He tilted his head.

"Spain!" Lawson yelled against this uproar. *"¡España!"*

The black man looked at Lawson, but the hieroglyph of recognition was not among those that glinted in his eyes. As if to dislodge the wailing of the city, he shook his head. Then, still crouching lizard-fashion on the wall, he began methodically banging his head against its stones. Lawson, helplessly aghast, watched him until he had knocked himself insensible in a sickening, repetitive spattering of blood.

But Lawson was the only one who watched. When he approached the man to see if he had killed himself, Lawson's eyes were seduced away from the African by a movement in the river. A bundle of some sort was floating in the greasy waters below the wall—an infant, clad only in a shirt. The tie-strings on the shirt trailed out behind the child like the severed, wavering legs of a water-walker. Lawson wondered if, in Spain, they even had water-walkers. . . .

Meanwhile, still growing in volume, there crooned above the highrises and Moorish gardens the important air-raid siren of four hundred thousand human voices. Lawson cursed the sound. Then he covered his face and wept.

II

The city was Seville. The river was the Guadalquivir. Lynchburg and the James River, around which Lawson had grown up as the eldest child of an itinerant fundamentalist preacher, were several thousand miles and one helluva big ocean away. You couldn't get there by swimming, and if you imagined that your loved ones would be waiting for you when you got back, you were probably fantasizing the nature of the world's changed reality. No one was where he or she belonged anymore, and Lawson knew himself lucky even to realize where he was. Most of the dispossessed, displaced people inhabiting Seville today *didn't* know that much; all they knew was the intolerable cruelty of their uprooting, the pain of separation from husbands, wives, children, lovers, friends. These things, and fear.

The bodies of infants floated in the Guadalquivir; and Lawson, from his early reconnoiterings of the city on a motor scooter that he had found near the Jardines de Cristina park, knew that thousands of adults already lay dead on streets and in apartment buildings—victims of panic-inspired beatings or their own traumatized hearts. Who knew exactly what was going on in the morning's chaos? Babel had come again and with it, as part of the package, the utter dissolution of all family and societal ties. You couldn't go around a corner without encountering a child of some exotic ethnic caste, her face snot-glazed, sobbing loudly or maybe running through a crush of bodies calling out names in an alien tongue.

What were you supposed to do? Wheeling by on his motor scooter, Lawson either ignored these children or searched their faces to see how much they resembled his daughters.

Where was Marlena now? Where were Karen and Hannah? Just as he played deaf to the cries of the children in the boulevards, Lawson had to harden himself against the implications of these questions. As dialects of German, Chinese, Bantu, Russian, Celtic, and a hundred other languages rattled in his ears, his scooter rattled past a host of cars and buses with uncertain-seeming drivers at their wheels. Probably he too should have chosen an enclosed vehicle. If these frustrated and angry drivers, raging in polyglot defiance, decided to run over him, they could do so with impunity. Who would stop them?

Maybe—in Istanbul, or La Paz, or Mangalore, or Jönköping, or Boise City, or Kaesŏng—his own wife and children had already lost their lives to people made murderous by fear or the absence of helmeted men with pistols and billy sticks. Maybe Marlena and his children were dead. . . .

I'm in Seville, Lawson told himself, cruising. He had determined the name of the city soon after mounting the motor scooter and going by a sign that said *Plaza de Toros de Sevilla.* A circular stadium of considerable size near the river. The bullring. Lawson's Spanish was just good enough to decipher the signs and posters plastered on its walls. *Corrida a las cinco de la tarde.* (García Lorca, he thought, unsure of where the name had come from.) *Sombra y sol.* That morning, then, he took the scooter around the stadium three or four times and then shot off toward the center of the city.

Lawson wanted nothing to do with the nondescript highrises across the Gaudalquivir but had no real idea what he was going to do on the Moorish and Gothic side of the river, either. All he knew was that the empty bullring, with its dormant potential for death, frightened him. On the other hand, how did you go about establishing order in a city whose population had not willingly chosen to be there?

Seville's population, Lawson felt sure, had been redistributed across the face of the globe, like chess pieces flung from a height. The population of every other human community on Earth had undergone similar displacements. The result, as if by malevolent design, was chaos and suffering. Your ears eventually tried to shut out the audible manifestations of this pain, but your eyes held you accountable and you hated yourself for ignoring the wailing Arab child, the assaulted Polynesian woman, the blue-eyed old man bleeding from the palms as he prayed in the shadow of a department-store awning. Very nearly, you hated yourself for surviving.

Early in the afternoon, at the entrance to the Calle de Sierpes, Lawson got off his scooter and propped it against a wall. Then he waded into the crowd and lifted his right arm above his head.

"I speak English!" he called. "*¡Y hablo un poco Español!* Any who speak English or Spanish please come to me!"

A man who might have been Vietnamese or Kampuchean, or even Malaysian, stole Lawson's motor scooter and rode it in a wobbling zigzag down the Street of the Serpents. A heavyset blonde woman with red cheeks glared at Lawson from a doorway, and a twelve- or thirteen-year-old boy who appeared to be Italian clutched hungrily at Lawson's belt, seeking purchase on an adult, hoping for commiseration. Although he did not try to brush the boy's hand away, Lawson avoided his eyes.

"English! English here! *¡Un poco Español también!*"

Farther down Sierpes, Lawson saw another man with his hand in the air; he was calling aloud in a crisp but melodic Slavic dialect, and already he had succeeded in attracting two or three other people to him. In fact, pockets of like-speaking people seemed to be forming in the crowded commercial avenue, causing Lawson to fear that he had put up his hand too late to end his own isolation. What if those who spoke either English or Spanish had already gathered into survival-conscious groups? What if they had already made their way into the countryside, where the competition for food and drink might be a little less predatory? If they had, he would be a lost, solitary Virginian in this Babel. Reduced to sign language and guttural noises to make his wants known, he would die a cipher. . . .

"*Signore,*" the boy hanging on his belt cried. "*Signore.*"

Lawson let his eyes drift to the boy's face. "*Ciao,*" he said. It was the only word of Italian he knew, or the only word that came immediately to mind, and he spoke it much louder than he meant.

The boy shook his head vehemently, pulled harder on Lawson's belt. His words tumbled out like the contents of an unburdened closet into a darkened room, not a single one of them distinct or recognizable.

"English!" Lawson shouted. "English here!"

"English here, too, man!" a voice responded from the milling crush of people at the mouth of Sierpes. "Hang on a minute, I'm coming to you!"

A small muscular man with a large head and not much chin stepped daintily through an opening in the crowd and put out his hand to Lawson. His grip was firm. As he shook hands, he placed his left arm over the shoulder of the Italian boy hanging on to Lawson's belt. The boy stopped talking and gaped at the newcomer.

"Dai Secombe," the man said. "I went to bed in Aberystwyth, where I teach philosophy, and I wake up in Spain. Pleased to meet you, Mr.—"

"Lawson," Lawson said.

The boy began babbling again, his hand shifting from Lawson's belt to the Welshman's flannel shirt facing. Secombe took the boy's hands in his own. "I've got you, lad. There's a ragged crew of your compatriots in a pool-hall pub right down this lane. Come on, then, I'll take you." He glanced at Lawson. "Wait for me, sir. I'll be right back."

Secombe and the boy disappeared, but in less than five minutes the Welshman had returned. He introduced himself all over again. "To go to bed in Aberystwyth and to wake up in Seville," he said, "is pretty damn harrowing. I'm glad to be alive, sir."

"Do you have a family?"

"Only my father. He's eighty-four."

"You're lucky. Not to have anyone else to worry about, I mean."

"Perhaps," Dai Secombe said, a sudden trace of sharpness in his voice. "Yesterday I would not've thought so."

The two men stared at each other as the wail of the city modulated into a less hysterical but still inhuman drone. People surged around them, scrutinized them from foyers and balconies, took their measure. Out of the corner of his eye Lawson was aware of a moonfaced woman in summer deerskins slumping abruptly and probably painfully to the street. An Eskimo woman—the conceit was almost comic, but the woman herself was dying and a child with a Swedish-steel switchblade was already freeing a necklace of teeth and shells from her throat.

Lawson turned away from Secombe to watch the plundering of the Eskimo woman's body. Enraged, he took off his wristwatch and threw it at the boy's head, scoring a glancing sort of hit on his ear.

"You little jackal, get away from there!"

The red-cheeked woman who had been glaring at Lawson applied her foot to the rump of the boy with the switchblade and pushed him over. Then she retrieved the thrown watch, hoisted her skirts, and retreated into the dim interior of the café whose door she had been haunting.

"In this climate, in this environment," Dai Secombe told Lawson, "an Eskimo is doomed. It's as much psychological and emotional as it is physical. There may be a few others who've already died for similar reasons. Not much we can do, sir."

Lawson turned back to the Welshman with a mixture of awe and disdain. How had this curly-haired lump of a man, in the space of no more than three or four hours, come to respond so lackadaisically to the deaths of his fellows? Was it merely because the sky was still blue and the edifices of another age still stood?

Pointedly, Secombe said, "That was a needless forfeiture of your watch, Lawson."

"How the hell did that poor woman get here?" Lawson demanded, his gesture taking in the entire city. "How the hell did any of us get here?" The stench of open wounds and the first sweet hints of decomposition mocked the luxury of his ardor.

"Good questions," the Welshman responded, taking Lawson's arm and leading him out of the Calle de Sierpes. "It's a pity I can't answer 'em."

III

That night they ate fried fish and drank beer together in a dirty little apartment over a shop whose glass display cases were filled with a variety of latex contraceptives. They had obtained the fish from a *pescadería* voluntarily tended by men and women of Greek and Yugoslavian citizenship, people who had run similar shops in their own countries. The beer they had taken from one of the classier bars on the Street of the Serpents. Both the fish and the beer were at room temperature, but tasted none the worse for that.

With the fall of evening, however, the wail that during the day had subsided into a whine began to reverberate again with its first full burden of grief. If the noise was not quite so loud as it had been that morning, Lawson thought, it was probably because the city contained fewer people. Many had died, and a great many more, unmindful of the distances involved, had set out to return to their homelands.

Lawson chewed a piece of *adobo* and washed this down with a swig of the vaguely bitter *Cruz del Campo* beer.

"Isn't this fine?" Secombe said, his butt on the tiles of the room's one windowsill. "Dinner over a Durex shop. And this a Catholic country, too."

"I was raised a Baptist," Lawson said, realizing at once that his confession was a non sequitur.

"Oh," Secombe put in immediately. "Then I imagine you could get all the condoms you wanted."

"Sure. For a quarter. In almost any gas-station restroom."

"Sorry," Secombe said.

They ate for a while in silence. Lawson's back was to a cool plaster wall; he leaned his head against it, too, and released a sharp moan from his chest. Then, sustaining the sound, he moaned again, adding his own strand of grief to the cacophonous harmonies already afloat over the city. He was no different from all the bereaved others who shared his pain by concentrating on their own.

"What did you do in . . . in Lynchburg?" Secombe suddenly asked.

"Campus liaison for the Veterans Administration. I traveled to four different colleges in the area straightening out people's problems with the GI Bill. I tried to see to it that— Sweet Jesus, Secombe, who cares? I miss my wife. I'm afraid my girls are dead."

"Karen and Hannah?"

"They're three and five. I've taught them to play chess. Karen's good enough to beat me occasionally if I spot her my queen. Hannah knows the moves, but she hasn't got her sister's patience—she's only three, you know. Yeah. Sometimes she sweeps the pieces off the board and folds her arms, and we play hell trying to find them all. There'll be pawns under the sofa, horsemen upside down in the shag—" Lawson stopped.

"She levels them," Secombe said. "As we've all been leveled. The knight's no more than the pawn, the king no more than the bishop."

Lawson could tell that the Welshman was trying to turn aside the ruinous thrust of his grief. But he brushed the metaphor aside: "I don't think we've been 'leveled,' Secombe."

"Certainly we have. Guess who I saw this morning near the cathedral when I first woke up."

"God only knows."

"God and Dai Secombe, sir. I saw the Marxist dictator of . . . oh, you know, that little African country where there's just been a coup. I recognized the bastard from the telly broadcasts during the purge trials there. There he was, though, in white ducks and a ribbed T-shirt—terrified, Lawson, and as powerless as you and I. He'd been quite decidedly leveled; you'd better believe he had."

"I'll bet he's alive tonight, Secombe."

The Welshman's eyes flickered with a sudden insight. He extended the greasy cone of newspaper from the *pescadería*. "Another piece of fish, Lawson? Come on, then, there's only one more."

"To be leveled, Secombe, is to be put on a par with everyone else. Your dictator, even deprived of office, is a grown man. What about infant children? Toddlers and preadolescents? And what about people like that Eskimo woman who haven't got a chance in an unfamiliar environment, even if its inhabitants don't happen to be hostile? . . . I saw a man knock his brains out on a stone wall this morning because he took a look around and knew he couldn't make it here. Maybe he thought he was in Hell, Secombe. I don't know. But his chance certainly wasn't ours."

"He knew he couldn't adjust."

"Of course he couldn't adjust. Don't give me that bullshit about leveling!"

Secombe turned the cone of newspaper around and withdrew the last piece of fish. "I'm going to eat this myself, if you don't mind." He ate. As he was chewing, he said, "I didn't think that Virginia Baptists were so free with their tongues, Lawson. Tsk, tsk. Undercuts my preconceptions."

"I've fallen away."

"Haven't we all."

Lawson took a final swig of warm beer. Then he hurled the bottle across the room. Fragments of amber glass went everywhere. "God!" he cried. "God, God, God!" Weeping, he was no different from three quarters of Seville's new citizens-by-chance. Why, then, as he sobbed, did he shoot such guilty and threatening glances at the Welshman?

"Go ahead," Secombe advised him, waving the empty cone of newspaper. "I feel a little that way myself."

IV

In the morning an oddly blithe woman of forty-five or so accosted them in the alley outside the contraceptive shop. A military pistol in a patent-leather holster was strapped about her skirt. Her seeming airiness, Lawson quickly realized, was a function of her appearance and her movements; her eyes were as grim and frightened as everyone else's. But, as soon as they came out of the shop onto the cobblestones, she approached them fearlessly, hailing Secombe almost as if he were an old friend.

"You left us yesterday, Mr. Secombe. Why?"

"I saw everything dissolving into cliques."

"Dissolving? Coming together, don't you mean?"

Secombe smiled noncommittally, then introduced the woman to Lawson as Mrs. Alexander. "She's one of your own, Lawson. She's from Wyoming or some such place. I met her outside the cathedral yesterday morning when the first self-appointed muezzins started calling their language-mates together. She didn't have a pistol then."

"I got it from one of the Guardia Civil stations," Mrs. Alexander said. "And I feel lots better just having it, let me tell you." She looked at Lawson. "Are you in the Air Force?"

"Not anymore. These are the clothes I woke up in."

"My husband's in the Air Force. Or was. We were stationed at Warren in Cheyenne. I'm originally from upstate New York. And these are the clothes *I* woke up in." A riding skirt, a blouse, low-cut rubber-soled shoes. "I think they tried to give us the most serviceable clothes we had in our wardrobes—but they succeeded better in some cases than others."

"'They'?" Secombe asked.

"Whoever's done this. It's just a manner of speaking."

"What do you want?" Secombe asked Mrs. Alexander. His brusqueness of tone surprised Lawson.

Smiling, she replied, "The word for today is Exportadora. We're trying to get as many English-speaking people as we can to Exportadora. That's where the commercial center for American servicemen and their families in Seville is located, and it's just off one of the major boulevards to the south of here."

On a piece of paper sack Mrs. Alexander drew them a crude map and explained that her husband had once been stationed in Zaragoza in the north of Spain. Yesterday she had recalled that Seville was one of the four Spanish cities supporting the American military presence, and with persistence and a little luck a pair of carefully briefed English-speaking DPs (the abbreviation was Mrs. Alexander's) had discovered the site of the American PX and commissary just before nightfall. Looting the place when they arrived had been an impossibly mixed crew of foreigners, busily hauling American merchandise out of the ancient buildings. But Mrs. Alexander's DPs had run off the looters by the simple expedient of revving the engine of their commandeered taxicab and blowing its horn as if to announce Armageddon. In ten minutes the little American enclave had emptied of all human beings but the two men in the cab. After that, as English-speaking DPs all over the city learned of Exportadora's existence and sought to reach it, the place had begun to fill up again.

"Is there an air base in Seville?" Lawson asked the woman.

"No, not really. The base itself is near Morón de la Frontera, about thirty miles away, but Seville is where the real action is." After a brief pause, lifting her eyebrows, she corrected herself: "Was."

She thrust her map into Secombe's hands. "Here. Go on out to Exportadora. I'm going to look around for more of us. You're the first people I've found this morning. Others are looking, too, though. Maybe things'll soon start making some sense."

Secombe shook his head. "Us. Them. There isn't anybody now who isn't a 'DP,' you know. This regrouping on the basis of tired cultural affiliations is probably a mistake. I don't like it."

"You took up with Mr. Lawson, didn't you?"

"Out of pity only, I assure you. He looked lost. Moreover, you've got to have companionship of *some* sort—especially when you're in a strange place."

"Sure. That's why the word for today is Exportadora."

"It's a mistake, Mrs. Alexander."

"Why?"

"For the same reason your mysterious 'they' saw fit to displace us to begin with, I'd venture. It's a feeling I have."

"Old cultural affiliations are a source of stability," Mrs. Alexander said earnestly. As she talked, Lawson took the rumpled map out of Secombe's fingers. "This chaos around us won't go away until people have settled themselves into units—it's a natural process, it's beginning already. Why, walking along the river this morning, I saw several groups of like-speaking people burying yesterday's dead. The city's churches and chapels have begun to fill up, too. You can still hear the frightened and the heartbroken keening in solitary rooms, of course—but it can't go on forever. They'll either make connection or die. I'm not one of those who wish to die, Mr. Secombe."

"Who wishes that?" Lawson put in, annoyed by the shallow metaphysical drift of this exchange and by Secombe's irrationality. Although Mrs. Alexander was right, she didn't have to defend her position at such length. The map was her most important contribution to the return of order in their lives, and Lawson wanted her to let them use that map.

"Come on, Secombe," he said. "Let's get out to this Exportadora. It's probably the only chance we have of making it home."

"I don't think there's any chance of our making it home again, Lawson. Ever."

Perceiving that Mrs. Alexander was about to ask the Welshman why, Lawson turned on his heel and took several steps down the alley. "Come on, Secombe. We have to try. What the hell are you going to do in this flip-flopped city all by yourself?"

"Look for somebody else to talk to, I suppose."

But in a moment Secombe was at Lawson's side helping him decipher the smudged geometries of Mrs. Alexander's map, and the woman herself, before heading back to Sierpes to look for more of her own kind, called out, "It'll only take you twenty or so minutes, on foot. Good luck. See you later."

Walking, they passed a white-skinned child lying in an alley doorway opening onto a courtyard festooned with two-day-old washing and populated by a pack of orphaned dogs. The child's head was covered by a coat, but she did appear to be breathing. Lawson was not even tempted to examine her more closely, however. He kept his eyes resolutely on the map.

V

The newsstand in the small American enclave had not been looted. On Lawson's second day at Exportadora it still contained quality paperbacks, the most recent American news and entertainment magazines, and a variety of tabloids, including the military paper

The Stars and Stripes. No one knew how old these publications were because no one knew over what length of time the redistribution of the world's population had taken place. How long had everyone slept? And what about the discrepancies among time zones and the differences among people's waking hours within the same time zones? These questions were academic now, it seemed to Lawson, because the agency of transfer had apparently encompassed every single human being alive on Earth.

Thumbing desultorily through a copy of *Stars and Stripes,* he encountered an article on the problems of military hospitals and wondered how many of the world's sick had awakened in the open, doomed to immediate death because the care they required was nowhere at hand. The smell of spilled tobacco and melted Life Savers made the newsstand a pleasant place to contemplate these horrors; and, even as his conscience nagged and a contingent of impatient DPs awaited him, Lawson perversely continued to flip through the newspaper.

Secombe's squat form appeared in the doorway. "I thought you were looking for a local roadmap."

"Found it already, just skimmin' the news."

"Come on, if you would. The folks're ready to be off."

Reluctantly, Lawson followed Secombe outside, where the raw Andalusian sunlight broke like invisible surf against the pavement and the fragile-seeming shell of the Air Force bus. It was of the Bluebird shuttle variety, and Lawson remembered summer camp at Eglin Air Force Base in Florida and bus rides from his squadron's minimum-maintenance ROTC barracks to the survival-training camps near the swamp. That had been a long time ago, but this Bluebird might have hailed from an even more distant era. It was as boxy and sheepish-looking as if it had come off a 1954 assembly line, and it appeared to be made out of warped tin rather than steel. The people inside the bus had opened all its windows, and many of those on the driver's side were watching Secombe and Lawson approach.

"Move your asses!" a man shouted at them. "Let's get some wind blowing through this thing before we all suffo-damn-cate."

"Just keep talking," Secombe advised him. "That should do fine."

Aboard the bus was a motley lot of Americans, Britishers, and Australians, with two or three English-speaking Europeans and an Oxford-educated native of India to lend the group ballast. Lawson took up a window seat over the hump of one of the bus's rear tires, and Secombe squeezed in beside him. A few people introduced themselves; others, lost in fitful reveries, ignored them altogether. The most unsettling thing about the contingent to Lawson was the absence of children. Although about equally divided between men and women, the group contained no boys or girls any younger than their early teens.

Lawson opened the map of southern Spain he had found in the newsstand and traced his finger along a highway route leading out of Seville to two small American enclaves outside the city, Santa Clara and San Pablo. Farther to the south were Jerez and the port city of Cádiz. Lawson's heart misgave him; the names were all so foreign, so formidable in what they evoked, and he felt this entire enterprise to be hopeless. . . .

About midway along the right-hand side of the bus a black woman was sobbing into the hem of her blouse, and a man perched on the Bluebird's long rear seat had his hands clasped to his ears and his head canted forward to touch his knees. Lawson folded up the map and stuck it into the crevice between the seat and the side of the bus.

"The bottom-line common denominator here isn't our all speaking English," Secombe whispered. "It's what we're suffering."

Driven by one of Mrs. Alexander's original explorers, a doctor from Ivanhoe, New South Wales, the Bluebird shuddered and lurched forward. In a moment it had left Exportadora and begun banging along one of the wide avenues that would lead it out of town.

"And our suffering," Secombe went on, still whispering, "unites us with all those poor souls raving in the streets and sleeping face-down in their own vomit. You felt that the other night above the condom shop, Lawson. I know you did, talking of your daughters. So why are you so quick to go looking for what you aren't likely to find? Why are you so ready to unite yourself with this artificial family born out of catastrophe? Do you really think you're going to catch a flight home to Lynchburg? Do you really think the bird driving this sardine can—who ought to be out in the streets plying his trade instead of running a shuttle service—d'you really think he's ever going to get back to Australia?"

"Secombe—"

"Do you, Lawson?"

Lawson clapped a hand over the Welshman's knee and wobbled it back and forth. "You wouldn't be badgering me like this if you had a family of your own. What the hell do you want us to do? Stay here forever?"

"I don't know, exactly." He removed Lawson's hand from his knee. "But I do have a father, sir, and I happen to be fond of him. . . . All I know for certain is that things are *supposed* to be different now. We shouldn't be rushing to restore what we already had."

"Shit," Lawson murmured. He leaned his head against the bottom edge of the open window beside him.

From deep within the city came the brittle noise of gunshots. The Bluebird's driver, in response to this sound and to the vegetable carts and automobiles that had been moved into the streets as obstacles, began wheeling and cornering like a stock-car jockey. The bus clanked and stuttered alarmingly. It growled through an intersection below a stone bridge, leapt over that bridge like something living, and roared down into a semi-industrial suburb of Seville where a Coca-Cola bottling factory and a local brewery lifted huge competing signs.

On top of one of these buildings Lawson saw a man with a rifle taking unhurried potshots at anyone who came into his sights. Several people already lay dead.

And a moment later the Bluebird's front window shattered, another bullet ricocheted off its flank, and everyone in the bus was either shouting or weeping. The next time Lawson looked, the bus's front window appeared to have woven inside it a large and exceedingly intricate spider's web.

The Bluebird careened madly, but the doctor from Ivanhoe kept it upright and turned it with considerable skill onto the highway to San Pablo. Here the bus eased into a quiet and rhythmic cruising that made this final incident in Seville—except for the evidence of the front window—seem only the cottony aftertaste of nightmare. At last they were on their way. Maybe.

"Another good reason for trying to get home," Lawson said.

"What makes you think it's going to be different there?"

Irritably Lawson turned on the Welshman. "I thought your idea was that this change was some kind of *improvement.*"

"Perhaps it will be. Eventually."

Lawson made a dismissive noise and looked at the olive orchard spinning by on his left. Who would harvest the crop? Who would set the aircraft factories, the distilleries, the chemical and textile plants running again? Who would see to it that seed was sown in the empty fields?

Maybe Secombe had something. Maybe, when you ran for home, you ran from the new reality at hand. The effects of this new reality's advent were not going to go away very soon, no matter what you did—but seeking to reestablish yesterday's order would probably create an even nastier entropic pattern than would accepting the present chaos and working to rein it in. How, though, did you best rein it in? Maybe by trying to get back home . . .

Lawson shook his head and thought of Marlena, Karen, Hannah; of the distant mist-softened cradle of the Blue Ridge. Lord. That was country much easier to get in tune with than the harsh white-sky bleakness of this Andalusian valley. If you stay here, Lawson told himself, the pain will *never* go away.

They passed Santa Clara, which was a housing area for the officers and senior NCOs who had been stationed at Morón. With its neatly trimmed hedgerows, tall aluminum streetlamps, and low-roofed houses with carports and picture windows, Santa Clara resembled a middle-class exurbia in New Jersey or Ohio. Black smoke was curling over the area, however, and the people on the streets and lawns were definitely not Americans—they were transplanted Dutch South Africans, Amazonian tribesmen, Poles, Ethiopians, God-only-knew-what. All Lawson could accurately deduce was that a few of these people had moved into the vacant houses—maybe they had awakened in them—and that others had aimlessly set bonfires about the area's neighborhoods. These fires, because there was no wind, burned with a maddening slowness and lack of urgency.

"Little America," Secombe said aloud.

"That's in Antarctica," Lawson responded sarcastically.

"Right. No matter where it happens to be."

"Up yours."

Their destination was now San Pablo, where the Americans had hospital facilities, a library, a movie theater, a snackbar, a commissary, and, in conjunction with the Spaniards, a small commercial and military airfield. San Pablo lay only a few more miles down the road, and Lawson contemplated the idea of a flight to Portugal. What would be the chances, supposing you actually reached Lisbon, of crossing the Atlantic, either by sea or air, and reaching one of the United States's coastal cities? One in a hundred? One in a thousand? Less than that?

A couple of seats behind the driver, an Englishman with a crisp-looking moustache and an American woman with a distinct Southwestern accent were arguing the merits of bypassing San Pablo and heading on to Gibraltar, a British possession. The Englishman seemed to feel that Gibraltar would have escaped the upheaval to which the remainder of the world had fallen victim, whereas the American woman thought he was crazy. A shouting match involving five or six other passengers ensued. Finally, his patience at an end, the Bluebird's driver put his elbow on the horn and held it there until everyone had shut up.

"It's San Pablo," he announced. "Not Gibraltar or anywhere else. There'll be a plane waitin' for us when we get there."

VI

Two aircraft were waiting, a pair of patched-up DC-7s that had once belonged to the Spanish airline known as Iberia. Mrs. Alexander had recruited one of her pilots from the DPs who had shown up at Exportadora; the other, a retired TWA veteran from Riverside, California, had made it by himself to the airfield by virtue of a prior acquaintance with Seville and its American military installations. Both men were eager to carry passengers home, one via a stopover in Lisbon and the other by using Madrid as a stepping-stone to the British Isles. The hope was that they could transfer their passengers to jet aircraft at these cities' more cosmopolitan airports, but no one spoke very much about the real obstacles to success that had already begun stalking them: civil chaos, delay, inadequate communications, fuel shortages, mechanical hangups, doubt and ignorance, a thousand other things.

At twilight, then, Lawson stood next to Dai Secombe at the chain link fence fronting San Pablo's pothole-riven runway and watched the evening light glimmer off the wings of the DC-7s. Bathed in a muted dazzle, the two old airplanes were almost beautiful. Even though Mrs. Alexander had informed the DPs that they must spend the night in the installation's movie theater, so that the Bluebird could make several more shuttle runs to Exportadora, Lawson truly believed that he was bound for home.

"Goodbye," Secombe told him.

"Goodbye? . . . Oh, because you'll be on the other flight?"

"No, I'm telling you goodbye, Lawson, because I'm leaving. Right now, you see. This very minute."

"Where are you going?"

"Back into the city."

"How? What for?"

"I'll walk, I suppose. As for why, it has something to do with wanting to appease Mrs. Alexander's 'they,' also with finding out what's to become of us all. Seville's the place for that, I think."

"Then why'd you even come out here?"

"To say goodbye, you bloody imbecile." Secombe laughed, grabbed Lawson's hand, shook it heartily. "Since I couldn't manage to change your mind."

With that, he turned and walked along the chain link fence until he had found the roadway past the installation's commissary. Lawson watched him disappear behind the building's complicated system of loading ramps. After a time the Welshman reappeared on the other side, but, against the vast Spanish sky, his compact striding form rapidly dwindled to an imperceptible smudge. A smudge on the darkness.

"Goodbye," Lawson said.

That night, slumped in a lumpy theater chair, he slept with nearly sixty other people in San Pablo's movie house. A teenage boy, over only a few objections, insisted on showing all the old movies still in tins in the projection room. As a result, Lawson awoke once in the middle of *Apocalypse Now* and another time near the end of Kubrick's *Left Hand of Darkness*. The ice on the screen, dunelike *sastrugi* ranged from horizon to horizon, chilled him, touching a sensitive spot in his memory. "Little America," he murmured. Then he went back to sleep.

VII

With the passengers bound for Lisbon, Lawson stood at the fence where he had stood with Secombe, and watched the silver pinwheeling of propellers as the aircraft's engines engaged. The DC-7 flying to Madrid would not leave until much later that day, primarily because it still had several vacant seats and Mrs. Alexander felt sure that more English-speaking DPs could still be found in the city.

The people at the gate with Lawson shifted uneasily and whispered among themselves. The engines of their savior airplane whined deafeningly, and the runway seemed to tremble. What woebegone eyes the women had, Lawson thought, and the men were as scraggly as railroad hoboes. Feeling his jaw, he understood that he was no more handsome or well-groomed than any of those he waited with. And, like them, he was impatient for the signal to board, for the thumbs-up sign indicating that their airplane had passed its latest rudimentary ground tests.

At least, he consoled himself, you're not eating potato chips at ten-thirty in the morning. Disgustedly, he turned aside from a jut-eared man who was doing just that.

"There's more people here than our plane's supposed to carry," the potato-chip cruncher said. "That could be dangerous."

"But it isn't really that far to Lisbon, is it?" a woman replied. "And none of us has any luggage."

"Yeah, but—" The man gagged on a chip, coughed, tried to speak again. Facing deliberately away, Lawson felt the man's words would acquire eloquence only if he suddenly volunteered to ride in the DC-7's unpressurized baggage compartment.

As it was, the signal came to board and the jut-eared man had no chance to finish his remarks. He threw his cellophane sack to the ground, and Lawson heard it crackling underfoot as people crowded through the gate onto the grassy verge of the runway.

In order to fix the anomaly of San Pablo in his memory, Lawson turned around and walked backward across the field. He saw that bringing up the rear were four men with automatic weapons—weapons procured, most likely, from the installation's Air Police station. These men, like Lawson, were walking backward, but with their guns as well as their eyes trained on the weirdly constituted band of people who had just appeared, seemingly out of nowhere, along the airfield's fence.

One of these people wore nothing but a ragged pair of shorts, another an ankle-length burnoose, another a pair of trousers belted with a rope. One of their number was a doe-eyed young woman with an exposed torso and a circlet of bright coral on her wrist. But there were others, too, and they all seemed to have been drawn to the runway by the airplane's engine whine; they moved along the fence like desperate ghosts. As the first members of Lawson's group mounted into the plane, even more of these people appeared—an assembly of nomads, hunters, hodcarriers, fishers, herdspeople. Apparently they all understood what an airplane was for, and one of the swarthiest men among them ventured out onto the runway with his arms thrown out imploringly.

"Where you go?" he shouted. "Where you go?"

"There's no more room!" responded a blue-jean-clad man with a machine gun. "Get back! You'll have to wait for another flight!"

Oh, sure, Lawson thought, the one to Madrid. He was at the base of the airplane's mobile stairway. The jut-eared man who had been eating potato chips nodded brusquely at him.

"You'd better get on up there," he shouted over the robust hiccoughing of the airplane's engines, "before we have unwanted company breathing down our necks!"

"After you." Lawson stepped aside.

Behind the swarthy man importuning the armed guards for a seat on the airplane, there clamored thirty or more insistent people, their only real resemblance to one another their longing for a way out. "Where you go? Where you go?" the bravest and most desperate among them yelled, but they all wanted to board the airplane that Mrs. Alexander's charges had already laid claim to; and most of them could see that it was too late to accomplish their purpose without some kind of risk-taking. The man who had been shouting in English, along with four or five others, broke into an assertive dogtrot toward the plane. Although their cries continued to be modestly beseeching, Lawson could tell that the passengers' guards now believed themselves under direct attack.

A burst of machine-gun fire sounded above the field and echoed away like rain drumming on a tin roof. The man who had been asking, "Where you go?" pitched forward on his face. Others fell beside him, including the woman with the coral bracelet. Panicked or prodded by this evidence of their assailants' mortality, one of the guards raked the chain link fence with his weapon, bringing down some of those who had already begun to retreat and summoning forth both screams and the distressingly incongruous sound of popping wire. Then, eerily, it was quiet again.

"Get on that airplane!" a guard shouted to Lawson. He was the only passenger still left on the ground, and everyone wanted him inside the plane so that the mobile stairway could be rolled away.

"I don't think so," Lawson said to himself.

Hunching forward like a man under fire, he ran toward the gate and the crude mandala of bodies partially blocking it. The slaughter he had just witnessed struck him as abysmally repetitive of a great deal of recent history, and he did not wish to belong to that history anymore. Further, the airplane behind him was a gross iron-plated emblem of the burden he no longer cared to bear—even if it also seemed to represent the promise of passage home.

"Hey, where the hell you think you're goin'?"

Lawson did not answer. He stepped gingerly through the corpses on the runway's margin, halted on the other side of the fence, and, his eyes misted with glare and poignant bewilderment, turned to watch the DC-7 taxi down the scrub-lined length of concrete to the very end of the field. There the airplane negotiated a turn and started back the way it had come. Soon it was hurtling along like a colossal metal dragonfly, building speed. When it lifted from the ground, its tires screaming shrilly with the last series of bumps before takeoff, Lawson held his breath.

Then the airplane's right wing dipped, dipped again, struck the ground, and broke off like a piece of balsa wood, splintering brilliantly. After that, the airplane went flipping, cartwheeling, across the end of the tarmac and into the desolate open field beyond, where its shell and remaining wing were suddenly engulfed in flames. You could hear people frying in that inferno; you could smell gasoline and burnt flesh.

"Jesus," Lawson said.

He loped away from the airfield's fence, hurried through the short grass behind the San Pablo library, and joined a group of those who had just fled the English-speaking guards' automatic-weapon fire. He met them on the highway going back to Seville and walked among them as merely another of their number. Although several people viewed his 1505 trousers with suspicion, no one argued that he did not belong, and no one threatened to cut his throat for him.

As hangdog and exotically nondescript as most of his companions, Lawson watched his tennis shoes track the pavement like the feet of a mechanical toy. He wondered what he was going to do back in Seville. Successfully dodge bullets and eat fried fish, if he was lucky. Talk with Secombe again, if he could find the man. And, if he had any sense, try to organize his life around some purpose other than the insane and hopeless one of returning to Lynchburg. What purpose, though? What purpose beyond the basic animal purpose of staying alive?

"Are any of you hungry?" Lawson asked.

He was regarded with suspicious curiosity.

"Hungry," he repeated. "*¿Tiene hambre?*"

English? Spanish? Neither worked. What languages did they have, these refugees from an enigma? It looked as if they had all tried to speak together before and found the task impossible—because, moving along the asphalt under the hot Andalusian sun, they now relied on gestures and easily interpretable noises to express themselves.

Perceiving this, Lawson brought the fingers of his right hand to his mouth and clacked his teeth to indicate chewing.

He was understood. A thin barefoot man in a capacious linen shirt and trousers led Lawson off the highway into an orchard of orange trees. The fruit was not yet completely ripe, and was sour because of its greenness, but all twelve or thirteen of Lawson's crew ate, letting the juice run down their arms. When they again took up the trek to Seville, Lawson's mind was almost absolutely blank with satiety. The only thing rattling about in it now was the fear that he would not know what to do once they arrived. He never did find out if the day's other scheduled flight, the one to Madrid, made it safely to its destination, but the matter struck him now as of little import. He wiped his sticky mouth and trudged along numbly.

VIII

He lived above the contraceptive shop. In the mornings he walked through the alley to a bakery that a woman with calm Mongolian features had taken over. In return for a daily allotment of bread and a percentage of the goods brought in for barter, Lawson swept the bakery's floor, washed the utensils that were dirtied each day, and kept the shop's front counter. His most rewarding skill, in fact, was communicating with those who entered to buy something. He had an uncanny grasp of several varieties of sign language, and, on occasion, he found himself speaking a monosyllabic patois whose derivation was a complete mystery to him. Sometimes he thought that he had invented it himself; sometimes he believed that he had learned it from the transplanted Sevillanos among whom he now lived.

English, on the other hand, seemed to leak slowly out of his mind, a thick, unrecoverable fluid.

The first three or four weeks of chaos following The Change had, by this time, run their course, a circumstance that surprised Lawson. Still, it was true. Now you could lie down at night on your pallet without hearing pistol reports or fearing that some benighted freak was going to set fire to your staircase. Most of the city's essential services—electricity, water, and sewerage—were working again, albeit uncertainly, and agricultural goods were coming in from the countryside. People had gone back to doing what they knew best, while those whose previous jobs had had little to do with the basics of day-to-day survival were now apprenticing as bricklayers, carpenters, bakers, fishers, water and power technicians. That men and women chose to live separately and that children were as rare as sapphires, no one seemed to find disturbing or unnatural. A new pattern was evolving. You lived among your fellows without tension or quarrel, and you formed no dangerously intimate relationships.

One night, while standing at his window, Lawson struck a loose tile below the casement. He removed the tile and set it on the floor. Every night for nearly two months he pried away at least one tile and, careful not to chip or break it, stacked it near an inner wall with those he had already removed.

After completing this task, as he lay on his pallet, he would often hear a man or a woman somewhere in the city singing a high, sweet song whose words had no significance for him. Sometimes a pair of voices would answer each other, always in different languages. Then, near the end of the summer, as Lawson stood staring at the lathing and the wall beams he had methodically exposed, he was moved to sing a melancholy song of his own. And he sang it without knowing what it meant.

The days grew cooler. Lawson took to leaving the bakery during its midafternoon closing and proceeding by way of the Calle de Sierpes to a *bodega* across from the bullring. A crew of silent laborers, who worked very purposively in spite of their seeming to have no single boss, was dismantling the Plaza de Toros, and Lawson liked to watch as he drank his wine and ate the breadsticks he had brought with him.

Other crews about the city were carefully taking down the government buildings, banks, and *barrio* chapels that no one frequented anymore, preserving the bricks, tiles, and beams as if in the hope of some still unspecified future construction. By this time Lawson himself had knocked out the rear wall of his room over the contraceptive shop, and he felt a strong sense of identification with the laborers craftily gutting the bullring of its railings and barricades. Eventually, of course, everything would have to come down. Everything.

The rainy season began. The wind and the cold. Lawson continued to visit the sidewalk café near the ruins of the stadium; and because the bullring's destruction went forward even in wet weather, he wore an overcoat he had recently acquired and staked out a nicely sheltered table under the *bodega*'s awning. This was where he customarily sat.

One particularly gusty day, rain pouring down, he shook out his umbrella and sat down at this table only to find another man sitting across from him. Upon the table was a wooden game board of some kind, divided into squares.

"Hello, Lawson," the interloper said.

Lawson blinked and licked his lips thoughtfully. Although he had not called his family to mind in some time, and wondered now if he had ever really married and fathered children, Dai Secombe's face had occasionally floated up before him in the dark of his room. But now Lawson could not remember the Welshman's name, or his nationality, and he had no notion of what to say to him. The first words he spoke, therefore, came out sounding like dream babble, or a voice played backward on the phonograph. In order to say hello he was forced to the indignity, almost comic, of making a childlike motion with his hand.

Secombe, pointing to the game board, indicated that they should play. From a carved wooden box with a velvet lining he emptied the pieces onto the table, then arranged them on both sides of the board. Chess, Lawson thought vaguely, but he really did not recognize the pieces—they seemed changed from what he believed they should look like. And when it came his turn to move, Secombe had to demonstrate the capabilities of all the major pieces before he, Lawson, could essay even the most timid advance. The piece that most reminded him of a knight had to be moved according to two distinct sets of criteria, depending on whether it started from a black square or a white one; the "rooks," on the other hand, were able, at certain times, to *jump* an opponent's intervening pieces. The game boggled Lawson's understanding. After ten or twelve moves he pushed his chair back and took a long bittersweet taste of wine. The rain continued to pour down like an endless curtain of deliquescent beads.

"That's all right," Secombe said. "I haven't got it all down yet myself, quite. A Bhutanese fellow near where I live made the pieces, you see, and just recently taught me how to play."

With difficulty Lawson managed to frame a question: "What work have you been doing?"

"I'm in demolition. As we all will be soon. It's the only really constructive occupation going." The Welshman chuckled mildly, finished his own wine, and rose. Lifting his umbrella, he bid Lawson farewell with a word that, when Lawson later tried to repeat and intellectually encompass it, had no meaning at all.

Every afternoon of that dismal, rainy winter Lawson came back to the same table, but Secombe never showed up there again. Nor did Lawson miss him terribly. He had grown accustomed to the strange richness of his own company. Besides, if he wanted people to talk to, all he needed to do was remain behind the counter at the bakery.

IX

Spring came again. All of his room's interior walls were down, and it amused him to be able to see the porcelain chalice of the commode as he came up the stairs from the contraceptive shop.

The plaster that he had sledgehammered down would never be of use to anybody again, of course, but he had saved from the debris whatever was worth the salvage. With the return of good weather, men driving oxcarts were coming through the city's backstreets and alleys to collect these items. You never saw anyone trying to drive a motorized vehicle nowadays, probably because, over the winter, most of them had been hauled away. The scarcity of gasoline and replacement parts might well have been a factor, too—but, in truth, people seemed no longer to want to mess with internal-combustion engines. Ending pollution and noise had nothing to do with it, either. A person with dung on his shoes or front stoop was not very likely to be convinced of a vast improvement in the environment, and the clattering of wooden carts—the ringing of metal-rimmed wheels on cobblestone—could be as ear-wrenching as the hum and blare of motorized traffic. Still, Lawson liked to hear the oxcarts turn into his alley. More than once, called out by the noise, he had helped their drivers load them with masonry, doors, window sashes, even ornate carven mantels.

At the bakery the Mongolian woman with whom Lawson worked, and had worked for almost a year, caught the handle of his broom one day and told him her name. Speaking the odd quicksilver monosyllables of the dialect that nearly everyone in Seville had by now mastered, she asked him to call her Tij. Lawson did not know whether this was her name from before The Change or one she had recently invented for herself. Pleased in either case, he responded by telling her his own Christian name. He stumbled saying it, and when Tij also had trouble pronouncing the name, they laughed together about its uncommon awkwardness on their tongues.

A week later he had moved into the tenement building where Tij lived. They slept in the same "room" three flights up from a courtyard filled with clambering wisteria. Because all but the supporting walls on this floor had been knocked out, Lawson often felt that he was living in an open-bay barracks. People stepped over his pallet to get to the stairwell and dressed in front of him as if he were not even there. Always a quick study, he emulated their casual behavior.

And when the ice in his loins finally began to thaw, he turned in the darkness to Tij—without in the least worrying about propriety. Their coupling was invariably silent, and the release Lawson experienced was always a serene rather than a shuddering one. Afterwards, in the wisteria fragrance pervading their building, Tij and he lay beside each other like a pair of larval bumblebees as the moon rolled shadows over their naked sweat-gleaming bodies.

Each day after they had finished making and trading away their bread, Tij and Lawson closed the bakery and took long walks. Often they strolled among the hedge-enclosed pathways and the small wrought-iron fences at the base of the city's cathedral. From these paths, so overwhelmed were they by buttresses of stones and arcaded balconies, they could not even see the bronze weather vane of Faith atop the Giralda. But, evening after evening, Lawson insisted on returning to that place, and at last his persistence and his sense of expectation were rewarded by the sound of jackhammers biting into marble in each one of the cathedral's five tremendous naves. He and Tij, holding hands, entered.

Inside, men and women were at work removing the altar screens, the metalwork grilles, the oil paintings, sections of stained-glass windows, religious relics. Twelve or more oxcarts were parked beneath the vault of the cathedral, and the noise of the jackhammers echoed shatteringly from nave to nave, from floor to cavernous ceiling. The oxen stood so complacently in their traces that Lawson wondered if the drivers of the carts had somehow contrived to deafen the animals. Tij released Lawson's hand to cover her ears. He covered his own ears. It did no good. You could remain in the cathedral only if you accepted the noise and resolved to be a participant in the building's destruction. Many people had already made that decision. They were swarming through its chambered stone belly like a spectacularly efficient variety of stone-eating termite.

An albino man of indeterminate race—a man as pale as a termite—thrust his pickax at Lawson. Lawson uncovered his ears and took the pickax by its handle. Tij, a moment later, found a crowbar hanging precariously from the side of one of the oxcarts. With these tools the pair of them crossed the nave they had entered and halted in front of an imposing mausoleum. Straining against the cathedral's poor light and the strange linguistic static in his head, Lawson painstakingly deciphered the plaque near the tomb.

"Christopher Columbus is buried here," he said.

Tij did not hear him. He made a motion indicating that this was the place where they should start. Tij nodded her understanding. Together, Lawson thought, they would dismantle the mausoleum of the discoverer of the New World and bring his corrupt remains out into the street. After all these centuries they would free the man.

Then the bronze statue of Faith atop the bell tower would come down, followed by the lovely bell tower itself. After that, the flying buttresses, the balconies, the walls; every beautiful, tainted stone.

It would hurt like hell to destroy the cathedral, and it would take a long, long time—but, considering everything, it was the only meaningful option they had. Lawson raised his pickax.